CAUGHT IN THE NET

SABINE GAZED AT IT FOR A FEW MOMENTS IN SILENCE, AND THEN MUR-
MURED THE WORDS, "IT IS LOVELY!"

CAUGHT IN THE NET

Translated from the French of
EMILE GABORIAU

Illustrated by
JOHN SLOAN

Charles Scribner's Sons
New York 1913

COPYRIGHT, 1913, BY
CHARLES SCRIBNER'S SONS

CONTENTS

v

ILLUSTRATIONS

CAUGHT IN THE NET

CHAPTER I.

PUTTING ON THE SCREW.

THE cold on the 8th of February, 186—, was more intense than the Parisians had experienced during the whole of the severe winter which had preceded it, for at twelve o'clock on that day Chevalier's thermometer, so well known by the denizens of Paris, registered three degrees below zero. The sky was overcast and full of threatening signs of snow, while the moisture on the pavement and roads had frozen hard, rendering traffic of all kinds exceedingly hazardous. The whole great city wore an air of dreariness and desolation, for even when a thin crust of ice covers the waters of the Seine, the mind involuntarily turns to those who have neither food, shelter, nor fuel.

This bitterly cold day actually made the landlady of the Hôtel de Perou, though she was a hard, grasping woman from Auvergne, give a thought to the condition of her lodgers, and one quite different from her usual idea of obtaining the maximum of rent for the minimum of accommodation.

"The cold," remarked she to her husband, who was busily engaged in replenishing the stove with fuel, "is enough to frighten the wits out of a Polar bear. In this kind of weather I always feel very anxious, for it was during a winter like this that one of our lodgers hung himself, a trick which cost us fifty francs, in good, honest money, besides giving us a bad name in the neighborhood. The fact is, one never knows what lodgers are capable of doing. You should go up to the top floor, and see how they are getting on there."

" Pooh, pooh! " replied her husband, M. Loupins; " they will do well enough."

" Is that really your opinion? "

" I know that I am right. Daddy Tantaine went out as soon as it was light, and a short time afterward Paul Violaine came down. There is no one upstairs now but little Rose, and I expect that she has been wise enough to stick to her bed."

" Ah! " answered the landlady rather spitefully. " I have made up my mind regarding that young lady some time ago; she is a sight too pretty for this house, and so I tell you."

The Hôtel de Perou stands in the Rue de la Hachette, not twenty steps from the Place de Petit Pont; and no more cruelly sarcastic title could ever have been conferred on a building. The extreme shabbiness of the exterior of the house, the narrow, muddy street in which it stood, the dingy windows covered with mud, and repaired with every variety of patch,—all seemed to cry out to the passers by: " This is the chosen abode of misery and destitution."

The observer might have fancied it a robbers' den, but he would have been wrong; for the inhabitants were fairly honest. The Hôtel de Perou was one of those refuges, growing scarcer and more scarce every day, where unhappy men and women, who had been worsted in the battle of life, could find a shelter in return for the change remaining from the last five-franc piece. They treat it as the shipwrecked mariner uses the rock upon which he climbs from the whirl of the angry waters, and breathes a deep sigh of relief as he collects his forces for a fresh effort. However wretched existence may be, a protracted sojourn in such a shelter as the Hôtel de Perou would be out of the question. The chambers in every floor of the house are divided into small slips by partitions, covered with canvas and paper, and pleasantly termed rooms by M. Loupins. The partitions were in a terrible condition, rickety and unstable, and the paper with which they were covered torn and hanging down in tatters; but the state of the attics was even more deplorable, the ceilings of which were so low that the occupants had to stoop continually, while the dormer windows admitted but a small amount of light. A bedstead, with a straw mattress, a rickety table, and two broken chairs, formed the sole furniture of these rooms. Miserable as these dormitories were, the landlady asked and obtained twenty-two francs for them by the month, as there was a fireplace in each, which she always pointed out to intending tenants.

The young woman whom M. Loupins alluded to by the name of Rose was seated in one of these dreary dens on this bitter winter's day. Rose was an exquisitely beautiful girl about eighteen years of age. She was very fair; her long lashes partially concealed a pair of steely blue eyes, and to a certain extent relieved their hard expression. Her ripe, red lips, which seemed formed for love and kisses, permitted a glimpse of a row of pearly teeth. Her bright waving hair grew low down upon her forehead, and such of it as had escaped from the bondage of a cheap comb, with which it was fastened, hung in wild luxuriance over her exquisitely shaped neck and shoulders. She had thrown over her ragged print gown the patched coverlet of the bed, and, crouched upon the tattered hearthrug before the hearth, upon which a few sticks smouldered, giving out hardly a particle of heat, she was telling her fortune with a dirty pack of cards, endeavoring to console herself for the privations of the day by the promise of future prosperity. She had spread those arbiters of her destiny in a half circle before her, and divided them into threes, each of which had a peculiar meaning, and her breast rose and fell as she turned them up and read upon their faces good fortune or ill-luck. Absorbed in this task, she paid but little attention to the icy chillness of the atmosphere, which made her fingers stiff, and dyed her white hands purple.

"One, two, three," she murmured in a low voice. "A fair man, that's sure to be Paul. One, two, three, money to the house. One, two, three, troubles and vexations. One, two, three, the nine of spades; ah, dear! more hardships and misery,—always that wretched card turning up with its sad story!"

Rose seemed utterly downcast at the sight of the little pieces of painted cardboard, as though she had received certain intelligence of a coming misfortune. She soon, however, recovered herself, and was again shuffling the pack,—cut it, taking care to do so with her left hand, spread them out before her, and again commenced counting: one, two, three. This time the cards appeared to be more propitious, and held out promises of success for the future.

"I am loved," read she, as she gazed anxiously upon them,—"very much loved! Here is rejoicing, and a letter from a dark man! See, here he is,—the knave of clubs. Always the same," she continued; " I cannot strive against fate."

Then, rising to her feet, she drew from a crack in the wall, which formed a safe hiding-place for her secrets, a soiled and crumpled letter, and, unfolding it, she read for perhaps the hundredth time these words :—

"MADEMOISELLE,—

" To see you is to love you. I give you my word of honor that this is true. The wretched hovel where your charms are hidden is no fit abode for you. A home, worthy in every way to receive you, is at your service— Rue de Douai. It has been taken in your name, as I am straightforward in these matters. Think of my proposal, and make what inquiries you like concerning me. I have not yet attained my majority, but shall do so in five months and three days, when I shall inherit my mother's fortune. My father is wealthy, but old and infirm. From four to six in the afternoon of the next few days I will be in a carriage at the corner of the Place de Petit Pont.

GASTON DE GANDELU."

The cynical insolence of the letter, together with its entire want of form, was a perfect example of the style affected by those loiterers about town, known to the Parisians as "mashers;" and yet Rose did not appear at all disgusted by the reception of such an unworthily worded proposal, but, on the contrary, rather pleased by its contents. " If I only dared," mused she, with a sigh,—" ah, if I only dared!" For a time she sat deeply immersed in thought, with her face buried in her hands, until she was aroused from her meditations by the sound of an active and youthful step upon the creaking stairs. " He has come back," she gasped; and with the agile movement of a cat she again concealed the letter in its hiding-place, and she had scarcely done so, when Paul Violaine entered the miserable room. He was a young man of twenty-three, of slender figure, but admirably proportioned. His face was a perfect oval, and his complexion of just that slight olive tint which betrays the native of the south of France. A slight, silky moustache concealed his upper lip, and gave his features that air of manliness in which they would have otherwise been deficient. His curly chestnut hair fell gracefully over a brow upon which an expression of pride was visible, and enhanced the peculiar, restless glance of his large dark eyes. His physical beauty, which was fully equal to that of Rose, was increased by an aristocratic air, popularly believed to be only found in the scions of noble families. The landlady, in her moments of good humor, used to assert her belief that her lodger was a disguised prince; but if this were the case, he was certainly one that had been overtaken by poverty. His dress, to which the closest attention had been paid, revealed the state of destitution in which he was,—not the destitution which openly asks for alms, but the hidden poverty which shuns communication and blushes at a single glance of pity. In this almost Arctic winter he wore clothes rendered thin by the constant friction of the clothes brush, over which was a light overcoat about as thick as the web of a spider. His shoes were well blacked, but their condition told the piteous tale of long walks in search of employment, or of that good luck which seems to evade its pursuer.

Paul was holding a roll of manuscript in his hand, and as he entered the room he threw it on the bed with a despairing gesture. "A failure again!" exclaimed he, in accents of the utmost depression. "Nothing else but failures!"

The young woman rose hastily to her feet; she appeared to have forgotten the cards completely; the smile of satisfaction faded from her face and her features, and an expression of utter weariness took its place.

"What! no success?" she cried, affecting a surprise which was evidently assumed. "No success, after all your promises when you left me this morning?"

"This morning, Rose, a ray of hope had penetrated my heart; but I have been deceived, or rather I deceived myself, and I took my ardent desires for so many promises which were certain to be fulfilled. The people that I have been to have not even the kindness to say 'No' plain and flat; they listen to all you have to say, and as soon as your back is turned they forget your existence. The coin that passes around in this infernal town is indeed nothing but idle words, and that is all that poverty-stricken talent can expect."

A silence of some duration ensued, and Paul was too much absorbed in his own thoughts to notice the look of contempt with which Rose was regarding him. His helpless resignation to adverse circumstances appeared to have turned her to stone.

"A nice position we are in!" said she at last. "What do you think will become of us?"

"Alas! I do not know."

"Nor I. Yesterday Madame Loupins came to me and asked for the eleven francs we owe here; and told me plainly that if within three days we did not settle our account, she would turn us out; and I know enough of her to be sure that she will keep her word. The detestable old hag would do anything for the pleasure of seeing me on the streets."

"Alone and friendless in the world," muttered Paul,

paying but little attention to the young girl's words, "without a creature or a relative to care for you, or to lend you a helping hand."

"We have not a copper in the world," continued Rose with cruel persistency; "I have sold everything that I had, to preserve the rags that I am wearing. Not a scrap of wood remains, and we have not tasted food since yesterday morning."

To these words, which were uttered in a tone of the most bitter reproach, the young man made no reply, but clasped his icily cold hands against his forehead, as though in utter despair.

"Yes, that is a true picture of our position," resumed Rose coldly, her accents growing more and more contemptuous. "And I tell you that something must be done at once, some means discovered, I care not what, to relieve us from our present miserable state."

Paul tore off his overcoat, and held it toward her.

"Take it, and pawn it," exclaimed he; but the girl made no move.

"Is that all that you have to propose?" asked she, in the same glacial tone.

"They will lend you three francs upon it, and with that we can get bread and fuel."

"And after that is gone?"

"After that—oh, we will think of our next step, and shall have time to hit upon some plan. Time, a little time, is all that I require, Rose, to break asunder the bonds which seem to fetter me. Some day success must crown my efforts; and with success, Rose, dear, will come affluence, but in the meantime we must learn to wait."

"And where are the means to enable us to wait?"

" No matter; they will come. Only do what I tell you, and who can say what to-morrow——"

Paul was still too much absorbed in his own thoughts to notice the expression upon the young girl's face; for had he done so, he would at once have perceived that she was not in the humor to permit the matter to be shelved in this manner.

" To-morrow! " she broke in sarcastically. " To-morrow,—always the same pitiful cry. For months past we seem to have lived upon the word. Look you here, Paul, you are no longer a child, and ought to be able to look things straight in the face. What can I get on that threadbare coat of yours? Perhaps three francs at the outside. How many days will that last us? We will say three. And then, what then? Be-sides, can you not understand that your dress is too shabby for you to make an impression on the people you go to see? Well-dressed applicants only have at-tention, and to obtain money, you must appear not to need it; and, pray, what will people think of you if you have no overcoat? Without one you will look ridiculous, and can hardly venture into the streets."

" Hush! " cried Paul, " for pity's sake, hush! for your words only prove to me more plainly that you are like the rest of the world, and that want of success is a pernicious crime in your eyes. You once had con-fidence in me, and then you spoke in a very different strain."

" Once indeed! but then I did not know——"

" No, Rose, it was not what you were then ignorant of; but it was that in those days you loved me."

" Great heavens! I ask you, have I left one stone unturned? Have I not gone from publisher to publisher to sell those songs of my own composing—those songs that you sing so well? I have endeavored to get pupils. What fresh efforts can I try? What would *you* do, were you in my place? Tell me, I beg you."

And as Paul spoke, he grew more and more excited, while Rose still maintained her manner of exasperating coolness.

"I know not," she replied, after a brief pause; "but if I was a man, I do not think that I would permit the woman, for whom I pretended that I had the most sincere affection, to be in want of the actual necessities of life. I would strain every effort to obtain them."

"I have no trade; I am no mechanic," broke in Paul passionately.

"Then I would learn one. Pray how much does a man earn who climbs the ladder with a bricklayer's hod upon his shoulders? It may be hard work, I allow, but surely the business is not difficult to learn. You have, or say you have, great musical talents. I say nothing about them; but had I any vocal powers and if there was not a morsel to eat in the house, I would go and sing in the taverns or even in the public streets, and would earn money, and care little for the means by which I made it."

"When you say those things, you seem to forget that I am an honest man."

"One would really suppose that I had suggested some questionable act to you. Your reply, Paul, plainly proves to me that you are one of those who, for want of determination, fall, helpless, by the wayside in the journey of life. They flaunt their rags and tatters in the eyes of the world, and with saddened hearts and empty stomachs utter the boast, 'I am an honest man.'

Do you think that, in order to be rich, you must per-
force be a rogue? This is simple imbecility."

She uttered this tirade in clear and vibrant accents,
and her eyes gleamed with the fire of savage resolution.
Her nature was one of those cruel and energetic ones,
which lead a woman to hurl a man from the brink of
the abyss to which she has conducted him, and to forget him before he has ever reached the bottom.

This torrent of sarcasm brought out Paul's real
nature. His face flushed, and rage began to gain the
mastery over him. " Can you not work? " he asked.
" Why do you not do something instead of talking so
much? "

"That is not at all the same kind of thing," answered
she coolly. " I was not made for work."

Paul made a threatening gesture. " You wretch! "
exclaimed he.

" You are wrong," she replied. " I am not a wretch;
I am simply hungry."

There seemed every prospect of an angry scene,
when a slight sound attracted the attention of the
disputants, and, turning round, they saw an old man
standing upon the threshold of their open door. He
was tall, but stooped a good deal. He had high, thick
brows, and a red nose; a long, thick, grizzly beard
covered the rest of his countenance. He wore a pair
of spectacles with colored glasses, which, to a great
extent, concealed the expression of his face. His whole
attire indicated extreme poverty. He wore a greasy
coat, much frayed and torn at the pockets, and which
had carried away with it marks of all the walls against
which it had been rubbed when he had indulged a little
too freely in the cheerful glass. He seemed to belong
to that class who consider it a work of supererogation

to disrobe before going to bed, and who just turn in
on such spot as the fancy of the moment may dictate.
Paul and Rose both recognized the old man from having continually met him when ascending or descending
the staircase, and knew that he rented the back attic,
and was called Daddy Tantaine. In an instant the idea
flashed across Paul's mind that the dilapidated state of
the partition permitted every word spoken in one attic
to be overheard in the other, and this did not tend to
soothe his exasperated feelings.

"What do you want here, sir?" asked he angrily.
"And, pray, who gave you permission to enter my
room without leave?"

The old man did not seem at all put out by the
threatening language of his questioner. "I should be
telling a fib," answered he calmly, "if I were to tell
you that, being in my own room and hearing you quarrelling, I did not hear every word of what you have
been saying."

"Sir!"

"Stop a bit, and don't be in such a hurry, my young
friend. You seem disposed to quarrel, and, on my
faith, I am not surprised; for when there is no corn in
the manger, the best tempered horse will bite and
kick."

He uttered these words in the most soothing accents,
and appeared utterly unconscious of having committed
any breach of etiquette in entering the room.

"Well, sir," said Paul, a flush of shame passing
across his face, "you see now how poverty can drag
a man down. Are you satisfied?"

"Come, come, my young friend," answered Daddy
Tantaine, "you should not get angry; and if I did step
in without any notice, it was because, as a neighbor,

I find I might venture on such a liberty; for when I heard how embarrassed you were, I said to myself, 'Tantaine, perhaps you can help this pretty pair out of the scrape they have got into.'"

The promise of assistance from a person who had not certainly the outward appearance of a capitalist seemed so ludicrous to Rose that she could not restrain a smile, for she fancied that if their old neighbor was to present them with half his fortune, it might possibly amount to twenty centimes or thereabouts.

Paul had formed a somewhat similar idea, but he was a little touched by this act of friendliness on the part of a man who doubtless knew that money lent under similar circumstances was but seldom returned.

"Ah, sir!" said he, and this time he spoke in softer accents, "what can you possibly do for us?"

"Who can say?"

"You can see how hard we are pushed. We are in want of almost everything. Have we not reached the *acme* of misery?"

The old man raised his hand to heaven, as if to seek for aid from above.

"You have indeed come to a terrible pass," murmured he; "but all is not yet lost. The pearl which lies in the depths of the ocean is not lost for ever; for may not some skillful diver bring it to the surface? A fisherman may not be able to do much with it, but he knows something of its value, and hands it over to the dealer in precious stones."

He intensified his speech by a little significant laugh, the meaning of which was lost upon the two young people who, though their evil instincts led them to be greedy and covetous, were yet unskilled in the world's ways.

"I should," remarked Paul, "be a fool if I did not accept the offer of your kind assistance."

"There, then, that is right; and now the first thing to do is to have a really good feed. You must get in some wood too, for it is frightfully cold. My old bones are half frozen; and afterward we will talk of a fresh rig out for you both."

"Yes," remarked Rose with a faint sigh; "but to do all that, we want a lot of money."

"Well, how do you know that I can't find it?"

Daddy Tantaine unbuttoned his great coat with grave deliberation, and drew from an inner pocket a small scrap of paper which had been fastened to the lining by a pin. This he unfolded with the greatest care and laid upon the table.

"A banknote for five hundred francs!" exclaimed Rose, with extreme surprise. Paul did not utter a word. Had he seen the woodwork of the chair upon which he was leaning burst into flower and leaf, he could not have looked more surprised. Who could have expected to find such a sum concealed beneath the old man's tatters, and how could he have obtained so much money? The idea that some robbery had been committed at once occurred to both the young people, and they exchanged a meaning glance, which, however, did not escape the observation of their visitor.

"Pooh, pooh!" said he, without appearing in the slightest degree annoyed. "You must not give way to evil thoughts or suspicions. It is a fact that banknotes for five hundred francs don't often grow out of a ragged pocket like mine. But I got this fellow honestly,—that I can guarantee."

Rose paid no attention to his words; indeed, she took no interest in them. The note was there, and that was enough for her. She took it up and smoothed it out as though the crisp paper communicated a pleasant sensation to her fingers.

"I must tell you," resumed Daddy Tantaine, "that I am employed by a sheriff's officer, and that, in addition, I do a little bill collecting for various persons. By these means I have often comparatively large sums in my possession, and I can lend you five hundred francs for a short time without any inconvenience to myself."

Paul's necessities and conscience were fighting a hard battle, and he remained silent, as a person generally does before arriving at a momentous decision.

At length he broke the silence. "No," said he, "your offer is one that I cannot accept, for I feel——"

"This is no time, my dear Paul, to talk of feelings," interrupted Rose; "besides, can you not see that our refusal to accept the loan annoys this worthy gentleman?"

"The young lady is quite right," returned Daddy Tantaine. "Come, let us say that the matter is settled. Go out and get in something to eat, sharp, for it has struck four some time ago."

At these words, Rose started, and a scarlet flush spread over her cheek. "Four o'clock," repeated she, thinking of her letter; but after a moment's reflection she stepped up to the cracked mirror, and, arranging her tattered skirts, took up the banknote and left the room.

"She is a rare beauty," remarked Daddy Tantaine with the air of one who was an authority in such matters, "and as clever as they make them. Ah! if she had only some one to give her a hint, she might rise to any height."

Paul's ideas were in such a wild state of confusion, that he could make no reply; and, now that he was no longer held in thrall by Rose's presence, he began to be terrified at what had taken place, for he imagined that he caught a sinister expression in the old man's face which made him very suspicious of the wisdom of the course he had been persuaded to pursue. Was there ever such an unheard-of event as an old man of such a poverty-stricken appearance showering bank-notes upon the heads of perfect strangers? There was certainly something mysterious in the affair, and Paul made up his mind that he would do his utmost to avoid being compromised.

" I have thought the matter over," said he resolutely; " and it is impossible for me to accept the loan of a sum which it would be difficult for me to repay."

" My dear young friend, that is not the way to talk. If you do not have a good opinion of yourself, all the world will judge you according to your own estimation. Your inexperience has, up to this time, been the sole cause of your failure. Poverty soon changes a boy into a man as straw ripens fruit; but the first thing you must do is to put all confidence in me. You can repay the five hundred francs at your convenience, but I must have six per cent. for my money and your note of hand."

" But really——," began Paul.

" I am looking at the matter in a purely business light, so we can drop sentiment."

Paul had so little experience in the ways of the world, that the mere fact of giving his acceptance for the money borrowed put him at once at his ease, though he knew well that his name was not a very valuable addition to the slip of paper.

Daddy Tantaine, after a short search through his pockets, discovered a bill stamp, and, placing it on the table, said, " Write as I shall dictate :—

' On the 8th of June, 188—, I promise to pay to M. Tantaine or order the sum of five hundred francs for value received, such sum to bear interest at the rate of six per cent. per annum.
' Frs. 500.

‘ PAUL VIOLAINE.’ ”

The young man had just completed his signature when Rose made her appearance, bearing a plentiful stock of provisions in her arms. Her eyes had a strange radiance in them, which Paul, however, did not notice, as he was engaged in watching the old man, who, after carefully inspecting the document, secured it in one of the pockets of his ragged coat.

" You will, of course, understand, sir," remarked Paul, " that there is not much chance of my being able to save sufficient to meet this bill in four months, so that the date is a mere form."

A smile of benevolence passed over Daddy Tantaine's features. " And suppose," said he, " that I, the lender, was to put the borrower in a position to repay the advance before a month had passed ? "

" Ah ! but that is not possible."

" I do not say, my young friend, that I could do this myself; but I have a good friend whose hand reaches a long way. If I had only listened to his advice when I was younger, you would not have caught me to-day in the Hôtel de Perou. Shall I introduce you to him ? "

" Am I a perfect fool, to throw away such a chance ? "

" Good ! I shall see him this evening, and will mention your name to him. Call on him at noon to-morrow, and if he takes a fancy to you,—decides to push you, your future is assured, and you will have no doubts as to getting on."

He took out a card from his pocket and handed it to Paul, adding, " The name of my friend is Mascarin."

Meanwhile Rose, with a true Parisian's handiness, had contrived to restore order from chaos, and had arranged the table, with its one or two pieces of broken crockery, with scraps of brown paper instead of plates. A fresh supply of wood crackled bravely on the hearth, and two candles, one of which was placed in a chipped bottle, and the other in a tarnished candlestick belonging to the porter of the hotel. In the eyes of both the young people the spectacle was a truly delightful one, and Paul's heart swelled with triumph. The business had been satisfactorily concluded, and all his misgivings were at an end.

" Come, let us gather round the festive board," said he joyously. " This is breakfast and dinner in one. Rose, be seated; and you, my dear friend, will surely share with us the repast we owe to you? "

With many protestations of regret, however, Daddy Tantaine pleaded an important engagement at the other end of Paris. " And," added he, " it is absolutely necessary that I should see Mascarin this evening, for I must try my best to make him look on you with a favorable eye."

Rose was very glad when the old man took his departure, for his ugliness, the shabbiness of his dress, and his general aspect of dirt, drove away all the feelings of gratitude she ought to have evinced, and inspired in her loathing and repugnance; and she fancied that his eyes, though veiled by his colored glasses, could detect the minutest secrets of her heart; but still this did not prevent her putting on a sweet smile and entreating him to remain.

But Daddy Tantaine was resolute; and after impressing upon Paul the necessity of punctuality, he went away, repeating, as he passed through the door, " May good appetite be present at your little feast, my dears."

As soon, however, as the door was closed he bent down and listened. The young people were as merry as larks, and their laughter filled the bare attic of the Hôtel de Perou. Why should not Paul have been in good spirits? He had in his pocket the address of the man who was to make his fortune, and on the chimneypiece was the balance of the banknote, which seemed to him an inexhaustible sum. Rose, too, was delighted, and could not refrain from jeering at their benefactor, whom she stigmatized as " an old idiot."

" Laugh while you can, my dears!" muttered Daddy Tantaine; " for this may be the last time you will do so."

With these words he crept down the dark staircase, which was only lighted up on Sundays, owing to the high price of gas, and, peeping through the glass door of the porter's lodge, saw Madame Loupins engaged in cooking; and, with the timid knock of a man who has learned his lesson in poverty's grammar, he entered.

" Here is my rent, madame," said he, placing on the table ten francs and twenty centimes. Then, as the woman was scribbling a receipt, he launched into a statement of his own affairs, and told her that he had come into a little property which would enable him to live in comfort during his few remaining years on earth; and—evidently fearing that his well-known poverty might cause Madame Loupins to discredit his assertions—drew out his pocketbook and exhibited several banknotes. This exhibition of wealth so surprised the landlady, that when the old man left she insisted on lighting him to the door. He turned eastward as soon as he had left the house, and, glancing at the names of the shops, entered a grocer's establishment at the corner of the Rue de Petit Pont. This grocer, thanks to a certain cheap wine, manufactured for him by a chemist at Berçy, had achieved a certain notoriety in that quarter. He was very stout and pompous, a widower, and a sergeant in the National Guard. His name was Melusin. In all poor districts five o'clock is a busy hour for the shopkeepers, for the workmen are returning from their labors, and their wives are busy in their preparations for their evening meal. M. Melusin was so busily engaged, giving orders and seeing that they were executed, that he did not even notice the entrance of Daddy Tantaine; but had he done so, he would not have put himself out for so poorly dressed a customer. But the old man had left behind him in the Hôtel de Perou every sign of humility and servility, and, making his way to the least crowded portion of the shop, he called out in imperative accents, " M. Melusin ! "

Very much surprised, the grocer ceased his avocation and hastened to obey the summons. " How the deuce does the man know me ? " muttered he, forgetting that his name was over the door in gilt letters fully six inches long.

" Sir," said Daddy Tantaine, without giving the grocer time to speak, " did not a young woman come here about half an hour ago and change a note for five hundred francs ? "

"Most certainly," answered M. Melusin; "but how did you know that? Ah, I have it!" he added, striking his forehead; "there has been a robbery, and you are in pursuit of the criminal. I must confess that the girl looked so poor, that I guessed there was something wrong. I saw her fingers tremble."

"Pardon me," returned Daddy Tantaine. "I have said nothing about a robbery. I only wished to ask you if you would know the girl again?"

"Perfectly—a really splendid girl, with hair that you do not see every day. I have reason to believe that she lives in the Rue Hachette. The police are not very popular with the shopkeeping class; but the latter, desirous of keeping down crime, generally afford plenty of information, and in the interests of virtue will even risk losing customers, who go off in a huff at not being attended to while they are talking to the officers of justice. Shall I," continued the grocer, "send one of the errand boys to the nearest police station?"

"No, thank you," replied Daddy Tantaine. "I should prefer your keeping the matter quiet until I communicate with you once more."

"Yes, yes, I see; a false step just now would put them on their guard."

"Just so. Now, will you let me have the number of the note, if you still have it? I wish you also to make a note of the date as well as the number."

"Yes, yes, I see," returned the grocer. "You may require my books as corroborative evidence; that is often the way. Excuse me; I will be back directly."

All that Daddy Tantaine had desired was executed with the greatest rapidity, and he and the grocer parted on the best terms, and the tradesman watched his visitor's departure, perfectly satisfied that he had been assisting a police officer who had deemed it fit to assume a disguise. Daddy Tantaine cared little what he thought, and, gaining the Place de Petit Pont, stopped and gazed around as if he was waiting for some one. Twice he walked round it in vain; but in his third circuit he came to a halt with an exclamation of satisfaction, for he had seen the person of whom he had been in search, who was a detestable looking youth of about eighteen years of age, though so thin and stunted that he hardly appeared to be fifteen.

The lad was leaning against the wall of the Quay St. Michel, openly asking alms, but keeping a sharp lookout for the police. At the first glance it was easy to detect in him the hideous outgrowth of the great city, the regular young rough of Paris, who, at eight years of age, smokes the butt ends of cigars picked up at the tavern doors and gets tipsy on coarse spirits. He had a thin crop of sandy hair, his complexion was dull and colorless, and a sneer curled the corners of his mouth, which had a thick, hanging underlip, and his eyes had an expression in them of revolting cynicism. His dress was tattered and dirty, and he had rolled up the sleeve of his right arm, exhibiting a deformed limb, sufficiently repulsive to excite the pity of the passers by. He was repeating a monotonous whine, in which the words " poor workman, arm destroyed by machinery, aged mother to support," occurred continually.

Daddy Tantaine walked straight up to the youth, and with a sound cuff sent his hat flying.

The lad turned sharply round, evidently in a terrible rage; but, recognizing his assailant, shrank back, and muttered to himself, " Landed! " In an instant he restored his arm to its originally healthy condition, and, picking up his cap, replaced it on his head, and humbly waited for fresh orders.

"Is this the way you execute your errands?" asked Daddy Tantaine, snarling.

"What errands? I have heard of none!"

"Never you mind that. Did not M. Mascarin, on my recommendation, put you in a way of earning your livelihood? and did you not promise to give up begging?"

"Beg pardon, guv'nor, I meant to be on the square, but I didn't like to waste time while I was a-waiting. I don't like a-being idle and I have copped seven browns."

"Toto Chupin," said the old man, with great severity, "you will certainly come to a bad end. But come, give your report. What have you seen?"

During this conversation they were walking slowly along the quay, and had passed the Hôtel Dieu.

"Well, guv'nor," replied the young rogue, "I just saw what you said I should. At four sharp, a carriage drove into the Place, and pulled up bang opposite the wigfaker's. Dash me, if it weren't a swell turnout! —horse, coachman, and all, in real slap-up style. It waited so long that I thought it had taken root there."

"Come, get on! Was there any one inside?"

"I should think there was! I twigged him at once, by the description you gave me. I never see a cove togged out as he was,—tall hat, light sit-down-upons, and a short coat—wasn't it cut short! but in really bang-up style. To be certain, I went right up to him, for it was getting dark, and had a good look at him. He had got out of the trap, and was marching up and down the pavement, with an unlighted cigar stuck in his mouth. I took a match, and said, 'Have a light,

my noble swell?' and hanged if he didn't give me ten
centimes! My! ain't he ugly!—short, shrivelled up,
and knock-kneed, with a glass in his eye, and altogether
precious like a monkey."

Daddy Tantaine began to grow impatient with all
this rigmarole. " Come, tell me what took place," said
he angrily.

" Precious little. The young swell didn't seem to
care about dirtying his trotter-cases; he kept slashing
about with his cane, and staring at all the gals. What
an ass that masher is! Wouldn't I have liked to have
punched his head! If you ever want to hide him,
daddy, please think of yours truly. He wouldn't stand
up to me for five minutes."

" Go on, my lad; go on."

" Well, we had waited half an hour, when all at once
a woman came sharp round the corner, and stops before the masher. Wasn't she a fine gal! and hadn't
she a pair of sparklers! but she had awfully seedy togs
on. But they spoke in whispers."

" So you did not hear what they said?"

" Do you take me for a flat? The gal said, 'Do
you understand?—to-morrow.' Then the swell chap,
says he, 'Do you promise?' and the gal, she answers
back, ' Yes, at noon.' Then they parted. She went off
to the Rue Hachette, and the masher tumbled into his
wheelbox. The jarvey cracked his whip, and off they
went in a brace of shakes. Now hand over them five
francs."

Daddy Tantaine did not seem surprised at this request, and he gave over the money to the young loafer,
with the words, " When I promise, I pay down on the
nail; but remember, Toto Chupin, you'll come to grief one
day. Good-night. Our ways lie in different directions."

The old man, however, lingered until he had seen the lad go off toward the Jardin des Plantes, and then, turning round, went back by the way he had come. "I have not lost my day," murmured he. "All the improbabilities have turned out certaities, and matters are going straight. Won't Flavia be awfully pleased?"

CHAPTER II.

A REGISTRY OFFICE.

THE establishment of the influential friend of Daddy Tantaine was situated in the Rue Montorgeuil, not far from the Passage de la Reine Hortense. M. B. Mascarin has a registry office for the engagement of both male and female servants. Two boards fastened upon each side of the door announce the hours of opening and closing, and give a list of those whose names are on the books; they further inform the public that the establishment was founded in 1844, and is still in the same hands. It was the long existence of M. Mascarin in a business which is usually very short-lived that had obtained for him a great amount of confidence, not only in the quarter in which he resided, but throughout the whole of Paris. Employers say that he sends them the best of servants, and the domestics in their turn assert that he only despatches them to good places. But M. Mascarin has still further claims on the public esteem; for it was he who, in 1845, founded and carried out a project which had for its aim and end the securing of a shelter for servants out of place. The better to carry out this, Mascarin took a partner, and gave him the charge of a furnished house close to the office.   Worthy as these projects were, Mascarin contrived to draw considerable profit from them, and was the owner of the house before which, in the noon of the day following the events we have described, Paul Violaine might have been seen standing.   The five hundred francs of old Tantaine, or at any rate a portion of them, had been well spent, and his clothes did credit to his own taste and the skill of his tailor.   Indeed, in his fine feathers he looked so handsome, that many women turned to gaze after him. He however took but little notice of this, for he was too full of anxiety, having grave doubts as to the power of the man whom Tantaine had asserted could, if he liked, make his fortune.   " A registry office ! " muttered he scornfully.   " Is he going to propose a berth of a hundred francs a month to me ? "   He was much agitated at the thoughts of the impending inter-view, and, before entering the house, gazed upon its exterior with great interest.   The house much resem-bled its neighbors.   The entrances to the Registry Office and the Servants' Home were in a courtyard, at the arched entrance to which stood a vendor of roast chest-nuts.

" There is no use in remaining here," said Paul. Summoning, therefore, all his resolution, he crossed the courtyard, and, ascending a flight of stairs, paused before a door upon which " OFFICE " was written. " Come in ! " responded at once to his knock.   He pushed open the door, and entered a room, which closely resembled all other similar offices.   There were seats all round the room, polished by frequent use. At the end was a sort of compartment shut in by a green baize curtain, jestingly termed " the Confes-sional " by the frequenters of the office.   Between the windows was a tin plate, with the words, "All fees to be paid in advance," in large letters upon it. In one corner a gentleman was seated at a writing table, who, as he made entries in a ledger, was talking to a woman who stood beside him.

"M. Mascarin?" asked Paul hesitatingly.

"What do you want with him?" asked the man, without looking up from his work. "Do you wish to enter your name? We have now vacancies for three bookkeepers, a cashier, a confidential clerk—six other good situations. Can you give good references?"

These words seemed to be uttered by rote.

"I beg your pardon," returned Paul; "but I should like to see M. Mascarin. One of his friends sent me here."

This statement evidently impressed the official, and he replied almost politely, "M. Mascarin is much occupied at present, sir; but he will soon be disengaged. Pray be seated."

Paul sat down on a bench, and examined the man who had just spoken with some curiosity. M. Mascarin's partner was a tall and athletic man, evidently enjoying the best of health, and wearing a large moustache elaborately waxed and pointed. His whole appearance betokened the old soldier. He had, so he asserted, served in the cavalry, and it was there that he had acquired the *soubriquet* by which he was known —Beaumarchef, his original name being David. He was about forty-five, but was still considered a very good-looking fellow. The entries that he was making in the ledger did not prevent him from keeping up a conversation with the woman standing by him. The woman, who seemed to be a cross between a cook and a market-woman, might be described as a thoroughly jovial soul. She seasoned her conversation with pinches of snuff, and spoke with a strong Alsatian brogue.

"Now, look here," said Beaumarchef; "do you really mean to say that you want a place?"

"I do that."

"You said that six months ago. We got you a splendid one, and three days afterward you chucked up the whole concern."

"And why shouldn't I? There was no need to work then; but now it is another pair of shoes, for I have spent nearly all I had saved."

Beaumarchef laid down his pen, and eyed her curiously for a second or two; then he said,—

"You've been making a fool of yourself somehow, I expect."

She half turned away her head, and began to complain of the hardness of the terms and of the meanness of the mistresses, who, instead of allowing their cooks to do the marketing, did it themselves, and so cheated their servants out of their commissions.

Beaumarchef nodded, just as he had done half an hour before to a lady who had complained bitterly of the misconduct of her servants. He was compelled by his position to sympathize with both sides.

The woman had now finished her tirade, and drawing the amount of the fee from a well-filled purse, placed it on the table, saying,—

"Please, M. Beaumarchef, register my name as Caroline Scheumal, and get me a real good place. It must be a cook, you understand, and I want to do the marketing without the missus dodging around."

"Well, I'll do my best."

"Try and find me a wealthy widower, or a young woman married to a very old fellow. Now, do look round; I'll drop in again to-morrow;" and with a farewell pinch of snuff, she left the office.

Paul listened to this conversation with feelings of anger and humiliation, and in his heart cursed old Tantaine for having introduced him into such company. He was seeking for some plausible excuse for withdrawal, when the door at the end of the room was thrown open, and two men came in, talking as they did so. The one was young and well dressed, with an easy, swaggering manner, which ignorant people mistake for good breeding. He had a many-colored rosette at his buttonhole, showing that he was the knight of more than one foreign order. The other was an elderly man, with an unmistakable legal air about him. He was dressed in a quilted dressing-gown, fur-lined shoes, and had on his head an embroidered cap, most likely the work of the hands of some one dear to him. He wore a white cravat, and his sight compelled him to use colored glasses.

"Then, my dear sir," said the younger man, "I may venture to entertain hopes?"

"Remember, Marquis," returned the other, "that if I were acting alone, what you require would be at once at your disposal. Unfortunately, I have others to consult."

"I place myself entirely in your hands," replied the Marquis.

The appearance of the fashionably dressed young man reconciled Paul to the place in which he was.

"A Marquis!" he murmured; "and the other swell-looking fellow must be M. Mascarin."

Paul was about to step forward, when Beaumarchef respectfully accosted the last comer,—

"Who do you think, sir," said he, "I have just seen?"

"Tell me quickly," was the impatient reply.

"Caroline Schimmel; you know who I mean."

"What! the woman who was in the service of the Duchess of Champdoce?"

"Exactly so."

M. Mascarin uttered an exclamation of delight.

"Where is she living now?"

Beaumarchef was utterly overwhelmed by this simple question. For the first time in his life he had omitted to take a client's address. This omission made Mascarin so angry that he forgot all his good manners, and broke out with an oath that would have shamed a London cabman,—

"How could you be such an infernal fool? We have been hunting for this woman for five months. You knew this as well as I did, and yet, when chance brings her to you, you let her slip through your fingers and vanish again."

"She'll be back again, sir; never fear. She won't fling away the money that she has paid for fees."

"And what do you think that she cares for ten sous or ten francs? She'll be back when she thinks she will; but a woman who drinks and is off her head nearly all the year round——"

Inspired by a sudden thought, Beaumarchef made a clutch at his hat.

"She has only just gone," said he; "I can easily overtake her."

But Mascarin arrested his progress.

"You are not a good bloodhound. Take Toto Chupin with you; he is outside with his chestnuts, and is as fly as they make them. If you catch her up, don't say a word, but follow her up, and see where she goes. I want to know her whole daily life. Remember that no item, however unimportant it may seem, is not of consequence."

Beaumarchef disappeared in an instant, and Mascarin continued to grumble.

" What a fool! " he murmured. " If I could only do everything myself. I worried my life out for months, trying to find the clue to the mystery which this woman holds, and now she has again escaped me."

Paul, who saw that his presence was not remarked, coughed to draw attention to it. In an instant Mascarin turned quickly round.

"Excuse me," said Paul; but the set smile had already resumed its place upon Mascarin's countenance.

" You are," remarked he, civilly, " Paul Violaine, are you not? "

The young man bowed in assent.

" Forgive my absence for an instant. I will be back directly," said Mascarin.

He passed through the door, and in another instant Paul heard his name called.

Compared to the outer chamber, Mascarin's office was quite a luxurious apartment, for the windows were bright, the paper on the walls fresh, and the floor carpeted. But few of the visitors to the office could boast of having been admitted into this sanctum; for generally business was conducted at Beaumarchef's table in the outer room. Paul, however, who was unacquainted with the prevailing rule, was not aware of the distinction with which he had been received. Mascarin, on his visitor's entrance, was comfortably seated in an armchair before the fire, with his elbow on his desk—and what a spectacle did that desk present! It was a perfect world in itself, and indicated that its proprietor was a man of many trades. It was piled with books and documents, while a great deal of the space was occupied by square pieces of cardboard, upon each of which was a name in large letters, while underneath was writing in very minute characters.

With a benevolent gesture, Mascarin pointed to an armchair, and in encouraging tones said, "And now let us talk."

It was plain to Paul that Mascarin was not acting, but that the kind and patriarchal expression upon his face was natural to it, and the young man felt that he could safely intrust his whole future to him.

"I have heard," commenced Mascarin, "that your means of livelihood are very precarious, or rather that you have none, and are ready to take the first one that offers you a means of subsistence. That, at least, is what I hear from my poor friend Tantaine."

"He has explained my case exactly."

"Good; only before proceeding to the future, let us speak of the past."

Paul gave a start, which Mascarin noticed, for he added,—

"You will excuse the freedom I am taking; but it is absolutely necessary that I should know to what I am binding myself. Tantaine tells me that you are a charming young man, strictly honest, and well educated; and now that I have had the pleasure of meeting you, I am sure that he is right; but I can only deal with proofs, and must be quite certain before I act on your behalf with third parties."

"I have nothing to conceal, sir, and am ready to answer any questions," responded Paul.

A slight smile, which Paul did not detect, played round the corners of Mascarin's mouth, and, with a gesture, with which all who knew him were familiar, he pushed back his glasses on his nose.

"I thank you," answered he; "it is not so easy as you may suppose to hide anything from me." He took one of the packets of pasteboard slips from his desk, and shuffling them like a pack of cards, continued, "Your name is Marie Paul Violaine. You were born at Poitiers, in the Rue des Vignes, on the 5th of January, 1843, and are therefore in your twenty-fourth year."

"That is quite correct, sir."

"You are an illegitimate child?"

The first question had surprised Paul; the second absolutely astounded him.

"Quite true, sir," replied he, not attempting to hide his surprise; "but I had no idea that M. Tantaine was so well informed; the partition which divided our rooms must have been thinner than I thought."

Mascarin took no notice of this remark, but continued to shuffle and examine his pieces of cardboard. Had Paul caught a clear glimpse of these, he would have seen his initials in the corner of each.

"Your mother," went on Mascarin, "kept, for the last fifteen years of her life, a little haberdasher's shop."

"Just so."

"But a business of that description in a town like Poitiers, does not bring in very remunerative results, and luckily she received for your support and education a sum of one thousand francs per year."

This time Paul started from his seat, for he was sure that Tantaine could not have learned this secret at the Hôtel de Perou.

"Merciful powers, sir!" cried he; "who could have told you a thing that has never passed my lips since my arrival in Paris, and of which even Rose is entirely ignorant?"

Mascarin raised his shoulders.

"You can easily comprehend," remarked he, "that a man in my line of business has to learn many things. If I did not take the greatest precautions, I should be deceived daily, and so lead others into error."

Paul had not been more than an hour in the office, but the directions given to Beaumarchef had already taught him how many of these events were arranged.

"Though I may be curious," went on Mascarin, "I am the symbol of discretion; so answer me frankly: How did your mother receive this annuity?"

"Through a Parisian solicitor."

"Do you know him?"

"Not at all," answered Paul, who had begun to grow uneasy under this questioning, for a kind of vague apprehension was aroused in his mind, and he could not see the utility of any of these interrogations. There was, however, nothing in Mascarin's manner to justify the misgivings of the young man, for he appeared to ask all these questions in quite a matter-of-course way, as if they were purely affairs of business.

After a protracted silence, Mascarin resumed,—

"I am half inclined to believe that the solicitor sent the money on his own account."

"No, sir," answered Paul. "I am sure you are mistaken."

"Why are you so certain?"

"Because my mother, who was the incarnation of truth, often assured me that my father died before my birth. Poor mother! I loved and respected her too much to question her on these matters. One day, however, impelled by an unworthy feeling of curiosity, I

HE TOOK ONE OF THE PACKETS OF PASTEBOARD SLIPS FROM HIS
DESK, AND SHUFFLING THEM LIKE A PACK OF CARDS, CONTINUED,
"YOUR NAME IS MARIE PAUL VIOLAINE"

dared to ask her the name of our protector. She burst into tears, and then I felt how mean and cruel I had been. I never learned his name but I know that he was not my father."

Mascarin affected not to notice the emotion of his young client.

" Did the allowance cease at your mother's death? " continued he.

"No; it was stopped when I came of age. My mother told me that this would be the case; but it seems only yesterday that she spoke to me of it. It was on my birthday, and she had prepared a little treat for my supper; for in spite of the affliction my birth had caused her, she loved me fondly. Poor mother! 'Paul,' said she, 'at your birth a genuine friend promised to help me to bring up and educate you, and he kept his word. But you are now twenty-one, and must expect nothing more from him. My son, you are a man now, and I have only you to look to. Work and earn an honest livelihood——' "

Paul could proceed no farther, for his emotions choked him.

" My mother died suddenly some ten months after this conversation—without time to communicate anything to me, and I was left perfectly alone in the world; and were I to die to-morrow, there would not be a soul to follow me to my grave."

Mascarin put on a sympathetic look.

" Not quite so bad as that, my young friend; I trust that you have one now."

Mascarin rose from his seat, and for a few minutes paced up and down the room, and then halted, with his arms folded, before the young man.

" You have heard me," said he, " and I will not put

any further questions which it will but pain you to reply to, for I only wished to take your measure, and to judge of your truth from your replies. You will ask why? Ah, that is a question I cannot answer to-day, but you shall know later on. Be assured, however, that I know everything about you, but I cannot tell you by what means. Say it has all happened by chance. Chance has broad shoulders, and can bear a great deal."

This ambiguous speech caused a thrill of terror to pass through Paul, which was plainly visible on his expressive features.

"Are you alarmed?" asked Mascarin, readjusting his spectacles.

"I am much surprised, sir," stammered Paul.

"Come, come! what can a man in your circumstances have to fear? There is no use in racking your brain; you will find out all you want quickly enough, and had best make up your mind to place yourself in my hands without reserve, for my sole desire is to be of service to you."

These words were uttered in the most benevolent manner; and as he resumed his seat, he added,—

"Now let us talk of yourself. Your mother, whom you justly say was a thoroughly good woman, pinched herself in order to keep you at college at Poitiers. You entered a solicitor's office at eighteen, I think?"

"Yes, sir."

"But your mother's desire was to see you established at Loudon or Cevray. Perhaps she hoped that her wealthy friend would aid you still further. Unluckily, however, you had no inclination for the law."

Paul smiled, but Mascarin went on with some little severity.

"I repeat, unfortunately; and I think that by this

time you have gone through enough to be of my opinion. What did you do instead of studying law? You did—what? You wasted your time over music, and composed songs, and, I know, an opera, and thought yourself a perfect genius."

Paul had listened up to this time with patience, but at this sarcasm he endeavored to protest; but it was in vain, for Mascarin went on pitilessly,—

"One day you abandoned the study of the law, and told your mother that until you had made your name as a musical composer you would give lessons on the piano; but you could obtain no pupils, and—well, just look in the glass yourself, and say if you think that your age and appearance would justify parents in intrusting their daughters to your tuition?"

Mascarin stopped for a moment and consulted his notes afresh.

"Your departure from Poitiers," he went on, "was your last act of folly. The very day after your mother's death you collected together all her scanty savings, and took the train to Paris."

"Then, sir, I had hoped——"

"What, to arrive at fortune by the road of talent? Foolish boy! Every year a thousand poor wretches have been thus intoxicated by their provincial celebrity, and have started for Paris, buoyed up by similar hopes. Do you know the end of them? At the end of ten years—I give them no longer—nine out of ten die of starvation and disappointment, and the other joins the criminal army."

Paul had often repeated this to himself, and could, therefore, make no reply.

"But," went on Mascarin, "you did not leave Poitiers alone; you carried off with you a young girl named Rose Pigoreau."

"Pray, let me explain."

"It would be useless. The fact speaks for itself. In six months your little store had disappeared; then came poverty and starvation, and at last, in the Hôtel de Perou, your thoughts turned to suicide, and you were only saved by my old friend Tantaine."

Paul felt his temper rising, for these plain truths were hard to bear; but fear lest he should lose his protector kept him silent.

"I admit everything, sir," said he calmly. "I was a fool, and almost mad, but experience has taught me a bitter lesson. I am here to-day, and this fact should tell you that I have given up all my vain hallucinations."

"Will you give up Rose Pigoreau?"

As this abrupt question was put to him, Paul turned pale with anger.

"I love Rose," answered he coldly; "she believes in me, and has shared my troubles with courage, and one day she shall be my wife."

Raising his velvet cap from his head, Mascarin bowed with an ironical air, saying, "Is that so? Then I beg a thousand pardons. It is urgent that you should have immediate employment. Pray, what can you do? Not much of anything, I fancy;—like most college bred boys, you can do a little of everything, and nothing well. Had I a son, and an enormous income, I would have him taught a trade."

Paul bit his lips; but he knew the portrait was a true one.

"And now," continued Mascarin, "I have come to your aid, and what do you say to a situation with a salary of twelve thousand francs?"

This sum was so much greater than Paul had dared to hope, that he believed Mascarin was amusing himself at his expense.

"It is not kind of you to laugh at me, under the present circumstances," remarked he.

Mascarin was not laughing at him; but it was fully half an hour before he could prove this to Paul.

"You would like more proof of what I say," said he, after a long conversation. "Very well, then; shall I advance your first month's salary?" And as he spoke, he took a thousand-franc note from his desk, and offered it to Paul. The young man rejected the note; but the force of the argument struck him; and he asked if he was capable of carrying out the duties which such a salary doubtless demanded.

"Were I not certain of your abilities, I should not offer it to you," replied Mascarin. "I am in a hurry now, or I would explain the whole affair; but I must defer doing so until to-morrow, when please come at the same hour as you did to-day."

Even in his state of surprise and stupefaction, Paul felt that this was a signal for him to depart.

"A moment more," said Mascarin. "You understand that you can no longer remain at the Hôtel de Perou? Try and find a room in this neighborhood; and when you have done so, leave the address at the office. Good-bye, my young friend, until to-morrow, and learn to bear good fortune."

For a few minutes Mascarin stood at the door of the office watching Paul, who departed almost staggering beneath the burden of so many conflicting emotions; and when he saw him disappear round the corner, he ran to a glazed door which led to his bed chamber, and in a loud whisper called, " Come in, Hortebise. He has gone."

A man obeyed the summons at once, and hurriedly drew up a chair to the fire. " My feet are almost frozen," exclaimed he; " I should not know it if any one was to chop them off. Your room, my dear Baptiste, is a perfect refrigerator. Another time, please, have a fire lighted in it."

This speech, however, did not disturb Mascarin's line of thought. " Did you hear all? " asked he.

" I saw and heard all that you did."

" And what do you think of the lad? "

" I think that Daddy Tantaine is a man of observation and powerful will, and that he will mould this child between his fingers like wax."

CHAPTER III.

THE OPINION OF DR. HORTEBISE.

DR. HORTEBISE, who had addressed Mascarin so familiarly by his Christian name of Baptiste, was about fifty-six years of age, but he carried his years so well, that he always passed for forty-nine. He had a heavy pair of red, sensual-looking lips, his hair was untinted by gray, and his eyes still lustrous. A man who moved in the best society, eloquent in manner, a brilliant conversationalist, and vivid in his perceptions, he concealed under the veil of good-humored sarcasm the utmost cynicism of mind. He was very popular and much sought after. He had but few faults, but quite a catalogue of appalling vices. Under this Epicurean exterior lurked, it was reported, the man of talent and the celebrated physician. He was not a hard-working man, simply because he achieved the same results without toil or labor. He had recently taken to homœopathy, and started a medical journal, which he named *The Globule,* which died at its fifth number. His conversion made all society laugh, and he joined in the ridicule, thus showing the sincerity of his views, for he was never able to take the round of life seriously. To-day, however, Mascarin, well as he knew his friend, seemed piqued at his air of levity.

"When I asked you to come here to-day," said he, "and when I begged you to conceal yourself in my bedroom——"

"Where I was half frozen," broke in Hortebise.

"It was," went on Mascarin, "because I desired your advice. We have started on a serious undertaking,—an undertaking full of peril both to you and to myself."

"Pooh! I have perfect confidence in you,—whatever you do is done well, and you are not the man to fling away your trump cards."

"True; but I may lose the game, after all, and then——"

The doctor merely shook a large gold locket that depended from his watch chain.

This movement seemed to annoy Mascarin a great deal. "Why do you flash that trinket at me?" asked he. "We have known each other for five and twenty years,—what do you mean to imply? Do you mean that the locket contains the likeness of some one that you intend to make use of later on? I think that you might render such a step unnecessary by giving me your present advice and attention."

Hortebise threw himself back in his chair with an expression of resignation. "If you want advice," remarked he, "why not apply to our worthy friend Catenac?—he knows something of business, as he is a lawyer."

The name of Catenac seemed to irritate Mascarin so much, that, calm and self-contained as he usually was, he pulled off his cap and dashed it on his desk.

"Are you speaking seriously?" said he angrily.

"Why should I not be in earnest?"

Mascarin removed his glasses, as though without them he could the more easily peer into the depths of the soul of the man before him.

"Because," replied he slowly, "both you and I distrust Catenac. When did you see him last?"

"More than three months ago."

"True, and I allow that he seems to be acting fairly toward his old associates; but you will admit that, in keeping away thus, his conduct is without excuse, for he has made his fortune; and though he pretends to be poor, he is certainly a man of wealth."

"Do you really think so?"

"Were he here, I would force him to acknowledge that he is worth a million, at least."

"A million!" exclaimed the doctor, with sudden animation.

"Yes, certainly. You and I, Hortebise, have indulged our every whim, and have spent gold like water, while our friend garnered his harvest and stored it away. But poor Catenac has no expensive tastes, nor does he care for women or the pleasures of the table. While we indulged in every pleasure, he lent out his money at usurious interest. But, stop,—how much do you spend per annum?"

"That is a hard question to answer; but, say, forty thousand francs."

"More, a great deal more; but calculate what a capital sum that would amount to during the twenty years we have done business together."

The doctor was not clever at figures; he made several vain attempts to solve the problem, and at last gave it up in despair. "Forty and forty," muttered he, tapping the tips of his fingers, are eighty, then forty——"

"Call it eight hundred thousand francs," broke in Mascarin. "Say I drew the same amount as you did. We have spent ours, and Catenac has saved his, and grown rich; hence my distrust. Our interests are no longer identical. He certainly comes here every month, but it is only to claim his share; he consents to take his share of the profits, but shirks the risks. It is fully ten years since he brought in any business. I don't trust him at all. He always declines to join in any scheme that we propose, and sees danger in everything."

"He would not betray us, however."

Mascarin took a few moments for reflection. "I think," said he, "that Catenac is afraid of us. He knows that the ruin of me would entail the destruction of the other two. This is our only safeguard; but if he dare not injure us openly, he is quite capable of working against us in secret. Do you remember what he said the last time he was here? That we ought to close our business and retire. How should *we* live? for he is rich and we are poor. What on earth are you doing, Hortebise?" he added, for the physician, who had the reputation of being worth an enormous amount, had taken out his purse, and was going over the contents.

"I have exactly three hundred and twenty-seven francs!" answered he with a laugh. "What is the state of your finances?"

Mascarin made a grimace. "I am not so well off as you; and besides," he continued in a low voice, as though speaking to himself, "I have certain ties which you do not possess."

For the first time during this interview a cloud spread over the doctor's countenance.

"Great heavens!" said he, "and I was depending on you for three thousand francs, which I require urgently."

Mascarin smiled slyly at the doctor's uneasiness. "Don't worry," he answered. "You can have that; there ought to be some six or eight thousand francs in the safe. But that is all, and that is the last of our common capital,—this after twenty years of toil, danger, and anxiety, and we have not twenty years before us to make a fresh fortune in."

"Yes," continued Mascarin, "we are getting old, and therefore have the greater reason for making one grand stroke to assure our fortune. Were I to fall ill to-morrow, all would go to smash."

"Quite true," returned the doctor, with a slight shudder.

"We must, and that is certain, venture on a bold stroke. I have said this for years, and woven a web of gigantic proportions. Do you now know why at this last moment I appeal to you, and not to Catenac for assistance? If only one out of the two operations that I have fully explained to you succeeds, our fortune is made."

"I follow you exactly."

"The question now is whether the chance of success

is sufficiently great to warrant our going on with these undertakings. Think it over, and let me have your opinion."

An acute observer could easily have seen that the doctor was a man of resource, and a thoroughly competent adviser, for the reason that his coolness never deserted him. Compelled to choose between the use of the contents of his locket, or the continuance of a life of luxurious ease, the smile vanished from the doctor's face, and he began to reflect profoundly. Leaning back in his chair, with his feet resting on the fender, he carefully studied every combination in the undertaking, as a general inspects the position taken up by the enemy, when a battle is impending, upon which the fate of an empire may hinge. That this analysis took a favorable turn, was evident, for Mascarin soon saw a smile appear upon the doctor's lips. "We must make the attack at once," said he; "but make no mistake; the projects you propose are most dangerous, and a single error upon our side would entail destruction; but we must take some risk. The odds are against us, but still we may win. Under these circumstances, and as necessity cheers us on, I say, *Forward!*" As he said this, he rose to his feet, and extending his hand toward his friend, exclaimed, "I am entirely at your disposal."

Mascarin seemed relieved by the doctor's decision, for he was in that frame of mind when, however self-reliant a man may be, he has a disinclination to be left alone, and the aid of a stout ally is of the utmost service.

"Have you considered every point carefully?" asked he. "You know that we can only act at present upon one of these undertakings, and that is the one of which the Marquis de Croisenois——"

" I know that."

" With reference to the affair of the Duke de Champdoce, I have still to gather together certain things
necessary for the ultimate success of the scheme. There
is a mystery in the lives of the Duke and Duchess,—
of this there is no doubt,—but what is this secret? I
would lay my life that I have hit upon the correct
solution; but I want no suspicions, no probabilities; I
want absolute certainties. And now," continued he,
" this brings us back to the first question. What do
you think of Paul Violaine?"

Hortebise walked up and down the room two or
three times, and finally stopped opposite to his friend.
" I think," said he, " that the lad has many of the
qualities we want, and we might find it hard to discover
one better suited for our purpose. Besides, he is a
bastard, knows nothing of his father, and therefore
leaves a wide field for conjecture; for every natural
son has the right to consider himself, if he likes, the
offspring of a monarch. He has no family or any one
to look after him, which assures us that whatever may
happen, there is no one to call us to account. He is
not overwise, but has a certain amount of talent, and
any quantity of ridiculous self-conceit. He is wonderfully handsome, which will make matters easier, but—"

" Ah, there is a ' but ' then? "

" More than one," answered the doctor, " for there
are three for certain. First, there is Rose Pigoreau,
whose beauty has so captivated our old friend Tantaine,—she certainly appears to be a danger in the
future."

" Be easy," returned Mascarin; " we will quickly
remove this young woman from our road."

" Good; but do not be too confident," answered

Hortebise, in his usual tone. "The danger from her is not the one you think, and which you are trying to avoid. You think Paul loves her. You are wrong. He would drop her to-morrow, so that he could please his self-indulgence. But the woman who thinks that she hates her lover often deceives herself; and Rose is simply tired of poverty. Give her a little amount of comfort, good living, and luxury, and you will see her give them all up to come back to Paul. Yes, I tell you, she will harass and annoy him, as women of her class who have nothing to love always do. She will even go to Flavia to claim him."

"She had better not," retorted Mascarin, in threatening accents.

"Why, how could you prevent it? She has known Paul from his infancy. She knew his mother; she was perhaps brought up by her, perhaps even lived in the same street. Look out, I say, for danger from that quarter."

"You may be right, and I will take my precautions."

It was sufficient for Mascarin to be assured of a danger to find means of warding it off.

"My second ' but,' " continued Hortebise, " is the idea of the mysterious protector of whom the young man spoke. His mother, he says, has reason to know that his father is dead, and I believe in the truth of the statement. In this case, what has become of the person who paid Madame Violaine her allowance?"

"You are right, quite right; these are the crevices in our armor; but I keep my eyes open, and nothing escapes me."

The doctor was growing rather weary, but he still went on courageously. "My third ' but ' " said he, " is perhaps the strongest. We must see the young fel-

low at once. It may be to-morrow, without even having prepared him or taught him his part. Suppose we
found that he was honest! Imagine—if he returned a
firm negative to all your dazzling offers!"

Mascarin rose to his feet in his turn. "I do not
think that there is any chance of that," said he.

"Why not, pray?"

"Because when Tantaine brought him to me, he
had studied him carefully. He is as weak as a woman,
and as vain as a journalist. Besides, he is ashamed at
being poor. No; I can mould him like wax into any
shape I like. He will be just what we wish."

"Are you sure," asked Hortebise, "that Flavia will
have nothing to say in this matter?"

"I had rather, with your permission, say nothing on
that head," returned Mascarin. He broke off his
speech and listened eagerly. "There is some one listening," said he. "Hark!"

The sound was repeated, and the doctor was about
to seek refuge in the inner room, when Mascarin laid
a detaining hand upon his arm.

"Stay," observed he, "it is only Beaumarchef;" and
as he spoke, he struck a gilded bell that stood on his
desk. In another instant Beaumarchef appeared, and
with an air in which familiarity was mingled with
respect, he saluted in military fashion.

"Ah," said the doctor pleasantly, "do you take your
nips of brandy regularly?"

"Only occasionally, sir," stammered the man.

"Too often, too often, my good fellow. Do you
think that your nose and eyelids are not real telltales?"

"But I assure you, sir——"

"Do you not remember I told you that you had
asthmatic symptoms? Why, the movement of your

pectoral muscles shows that your lungs are affected."

" But I have been running, sir."

Mascarin broke in upon this conversation, which he considered frivolous. " If he is out of breath," remarked he, " it is because he has been endeavoring to repair a great act of carelessness that he has committed. Well, Beaumarchef, how did you get on?"

" All right, sir," returned he, with a look of triumph.   " Good!"

" What are you talking about?" asked the doctor.

Mascarin gave his friend a meaning glance, and then, in a careless manner, replied, " Caroline Schimmel, a former servant of the Champdoce family, also patronizes our office. How did you find her, Beaumarchef?"

" Well, an idea occurred to me."

"Pooh! do you have ideas at your time of life?"

Beaumarchef put on an air of importance. " My idea was this," he went on: " as I left the office with Toto Chupin, I said to myself, the woman would certainly drop in at some pub. before she reached the boulevard."

" A sound argument," remarked the doctor.

" Therefore Toto and I took a squint into every one we passed, and before we got to the Rue Carreau we saw her in one, sure enough."

" And Toto is after her now?"

" Yes, sir; he said he would follow her like her shadow, and will bring in a report every day."

" I am very pleased with you, Beaumarchef," said Mascarin, rubbing his hands joyously.

Beaumarchef seemed highly flattered, but continued,—

" This is not all."

" What else is there to tell?"

"I met La Candéle on his way from the Place de Petit Pont, and he has just seen that young girl—you know whom I mean—driving off in a two-horse Victoria. He followed it, of course. She has been placed in a gorgeous apartment in the Rue Douai; and from what the porter says, she must be a rare beauty; and La Candéle raved about her, and says that she has the most magnificent eyes in the world."

"Ah," remarked Hortebise, "then Tantaine was right in his description of her."

"Of course he was," answered Mascarin with a slight frown, "and this proves the justice of the objection you made a little time back. A girl possessed of such dazzling beauty may even influence the fool who has carried her off to become dangerous."

Beaumarchef touched his master's arm kindly. "If you wish to get rid of the masher," said he, "I can show you a way;" and throwing himself into the position of a fencer, he made a lunge with his right arm, exclaiming, "One, two!"

"A Prussian quarrel," remarked Mascarin. "No; a duel would do us no good. We should still have the girl on our hands, and violent measures are always to be avoided." He took off his glasses, wiped them, and looking at the doctor intently, said, "Suppose we take an epidemic as our ally. If the girl had the small-pox, she would lose her beauty."

Cynical and hardened as the doctor was, he drew back in horror at this proposal. "Under certain circumstances," remarked he, "science might aid us; but Rose, even without her beauty, would be just as dangerous as she is now. It is *her* affection for Paul that we have to check, and not *his* for her; and the uglier a woman is, the more she clings to her lover."

" All this is worthy of consideration," returned Mascarin; " meanwhile we must take steps to guard ourselves from the impending danger. Have you finished
that report on Gandelu, Beaumarchef? What is his
position? "

" Head over ears in debt, sir, but not harassed by
his creditors because of his future prospects."

" Surely among these creditors there are some that
we could influence? " said Mascarin. " Find this out,
and report to me this evening; and farewell for the
present."

When again alone, the two confederates remained
silent for some time. The decisive moment had arrived. As yet they were not compromised; but if they
intended to carry out their plans, they must no longer
remain inactive; and both of these men had sufficient
experience to know that they must look at the position
boldly, and make up their minds at once. The pleasant smile upon the doctor's face faded away, and his
fingers played nervously with his locket. Mascarin
was the first to break the silence.

" Let us no longer hesitate," said he; " let us shut
our eyes to the danger and advance steadily. You
heard the promises made by the Marquis de Croisenois.
He will do as we wish, but under certain conditions.
Mademoiselle de Mussidan must be his bride."

" That will be impossible."

" Not so, if we desire it: and the proof of this is,
that before two o'clock the engagement between
Mademoiselle Sabine and the Baron de Breulh-Faverlay will be broken off."

The doctor heaved a deep sigh. " I can understand
Catenac's scruples. Ah! if, like him, I had a million! "

During this brief conversation Mascarin had gone

into his sleeping room and was busily engaged in changing his dress.

"If you are ready," remarked the doctor, "we will make a start."

In reply, Mascarin opened the door leading into the office. "Get a cab, Beaumarchef," said he.

CHAPTER IV.

A TRUSTWORTHY SERVANT.

In the city of Paris it is impossible to find a more fashionable quarter than the one which is bounded on the one side by the Rue Faubourg Saint Honoré and on the other by the Seine, and commences at the Place de la Concorde and ends at the Avenue de l'Impératrice. In this favored spot millionaires seem to bloom like the rhododendron in the sunny south. There are the magnificent palaces which they have erected for their accommodation, where the turf is ever verdant, and where the flowers bloom perennially; but the most gorgeous of all these mansions was the Hôtel de Mussidan, the last *chef d'œuvre* of Sevair, that skilful architect who died just as the world was beginning to recognize his talents. With a spacious courtyard in front and a magnificent garden in the rear, the Hôtel de Mussidan is as elegant as it is commodious. The exterior was extremely plain, and not disfigured by florid ornamentation. White marble steps, with a light and elegant railing at the sides, lead to the wide doors which open into the hall. The busy hum of the servants at work at an early hour in the yard tells that an ample establishment is kept up. There can be seen luxurious carriages, for occasions of ceremony, and the park phaeton, and the simple brougham which the Countess uses when she goes out shopping; and that carefully groomed thoroughbred is Mirette, the favorite riding horse of Mademoiselle Sabine. Mascarin and his confederate descended from their cab a little distance at the corner of the Avenue Matignon. Mascarin, in his dark suit, with his spotless white cravat and glittering spectacles, looked like some highly respectable functionary of State. Hortebise wore his usual smile, though his cheek was pale.

"Now," remarked Mascarin, "let me see,—on what footing do you stand with the Mussidans? Do they look upon you as a friend?"

"No, no; a poor doctor, whose ancestors were not among the Crusaders, could not be the intimate friend of such haughty nobles as the Mussidans."

"But the Countess knows you, and will not refuse to receive you, nor have you turned out as soon as you begin to speak; for, taking shelter behind some rogue without a name, you can shelter your own reputation. I will see the Count."

"Take care of him," said Hortebise thoughtfully. "He has a reputation for being a man of ungovernable temper, and, at the first word from you that he objects to, would throw you out of the window as soon as look at you."

Mascarin shrugged his shoulders. "I can bring him to reason," answered he.

The two confederates walked a little past the Hôtel de Mussidan, and the doctor explained the interior arrangements of the house.

"I," continued Mascarin, "will insist upon the

Count's breaking off his daughter's engagement with M. de Breulh-Faverlay, but shall not say a word about the Marquis de Croisenois, while you will take the opportunity of putting his pretensions before the Countess, and will not say a word of M. de Breulh-Faverlay."

"I have learned my lesson, and shall not forget it."

"You see, doctor, the beauty of the whole affair is, that the Countess will wonder how her husband will take her interference, while he will be at a loss how to break the news to his wife. How surprised they will be when they find that they have both the same end in view!"

There was something so droll in the whole affair, that the doctor burst into a loud laugh.

"We go by such different roads," said he, "that they will never suspect that we are working together. Faith! my dear Baptiste, you are much more clever than I thought."

"Don't praise me until you see that I am successful."

Mascarin stopped opposite to a *café* in the Faubourg Saint Honoré.

"Wait here for me, doctor," said he, "while I make a little call. If all is right, I will come for you again; then I will see the Count, and twenty minutes later do you go to the house and ask for the Countess."

The clock struck four as the worthy confederates parted, and Mascarin continued his way along the Faubourg Saint Honoré, and again stopped before a public house, which he entered, the master of which, Father Canon, was so well known in the neighborhood that he had not thought it worth while to have his name painted over the door. He did not profess to serve his best wine to casual customers, but for regu-

lar frequenters of his house, chiefly the servants of
noble families, he kept a better brand of wine. Mascarin's respectable appearance inclined the landlord to
step forward. Among Frenchmen, who are always
full of gayety, a serious exterior is ever an excellent
passport.

"What can I do for you, sir?" asked he with great
politeness.

"Can I see Florestan?"

"In Count de Mussidan's service, I believe?"

"Just so; I have an appointment with him here."

"He is downstairs in the band-room," replied the
landlord. "I will send for him."

"Don't trouble; I will go down," and, without waiting for permission, Mascarin descended some steps
that apparently led to a cellar.

"It appears to me," murmured Father Canon, "that
I have seen this cove's face before."

Mascarin pushed open a door at the bottom of the
flight of stairs, and a strange and appalling noise issued
from within (but this neither surprised nor alarmed
him), and entered a vaulted room arranged like a
café, with seats and tables, filled with customers. In
the centre, two men, in their shirt sleeves, with crimson
faces, were performing upon horns; while an old man,
with leather gaiters, buttoning to the knee, and a broad
leather belt, was whistling the air the hornplayers were
executing. As Mascarin politely took off his hat, the
performers ceased, and the old man discontinued his
whistling, while a well-built young fellow, with pumps
and stockings, and wearing a fashionable mustache,
exclaimed,—

"Aha, it is that good old Mascarin. I was expecting you; will you drink?"

Without waiting for further invitation Mascarin helped himself from a bottle that stood near.

" Did Father Canon tell you that I was here? " asked the young man, who was the Florestan Mascarin had been inquiring for. " You see," continued he, " that the police will not permit us to practise the horn; so, you observe, Father Canon has arranged this underground studio, from whence no sound reaches the upper world."

The hornplayers had now resumed their lessons, and Florestan was compelled to place both hands to the side of his mouth, in order to render himself audible, and to shout with all his might.

" That old fellow there is a huntsman in the service of the Duke de Champdoce, and is the finest hornplayer going. I have only had twenty lessons from him, and am getting on wonderfully."

" Ah! " exclaimed Mascarin, " when I have more time I must hear your performance; but to-day I am in a hurry, and want to say a few words to you in private."

" Certainly, but suppose we go upstairs and ask for a private room."

The rooms he referred to were not very luxuriously furnished, but were admirably suited for confidential communications; and had the walls been able to speak, they could have told many a strange tale.

Florestan and Mascarin seated themselves in one of these before a small table, upon which Father Canon placed a bottle of wine and two glasses.

" I asked you to meet me here, Florestan," began Mascarin, " because you can do me a little favor."

" Anything that is in my power I will do," said the young man.

" First, a few words regarding yourself. How do you get on with Count de Mussidan?"

Mascarin had adopted an air of familiarity which he knew would please his companion.

" I don't care about the place," replied Florestan, " and I am going to ask Beaumarchef to look out another one for me."

" I am surprised at that; all your predecessors said that the Count was a perfect gentleman——"

" Just try him yourself," broke in the valet. " In the first place he is as fickle as the wind, and awfully suspicious. He never leaves anything about,—no letters, no cigars, and no money. He spends half his time in locking things up, and goes to bed with his keys under his pillow."

" I allow that such suspicion on his part is most unpleasant."

" It is indeed, and besides he is awfully violent. He gets in a rage about nothing, and half a dozen times in the day he looks ready to murder you. On my word, I am really frightened at him."

This account, coupled with what he had heard from Hortebise seemed to render Mascarin very thoughtful.

" Is he always like this, or only at intervals?"

" He is always a beast, but he is worse after drink or losing at cards. He is never home until after four in the morning."

" And what does his wife say?"

This query made Florestan laugh.

" Madame does not bother herself about her lord and master, I can assure you. Sometimes they don't meet for weeks. All she wants is plenty of money. And ain't we just dunned!"

" But the Mussidans are wealthy?"

"Tremendously so, but at times there is not the value of a franc in the house. Then Madame is like a tigress, and would send to borrow from all her friends."

"But she must feel much humiliated?"

"Not a bit; when she wants a heavy amount, she sends off to the Duke de Champdoce, and he always parts; but she doesn't mince matters with him."

"It would seem as if you had known the contents of your mistress's letters?" remarked Mascarin with a smile.

"Of course I have; I like to know what is in the letters I carry about. She only says, 'My good friend, I want so much,' and back comes the money without a word. Of course it is easy to see that there has been something between them."

"Yes, evidently."

"And when master and missus do meet they only have rows, and such rows! When the working man has had a drop too much, he beats his wife, she screams, then they kiss and make it up; but the Mussidans say things to each other in cold blood that neither can ever forgive."

From the air with which Mascarin listened to these details, it almost seemed as if he had been aware of them before.

"Then," said he, "Mademoiselle Sabine is the only nice one in the house?"

"Yes, she is always gentle and considerate."

"Then you think that M. de Breulh-Faverlay will be a happy man?"

"Oh yes; but perhaps this marriage will——" but here Florestan interrupted himself and assumed an air of extreme caution. After looking carefully round, he lowered his voice, and continued, "Mademoiselle Sabine has been left so much to herself that she acts just as she thinks fit."

"Do you mean," asked Mascarin, "that the young lady has a lover?"

"Just so."

"But that must be wrong; and let me tell you that you ought not to repeat such a story."

The man grew quite excited.

"Story," repeated he; "I know what I know. If I spoke of a lover, it is because I have seen him with my own eyes, not once, but twice."

From the manner in which Mascarin received this intelligence, Florestan saw that he was interested in the highest degree.

"I'll tell you all about it," continued he. "The first time was when she went to mass; it came on to rain suddenly, and Modeste, her maid, begged me to go for an umbrella. As soon as I came back I went in and saw Mademoiselle Sabine standing by the receptacle for holy water, talking to a young fellow. Of course I dodged behind a pillar, and kept a watch on the pair——"

"But you don't found all your story on this?"

"I think you would, had you seen the way they looked into each other's eyes."

"What was he like?"

"Very good looking, about my height, with an aristocratic air."

"How about the second time?"

"Ah, that is a longer story. I went one day with Mademoiselle when she was going to see a friend in the Rue Marbœuf. She waited at a corner of the street, and beckoned me to her. 'Florestan,' said she,

' I forgot to post this letter; go and do so; I will wait
here for you.' "

" Of course you read it ? "

" No. I thought there was something wrong. She
wants to get rid of you, so, instead of posting it, I
slunk behind a tree and waited. I had hardly done
so, when the young fellow I had seen at the chapel
came round the corner; but I scarcely knew him. He
was dressed just like a working man, in a blouse all
over plaster. They talked for about ten minutes, and
Mademoiselle Sabine gave him what looked like a
photograph."

By this time the bottle was empty, and Florestan
was about to call for another, when Mascarin checked
him, saying,—

" Not to-day; it is growing late, and I must tell
you what I want you to do for me. Is the Count at
home now ? "

" Of course he is; he has not left his room for two
days, owing to having slipped going downstairs."

" Well, my lad, I must see your master; and if I
sent up my card, the odds are he would not see me,
so I rely upon you to show me up without announcing
me."

Florestan remained silent for a few minutes.

" It is no easy job," he muttered, " for the Count
does not like unexpected visitors, and the Countess is
with him just now. However, as I am not going to
stay, I'll chance it."

Mascarin rose from his seat.

" We must not be seen together," said he; " I'll
settle the score; do you go on, and I will follow
in five minutes. Remember we don't know each
other."

"I am fly; and mind you look out a good place for me."

Mascarin paid the bill, and then looked into the *café* to inform the doctor of his movements, and a few minutes later, Florestan in his most sonorous voice, threw open the door of his master's room and announced,—

"M. Mascarin."

CHAPTER V.

A FORGOTTEN CRIME.

BAPTISTE MASCARIN had been in so many strange situations, from which he had extricated himself with safety and credit, that he had the fullest self-confidence, but as he ascended the wide staircase of the Hôtel de Mussidan, he felt his heart beat quicker in anticipation of the struggle that was before him. It was twilight out of doors, but all within was a blaze of light. The library into which he was ushered was a vast apartment, furnished in severe taste. At the sound of the unaristocratic name of Mascarin, which seemed as much out of place as a drunkard's oath in the chamber of sleeping innocence, M. de Mussidan raised his head in sudden surprise. The Count was seated at the other end of the room, reading by the light of four candles placed in a magnificently wrought candelabra. He threw down his paper, and raising his glasses, gazed with astonishment at Mascarin, who, with his hat in his hand and his heart in his mouth, slowly crossed the room, muttering a few unintelligible apologies. He could make nothing, however, of his visitor, and said, "Whom do you wish to see, sir?"

"The Count de Mussidan," stuttered Mascarin; "and I hope that you will forgive this intrusion."

The Count cut his excuse short with a haughty wave of his hand. "Wait," said he imperiously. He then with evident pain rose from his seat, and crossing the room, rang the bell violently, and then reseated himself. Mascarin, who still remained in the centre of the room, inwardly wondered if after all he was to be turned out of the house. In another second the door opened, and the figure of the faithful Florestan appeared.

"Florestan," said the Count angrily, "this is the first time that you have permitted any one to enter this room without my permission; if this occurs again, you leave my service."

"I assure your lordship," began the man.

"Enough! I have spoken; you know what to expect."

During this brief colloquy, Mascarin studied the Count with the deepest attention.

The Count Octave de Mussidan in no way resembled the man sketched by Florestan. Since the time of Montaigne, a servant's portrait of his employer should always be distrusted. The Count looked fully sixty, though he was but fifty years of age; he was undersized, and he looked shrunk and shrivelled; he was nearly bald, and his long whiskers were perfectly white. The cares of life had imprinted deep furrows on his brow, and told too plainly the story of a man who, having drained the chalice of life to the bottom, was now ready to shiver the goblet. As Florestan left the room the Count turned to Mascarin, and in the same glacial tone observed, "And now, sir, explain this intrusion."

Mascarin had often been rebuffed, but never so cruelly as this. His vanity was sorely wounded, for he was vain, as all are who think that they possess some hidden influence, and he felt his temper giving way.

"Pompous idiot!" thought he; "we will see how he looks in a short time;" but his face did not betray this, and his manner remained cringing and obsequious. "You have heard my name, my lord, and I am a general business agent."

The Count was deceived by the honest accents which long practice had taught Mascarin to use, and he had neither a suspicion nor a presentiment.

"Ah!" said he majestically, "a business agent, are you? I presume you come on behalf of one of my creditors. Well, sir, as I have before told these people, your errand is a futile one. Why do they worry me when I unhesitatingly pay the extravagant interest they are pleased to demand? They know that they are all knaves. They are aware that I am rich, for I have inherited a great fortune, which is certainly without encumbrance; for though I could raise a million to-morrow upon my estates in Poitiers, I have up to this time not chosen to do so."

Mascarin had at length so recovered his self-command that he listened to this speech without a word, hoping to gain some information from it.

"You may tell this," continued the Count, "to those by whom you are employed."

"Excuse me, my lord——"

"But what?"

"I cannot allow——"

"I have nothing more to say; all will be settled as I promised, when I pay my daughter's dowry. You are aware that she will shortly be united to M. de Breulh-Faverlay."

There was no mistaking the order to go, contained in these words, but Mascarin did not offer to do so, but readjusting his spectacles, remarked in a perfectly calm voice,—

" It is this marriage that has brought me here."

The Count thought that his ears had deceived him. " What are you saying?" said he.

" I say," repeated the agent, " that I am sent to you in connection with this same marriage."

Neither the doctor nor Florestan had exaggerated the violence of the Count's temper. Upon hearing his daughter's name and marriage mentioned by this man, his face grew crimson and his eyes gleamed with a lurid fire.

" Get out of this!" cried he, angrily.

But this was an order that Mascarin had no intention of obeying.

" I assure you that what I have to say is of the utmost importance," said he.

This speech put the finishing touch to the Count's fury.

" You won't go, won't you?" said he; and in spite of the pain that at the moment evidently oppressed him, he stepped to the bell, but was arrested by Mascarin, uttering in a warning voice the words,—

" Take care; if you ring that bell, you will regret it to the last day of your life."

This was too much for the Count's patience, and letting go the bell rope, he snatched up a walking cane that was leaning against the chimneypiece, and made a rush toward his visitor. But Mascarin did not move or lift his hand in self-defence, contenting himself with saying calmly,—

"No violence, Count; remember Montlouis."

At this name the Count grew livid, and dropping the cane from his nerveless hand staggered back a pace or two. Had a spectre suddenly stood up before him with threatening hand, he could not have been more horrified.

"Montlouis!" he murmured; "Montlouis!"

But now Mascarin, thoroughly assured of the value of his weapon, had resumed all his humbleness of demeanor.

"Believe me, my lord," said he, "that I only mention this name on account of the immediate danger that threatens you."

The Count hardly seemed to pay attention to his visitor's words.

"It was not I," continued Mascarin, "who devised the project of bringing against you an act which was perhaps a mere accident. I am only a plenipotentiary from persons I despise, to you, for whom I entertain the very highest respect."

By this time the Count had somewhat recovered himself.

"I really do not understand you," said he, in a tone he vainly endeavored to render calm. "My sudden emotion is only too easily explained. I had a sad misfortune. I accidentally shot my secretary, and the poor young man bore the name you just now mentioned; but the court acquitted me of all blame in the matter."

The smile upon Mascarin's face was so full of sarcasm that the Count broke off.

"Those who sent me here," remarked the agent, slowly, "are well acquainted with the evidence produced in court; but unfortunately, they know the real facts, which certain honorable gentlemen had sense to conceal at any risk."

Again the Count started, but Mascarin went on implacably,—

"But reassure yourself, your friend did not betray you voluntarily. Providence, in her inscrutable decrees——"

The Count shuddered.

"In short, sir, in short——"

Up to this time Mascarin had remained standing, but now that he saw that his position was fully established, he drew up a chair and sat down. The Count grew more livid at this insolent act, but made no comment, and this entirely removed any doubts from the agent's mind.

"The event to which I have alluded had two eye-witnesses, the Baron de Clinchain, and a servant, named Ludovic Trofin, now in the employ of the Count du Commarin."

"I did not know what had become of Trofin."

"Perhaps not, but my people do. When he swore to keep the matter secret, he was unmarried, but a few years later, having entered the bonds of matrimony, he told all to his young wife. This woman turned out badly; she had several lovers, and through one of them the matter came to my employer's ears."

"And it was on the word of a lackey, and the gossip of a dissolute woman, that they have dared to accuse me."

No word of direct accusation had passed, and yet the Count sought to defend himself.

Mascarin saw all this, and smiled inwardly, as he replied, "We have other evidence than that of Ludovic."

"But," said the Count, who was sure of the fidelity of his friend, "you do not, I suppose, pretend that the Baron de Clinchain has deceived me?"

The state of mental anxiety and perturbation into which this man of the world had been thrown must have been very intense for him not to have perceived that every word he uttered put a fresh weapon in his adversary's hands.

"He has not denounced you by word of mouth," replied the agent. "He has done far more; he has written his testimony."

"It is a lie," exclaimed the Count.

Mascarin was not disturbed by this insult.

"The Baron has written," repeated he, "though he never thought that any eye save his own would read what he had penned. As you are aware, the Baron de Clinchain is a most methodical man, and punctilious to a degree."

"I allow that; continue."

"Consequently you will not be surprised to learn that from his earliest years he has kept a diary, and each day he puts down in the most minute manner everything that has occurred, even to the different conditions of his bodily health."

The Count knew of his friend's foible, and remembered that when they were young many a practical joke had been played upon his friend on this account, and now he began to perceive the dangerous ground upon which he stood.

"On learning the facts of the case from Ludovic's wife's lover," continued Mascarin, "my employers decided that if the tale was a true one, some mention of it would be found in the Baron's diary; and thanks to the ingenuity and skill of certain parties, they have

had in their possession for twenty-four hours the volume for the year 1842."

"Scoundrels!" muttered the Count.

"They find not one only, but three distinct statements relating to the affair in question."

The Count started again to his feet with so menacing a look, that the worthy Mascarin pushed back
his chair in anticipation of an immediate assault.

"Proofs!" gasped the Count.   "Give me proofs."

"Everything has been provided for, and the three
leaves by which you are so deeply compromised have
been cut from the book."

"Where are these pages?"

Mascarin at once put on an air of injured innocence.

"I have not seen them, but the leaves have been
photographed, and a print has been entrusted to me,
in order to enable you to recognize the writing."

As he spoke he produced three specimens of the
photographic art, wonderfully clear and full of fidelity.
The Count examined them with the utmost attention,
and then in a voice which trembled with emotion, he
said, "True enough, it is his handwriting."

Not a line upon Mascarin's face indicated the delight
with which he received this admission.

"Before continuing the subject," he observed placidly, "I consider it necessary for you to understand the
position taken up by the Baron de Clinchain. Do you
wish, my lord, to read these extracts, or shall I do so
for you?"

"Read," answered the Count, adding in a lower
voice, "I cannot see to do so."

Mascarin drew his chair nearer to the lights on the
table. "I perceive," said he, "that the first entry was
made on the evening after the—well, the accident.

This is it: 'October 26, 1842. Early this morning went out shooting with Octave de Mussidan. We were accompanied by Ludovic, a groom, and by a young man named Montlouis, whom Octave intends one day to make his steward. It was a splendid day, and by twelve o'clock I had killed a leash of hares. Octave was in excellent spirits, and by one o'clock we were in a thick cover not far from Bevron. I and Ludovic were a few yards in front of the others, when angry voices behind attracted our attention. Octave and Montlouis were arguing violently, and all at once the Count struck his future steward a violent blow. In another moment Montlouis came up to me. "What is the matter?" cried I. Instead of replying to my question, the unhappy young man turned back to his master, uttering a series of threats. Octave had evidently been reproaching him for some low intrigue he had been engaged in, and was reflecting upon the character of the woman. "At any rate," cried Montlouis, "she is quite as virtuous as Madame de Mussidan was before her marriage."

" ' As Octave heard these words, he raised the loaded gun he held in his hand and fired. Montlouis fell to the ground, bathed in blood. We all ran up to him, but he was quite dead, for the charge of shot had penetrated his heart. I was almost beside myself, but Octave's despair was terrible to witness. Tearing his hair, he knelt beside the dead man. Ludovic, however, maintained his calmness. "We must say that it was an accident," observed he quickly. "Thinking that Montlouis was not near, my master fired into cover."

" 'This was agreed to, and we carefully arranged what we should say. It was I who went before the magistrate and made a deposition, which was unhesitatingly received. But, oh, what a fearful day! My pulse is at eighty, and I feel I shall not sleep all night. Octave is half mad, and Heaven knows what will become of him.' "

The Count, from the depths of his armchair, listened without apparent emotion to this terrible revelation. He was quite crushed, and was searching for some means to exorcise the green spectre of the past, which had so suddenly confronted him. Mascarin never took his eyes off him. All at once the Count roused himself from his prostration, as a man awakes from a hideous dream. " This is sheer folly," cried he.

" It is folly," answered Mascarin, " that would carry much weight with it."

" And suppose I were to show you," returned the Count, " that all these entries are the offspring of a diseased mind? "

Mascarin shook his head with an air of affected grief. " There is no use, my lord, in indulging in vain hopes. We," he continued, wishing to associate himself with the Count, " we might of course admit that the Baron de Clinchain had made this entry in his diary in a moment of temporary insanity, were it not for the painful fact that there are others. Let me read them."

" Go on ; I am all attention."

" We find the following, three days later : ' Oct. 29th, 1842. I am most uneasy about my health. I feel shooting pains in all my joints. The derangement of my system arises entirely from this business of Octave's. I had to run the gauntlet of a second court, and the judge's eyes seemed to look me through and through. I also saw with much alarm that my second statement differs somewhat from the first one, so I have now learned it by heart. Ludovic is a sharp fellow, and quite self-possessed. I would like to have him in my household. I keep myself shut up in my house for fear of meeting friends who want to hear all the details of the accident. I believe I may say that I have repeated the story more than a couple of dozen times.' Now, my lord," added Mascarin, "what do you say to this?"

"Continue the reading of the extracts."

"The third allusion, though it is short, is still very important: 'November 3rd, 1842. Thank Heaven! all is over. I have just returned from the court. Octave has been acquitted. Ludovic has behaved wonderfully. He explained the reason of the misadventure in a way that was really surprising in an uneducated man, and there was not an atom of suspicion among judge, jury, or spectators. I have changed my mind; I would not have a fellow like Ludovic in my service; he is much too sharp. When I had been duly sworn, I gave my evidence. Though I was much agitated, I went through it all right; but when I got home I felt very ill, and discovered that my pulse was down to fifty. Ah, me! what terrible misfortunes are wrought by a momentary burst of anger. I now write this sentence in my diary: "*Never give way to first impulses.*"' These words," continued Mascarin, "were inscribed on every one of the pages following,—at least so those who examined the entries informed me."

Mascarin persisted in representing himself as the agent of others, but still the Count made no allusion to the persons in the background.

After a few moments the Count rose and limped up and down, as though he hoped by this means to collect his ideas, or perhaps in order to prevent his visitor from scanning his face too closely.

" Have you done? " asked he, all at once.

" Yes, my lord."

" Have you thought what an impartial judge would say? "

" I think I have."

" He would say," broke in the Count, " that no sane man would have written such things down, for there are certain secrets which we do not whisper even to ourselves, and it is hardly likely that any man would make such compromising entries in a diary which might be lost or stolen, and which would certainly be read by his heir. Do you think that a man of high position would record his perjury, which is a crime that would send him to penal servitude? "

Mascarin gazed upon the Count with an air of pity.

" You are not going the right way, my lord, to get out of your trouble. No lawyer would adopt your theory. If the remaining volumes of M. de Clinchain's diaries were produced in court, I imagine that other equally startling entries would be found in them."

The Count now appeared to have arrived at some decision, and to continue the conversation simply for the purpose of gaining time.

" Well," said he, " I will give up this idea; but how do I know that these documents are not forgeries? Nowadays, handwritings are easily facsimilied, when even bankers find it hard to distinguish between their own notes and counterfeit ones."

" That can be settled by seeing if certain leaves are missing from the Baron's diary."

" That does not prove much."

" Pardon me, it proves a great deal. This new line

of argument, I assure you, will avail you as little as the other. I am perfectly aware that the Baron de Clinchain will utter whatever words you may place in his mouth. Let us suppose that the leaves which have been torn out should fit into the book exactly. Would not that be a strong point?"

The Count smiled ironically, as though he had a crushing reply in reserve.

"And so this is your opinion, is it?" said he.

"It is indeed."

"Then all I have to do is to plead guilty. I did kill Montlouis, just as Clinchain describes, but——" and as he spoke he took a heavy volume from a shelf, and opening it at a certain place laid it before Mascarin, remarking,—"this is the criminal code; read. 'All proceedings in criminal law shall be cancelled after a lapse of ten years.'"

The Count de Mussidan evidently thought that he had crushed his adversary by this shattering blow; but it was not so, for instead of exhibiting any surprise, Mascarin's smile was as bland as ever.

"I, too, know a little of the law," said he. "The very first day this matter was brought to me, I turned to this page and read what you have just shown me to my employers."

"And what did they say?"

"That they knew all this, but that you would be glad to compromise the affair, even at the expense of half your fortune."

The agent's manner was so confident that the Count felt they had discovered some means of turning this crime of his early days to advantage; but he was still sufficiently master of himself to show no emotion.

"No," replied he, "it is not such an easy matter as

you think to get hold of half my fortune. I fancy that your friends' demands will assume a more modest tone, the more so when I repeat that these morsels of paper, stolen from my friend's diary, are absolutely worthless."

" Do you think so ? "

" Certainly, for the law on this matter speaks plainly enough."

Mascarin readjusted his glasses, a sure indication that he was going to make an important reply.

" You are quite right, my lord," said he, slowly. " There is no intention of taking you before any court, for there is no penalty now for a crime committed twenty-three years ago; but the miserable wretches whom I blush to act for have arranged a plan which will be disagreeable in the highest degree both for you and the Baron."

" Pray tell me what this clever plan is."

" Most certainly. I came here to-day for this very purpose. Let us first conclude that you have rejected the request with which I approached you."

" Do you call this style of thing a request ? "

" What is the use of quarrelling over words. Well, to-morrow, my clients—though I am ashamed to speak of them as such—will send to a well known morning paper a tale, with the title, ' Story of a Day's Shooting.' Of course only initials will be used for the names, but no doubt will exist as to the identity of the actors in the tragedy."

" You forget that in actions for libel proofs are not admitted."

Mascarin shrugged his shoulders.

" My employers forget nothing," remarked he; " and it is upon this very point that they have based their plans. For this reason they introduce into the matter a fifth party, of course an accomplice, whose name is introduced into the story in the paper. Upon the day of its appearance, this man lodges a complaint against the journal, and insists on proving in a court of justice, that he did not form one of the shooting-party."

" Well, what happens then? "

" Then, my lord, this man insists that the journal should give a retraction of the injurious statement and summons as witnesses both yourself and the Baron de Clinchain, and as a conclusion, Ludovic; and as he claims damages, he employs a lawyer, who is one of the confederates and behind the scenes. The lawyer will speak something to this effect: 'That the Count de Mussidan is clearly a murderer; that the Baron de Clinchain is a perjurer, as proved by his own handwriting; Ludovic has been tampered with, but my client, an honorable man, must not be classed with these, etc., etc.' Have I made myself understood? "

Indeed, he had, and with such cold and merciless logic that it seemed hopeless to expect to escape from the net that had been spread.

As these thoughts passed through the Count's brain, he saw at a glance the whole terrible notoriety that the case would cause, and society gloating over the details. Yet such was the obstinacy of his disposition, and so impatient was he of control, that the more desperate his position seemed, the fiercer was his resistance. He knew the world well, and he also knew that the cutthroats who demanded his money with threats had every reason to dread the lynx eye of the law. If he refused to listen to them, as his heart urged him, perhaps they would not dare to carry out their threats. Had he alone been concerned in the matter, he would have resisted to the last, and fought it out to the last

drop or his blood, and as a preliminary, would have
beaten the sneering rogue before him to a jelly; but
how dared he expose his friend Clinchain, who had
already braved so much for him? As he paced up and
down the library, these and many other thoughts swept
across his brain, and he was undecided whether to submit to these extortions or throw the agent out of the
window. His excited demeanor and the occasional in-
terjections that burst from his lips showed Mascarin
that the account of him was not exaggerated, and that
when led by passion he would as soon shoot a fellow-
creature as a rabbit. And yet, though he knew not
whether he should make his exit by the door or the
window, he sat twirling his fingers with the most un-
concerned air imaginable. At last the Count gave ear
to prudence. He stopped in front of the agent, and,
taking no pains to hide his contempt, said,—

"Come, let us make an end of this. How much do
you want for these papers?"

"Oh, my lord!" exclaimed Mascarin; "surely you
do not think that I could be guilty——?"

M. de Mussidan shrugged his shoulders. "Pray, do
not take me for a fool," said he, "but name your sum."

Mascarin seemed a little embarrassed, and hesitated.
"We don't want money," answered he at length.

"Not money!" replied the Count.

"We want something that is of no importance to
you, but of the utmost value to those who despatched
me here. I am commissioned to inform you that my
clients desire that you should break off the engagement
between your daughter and M. de Breulh-Faverlay, and
that the missing paper will be handed to you on the
completion of her marriage with any one else whom you
may deem worthy of such an honor."

This demand, which was utterly unexpected, so astonished the Count that he could only exclaim, "Why, this is absolute madness!"

"No; it is plain, good sense, and a *bona fide* offer."

An idea suddenly flashed across the Count's mind. "Is it your intention," asked he, "to furnish me with a son-in-law too?"

"I am sure, my lord," answered Mascarin, looking the picture of disinterested honesty, "that, even to save yourself, you would never sacrifice your daughter."

"But——"

"You are entirely mistaken; it is M. de Breulh-Faverlay whom my clients wish to strike at, for they have taken an oath that he shall never wed a lady with a million for her dowry."

So surprised was the Count, that the whole aspect of the interview seemed to have changed, and he now combated his own objections instead of those of his unwelcome visitor. "M. de Breulh-Faverlay has my promise," remarked he; "but of course it is easy to find a pretext. The Countess, however, is in favor of the match, and the chief opposition to any change will come from her."

Mascarin did not think it wise to make any reply, and the Count continued, "My daughter also may not view this rupture with satisfaction."

Thanks to the information he had received from Florestan, Mascarin knew how much importance to attach to this. "Mademoiselle, at her age and with her tastes, is not likely to have her heart seriously engaged." For fully a quarter of an hour the Count still hesitated. He knew that he was entirely at the mercy of those miscreants, and his pride revolted at the idea of submission; but at length he yielded.

"I agree," said he. "My daughter shall not marry M. de Breulh-Faverlay."

Even in his hour of triumph, Mascarin's face did not change. He bowed profoundly, and left the room; but as he descended the stairs, he rubbed his hands, exclaiming, "If the doctor has made as good a job of it as I have, success is certain."

CHAPTER VI.

A MEDICAL ADVISER.

DOCTOR HORTEBISE did not find it necessary to resort to any of those expedients which Mascarin had found it advisable to use in order to reach Madame de Mussidan. As soon as he presented himself—that is, after a brief interval of five minutes—he was introduced into the presence of the Countess. He rather wondered at this, for Madame de Mussidan was one of those restless spirits that are seldom found at home, but are to be met with at exhibitions, on race-courses, at the *salons,* restaurants, shops, or theatres; or at the studio of some famous artist; or at the rooms of some musical professor who had discovered a new tenor; anywhere and everywhere, in fact, except at home. Hers was one of those restless natures constantly craving for excitement; and husband, home, and child were mere secondary objects in her eyes. She had many avocations; she was a patroness of half a dozen charitable institutions, but the chief thing that she did was to spend money. Gold seemed to melt in her grasp like so much snow, and she never knew what became of

the sums she lavished so profusely. Husband and wife
had long been almost totally estranged, and led almost
separate existences. Dr. Hortebise was well aware of
this, in common with others who moved in society.
Upon the appearance of the doctor, the Countess
dropped the book she had been perusing, and gave vent
to an exclamation of delight. " Ah, doctor, this is
really very kind of you; " and at the same time signed
to the servant to place a chair for the visitor.

The Countess was tall and slender, and at forty-five
had the figure of a girl. She had an abundance of fair
hair, the color of which concealed the silver threads
which plentifully interspersed it. A subtle perfume
hung about her, and her pale blue eyes were full of
pride and cold disdain.

" You know how to time your visits so well, doctor! " said she. " I am thoroughly bored, and am utterly weary of books, for it always seems to me, when
I read, that I had perused the same thing before some-
where or other. You have arrived at so opportune a
moment, that you appear to be a favorite of timely
chance."

The doctor was indeed a favorite of chance; but the
name of chance was Baptiste Mascarin.

" I see so few visitors," continued Madame de Mussidan, " that hardly any one comes to see me. I must
really set aside one day in the week for my at home;
for when I do happen to stay at home, I feel fearfully
dull and lonely. For two mortal hours I have been in
this room. I have been nursing the Count."

The doctor knew better than this; but he smiled
pleasantly, and said, " Perfectly so," exactly at the
right moment.

" Yes," continued the Countess, " my husband

slipped on the stairs, and hurt himself very much. Our doctor says it is nothing; but then I put little faith in what doctors say."

" I know that by experience, madame," replied Hortebise.

" Present company of course always excepted; but, do you know, I once really believed in you; but your sudden conversion to homeopathy quite frightened me."

The doctor smiled. " It is as safe a mode of practice as any other."

" Do you really think so? "

" I am perfectly sure of it."

" Well, now that you *are* here, I am half inclined to ask your advice."

" I trust that you are not suffering."

" No, thank heaven; I have never any cause to complain of my health; but I am very anxious about Sabine's state."

Her affectation of maternal solicitude was a charming pendant to her display of conjugal affection, and again the doctor's expression of assent came in in the right place.

" Yes, for a month, doctor, I have hardly seen Sabine, I have been so much engaged; but yesterday I met her, and was quite shocked at the change in her appearance."

" Did you ask her what ailed her? "

" Of course, and she said, ' Nothing,' adding that she was perfectly well."

" Perhaps something had vexed her? "

" She,—why, don't you know that every one likes her, and that she is one of the happiest girls in Paris; but I want you to see her in spite of that." She rang the bell as she spoke, and as soon as the footman made his appearance, said, "Lubin, ask Mademoiselle to have the goodness to step downstairs."

"Mademoiselle has gone out, madame."

"Indeed! how long ago?"

"About three o'clock, madame."

"Who went with her?"

"Her maid, Modeste."

"Did Mademoiselle say where she was going to?"

"No, madame."

"Very well, you can go."

Even the imperturbable doctor was rather surprised at a girl of eighteen being permitted so much freedom.

"It is most annoying," said the Countess. "However, let us hope that the trifling indisposition, regarding which I wished to consult you, will not prevent her marriage."

Here was the opening that Hortebise desired.

"Is Mademoiselle going to be married?" asked he with an air of respectful curiosity.

"Hush!" replied Madame de Mussidan, placing her finger on her lips; "this is a profound secret, and there is nothing definitely arranged; but you, as a doctor, are a perfect father confessor, and I feel that I can trust you. Let me whisper to you that it is quite possible that Sabine will be Madame de Breulh-Faverlay before the close of the year."

Hortebise had not Mascarin's courage; indeed, he was frequently terrified at his confederate's projects; but having once given in his adherence, he was to be relied on, and did not hesitate for a moment. "I confess, madame, that I heard that mentioned before;" returned he cautiously.

"And, pray, who was your informant?"

"Oh, I have had it from many sources; and let me say at once that it was this marriage, and no mere chance, that brought me here to-day."

Madame de Mussidan liked the doctor and his pleasant and witty conversation very much, and was always charmed to see him; but it was intolerable that he should venture to interfere in her daughter's marriage. "Really, sir, you confer a great honor upon the Count and myself," answered she haughtily.

Her severe manner, however, did not cause the doctor to lose his temper. He had come to say certain things in a certain manner. He had learned his part, and nothing that the Countess could say would prevent his playing it.

"I assure you, madame," returned he, "that when I accepted the mission with which I am charged, I only did so from my feelings of respect to you and yours."

"You are really very kind," answered the Countess superciliously.

"And I am sure, madame, that after you have heard what I have to say, you will have even more reason to agree with me." His manner as he said this was so peculiar, that the Countess started as though she had received a galvanic shock. "For more than twenty-five years," pursued the doctor, "I have been the constant depositary of strange family secrets, and some of them have been very terrible ones. I have often found myself in a very delicate position, but never in such an embarrassing one as I am now."

"You alarm me," said the Countess, dropping her impatient manner.

"If, madame, what I have come to relate to you are the mere ravings of a lunatic, I will offer my most sincere apologies; but if, on the contrary, his statements are true—and he has irrefragable proofs in his possession,—then, madame——"

" What then, doctor?"

" Then, madame, I can only say, make every use of me, for I will willingly place my life at your disposal."

The Countess uttered a laugh as artificial as the tears of long-expectant heirs. " Really," said she, " your solemn air and tones almost kill me with laughter."

" She laughs too heartily, and at the wrong time. Mascarin is right," thought the doctor. " I trust, madame," continued he, " that I too may laugh at my own imaginary fears; but whatever may be the result, permit me to remind you that a little time back you said that a doctor was a father confessor: for, like a priest, the physician only hears secrets in order to forget them. He is also more fitted to console and advise, for, as his profession brings him into contact with the frailties and passions of the world, he can comprehend and excuse."

" And you must not forget, doctor, that like the priest also, he preaches very long sermons."

As she uttered this sarcasm, there was a jesting look upon her features, but it elicited no smile from Hortebise, who, as he proceeded, grew more grave.

" I may be foolish," he said; " but I had better be that than reopen some old wound."

" Do not be afraid, doctor; speak out."

" Then, I will begin by asking if you have any remembrance of a young man in your own sphere of society, who, at the time of your marriage, was well known in every Parisian *salon*. I speak of the Marquis de Croisenois."

The Countess leaned back in her chair, and contracted her brow, and pursed up her lips, as though vainly endeavoring to remember the name.

" The Marquis de Croisenois? " repeated she. " It seems as if——no—wait a moment. No; I cannot say that I can call any such person to mind."

The doctor felt that he must give the spur to this rebellious memory.

" Yes, Croisenois," he repeated. " His Christian name was George, and he had a brother Henry, whom you certainly must know, for this winter I saw him at the Duchess de Laumeuse's, dancing with your daughter."

" You are right; I remember the name now."

Her manner was indifferent and careless as she said this.

" Then perhaps you also recollect that some twenty-three years ago, George de Croisenois vanished suddenly. This disappearance caused a terrible commotion at the time, and was one of the chief topics of society."

" Ah! indeed? " mused the Countess.

" He was last seen at the Café de Paris, where he dined with some friends. About nine he got up to leave. One of his friends proposed to go with him, but he begged him not to do so, saying, ' Perhaps I shall see you later on at the opera, but do not count on me.' The general impression was that he was going to some love tryst."

" His friends thought that, I suppose."

" Yes, for he was attired with more care than usual, though he was always one of the best dressed men in Paris. He went out alone, and was never seen again."

" Never again," repeated the Countess, a slight shade passing across her brow.

"Never again," echoed the unmoved doctor. "At first his friends merely thought his absence strange; but at the end of a week they grew anxious."

"You go very much into details."

"I heard them all at the time, madame, and they were only brought back to my memory this morning. All are to be found in the records of a minute search that the authorities caused to be made into the affair. The friends of De Croisenois had commenced the search; but when they found their efforts useless, they called in the aid of the police. The first idea was suicide: George might have gone into some lonely spot and blown out his brains. There was no reason for this; he had ample means, and always appeared contented and happy. Then it was believed that a murder had been committed, and fresh inquiries were instituted, but nothing could be discovered—nothing."

The Countess affected to stifle a yawn, and repeated like an echo, "Nothing."

"Three months later, when the police had given up the matter in despair, one of George de Croisenois' friends received a letter from him."

"He was not dead then, after all?"

Dr. Hortebise made a mental note of the tone and manner of the Countess, to consider over at his leisure.

"Who can say?" returned he. "The envelope bore the Cairo post-mark. In it George declared that, bored with Parisian life, he was going to start on an exploring expedition to Central Africa, and that no one need be anxious about him. People thought this letter highly suspicious. A man does not start upon such an expedition as this without money; and it was conclusively proved that on the day of De Croisenois' disappearance he had not more than a thousand francs about him, half of which was in Spanish doubloons, won at whist before dinner. The letter was therefore regarded as a trick to turn the police off the scent; but the best experts asserted that the handwriting was George's own. Two detectives were at once despatched to Cairo, but neither there nor anywhere on the road were any traces of the missing man discovered."

As the doctor spoke, he kept his eyes riveted on the Countess, but her face was impassable.

" Is that all? " asked she.

Dr. Hortebise paused a few moments before he replied, and then answered slowly,—

" A man came to me yesterday, and asserts that you can tell me what has become of George de Croisenois."

A man could not have displayed the nerve evinced by this frail and tender woman, for however callous he may be, some feature will betray the torture he is enduring; but a woman can often turn a smiling face upon the person who is racking her very soul. At the mere name of Montlouis the Count had staggered, as though crushed down by a blow from a sledge hammer; but at this accusation of Hortebise the Countess burst into a peal of laughter, apparently perfectly frank and natural, which utterly prevented her from replying.

" My dear doctor," said she at length, as soon as she could manage to speak, " your tale is highly sensational and amusing, but I really think that you ought to consult a *clairvoyant,* and not a matter-of-fact person like me, about the fate of George de Croisenois."

But the doctor, who was ready with his retort, and, not at all disconcerted by the cachinations of the Countess, heaved a deep sigh, as though a great load had been removed from his heart, and, with an air of extreme delight, exclaimed, "Thank Heaven! then I was deceived."

He uttered these words with an affectation of such sincerity that the Countess fell into the trap.

"Come," said she, with a winning smile, "tell me who it is that says I know so much."

"Pooh! pooh!" returned Hortebise. "What good would that do? He has made a fool of me, and caused me to risk losing your good opinion. Is not that enough? To-morrow, when he comes to my house, my servants will refuse to admit him; but if I were to do as my inclinations lead me, I should hand him over to the police."

"That would never do," returned the Countess, "for that would change a mere nothing into a matter of importance. Tell me the name of your mysterious informer. Do I know him?"

"It is impossible that you could do so, madame, for he is far below you in the social grade. You would learn nothing from his name. He is a man I once helped, and is called Daddy Tantaine."

"A mere nickname, of course."

"He is miserably poor, a cynic, philosopher, but as sharp as a needle; and this last fact causes me great uneasiness, for at first I thought that he had been sent to me by some one far above him in position, but——"

"But, doctor," interposed the Countess, "you spoke to me of proofs, of threats, of certain mysterious persons."

"I simply repeated Daddy Tantaine's words. The old idiot said to me, 'Madame de Mussidan knows all about the fate of the Marquis, and this is clearly proved by letters that she has received from him, as well as from the Duke de Champdoce.'"

This time the arrow went home. She grew deadly pale, and started to her feet with her eyes dilated with horror.

"My letters!" exclaimed she hoarsely.

Hortebise appeared utterly overwhelmed by this display of consternation, of which he was the innocent cause.

"Your letters, madame," replied he with evident hesitation, "this double-dyed scoundrel declares he has in his possession."

With a cry like that of a wounded lioness, the Countess, taking no notice of the doctor's presence, rushed from the room. Her rapid footfall could be heard on the stairs, and the rustle of her silken skirts against the banisters. As soon as he was left alone, the doctor rose from his seat with a cynical smile upon his face.

"You may search," mused he, "but you will find that the birds have flown." He walked up to one of the windows, and drummed on the glass with his fingers. "People say," remarked he, "that Mascarin never makes a mistake. One cannot help admiring his diabolical sagacity and unfailing logic. From the most trivial event he forges a long chain of evidence, as the botanist is able, as he picks up a withered leaf, to describe in detail the tree it came from. A pity, almost, that he did not turn his talents to some nobler end; but no; he is now upstairs putting the Count on the rack, while I am inflicting tortures on the Countess. What a shameful business we are carrying on! There are moments when I think that I have paid dearly for my life of luxury, for I know well," he added, half consciously fingering his locket, "that some day we shall meet some one stronger than ourselves, and then the inevitable will ensue."

The reappearance of the Countess broke the chain of his thoughts. Her hair was disturbed, her eyes had a wild look in them, and everything about her betrayed the state of agitation she was in.

"Robbed! robbed!" cried she, as she entered the room. Her excitement was so extreme that she spoke aloud, forgetting that the door was open, and that the lackey in the ante-room could hear all she said. Luckily Hortebise did not lose his presence of mind, and, with the ease of a leading actor repairing the error of a subordinate, he closed the door.

"What have you lost?" asked he.

"My letters; they are all gone."

She staggered on to a couch, and in broken accents went on. "And yet these letters were in an iron casket closed by a secret spring; that casket was in a drawer, the key of which never leaves me."

"Good heavens!" exclaimed Hortebise in affected tones, "then Tantaine spoke the truth."

"He did," answered the Countess hoarsely. "Yes," she continued, "I am the bondslave to people whose names I do not even know, who can control my every movement and action."

She hid her face in her hands as though her pride sought to conceal her despair.

"Are these letters, then, so terribly compromising?" asked the doctor.

"I am utterly lost," cried she. "In my younger days I had no experience; I only thought of vengeance, and lately the weapons I forged myself have been turned against me. I dug a pitfall for my adversaries and have fallen into it myself."

Hortebise did not attempt to stay the torrent of her words, for the Countess was in one of those moods of utter despair when the inner feelings of the soul are made manifest, as during a violent tempest the weeds of ocean are hurled up to the surface of the troubled waters.

" I would sooner be lying in my grave a thousand times," wailed she, " than see these letters in my husband's hands. Poor Octave! have I not caused him sufficient annoyance already without this crowning sorrow? Well, Dr. Hortebise, I am menaced with the production of these letters, and they will be handed to my husband unless I agree to certain terms. What are they? Of course money is required; tell me to what amount."

The doctor shook his head.

" Not money?" cried the Countess; " what, then, do they require? Speak, and do not torture me more."

Sometimes Hortebise confessed to Mascarin that, putting his interests on one side, he pitied his victims; but he showed no sign of this feeling, and went on,—

" The value of what they require, madame, is best estimated by yourself."

" Tell me what it is; I can bear anything now."

" These compromising letters will be placed in your hands upon the day on which your daughter marries Henry de Croisenois, the brother of George."

Madame de Mussidan's astonishment was so great that she stood as though petrified into a statue.

" I am commissioned to inform you, madame, that every delay necessary for altering any arrangements that may exist will be accorded you; but, remember, if your daughter marries any one else than Henry de Croisenois, the letters will be at once placed in your husband's hands."

As he spoke the doctor watched her narrowly. The Countess crossed the room, faint and dizzy, and rested her head on the mantelpiece.

"And that is all?" asked she. "What you ask me to do is utterly impossible: and perhaps it is for the best, for I shall have no long agony of suspense to endure. Go, doctor, and tell the villain who holds my letters that he can take them to the Count at once."

The Countess spoke in such a decided tone that Hortebise was a little puzzled.

"Can it be true," she continued, "that scoundrels exist in our country who are viler than the most cowardly murderers,—men who trade in the shameful secrets that they have learned, and batten upon the money they earn by their odious trade? I heard of such creatures before, but declined to believe it; for I said to myself that such an idea only existed in the unhealthy imaginations of novel writers. It seems, however, that I was in error; but do not let these villains rejoice too soon; they will reap but a scanty harvest. There is one asylum left for me where they cannot molest me."

"Ah, madame!" exclaimed the doctor in imploring accents; but she paid no attention to his remonstrances, and went on with increasing violence,—

"Do the miserable wretches think that I fear death? For years I have prayed for it as a final mercy from the heaven I have so deeply offended. I long for the quiet of the sepulchre. You are surprised at hearing one like me speak in this way,—one who has all her life been admired and flattered,—I, Diana de Laurebourg, Countess de Mussidan. Even in the hours of my greatest triumphs my soul shuddered at the thought of the grim spectre hidden away in the past; and I

wished that death would come and relieve my sufferings. My eccentricities have often surprised my friends,
who asked if sometimes I were not a little mad. Mad?
Yes, I am mad! They do not know that I seek oblivion
in excitement, and that I dare not be alone. But I
have learned by this time that I must stifle the voice of
conscience."

She spoke like a woman utterly bereft of hope, who
had resolved on the final sacrifice. Her clear voice
rang through the room, and Hortebise turned pale as
he heard the footsteps of the servants pacing to and
fro outside the door, as they made preparations for
dinner.

" All my life has been one continual struggle," resumed she,—" a struggle which has cost me sore ; but
now all is over, and to-night, for the first time for
many years, Diana de Mussidan will sleep a calm and
untroubled sleep."

The excitement of the Countess had risen to so high
a pitch that the doctor asked himself how he could
allay a tempest which he had not foreseen ; for her loud
tones would certainly alarm the servants, who would
hasten to acquaint the Count, who was himself stretched
upon the rack ; then the entire plot would be laid bare,
and all would be lost.

Madame de Mussidan was about to rush from the
room, when the doctor, perceiving that he must act
decisively, seized her by both wrists, and, almost by
force, caused her to resume her seat.

" In Heaven's name, madame," he whispered, " for
your daughter's sake, listen to me. Do not throw up
all; am not I here ready to do your bidding, whatever
it may be? Rely upon me,—rely upon the knowledge
of a man of the world, and of one who still possesses

some portion of what is called heart.   Cannot we form an alliance to ward off this attack?"

The doctor continued in this strain, endeavoring to reassure the Countess as much as he had previously endeavored to terrify her, and soon had the satisfaction of seeing his efforts crowned with success; for Madame de Mussidan listened to his flow of language, hardly comprehending its import, but feeling calmer as he went on; and in a quarter of an hour he had persuaded her to look the situation boldly in the face. Then Hortebise breathed more freely, and, wiping the perspiration from his brow, felt that he had gained the victory.

"It is a nefarious plot," said the Countess.

"So it is, madame; but the facts remain.   Only tell me one thing, have you any special objection to M. de Croisenois paying his addresses to your daughter?"

"Certainly not."

"He comes from a good family, is well educated, handsome, popular, and only thirty-four.   If you remember, George was his senior by fifteen years.   Why, then, is not the marriage a suitable one?   Certainly, he has led rather a fast life; but what young man is immaculate?   They say that he is deeply in debt; but then your daughter has enough for both.   Besides, his brother left behind him a considerable fortune, not far short of two millions, I believe; and to this, of course, Henry will eventually succeed."

Madame de Mussidan was too overwhelmed by what she had already gone through to offer any further exposition of her feelings on the subject.

"All this is very well," answered she; "but the Count has decided that Sabine is to become the wife of

M. de Breulh-Faverlay, and I have no voice in the matter."

" But if you exerted your influence? "

The Countess shook her head. " Once on a time," said she sadly, " I reigned supreme over Octave's heart; I was the leading spirit of his existence. Then he loved me; but I was insensible to the depths of his affection, and wore out a love that would have lasted as long as life itself. Yes, in my folly I slew it, and now——" She paused for a moment as if to collect her ideas, and then added more slowly : " and now our lives are separate ones. I do not complain; it is all my own fault; he is just and generous."

" But surely you can make the effort? "

" But suppose Sabine loves M. de Breulh-Faverlay?"

" But, madame, a mother can always influence her daughter."

The Countess seized the doctor's hand, and grasped it so tightly that he could hardly bear the pain.

" I must," said she in a hoarse whisper, " divulge to you the whole extent of my unhappiness. I am estranged from my husband, and my daughter dislikes and despises me. Some people think that life can be divided into two portions, one consecrated to pleasure and excitement, and the other to domestic peace and happiness; but the idea is a false one. As youth has been, so will be age, either a reward or an expiation."

Dr. Hortebise did not care to follow this train of argument—for the Count might enter at any moment, or a servant might come in to announce dinner—and only sought to soothe the excited feelings of Madame de Mussidan, and to prove to her that she was frightened by shadows, and that in reality she was not estranged from her husband, nor did her daughter dislike her; and finally a ray of hope illuminated the saddened heart of the unfortunate lady.

"Ah, doctor!" said she, "it is only misfortune that teaches us to know our true friends."

The Countess, like her husband, had now laid down her arms; she had made a longer fight of it, but in both cases the result had been the same. She promised that she would commence operations the next day, and do her utmost to break off the present engagement.

Dr. Hortebise was well satisfied with his morning's work, and promised the unhappy lady that he would do his best to keep that scoundrel, Tantaine, quiet, and would bring her news of what was passing from day to day.

Hortebise then took his leave, quite worn out with the severe conflict he had waged during his two hours' interview with the Countess. In spite of the extreme cold, the air outside seemed to refresh him considerably, and he inhaled it with the happy feeling that he had performed his duty in a manner worthy of all praise. He walked up the Rue de Faubourg Saint Honoré, and again entered the *café* where he and his worthy confederate had agreed to meet. Mascarin was there, an untasted cutlet before him, and his face hidden by a newspaper which his anxiety would not permit him to peruse. His suspense was terrible. Had Hortebise failed? had he encountered one of those unforeseen obstacles which, like a minute grain of sand, utterly hinders the working of a piece of delicate machinery?

"Well, what news?" said he eagerly, as soon as he caught sight of the doctor.

" Success, perfect success! " said Hortebise gayly.
" But," added he, as he sank exhausted upon a seat,
" the battle has been a hard one."

CHAPTER VII.

IN THE STUDIO.

STAGGERING like a drunken man, Paul Violaine descended the stairs when his interview with Mascarin
had been concluded. The sudden and unexpected good
fortune which had fallen so opportunely at his feet had
for the moment absolutely stunned him. He was now
removed from a position which had caused him to gaze
with longing upon the still waters of the Seine, to one
of comparative affluence. " Mascarin," said he to himself, " has offered me an appointment bringing in
twelve thousand francs per annum, and proposed to
give me the first month's salary in advance."

Certainly it was enough to bewilder any man, and
Paul was utterly dazed. He went over all the events
that had occurred during the day—the sudden appearance of old Tantaine, with his loan of five hundred
francs, and the strange man who knew the whole history of his life, and who, without making any conditions, had offered him a valuable situation. Paul was
in no particular hurry to get back to the Hôtel de
Perou, for he said to himself that Rose could wait. A
feeling of restlessness had seized upon him. He wanted
to squander money, and to have the sympathy of some
companions,—but where should he go, for he had no
friends? Searching the records of his memory, he remembered that, when poverty had first overtaken him,
he had borrowed twenty francs from a young fellow

of his own age, named André. Some gold coins still jingled in his pocket, and he could have a thousand francs for the asking. Would it not add to his importance if he were to go and pay this debt? Unluckily his creditor lived a long distance off in the Rue de la Tour d'Auvergne. He, however, hailed a passing cab, and was driven to André's address. This young man was only a casual acquaintance, whom Paul had picked up one day in a small wine-shop to which he used to take Rose when he first arrived in Paris. André, with whose other name Paul was unacquainted, was an artist, and, in addition, was an ornamental sculptor, and executed those wonderful decorations on the outside of houses in which builders delight. The trade is not a pleasant one, for it necessitates working at dizzy heights, on scaffolds that vibrate with every footstep, and exposes you to the heat of summer and the frosts of winter. The business, however, is well paid, and André got a good price for his stone figures and wreaths. But all the money he earned went in the study of the painter's art, which was the secret desire of his soul. He had taken a studio, and twice his pictures had been exhibited at the *Salon,* and orders began to come in. Many of his brother artists predicted a glorious future for him. When the cab stopped, Paul threw the fare to the driver, and asked the clean-looking portress, who was polishing the brasswork on the door, if M. André was at home.

" He is, sir," replied the old woman, adding, with much volubility, " and you are likely to find him in, for he has so much work; but he is such a good and quiet young man, and so regular in his habits! I don't believe he owes a penny in the world; and as for drink, why he is a perfect Anchorite. Then he has very few acquaintances,—one young lady, whose face for a month past I have tried to see, but failed, because she wears a veil, comes to see him, accompanied by her maid."

" Good heavens, woman ! " cried Paul impatiently, " will you tell me where to find M. André ? "

" Fourth floor, first door to the right," answered the portress, angry at being interrupted ; and as Paul ran up the stairs, she muttered, " A young chap with no manners, taking the words out of a body's mouth like that ! Next time he comes, I'll serve him out somehow."

Paul found the door, with a card with the word " André " marked upon it nailed up, and rapped on the panel. He heard the sound of a piece of furniture being moved, and the jingle of rings being passed along a rod ; then a clear, youthful voice answered, " Come in ! "

Paul entered, and found himself in a large, airy room, lighted by a skylight, and exquisitely clean and orderly. Sketches and drawings were suspended on the walls ; there was a handsome carpet from Tunis, and a comfortable lounge ; a mirror in a carved frame, which would have gladdened the heart of a connoisseur, stood upon the mantelpiece. An easel with a picture upon it, covered with a green baize curtain, stood in one corner. The young painter was in the centre of his studio, brush and palette in hand. He was a dark, handsome young man, well built and proportioned, with close-cut hair, and a curling beard flowing down over his chest. His face was full of expression, and the energy and vigor imprinted upon it formed a marked contrast to the appearance of Mascarin's *protégé*. Paul noticed that he did not wear the usual painter's blouse, but was carefully dressed in the prevailing fashion. As soon as he recognized Paul, André came forward with extended hand. "Ah," said he, "I am pleased to see you, for I often wondered what had become of you."

Paul was offended at this familiar greeting. "I have had many worries and disappointments," said he.

"And Rose," said André, "how is she—as pretty as ever, I suppose?"

"Yes, yes," answered Paul negligently; "but you must forgive me for having vanished so suddenly. I have come to repay your loan, with many thanks."

"Pshaw!" returned the painter, "I never thought of the matter again; pray, do not inconvenience yourself."

Again Paul felt annoyed, for he fancied that under the cloak of assumed generosity the painter meant to humiliate him; and the opportunity of airing his newly-found grandeur occurred to him.

"It was a convenience to me, certainly," said he, "but I am all right now, having a salary of twelve thousand francs."

He thought that the artist would be dazzled, and that the mention of this sum would draw from him some exclamations of surprise and envy. André, however, made no reply, and Paul was obliged to wind up with the lame conclusion, "And at my age that is not so bad."

"I should call it superb. Should I be indiscreet in asking what you are doing?"

The question was a most natural one, but Paul could not reply to it, as he was entirely ignorant as to what his employment was to be, and he felt as angry as if the painter had wantonly insulted him.

"I work for it," said he, drawing himself up with

such a strange expression of voice and feature that
André could not fail to notice it.

"I work too," remarked he; "I am never idle."

"But I have to work very hard," returned Paul,
"for I have not, like you, a friend or protector to interest himself in me."

Paul, who had not a particle of gratitude in his
disposition, had entirely forgotten Mascarin.

The artist was much amused by this speech. "And
where do you think that a foundling, as I am, would
find a protector?"

Paul opened his eyes. "What," said he, "are you
one of those?"

"I am; I make no secret of it, hoping that there is
no occasion for me to feel shame, though there may be
for grief. All my friends know this; and I am surprised that you are not aware that I am simply a
foundling from the Hôpital de Vendôme. Up to twelve
years of age I was perfectly happy, and the masters
praised me for the knack I had of acquiring knowledge.
I used to work in the garden by day, and in the evening
I wasted reams of paper; for I had made up my mind
to be an artist. But nothing goes easily in this world,
and one day the lady superintendent conceived the idea
of apprenticing me to a tanner."

Paul, who had taken a seat on the divan in order
to listen, here commenced making a cigarette; but
André stopped him. "Excuse me; but will you oblige
me by not smoking?"

Paul tossed the cigarette aside, though he was a little surprised, as the painter was an inveterate smoker.
"All right," said he, "but continue your story."

"I will; it is a long one. I hated the tanner's business from the very beginning. Almost the first day

an awkward workman scalded me so severely that the traces still remain." As he spoke he rolled up his shirt sleeve, and exhibited a scar that covered nearly all one side of his arm. "Horrified at such a commencement, I entreated the lady superintendent, a hideous old woman in spectacles, to apprentice me to some other trade, but she sternly refused. She had made up her mind that I should be a tanner."

"That was nasty of her," remarked Paul.

"It was, indeed; but from that day I made up my mind, and I determined to run away as soon as I could get a little money together. I therefore stuck steadily to the business, and by the end of the year, by means of the strictest economy, I found myself master of thirty francs. This, I thought, would do, and, with a bundle containing a change of linen, I started on foot for Paris. I was only thirteen, but I had been gifted by Providence with plenty of that strong will called by many obstinacy. I had made up my mind to be a painter."

"And you kept your vow?"

"But with the greatest difficulty. Ah! I can close my eyes and see the place where I slept the first night I came to Paris. I was so exhausted that I did not awake for twelve hours. I ordered a good breakfast; and finding funds at a very low ebb, I started in search of work."

Paul smiled. He, too, remembered *his* first day in Paris. He was twenty-two years of age, and had forty francs in his pocket.

"I wanted to make money—for I felt I needed it— to enable me to pursue my studies. A stout man was seated near me at breakfast, and to him I addressed myself.

" ' Look here,' said I, ' I am thirteen, and much stronger than I look. I can read and write. Tell me how I can earn a living.'

" He looked steadily at me, and in a rough voice answered, ' Go to the market to-morrow morning, and try if one of the master masons, who are on the lookout for hands, will employ you.' "

" And you went? "

" I did; and was eagerly watching the head masons, when I perceived my stout friend coming toward me.

" ' I like the looks of you, my lad,' he said; ' I am an ornamental sculptor. Do you care to learn my trade? '

" When I heard this proposal, it seemed as if Paradise was opening before me, and I agreed with enthusiasm."

" And how about your painting? "

" That came later on. I worked hard at it in all my hours of leisure. I attended the evening schools, and worked steadily at my art and other branches of education. It was a very long time before I ventured to indulge in a glass of beer. ' No, no, André,' I would say to myself, ' beer costs six sous; lay the money by.' Finally, when I was earning from eighty to a hundred francs a week, I was able to give more time to the brush."

The recital of this life of toil and self-denial, so different from his own selfish and idle career, was inexpressibly mortifying to Paul; but he felt that he was called upon to say something.

" When one has talents like yours," said he, " success follows as a matter of course."

He rose to his feet, and affected to examine the sketches on the walls, though his attention was attracted to the covered picture on the easel. He remembered what the garrulous old portress had said about the veiled lady who sometimes visited the painter, and that there had been some delay in admitting him when he first knocked. Then he considered, for whom had the painter dressed himself with such care? and why had he requested him not to smoke? From all these facts Paul came to the conclusion that André was expecting the lady's visit, and that the veiled picture was her portrait. He therefore determined to see it; and with this end in view, he walked round the studio, admiring all the paintings on the walls, manœuvring in such a manner as to imperceptibly draw nearer to the easel.

"And this," said he, suddenly extending his hand toward the cover, "is, I presume, the gem of your studio?"

But André was by no means dull, and had divined Paul's intention, and grasped the young man's outstretched hand just as it touched the curtain.

"If I veil this picture," said he, "it is because I do not wish it to be seen."

"Excuse me," answered Paul, trying to pass over the matter as a jest, though in reality he was boiling over with rage at the manner and tone of the painter, and considered his caution utterly ridiculous.

"At any rate," said he to himself, "I will lengthen out my visit, and have a glimpse of the original instead of her picture;" and, with this amiable resolution, he sat down by the artist's table, and commenced an apparently interminable story, resolved not to attend to any hints his friend might throw out, who was glancing at the clock with the utmost anxiety, comparing it every now and then with his watch.

As Paul talked on, he saw close to him on the table

the photograph of a young lady, and, taking advantage of the artist's preoccupation, looked at it.

"Pretty, very pretty!" remarked he.

At these words the painter flushed crimson, and snatching away the photograph with some little degree of violence, thrust it between the leaves of a book.

André was so evidently in a passion, that Paul rose to his feet, and for a second or two the men looked into each other's eyes as two adversaries do when about to engage in a mortal duel. They knew but little of each other, and the same chance which had brought them together might separate them again at any moment, but each felt that the other exercised some influence over his life.

André was the first to recover himself.

"You must excuse me; but I was wrong to leave so precious an article about."

Paul bowed with the air of a man who accepts an apology which he considers his due; and André went on,—

"I very rarely receive any one except my friends; but to-day I have broken through my rule."

Paul interrupted him with a magniloquent wave of the hand.

"Believe me, sir," said he, in a voice which he endeavored to render cutting and sarcastic, "had it not been for the imperative duty I before alluded to, I should not have intruded."

And with these words he left the room, slamming the door behind him.

"The deuce take the impudent fool!" muttered André. "I was strongly tempted to pitch him out of the window."

Paul was in a furious rage for having visited the

studio with the kindly desire of humiliating the painter. He could not but feel that the tables had been turned upon himself.

"He shall not have it all his own way," muttered he; "for I will see the lady," and not reflecting on the meanness of his conduct, he crossed the street, and took up a position from which he could obtain a good view of the house where André resided. It was snowing; but Paul disregarded the inclemency of the weather in his eagerness to act the spy.

He had waited for fully half an hour, when a cab drove up. Two women alighted from it. The one was eminently aristocratic in appearance, while the other looked like a respectable servant. Paul drew closer; and, in spite of a thick veil, recognized the features he had seen in the photograph.

"Ah!" said he, "after all, Rose is more to my taste, and I will get back to her. We will pay up Loupins, and get out of his horrible den."

CHAPTER VIII.

MADEMOISELLE DE MUSSIDAN.

PAUL had not been the only watcher; for at the sound of the carriage wheels the ancient portress took up her position in the doorway, with her eyes fixed on the face of the young lady. When the two women had ascended the stairs, a sudden inspiration seized her, and she went out and spoke to the cabman.

"Nasty night," remarked she; "I don't envy you in such weather as this."

" You may well say that," replied the driver; " my feet are like lumps of ice."

" Have you come far? "

" Rather; I picked them up in the Champs Elysées, near the Avenue de Matignon."

" That is a distance."

" Yes; and only five sous for drink money. Hang your respectable women! "

" Oh! they are respectable, are they? "

" I'll answer for that. The other lot are far more open-handed. I know both of them."

And with these words and a knowing wink, he touched up his horse and drove away; and the portress, only half satisfied, went back to her lodge.

" Why that is the quarter where all the swells live," murmured she. " I'll tip the maid next time, and she'll let out everything."

After Paul's departure, André could not remain quiet; for it appeared to him as if each second was a century. He had thrown open the door of his studio, and ran to the head of the stairs at every sound.

At last their footsteps really sounded on the steps. The sweetest music in the world is the rustle of the beloved one's dress. Leaning over the banisters, he gazed fondly down. Soon she appeared, and in a short time had gained the open door of the studio.

" You see, André," said she, extending her hand, " you see that I am true to my time."

Pale, and trembling with emotion, André pressed the little hand to his lips.

" Ah! Mademoiselle Sabine, how kind you are! Thanks, a thousand thanks."

Yes, it was indeed Sabine, the scion of the lordly house of Mussidan, who had come to visit the poor foundling of the Hôtel de Vendôme in his studio, and who thus risked all that was most precious to her in the world, her honor and her reputation. Yes, regardless of the conventionalities among which she had been reared, dared to cross that social abyss which separates the Avenue de Matignon from the Rue de la Tour d'Auvergne. Cold reason finds no excuse for such a step, but the heart can easily solve this seeming riddle. Sabine and André had been lovers for more than two years. Their first acquaintance had commenced at the Château de Mussidan. At the end of the summer of 1865, André, whose constant application to work had told upon his health, determined to take a change, when his master, Jean Lanier, called him, and said,—

"If you wish for a change, and at the same time to earn three or four hundred francs, now is your time. An architect has written to me, asking me for a skilled stone carver, to do some work in the country at a magnificent mansion in the midst of the most superb scenery. Would you care about undertaking this?"

The proposal was a most acceptable one to André, and in a week's time he was on his way to his work with a prospect of living for a month in pure country air. Upon his arrival at the Château, he made a thorough examination of the work with which he had been entrusted. He saw that he could finish it with perfect ease, for it was only to restore the carved work on a balcony, which would not take more than a fortnight. He did not, however, press on the work, for the beautiful scenery enchanted him.

He made many exquisite sketches, and his health began to return to him. But there was another reason why he was in no haste to complete his task, one which he hardly ventured even to confess to himself: he had caught a glimpse of a young girl in the park of the Château who had caused a new feeling to spring up in his heart. It was Sabine de Mussidan. The Count, as the season came on, had gone to Germany, the Countess had flitted away to Luzon, and the daughter was sent to the dull old country mansion in charge of her old aunt. It was the old, old story; two young hearts loving with all the truth and energy of their natures. They had exchanged a few words on their first meeting, and on the next Sabine went on to the balcony and watched the rapid play of André's chisel with childish delight. For a long time they conversed, and Sabine was surprised at the education and refinement of the young workman. Utterly fresh, and without experience, Sabine could not understand her new sensations. André held, one night, a long converse with himself, and was at last obliged to confess that he loved her fondly. He ran the extent of his folly and madness, and recognized the barrier of birth and wealth that stood between them, and was overwhelmed with consternation.

The Château de Mussidan stands in a very lonely spot, and one of the roads leading to it passes through a dense forest, and therefore it had been arranged that André was to take his meals in the house. After a time Sabine began to feel that this isolation was a needless humiliation.

"Why can't M. André take his meals with us?" asked she of her aunt. "He is certainly more gentlemanlike than many of those who visit us, and I think that his conversation would entertain you."

The old lady was easily persuaded to adopt this suggestion, though at first it seemed an odd kind of thing to admit a mere working man to her table; but she was so bored with the loneliness of the place that she hailed with delight anything that would break its monotony.   André at once accepted the proposal, and the old lady would hardly believe her eyes when her guest entered the room with the dress and manners of a highbred gentleman.   "It is hardly to be believed," said she, as she was preparing to go to bed, "that a mere carver of stone should be so like a gentleman.   It seems to me that all distinctions of social rank have vanished.   It is time for me to die, or we are rapidly approaching a state of anarchy."

In spite of her prejudices, however, André contrived to win the old lady's heart, and won a complete victory by painting her portrait in full gala costume.   From that moment he was treated as one of the family, and, having no fear of a rebuff, was witty and sprightly in his manner.   Once he told the old lady the true story of his life.   Sabine was deeply interested, and marvelled at his energy and endurance, which had won for him a place on the ladder that leads to future eminence.   She saw in him the realization of all her girlish dreams, and finally confessed to herself that she loved him.   Both her father and mother had their own pleasures and pursuits, and Sabine was as much alone in the world as André.

The days now fled rapidly by.   Buried in this secluded country house, they were as free as the breeze that played through the trees of the forest, for the old lady rarely disturbed them.   After the morning meal, she would beg André to read the newspaper to her, and fell into a doze before he had been five minutes at the task.   Then the young people would slip quietly away, as merry as truants from school.   They wandered beneath the shade of the giant oaks, or climbed the rocks that stood by the river bank. Sometimes, seated in a dilapidated boat, they would drift down the stream with its flower-bedecked banks. The water was often almost covered with rushes and water lilies. Two months of enchantment thus fled past, two months of the intoxications of love, though the mention of the tender passion never rose to their lips from their hearts, where it was deeply imbedded. André had cast all reflections regarding the perils of the future to the winds, and only thanked heaven for the happiness that he was experiencing.

"Am I not too happy?" he would say to himself. "I fear this cannot last." And he was right. Anxious to justify his remaining at Mussidan after his task was completed, André determined to add to what he had already done a masterpiece of modern art, by carving a garland of fruit and flowers over the old balcony, and every morning he rose with the sun to proceed with his task.

One morning the valet came to him, saying that the old lady was desirous of seeing him, and begged him to lose no time, as the business was urgent. A presentiment of evil came like a chilly blast upon the young man's heart. He felt that his brief dream of happiness was at an end, and he followed the valet as a criminal follows his executioner to the scaffold.

As he opened the door in which Sabine's aunt was awaiting him, the old man whispered,—

"Have a care, sir, have a care. Madame is in a terrible state; I have not seen her like this since her husband died."

The old lady was in a terrible state of excitement, and in spite of rheumatic pains was walking up and down the room, gesticulating wildly, and striking her crutch-handled stick on the floor.

" And so," cried she in that haughty tone adopted by women of aristocratic lineage when addressing a supposed inferior, " you have, I hear, had the impudence to make love to my niece? "

André's pale face grew crimson as he stammered out,—

" Madame——"

" Gracious powers, fellow ! " cried the angry woman, " do you dare to deny this when your very face betrays you? Do you know that you are an insolent rogue even to venture to look on Sabine de Mussidan? How dare you ! Perhaps you thought that if you compromised her, we should be forced to submit to this ignoble alliance."

" On my honor, madame, I assure you——"

" On your honor ! To hear you speak, one would suppose that you were a gentleman. If my poor husband were alive, he would break every bone in your body; but I am satisfied with ordering you out of the house. Pack up your tools, and be off at once."

André stood as though petrified into stone. He took no notice of her imperious manner, but only realized the fact that he should never see Sabine again, and, turning deadly pale, staggered to a chair. The old lady was so surprised at the manner in which André received her communication, that for a time she too was bewildered, and could not utter a word.

" I am unfortunately of a violent temper," said she, speaking in more gentle accents, " and perhaps I have spoken too severely, for I am much to blame in this matter, as the priest of Berron said when he came to inform me of what was going on. I am so old that

I forgot what happens when young people are thrown together, and I was the only one who did not know what was going on when you were affording subject of gossip for the whole countryside; my niece——"

But here André started to his feet with a threatening look upon his face.

" I could strangle them all," cried he.

" That is right," returned the old lady, secretly pleased at his vigor and energy, " but you cannot silence every idle tongue. Fortunately, matters have not gone too far. Go away, and forget my niece."

She might as well have told the young man to go away and die.

" Madame!" cried he in accents of despair, " pray listen to me. I am young, and full of hope and courage."

The old lady was so touched by his evident sorrow, that the tears rolled down her wrinkled cheeks.

" What is the good of saying this to me?" asked she. " Sabine is not my daughter. All that I can do is never to say a word to her father and mother. Great heavens, if Mussidan should ever learn what has occurred! There, do go away. You have upset me so that I do not believe I shall eat a mouthful for the next two days."

André staggered out of the room. It seemed to him as if the flooring heaved and rolled beneath his feet. He could see nothing, but he felt some one take him by the hand. It was Sabine, pallid and cold as a marble statue.

" I have heard everything, André," murmured she.

" Yes," stammered he. " All is over, and I am dismissed."

" Where are you going to?"

"Heaven only knows, and when once I leave this place I care not."

"Do not be desperate," urged Sabine, laying her hand upon his arm.

His fixed glance terrified her as he muttered,—

"I cannot help it; I am driven to despair."

Never had Sabine appeared so lovely; her eyes gleamed with some generous impulse, and her face glowed.

"Suppose," said she, "I could give you a ray of future hope, what would you do then?"

"What would I *not* do then? All that a man could. I would fight my way through all opposition. Give me the hardest task, and I will fulfil it. If money is wanted, I will gain it; if a name, I will win it."

"There is one thing that you have forgotten, and that is patience."

"And that, Mademoiselle, I possess also. Do you not understand that with one word of hope from you I can live on?"

Sabine raised her head heavenwards. "Work!" she exclaimed. "Work and hope, for I swear that I will never wed other than you."

Here the voice of the old lady interrupted the lovers.

"Still lingering here!" she cried, in a voice like a trumpet call. André fled away with hope in his heart, and felt that he had now something to live for. No one knew exactly what happened after his departure. No doubt Sabine brought round her aunt to her way of thinking, for at her death, which happened two months afterward, she left the whole of her immense fortune directly to her niece, giving her the income while she remained single, and the capital on her marriage, whether with or without the consent of her par-

ents. Madame de Mussidan declared that the old lady
had gone crazy, but both André and Sabine knew what
she had intended, and sincerely mourned for the excellent woman, whose last act had been to smooth away
the difficulties from their path. André worked harder
than ever, and Sabine encouraged him by fresh promises. Sabine was even more free in Paris than at
Mussidan, and her attached maid, Modeste, would have
committed almost any crime to promote the happiness
of her beloved mistress. The lovers now corresponded
regularly, and Sabine, accompanied by Modeste, frequently visited the artist's studio, and never was a saint
treated with greater respect and adoration than was
Sabine by André.

CHAPTER IX.

˅OSE'S PROMOTION.

As soon as André had released her hand, Sabine took
off her hat, and, handing it to Modeste, remarked,—

"How am I looking to-day, André?"

The young painter hastened to reassure her on this
point, and she continued in joyous tones,—

"No, I do not want compliments; I want to know
if I look the right thing for sitting for my portrait."

Sabine was very beautiful, but hers was a different
style of beauty from that of Rose, whose ripe, sensu-
ous charms were fitted to captivate the admiration of
the voluptuary, while Sabine was of the most refined
and ethereal character. Rose fettered the body with
earthly trammels, while Sabine drew the soul heaven-

ward. Her beauty was not of the kind that dazzles, for
the air of proud reserve which she threw over it, in
some slight measure obscured its brilliancy.

She might have passed unnoticed, like the work of
a great master's brush hanging neglected over the altar
of a village church; but when the eye had once fathomed that hidden beauty, it never ceased to gaze on it
with admiration. She had a broad forehead, covered
with a wealth of chestnut hair, soft, lustrous eyes, and
an exquisitely chiselled mouth.

"Alas!" said André, "when I gaze upon you, I
have to confess how impossible it is to do you justice.
Before you came I had fancied that the portrait was
completed, but now I see that I have only made a
failure."

As he spoke, he drew aside the curtain, and the young
girl's portrait was revealed. It was by no means a
work of extraordinary merit. The artist was only
twenty-four years of age, and had been compelled to
interrupt his studies to toil for his daily bread, but it
was full of originality and genius. Sabine gazed at
it for a few moments in silence, and then murmured the
words,—

"It is lovely!"

But André was too discouraged to notice her praise.

"It is like," remarked he, "but a photograph also
has that merit. I have only got your features, but not
your expression; it is an utter failure. Shall I try
again?"

Sabine stopped him with a gesture of denial.

"You shall not try again," said she decidedly.

"And why not?" asked he in astonishment.

"Because this visit will be my last, André."

"The last?" stammered the painter. "In what way

have I so offended you, that you should inflict so terrible a punishment on me?"

"I do not wish to punish you. You asked for my portrait, and I yielded to your request; but let us talk reasonably. Do you not know that I am risking my reputation by coming here day after day?"

André made no reply, for this unexpected blow had almost stunned him.

"Besides," continued Mademoiselle de Mussidan, "what is to be done with the portrait? It must be hidden away, as if it were something we were ashamed of. Remember, on your success hangs our marriage."

"I do not forget that."

"Hasten then to gain all honor and distinction, for the world must agree with me in saying that my choice has been a wise one."

"I will do so."

"I fully believe you, dear André, and remember what I said to you a year ago. Achieve a name, then go to my father and ask for my hand. If he refuses, if my supplications do not move him, I will quit his roof forever."

"You are right," answered André. "I should indeed be a fool if I sacrificed a future happy life for a few hours of present enjoyment, and I will implicitly——"

"And now," said Sabine, "that we have agreed on this point, let us discuss our mutual interests, of which it seems that we have been a little negligent up till now."

André at once began to tell her of all that had befallen him since they had last met, his defeats and successes.

"I am in an awkward plight," said he. "Yesterday, that well known collector, Prince Crescenzi, came to my studio. One of my pictures took his fancy, and he ordered another from me, for which he would pay six thousand francs."

" That was quite a stroke of luck."

" Just so, but unfortunately he wants it directly. Then Jean Lamou, who has more in his hand than he can manage, has offered me the decoration of a palatial edifice that he is building for a great speculator, M. Gandelu. I am to engage all the workmen, and shall receive some seven or eight hundred francs a month."

" But how does this trouble you ? "

" I will tell you. I have twice seen M. Gandelu, and he wants me to begin work at once; but I cannot accept both, and must choose between them."

Sabine reflected.

" I should execute the Prince's commission," said she.

" So should I, only——"

The girl easily found the cause of his hesitation.

" Will you never forget that I am wealthy ? " replied she.

" The one would bring in the most money," he returned, " and the other most credit."

" Then accept the offer of M. Gandelu."

The old cuckoo-clock in the corner struck five.

" Before we part, dear André," resumed she, " I must tell you of a fresh trouble which threatens us; there is a project for marrying me to M. de Breulh-Faverlay."

" What, that very wealthy gentleman ? "

" Just so."

" Well, if I oppose my father's wishes, an explanation must ensue, and this just now I do not desire. I therefore intend to speak openly to M. de Breulh-Faverlay, who is an honorable, straightforward man; and when I tell him the real state of the case, he will withdraw his pretensions."

" But," replied André, " should he do so, another will come forward."

" That is very possible, and in his turn the successor will be dismissed."

" Ah!" murmured the unhappy man, " how terrible will be your life,—a scene of daily strife with your father and mother."

After a tender farewell, Sabine and Modeste left. André had wished to be permitted to go out and procure a vehicle, but this the young girl negatived, and took her leave, saying,—

" I shall see M. de Breulh-Faverlay to-morrow."

For a moment after he was left alone André felt very sad, but a happy thought flashed across his brain.

" Sabine," said he, " went away on foot, and I may follow her without injury to her reputation."

In another moment he was in the street, and caught a glimpse of Sabine and her maid under a lamp at the next corner. He crossed to the other side of the way and followed them cautiously.

" Perhaps," murmured he, " the time is not far distant when I shall have the right to be with her in her walks, and feel her arm pressed against mine."

By this time Sabine and her companion had reached the Rue Blanche, and hailing a cab, were rapidly driven away. André gazed after it, and as soon as it was out of sight, decided to return to his work. As he passed a brilliantly lighted shop, a fresh young voice saluted him.

" M. André, M. André."

He looked up in extreme surprise, and saw a young woman, dressed in the most extravagant style, standing by the door of a brougham, which glittered with fresh paint and varnish. In vain he tried to think who she could be, but at length his memory served him.

"Mademoiselle Rose," said he, "or I am much mistaken."

A shrill, squeaky voice replied, "Madame Zora Chantemille, if you please."

André turned sharply round and found himself face to face with a young man who had completed an order he was giving to the coachman.

"Ah, is that you?" said he.

"Yes, Chantemille is the name of the estate that I intend to settle on madame."

The painter examined the personage who had just addressed him with much curiosity. He was dressed in the height or rather the burlesque of fashion, wore an eyeglass, and an enormous locket on his chain. The face which surmounted all this grandeur was almost that of a monkey, and Toto Chupin had not exaggerated its ugliness when he likened it to that animal.

"Pooh," cried Rose, "what matters a name? All you have to do is to ask this gentleman, who is an old friend of mine, to dinner." And without waiting for a reply, she took André by the hand and led him into a brilliantly lighted hall. "You must dine with us," she exclaimed; "I will take no denial. Come, let me introduce you, M. André, M. Gaston de Gandelu. There, that is all settled."

The man bowed.

"André, André," repeated Gandelu; "why, the name is familiar to me,—and so is the face. Have I not met you at my father's house? Come in; we intend to have a jovial evening."

" I really cannot," pleaded André. " I have an engagement."

" Throw it over then; we intend to keep you, now that we have got you."

André hesitated for a moment, but he felt dispirited, and that he required rousing. " After all," thought he, " why should I refuse? If this young man's friends are like himself, the evening will be an amusing one."

" Come up," cried Rose, placing her foot upon the stairs. André was about to follow her, but was held back by Gandelu, whose face was radiant with delight.

" Was there ever such a girl? " whispered he; " but there, don't jump at conclusions. I have only had her in hand for a short time, but I am a real dab at starting a woman grandly, and it would be hard to find my equal in Paris, you may bet."

" That can be seen at a glance," answered André, concealing a smile.

" Well, look here, I began at once. Zora is a quaint name, is it not? It was my invention. She isn't a right down swell to-day, but I have ordered six dresses for her from Van Klopen; such swell gets up! You know Van Klopen, don't you, the best man-milliner in Paris. Such taste! such ideas! you never saw the like."

Rose had by this time reached her drawing-room. " André," said she, impatiently, " are you never coming up?"

" Quick, quick," said Gandelu, " let us go at once; if she gets into a temper she is sure to have a nervous attack, so let us hurry up."

Rose did all she could to dazzle André, and as a commencement exhibited to him her domestics, a cook and a maid; then he was shown every article of furniture, and not one was spared him. He was forced to admire the drawing-room suite covered with old gold silk, trimmed with blue, and to test the thickness of the curtains. Bearing aloft a large candelabra, and covering himself with wax, Gandelu led the way, telling them the price of everything like an energetic tradesman.

"That clock," said he, "cost me a hundred louis, and dirt cheap at the price. How funny that you should have known my father! Has he not a wonderful intellect? That flower stand was three hundred francs, absolutely given away. Take care of the governor, he is as sharp as a needle. He wanted me to have a profession, but no, thank you. Yes, that occasional table was a bargain at twenty louis. Six months ago I thought that the old man would have dropped off, but now the doctors say——" He stopped suddenly, for a loud noise was heard in the vestibule. "Here come the fellows I invited," cried he, and placing the candelabra on the table, he hurried from the room.

André was delighted at so grand an opportunity of studying the *genus* masher. Rose felt flattered by the admiration her fine rooms evidently caused.

"You see," cried she, "I have left Paul; he bothered me awfully, and ended by half starving me."

"Why, you are joking; he came here to-day, and said he was earning twelve thousand francs a year."

"Twelve thousand humbugs. A fellow that will take five hundred francs from an old scarecrow he never met before is——"

Rose broke off abruptly, for at that moment young Gandelu brought in his friends, and introduced them; they were all of the same type as their host, and André was about to study them more intently, when a white-waistcoated waiter threw open the door, exclaiming pompously, "Madame, the dinner is on the table."

CHAPTER X.

" YOU ARE A THIEF."

WHEN Mascarin was asked what was the best way to achieve certain results, his invariable reply was, " Keep moving, keep moving." He had one great advantage over other men, he put in practice the doctrines he preached, and at seven o'clock the morning after his interview with the Count de Mussidan he was hard at work in his room. A thick fog hung over the city, even penetrating into the office, which had begun to fill with clients. This crowd had but little interest for the head of the establishment, as it consisted chiefly of waiters from small eating houses, and cooks who knew little or nothing of what was going on in the houses where they were in service. Finding this to be the case, Mascarin handed them all over to Beaumarchef, and only occasionally nodded to the serviteur of some great family, who chanced to stroll in.

He was busily engaged in arranging those pieces of cardboard which had so puzzled Paul in his first visit, and was so much occupied with his task, that all he could do was to mutter broken exclamations: " What a stupendous undertaking! but I have to work single-handed, and hold in my hands all these threads, which for twenty years, with the patience of a spider, I have been weaving into a web. No one, seeing me here, would believe this. People who pass me by in the street say, ' That is Mascarin, who keeps a servants' registry office;' that is the way in which they look upon me. Let them laugh if they like; they little know the mighty power I wield in secret. No one suspects me, no, not one. I may seem too sanguine, it is true," he continued, still glancing over his papers, " or the net may break and some of the fishes slip out. That idiot, Mussidan, asked me if I was acquainted with the Penal Code. I should think I was, for no one has studied them more deeply than I have, and there is a clause in volume 3, chapter 2, which is always before me. Penal servitude for a term of years; and if I am convicted under Article 306, then it means a life sentence." He shuddered, but soon a smile of triumph shone over his face as he resumed, " Ah, but to send a man like Mascarin for change of air to Toulon, he must be caught, and that is not such an easy task. The day he scents danger he disappears, and leaves no trace behind him. I fear that I cannot look for too much from my companions, Catenac and Hortebise; I have up to now kept them back. Croisenois would never betray me, and as for Beaumarchef, La Candèle, Toto Chupin, and a few other poor devils, they would be a fine haul for the police. They couldn't split, simply because they know nothing." Mascarin chuckled, and then adjusting his spectacles with his favorite gesture, said, " I shall go on in the course I have commenced, straight as the flight of an arrow. I ought to make four millions through Croisenois. Paul shall marry Flavia, that is all arranged, and Flavia will make a grand duchess with her magnificent income."

He had by this time arranged his pasteboard squares, then he took a small notebook, alphabetically arranged, from a drawer, wrote a name or two in it, and then closing it said with a deadly smile, " There, my friends, you are all registered, though you little suspect it. You are all rich, and think that you are free, but you are wrong, for there is one man who owns you, soul and body, and that man is Baptiste Mascarin; and at his bidding, high as you hold your heads now, you will crawl to his feet in humble abasement." His musings were interrupted by a knock at the door. He struck the bell on his writing table, and the last sound of it had hardly died away, when Beaumarchef stood on the threshold.

"You desired me, sir," said he, with the utmost deference, "to complete my report regarding young M. Gandelu, and it so happens that the cook whom he has taken into his service in the new establishment he has started is on our list. She has just come to pay us eleven francs that she owed us, and is waiting outside. Is not this lucky?"

Mascarin made a little grimace. "You are an idiot, Beaumarchef," said he, "to be pleased at so trivial a matter. I have often told you that there is no such thing as luck or chance, and that all comes to those who work methodically."

Beaumarchef listened to his master's wisdom in silent surprise.

"And pray, who is this woman?" asked Mascarin.

"You will know her when you see her, sir. She is registered under class D, that is, for employment in rather fast establishments."

"Go and fetch her," observed Mascarin, and as the man left the room, he muttered, "Experience has taught me that it is madness to neglect the smallest precaution."

In another moment the woman appeared, and Mascarin at once addressed her with that air of friendly courtesy which made him so popular among such women. "Well, my good girl," said he, "and so you have got the sort of place you wanted, eh?"

"I hope so, sir, but you see I have only been with Madame Zora de Chantemille since yesterday."

"Ah, Zora de Chantemille, that is a fine name, indeed."

"It is only a fancy name, and she had an awful row over it with master. She wanted to be called Raphaela, but he stood out for Zora."

"Zora is a very pretty name," observed Mascarin solemnly.

"Yes, sir, just what the maid and I told her. She is a splendid woman, and doesn't she just squander the shiners? Thirty thousand francs have gone since yesterday."

"I can hardly credit it."

"Not cash, you understand, but tick. M. de Gandelu has not a sou of his own in the world, so a waiter at Potier's told me, and he knew what was what; but the governor is rolling in money. Yesterday they had a house-warming—the dinner, with wine, cost over a thousand francs."

Not seeing how to utilize any of this gossip, Mascarin made a gesture of dismissal, when the woman exclaimed,—

"Stop, sir, I have something to tell you."

"Well," said Mascarin, throwing himself back in his chair with an air of affected impatience, "let us have it."

"We had eight gents to dinner, all howling swells, but my master was the biggest masher of the lot. Madame was the only woman at table. Well, by ten o'clock, they had all had their whack of drink, and then they told the porter to keep the courtyard clear.

What do you think they did then? Why, they threw plates, glasses, knives, forks, and dishes bang out of the window. That is a regular swell fashion, so the waiter at Potier's told me, and was introduced into Paris by a Russian."

Mascarin closed his eyes and answered languidly, " Go on."

" Well, sir, there was one gent who was a blot on the whole affair. He was tall, shabbily dressed, and with no manners at all. He seemed all the time to be sneering at the rest. But didn't Madame make up to him just. She kept heaping up his plate and filling his glass. When the others got to cards, he sat down by my mistress, and began to talk."

" Could you hear what they said? "

" I should think so. I was in the bedroom, and they were near the door."

" Dear me," remarked Mascarin, appearing much shocked, " surely that was not right? "

" I don't care a rap whether it was right or not. I like to hear all about the people whom I engage with. They were talking about a M. Paul, who had been Madame's friend before, and whom the gentleman also knew. Madame said that this Paul was no great shakes, and that he had stolen twelve thousand francs."

Mascarin pricked up his ears, feeling that his patience was about to meet with its reward.

" Can you tell me the gentleman's name, to whom Madame said all this? " asked he.

" Not I. The others called him ' The painter.' "

This explanation did not satisfy Mascarin.

" Look here, my good girl," said he, " try and find out the fellow's name. I think he is an artist who owes me money."

"All right! Rely on me; and now I must be off, for I have breakfast to get ready, but I'll call again to-morrow;" and with a curtsy she left the room.

Mascarin struck his hand heavily on the table.

"Hortebise has a wonderful nose for sniffing out danger," said he. "This Rose and the young fool who is ruining himself for her must both be suppressed."

Beaumarchef again made a motion of executing a thrust with the rapier.

"Pooh, pooh!" answered his master; "don't be childish. I can do better than that. Rose calls herself nineteen, but she is more, she is of age, while Gandelu is still a minor. If old Gandelu had any pluck, he would put Article 354 in motion."

"Eh, sir?" said Beaumarchef, much mystified.

"Look here. Before twenty-four hours have elapsed I must know everything as to the habits and disposition of Gandelu senior. I want to know on what terms he is with his son."

"Good. I will set La Candèle to work."

"And as the young fellow will doubtless need money, contrive to let him know of our friend Verminet, the chairman of the Mutual Loan Society."

"But that is M. Tantaine's business."

Mascarin paid no heed to this, so occupied was he by his own thoughts.

"This young artist seems to have more brains than the rest of the set, but woe to him if he crosses my path. Go back to the outer office, Beaumarchef, I hear some clients coming in."

The man, however, did not obey.

"Pardon me, sir," said he, "but La Candèle, who is outside, will see to them. I have my report to make."

" Very good.   Sit down and go on."

Enchanted at this mark of condescension, Beaumarchef went on.   " Yesterday there was nothing of importance, but this morning Toto Chupin came."

" He had not lost Caroline Schimmel, I trust? "

" No, sir; he had even got into conversation with her."

" That is good.   He is a cunning little devil; a pity that he is not a trifle more honest."

" He is sure," continued Beaumarchef, " that the woman drinks, for she is always talking of persons following her about who menace her, and she is so afraid of being murdered that she never ventures out alone.   She lives with a respectable workingman and his wife, and pays well for her board, for she seems to have plenty of money."

" That is a nuisance," remarked Mascarin, evidently much annoyed.   " Where does she live? "

" At Montmartre, beyond the Château Rouge."

" Good.   Tantaine will inquire and see if Toto has made no mistake, and does not let the woman slip through his fingers."

" He won't do that, for he told me that he was on the right road to find out who she was, and where she got her money from.   But I ought to warn you against the young scamp, for I have found out that he robs us and sells our goods far below their value."

" What do you mean? "

" I have long had my suspicions, and yesterday I wormed it all out from a disreputable looking fellow, who came here to ask for his friend Chupin."

Men accustomed to danger are ever prompt in their decisions.   " Very well," returned Mascarin, " if this is the case, Master Chupin shall have a taste of prison fare."

Beaumarchef withdrew, but almost immediately re-appeared.

"Sir," said he, "a servant from M. de Croisenois is here with a note."

"Send the man in," said Mascarin.

The domestic was irreproachably dressed, and looked what he was, the servant of a nobleman.

He had something the appearance of an Englishman, with a high collar, reaching almost to his ears. His face was clean shaved, and of a ruddy hue. His coat was evidently the work of a London tailor, and his appearance was as stiff as though carved out of wood. Indeed, he looked like a very perfect piece of mechanism.

"My master," said he, "desired me to give this note into your own hands."

Under cover of breaking the seal, Mascarin viewed this model servant attentively. He was a stranger to him, for he had never supplied Croisenois with a domestic.

"It seems, my good fellow," said he, "that your master was up earlier than usual this morning?"

The man frowned a little at this familiar address, and then slowly replied,—

"When I took service with the Marquis, he agreed to give me fifteen louis over my wages for the privilege of calling me 'a good fellow,' but I permit no one to do so gratis. I think that my master is still asleep," continued the man solemnly. "He wrote the note on his return from the club."

"Is there any reply?"

"Yes, sir."

"Good; then wait a little."

And Mascarin, opening the note, read the following:

" My dear Friend,—

" Baccarat has served me an ugly turn, and in addition to all my ready cash I have given an I.O.U. for three thousand francs. To save my credit I must have this by twelve to-morrow."

" His credit," said Mascarin. " His credit! That is a fine joke indeed." The servant stood up stiffly erect, as one seeming to take no notice, and the agent continued reading the letter.

" Am I wrong in looking to you for this trifle? I do not think so. Indeed, I have an idea that you will send me a hundred and fifty louis over and above, so that I may not be left without a coin in my pocket. How goes the great affair? I await your decision on the brink of a precipice.
                    " Yours devotedly,
                              " Henry de Croisenois."

" And so," growled Mascarin, " he has flung away five thousand francs, and asks me to find it for him in my coffers. Ah, you fools, if I did not want the grand name that you have inherited from your ancestors, a name that you daily bespatter and soil, you might whistle for your five thousand francs."

However, as Croisenois was absolutely necessary to him, Mascarin slowly took from his safe five notes of a thousand francs each, and handed them to the man.

" Do you want a receipt? " asked the man.

" No; this letter is sufficient, but wait a bit; " and Mascarin, with an eye to the future, drew a twenty franc piece from his pocket, and placing it on the table, said in his most honeyed accents,—

"There, my friend, is something for yourself."

"No, sir," returned the man; "I always ask wages enough to prevent the necessity of accepting presents." And with this dignified reply he bowed with the stiff air of a Quaker, and walked rigidly out of the room.

The agent was absolutely thunderstruck. In all his thirty years' experience he had never come across anything like this.

"I can hardly believe my senses," muttered he; "where on earth did the Marquis pick this fellow up? Can it be that he is sharper than I fancied?"

Suddenly a new and terrifying idea flashed across his mind. "Can it be," said he, "that the fellow is not a real servant, after all? I have so many enemies that one day they may strive to crush me, and however skilfully I may play my cards, some one may hold a better hand." This idea alarmed him greatly, for he was in a position in which he had everything to fear; for when a great work is approaching completion, the anxiety of the promoter becomes stronger and stronger. "No, no," he continued; "I am getting too full of suspicions;" and with these words he endeavored to put aside the vague terrors which were creeping into his soul.

Suddenly Beaumarchef, evidently much excited, appeared upon the threshold.

"What, you here again!" cried Mascarin, angrily; "am I to have no peace to-day?"

"Sir, the young man is here."

"What young man? Paul Violaine?"

"Yes, sir."

"Why, I told him not to come until twelve; something must have gone wrong." He broke off his speech, for at the half-open door stood Paul. He was very pale, and his eyes had the expression of some hunted creature. His attire was in disorder and betokened a night spent in aimless wanderings to and fro.

"Ah, sir!" said he, as he caught sight of Mascarin.

"Leave us, Beaumarchef," said the latter, with an imperious wave of his hand; "and now, my dear boy, what is it?"

Paul sank into a chair.

"My life is ended," said he; "I am lost, dishonored for ever."

Mascarin put on a face of the most utter bewilderment, though he well knew the cause of Paul's utter prostration; but it was with the air of a ready sympathizer that he drew his chair nearer to that of Paul, and said,—

"Come, tell me all about it; what can possibly have happened to affect you thus?"

In deeply tragic tones, Paul replied,—

"Rose has deserted me."

Mascarin raised his hands to heaven.

"And is this the reason that you say you are dishonored? Do you not see that the future is full of promise?"

"I loved Rose," returned Paul, and his voice was so full of pathos that Mascarin could hardly repress a smile. "But this is not all," continued the unhappy boy, making a vain effort to restrain his tears; "I am accused of theft."

"Impossible!" exclaimed Mascarin.

"Yes, sir; and you who know everything are the only person in the world who can save me. You were so kind to me yesterday that I ventured to come here before the time appointed, in order to entreat your help."

"But what do you think I can do?"

"Everything, sir; but let me tell you the whole hideous complication."

Mascarin's face assumed an air of the deepest interest, as he answered, "Go on."

"After our interview," began Paul, "I went back to the Hôtel de Perou, and on the mantelpiece in my garret found this note from Rose."

He held it out as he spoke, but Mascarin made no effort to take it.

"In it," resumed Paul, "Rose tells me she no longer loves me, and begs me not to seek to see her again; and also that, wearied out with poverty, she has accepted the offer of unlimited supplies of money, a carriage, and diamonds."

"Are you surprised at this?" asked Mascarin, with a sneer.

"How could I anticipate such an infidelity, when only the evening before she swore by all she held most sacred that she loved me only? Why did she lie to me? Did she write to make the blow fall heavier? When I ascended the staircase, I was picturing to myself her joy when I told her of your kind promises to me. For more than an hour I remained in my garret, overwhelmed with the terrible thought that I should never see her again."

Mascarin watched Paul attentively, and came to the conclusion that his words were too fine for his grief to be sincere.

"But what about the accusation of theft?"

"I am coming to that," returned the young man. "I then determined to obey your injunctions and leave the Hôtel de Perou, with which I was more than ever disgusted. I went downstairs to settle with Madame

Loupins, when ah! hideous disgrace! As I handed her the two weeks' rent, she asked me with a contemptuous sneer, where I had stolen the money from?"

Mascarin secretly chuckled over the success of his plans thus announced by Paul.

"What did you say?" asked he.

"Nothing, sir; I was too horror-stricken; the man Loupins came up, and both he and his wife scowled at me threateningly. After a short pause, they asserted that they were perfectly sure that Rose and I had robbed M. Tantaine."

"But did you not deny this monstrous charge?"

"I was utterly bewildered, for I saw that every circumstance was against me. The evening before, Rose, in reply to Madame Loupin's importunities, had told her that she had no money, and did not know where to get any. But, as you perceive, on the very next day I appeared in a suit of new clothes, and was prepared to pay my debts, while Rose had left the house some hours before. Does not all this form a chain of strange coincidences? Rose changed the five hundred franc note that Tantaine had lent me at the shop of a grocer, named Melusin, and this suspicious fool was the first to raise a cry against us, and dared to assert that a detective had been ordered to watch us."

Mascarin knew all this story better than Paul, but here he interrupted his young friend.

"I do not understand you," said he, "nor whether your grief arises from indignation or remorse. Has there been a robbery?"

"How can I tell? I have never seen M. Tantaine from that day. There is a rumor that he has been plundered and important papers taken from him, and that he has consequently been arrested."

"Why did you not explain the facts?"

"It would have been of no use. It would clearly prove that Tantaine was no friend of mine, not even an acquaintance, and they would have laughed me to scorn had I declared that the evening before he came into my room and made me a present of five hundred francs."

"I think that I can solve the riddle," remarked Mascarin. "I know the old fellow so well."

Paul listened with breathless eagerness.

"Tantaine," resumed Mascarin, "is the best and kindest fellow in the world, but he is not quite right in the upper story. He was a wealthy man once, but his liberality was his ruin. He is as poor as a church-mouse now, but he is as anxious as ever to be charitable. Unfortunately in the place I procured for him he had a certain amount of petty cash at his disposal, and moved to pity at the sight of your sufferings, he gave you the money that really belonged to others. Then he sent in his accounts, and the deficiency was discovered. He lost his head, and declared that he had been robbed. You lived in the next room; you were known to be in abject poverty on the one day and in ample funds on the next; hence these suspicions."

All was too clear to Paul, and a cold shiver ran through his frame as he saw himself arrested, tried, and condemned.

"But," stammered he, "M. Tantaine holds my note of hand, which is a proof that I acted honestly."

"My poor boy, do you think that if he hoped to save himself at your expense he would produce it?"

"Luckily, sir, you know the real state of the case."

Mascarin shook his head.

"Would my story be credited?" asked he. "Justice

is not infallible, and I must confess that appearances
are against you."

Paul was crushed down beneath this weight of argument. " There is no resource for me then but death,"
murmured he, " for I will not live a dishonored man."

The conduct of Paul was precisely what Mascarin
had expected, and he felt that the moment had arrived
to strike a final blow.

" You must not give way to despair, my boy," said
he.

But Paul made no reply; he had lost the power of
hearing. Mascarin, however, had no time to lose, and
taking him by the arm, shook him roughly. " Rouse
yourself. A man in your position must help himself,
and bring forward proofs of his innocence."

" There is no use in fighting," replied Paul. " Have
you not just shown me that it is hopeless to endeavor
to prove my innocence? "

Mascarin grew impatient at this unnecessary exhibition of cowardice, but he concealed his feelings as best
he could.

" No, no," answered he; " I only wished to show
you the worst side of the affair."

" There is only one side."

" Not so, for it is only a supposition that Tantaine
had made away with money entrusted to him, and we
are not certain of it. And we only surmise that he
has been arrested, and thrown the blame on you. Before giving up the game, would it not be best to be
satisfied on these points? "

Paul felt a little reassured.

" I say nothing," continued Mascarin, " of the influence I exercise over Tantaine, and which may enable me to compel him to confess the truth."

Weak natures like Paul's are raised in a moment from the lowest depths of depression to the highest pitch of exultation, and he already considered that he was saved.

" Shall I ever be able to prove my gratitude to you? " said he impulsively.

Mascarin's face assumed a paternal expression.

" Perhaps you may," answered he; " and as a commencement you must entirely forget the past. Daylight dispels the hideous visions of the night. I offer you a fresh lease of life; will you become a new man? "

Paul heaved a deep sigh. " Rose," he murmured; " I cannot forget her."

Mascarin frowned. " What," said he, " do you still let your thoughts dwell on that woman? There are people who cringe to the hand that strikes them, and the more they are duped and deceived, the more they love. If you are made of this kind of stuff, we shall never get on. Go and find your faithless mistress, and beg her to come back and share your poverty, and see what she will say."

These sarcasms roused Paul. " I will be even with her some day," muttered he.

" Forget her; that is the easiest thing for you to do."

Even now Paul seemed to hesitate. " What," said his patron reproachfully, " have you no pride? "

" I have, sir."

" You have not, or you would never wish to hamper yourself with a woman like Rose. You should keep your hands free, if you want to fight your way through the battle of life."

" I will follow your advice, sir," said Paul hurriedly.

" Very soon you will thank Rose deeply for having

left you. You will climb high, I can tell you, if you will work as I bid you."

" Then," stammered Paul, " this situation at twelve thousand francs a year——"

" There never has been such a situation."

A ghastly pallor overspread Paul's countenance, as he saw himself again reduced to beggary.

" But, sir," he murmured, " will you not permit me to hope——"

" For twelve thousand francs! Be at ease, you shall have that and much more. I am getting old. I have no ties in the world—you shall be my adopted son."

A cloud settled on Paul's brow, for the idea that his life was to be passed in this office was most displeasing to him. Mascarin divined his inmost thoughts with perfect ease. " And the young fool does not know where to go for a crust of bread," thought he. " Ah, if there were no Flavia, no Champdoce; " then, speaking aloud, he resumed, " don't fancy, my dear boy, that I wish to condemn you to the treadmill that I am compelled to pass my life in. I have other views for you, far more worthy of your merits. I have taken a great liking to you, and I will do all I can to further your ambitious views. I was thinking a great deal of you, and in my head I raised the scaffolding of your future greatness. ' He is poor,' said I, ' and at his age, and with his tastes, this is a cruel thing. Why, pray, should I not find a wife for him among those heiresses who have a million or two to give the man they marry? When I talk like this, it is because I know of an heiress, and my friend, Dr. Hortebise, shall introduce her to you. She is nearly, if not quite, as pretty as Rose, and has the advantage of her in being well-born, well-educated, and wealthy. She has influential relatives, and if her husband should happen to be a poet, or a composer, she could assist him in becoming famous."

A flush came over Paul's face. This seemed like the realization of some of his former dreams.

" With regard to your birth," continued Mascarin, " I have devised a wonderful plan. Before '93, you know, every bastard was treated as a gentleman, as he might have been the son of some high and mighty personage. Who can say that your father may not have been of the noblest blood of France, and that he has not lands and wealth? He may even now be looking for you, in order to acknowledge you and make you his heir. Would you like to be a duke? "

" Ah, sir," stammered the young man.

Mascarin burst into a fit of laughter. " Up to now," said he, " we are only in the region of suppositions."

" Well, sir, what do you wish me to do? " asked Paul, after a short pause.

Mascarin put on a serious face. " I want absolute obedience from you," said he; " a blind and undeviating obedience, one that makes no objections and asks no questions."

" I will obey you, sir; but, oh! do not desert me."

Without making any reply, Mascarin rang for Beaumarchef, and as soon as the latter appeared, said, " I am going to Van Klopen's, and shall leave you in charge here." Then, turning to Paul, he added, " I always mean what I say; we will go and breakfast at a neighboring restaurant. I want to have a talk with you, and afterward—afterward, my boy, I will show you the girl I intend to be your wife. I am curious to know how you like her looks."

CHAPTER XI.

THE MAN-MILLINER.

GASTON DE GANDELU was much surprised at finding that André should be ignorant of the existence of Van Klopen, the best-known man in Paris. To assure oneself of this, it was only necessary to glance at his circulars, which were ornamented with the representations of medals won at all sorts of exhibitions in different quarters of the world, together with various decorations received from foreign potentates. One had been presented to him by the Queen of Spain, while he had a diploma appointing him the supplier to the Court of the Czar. The great Van Klopen was not an Alsatian, as was generally supposed, but a stout, handsome Dutchman, who, in the year 1850, had been a tailor in his small native town, and manufactured in cloth, purchased on credit, the long waistcoats and miraculous coats worn by the wealthy citizens of Rotterdam. Van Klopen, however, was not successful in his business, and was compelled to close his shop and abscond from his creditors. He took refuge in Paris, where he seemed likely to die of hunger. One day over a magnificent establishment in the Rue de Grammont appeared a signboard with the name of Van Klopen, dressmaker, and in the thousands of handbills distributed with the utmost profusion, he called himself the " Regenerator of Fashion." This was an idea that would have never originated in the brain of the phlegmatic Dutchman, and whence came the funds to carry on the business? On this point he was discreetly silent. The enterprise was at first far from a success, for during nearly a month Paris almost split its sides laughing at the absurd pretensions of the self-dubbed "Regenerator of Fashion." Van Klopen bent before the storm he had aroused, and in due time his advertisements brought him two customers, who were the first to blow the trumpet of his fame. One was the Duchess de Suirmeuse, a very great lady indeed, and renowned for her eccentricities and extravagant manner, while the other was an example of another class, being no less than the celebrated Jennie Fancy, who was at that time under the protection of the Count de Tremouselle; and for these two Van Klopen invented such dresses as had never been seen before. From this moment his success was certain; indeed, it was stupendous, and Paris resounded with his praises. Now he has achieved a world-wide reputation, and has nothing to fear from the attacks of his rivals. He would not execute orders for every one, saying that he must pick and choose his customers, and he did so, excising the names of such as he did not think would add to his reputation. Rank and wealth disputed the honor of being his customers. The haughtiest dames did not shrink from entrusting to him secrets of form and figure, which they even hid from their husbands. They endured without shrinking the touch of his coarse hands as he measured them. He was the rage, and his showrooms were a species of neutral ground, where women of all circles of society met and examined each other. The Duchess of —— did not shrink from being in the same room with the celebrated woman for whom the Baron de —— had blown out the few brains he possessed. Perhaps the Duchess thought that by employing the same costumier, she might also gain some of the venal beauteous attractions. Mademoiselle D——, of the Gymnase Theatre, who was well known to earn just one thousand francs per annum, took a delight in astonishing the haughty ladies of fashion by the reckless extravagance of her orders. Van Klopen, who was a born diplomatist, distributed his favors between his different customers; consequently he was termed the most charming and angelic of men. Many a time had he heard the most aristocratic lips let fall the words, "I shall die, Van Klopen, if my dress is not ready." On the evenings of the most aristocratic balls a long line of carriages blocked up the road in front of his establishment, and the finest women in Paris crowded the showrooms for a word of approval from him.

He gave credit to approved customers, and also, it was whispered, lent money to them. But woe to the woman who permitted herself to be entrapped in the snare of credit that he laid for her; for the woman who owed him a bill was practically lost, never knowing to what depths she might be degraded to obtain the money to settle her account. It was not surprising that such sudden prosperity should have turned Van Klopen's head. He was stout and ruddy, impudent, vain, and cynical. His admirers said that he was witty.

It was to this man's establishment that Mascarin conducted Paul after a sumptuous breakfast at Philipe's.

It is necessary to give a slight description of Van Klopen's establishment. Carpets of the most expensive description covered the stairs to his door on the first floor, at which stood the liveried menials resplendent in gold lace and scarlet. As soon as Mascarin made his appearance, one of these gorgeous creatures hastened to him and said, " M. Van Klopen is just now engaged with the Princess Korasoff, but as soon as he hears of your arrival he will manage to get rid of her. Will you wait for him in his private room? "

But Mascarin answered,—

" We are in no hurry, and may as well wait in the public room with the other customers. Are there many of them? "

" There are about a dozen ladies, sir."

" Good; I am sure that they will amuse me."

And, without wasting any more words, Mascarin opened a door which led into a magnificent drawing-room, decorated in very florid style. The paper on the walls almost disappeared beneath a variety of water-color sketches, representing ladies in every possible style of costume. Each picture had an explanatory note beneath it, such as " Costume of Mde. de C—— for a dinner at the Russian Ambassador's," " Ball costume of the Marchioness de V—— for a ball at the Hôtel de Ville," etc.

Paul, who was a little nervous at finding himself among such splendor, hesitated in the doorway; but Mascarin seized his young friend by the arm, and, as he drew him to a settee, whispered in his ear,—

" Keep your eyes about you; the heiress is here."

The ladies were at first a little surprised at this invasion of the room by the male element, but Paul's extreme beauty soon attracted their attention. The hum of conversation ceased, and Paul's embarrassment increased as he found a battery of twelve pairs of eyes directed full upon him.

Mascarin, however, was quite at his ease, and upon his entrance had made a graceful though rather old-

fashioned bow to the fair inmates of the room. His
coolness was partly due to the contempt he felt for the
human race in general, and also to his colored glasses,
which hid the expression of his countenance. When he
saw that Paul still kept his eyes on the ground, he
tapped him gently on the arm.

" Is this the first time you ever saw well-dressed
women? Surely you are not afraid of them. Look to
the right," continued Mascarin, " and you will see the
heiress."

A young girl, not more than eighteen, was seated
near one of the windows. She was not perhaps so
beautiful as Mascarin had described, but her face was
a very striking one nevertheless. She was slight and
good-looking, with the clear complexion of a brunette.
Her features were not perhaps very regular, but her
glossy black hair was a beauty in itself. She had a
pair of dark, melting eyes, and her wide, high forehead showed that she was gifted with great intelligence. There was an air of restrained voluptuousness
about her, and she seemed the very embodiment of
passion.

Paul felt insensibly attracted toward her. Their
eyes met, and both started at the same moment. Paul
was fascinated in an instant, and the girl's emotion
was so evident that she turned aside her head to conceal it.

The babel had now commenced again, and general
attention was being paid to a lady who was enthusiastically describing the last new costume which had
made its appearance in the Bois de Boulogne.

" It was simply miraculous," said she; " a real triumph of Van Klopen's art. The ladies of a certain
class are furious, and Henry de Croisenois tells me

that Jennie Fancy absolutely shed tears of rage. Imagine three green skirts of different shades, each draped——."

Mascarin, however, only paid attention to Paul and the young girl, and a sarcastic smile curled his lips.

"What do you think of her?" asked he.

"She is adorable!" answered Paul, enthusiastically.

"And immensely wealthy."

"I should fall at her feet if she had not a sou."

Mascarin gave a little cough, and adjusted his glasses.

"Should you, my lad?" said he to himself; "whether your admiration is for the girl or her money, you are in my grip."

Then he added, aloud,—

"Would you not like to know her name?"

"Tell me, I entreat you."

"Flavia."

Paul was in the seventh heaven, and now boldly turned his eyes on the girl, forgetting that owing to the numerous mirrors, she could see his every movement.

The door was at this moment opened quietly, and Van Klopen appeared on the threshold. He was about forty-four, and too stout for his height. His red, pimply face had an expression upon it of extreme insolence, and his accent was thoroughly Dutch. He was dressed in a ruby velvet dressing-gown, with a cravat with lace ends. A huge cluster-diamond ring blazed on his coarse, red hand.

"Who is the next one?" asked he, rudely.

The lady who had been talking so volubly rose to her feet, but the tailor cut her short, for, catching sight of Mascarin, he crossed the room, and greeted him with the utmost cordiality.

"What!" said he; "is it you that I have been keeping waiting? Pray pardon me. Pray go into my private room; and this gentleman is with you? Do me the favor, sir, to come with us."

He was about to follow his guests, when one of the ladies started forward.

"One word with you, sir, for goodness sake!" cried she.

Van Klopen turned sharply upon her.

"What is the matter?" asked he.

"My bill for three thousand francs falls due to-morrow."

"Very likely."

"But I can't meet it."

"That is not my affair."

"I have come to beg you will renew it for two months, or say one month, on whatever terms you like."

"In two months," answered the man brutally, "you will be no more able to pay than you are to-day. If you can't pay it, it will be noted."

"Merciful powers! then my husband will learn all."

"Just so; that will be what I want; for he will then have to pay me."

The wretched woman grew deadly pale.

"My husband will pay you," said she; "but I shall be lost."

"That is not my lookout. I have partners whose interests I have to consult."

"Do not say that, sir! He has paid my debts once, and if he should be angry and take my children from me——Dear M. Van Klopen, be merciful!"

She wrung her hands, and the tears coursed down her cheeks; but the tailor was perfectly unmoved.

" When a woman has a family of children, one ought to have in a needlewoman by the hour."

She did not desist from her efforts to soften him, and, seizing his hand, strove to carry it to her lips.

" Ah! I shall never dare to go home," wailed she; " never have the courage to tell my husband."

" If you are afraid of your own husband, go to some one else's," said he roughly; and tearing himself from her, he followed Mascarin and Paul.

" Did you hear that?" asked he, as soon as he had closed the door of his room with an angry slam. " These things occasionally occur, and are not particularly pleasant."

Paul looked on in disgust. If he had possessed three thousand francs, he would have given them to this unhappy woman, whose sobs he could still hear in the passage.

" It is most painful," remarked he.

" My dear sir," said the tailor, " you attach too much importance to these hysterical outbursts. If you were in my place, you would soon have to put their right value on them. As I said before, I have to look after my own and my partners' interests. These dear creatures care for nothing but dress; father, husband, and children are as nothing in comparison. You cannot imagine what a woman will do in order to get a new dress, in which to outshine her rival. They only talk of their families when they are called on to pay up."

Paul still continued to plead for some money for the poor lady, and the discussion was getting so warm that Mascarin felt bound to interfere.

" Perhaps," said he, "you have been a little hard."

" Pooh," returned the tailor; " I know my customer;

and to-morrow my account will be settled, and I know very well where the money will come from. Then she will give me another order, and we shall have the whole comedy over again. I know what I am about." And taking Mascarin into the window, he made some confidential communication, at which they both laughed heartily.

Paul, not wishing to appear to listen, examined the consulting-room, as Van Klopen termed it. He saw a great number of large scissors, yard measures, and patterns of material, and heaps of fashion plates.

By this time the two men had finished their conversation.

" I had," said Mascarin, as they returned to the fireplace, " I had meant to glance through the books; but you have so many customers waiting, that I had better defer doing so."

" Is that all that hinders you?" returned Van Klopen, carelessly. " Wait a moment."

He left the room, and in another moment his voice was heard.

" I am sorry, ladies, very sorry, on my word; but I am busy with my silk mercer. I shall not be very long."

" We will wait," returned the ladies in chorus.

" That is the way," remarked Van Klopen, as he returned to the consulting-room. " Be civil to women, and they turn their backs on you; try and keep them off, and they run after you. If I was to put up ' no admittance ' over my door, the street would be blocked up with women. Business has never been better," continued the tailor, producing a huge ledger. " Within the last ten days we have had in orders amounting to eighty-seven thousand francs."

" Good! " answered Mascarin; " but let us have a look at the column headed ' Doubtful.' "

" Here you are," returned the arbiter of fashion, as he turned over the leaves. " Mademoiselle Virginie Cluhe has ordered five theatrical costumes, two dinner, and three morning dresses."

" That is a heavy order."

" I wanted for that reason to consult you. She doesn't owe us much—perhaps a thousand francs or so."

" That is too much, for I hear that her friend has come to grief. Do not decline the order, but avoid taking fresh ones."

Van Klopen made a few mysterious signs in the margin of his ledger.

" On the 6th of this month the Countess de Mussidan gave us an order—a perfectly plain dress for her daughter. Her account is a very heavy one, and the Count has warned us that he will not pay it."

" Never mind that. Go on with the order, but press for payment."

" On the 7th a new customer came—Mademoiselle Flavia, the daughter of Martin Rigal, the banker."

When Paul heard this name, he could not repress a start, of which, however, Mascarin affected to take no notice.

" My good friend," said he, turning to Van Klopen, " I confide this young lady to you; give her your whole stock if she asks for it."

By the look of surprise which appeared upon the tailor's face, Paul could see that Mascarin was not prodigal of such recommendations.

" You shall be obeyed," said Van Klopen, with a bow.

"On the 8th a young gentleman of the name of Gaston de Gandelu was introduced by Lupeaux, the jeweller. His father is, I hear, very wealthy, and he will come into money on attaining his majority, which is near at hand. He brought with him a lady," continued the tailor, "and said her name was Zora de Chantemille, a tremendously pretty girl."

"That young man is always in my way," said Mascarin. "I would give something to get him out of Paris."

Van Klopen reflected for a moment. "I don't think that would be difficult," remarked he; "that young fellow is capable of any act of folly for that fair girl."

"I think so too."

"Then the matter is easy. I will open an account with him; then, after a little, I will affect doubts as to his solvency, and ask for a bill; and we shall then place our young friend in the hands of the Mutual Loan Society, and M. Verminet will easily persuade him to write his name across the bottom of a piece of stamped paper. He will bring it to me; I will accept it, and then we shall have him hard and fast."

"I should have proposed another course."

"I see no other way, however." He suddenly stopped, for a loud noise was heard in the ante-room, and the sound of voices in loud contention.

"I should like to know," said Van Klopen, rising to his feet, "who the impudent scoundrel is, who comes here kicking up a row. I expect that it is some fool of a husband."

"Go and see what it is," suggested Mascarin.

"Not I! My servants are paid to spare me such annoyances."

Presently the noise ceased.

" And now," resumed Mascarin, " let us return to our own affairs. Under the circumstances, your proposal appears to be a good one. How about writing in another name? A little forgery would make our hands stronger." He rose, and taking the tailor into the window recess, again whispered to him.

During this conversation Paul's cheek had grown paler and paler, for, occupied as he was, he could not fail to comprehend something of what was going on. During the breakfast Mascarin had partially disclosed many strange secrets, and since then he had been even more enlightened. It was but too evident to him that his protector was engaged in some dark and insidious plot, and Paul felt that he was standing over a mine which might explode at any moment. He now began to fancy that there was some mysterious link between the woman Schimmel, who was so carefully watched, and the Marquis de Croisenois, so haughty, and yet on such intimate terms with the proprietor of the registry office. Then there was the Countess de Mussidan, Flavia, the rich heiress, and Gaston de Gandelu, who was to be led into a crime the result of which would be penal servitude,—all jumbled and mixed up together in one strange phantasmagoria. Was he, Paul, to be a mere tool in such hands? Toward what a precipice was he being impelled! Mascarin and Van Klopen were not friends, as he had at first supposed, but confederates in villainy. Too late did he begin to see collusion between Mascarin and Tantaine, which had resulted in his being accused of theft during his absence. But the web had been woven too securely, and should he struggle to break through it, he might find himself exposed to even more terrible dangers. He felt horrified at his position, but with this there was mingled no horror of the criminality of his associates, for the skilful hand of Mascarin had unwound and mastered all the bad materials of his nature. He was dazzled at the glorious future held out before him, and said to himself that a man like Mascarin, unfettered by law, either human or Divine, would be most likely to achieve his ends. " I should be in no danger," mused he to himself, " if I yield myself up to the impetuous stream which is already carrying me along, for Mascarin is practised swimmer enough to keep both my head and his own above water."

Little did Paul think that every fleeting expression in his countenance was caught up and treasured by the wily Mascarin; and it was intentionally that he had permitted Paul to listen to this compromising conversation. He had decided that very morning, that if Paul was to be a useful tool, he must be at once set face to face with the grim realities of the position.

" Now," said he, " for the really serious reason for my visit. How do we stand now with regard to the Viscountess Bois Arden?"

Van Klopen gave his shoulders a shrug as he answered, " She is all right. I have just sent her several most expensive costumes."

" How much does she owe you? "

" Say twenty-five thousand francs. She has owed us more than that before."

" Really," remarked Mascarin, " that woman has been grossly libelled; she is vain, frivolous, and fond of admiration, but nothing more. For a whole fortnight I have been prying into her life, but I can't hit upon anything in it to give us a pull over her. The debt may help us, however. Does her husband know that she has an account with us?"

"Of course he does not; he is most liberal to her, and if he inquired——"

"Then we are all right; we will send in the bill to him."

"But, my good sir," urged Van Klopen, "it was only last week that she paid us a heavy sum on account."

"The more reason to press her, for she must be hard up."

Van Klopen would have argued further, but an imperious sign from Mascarin reduced him to silence.

"Listen to me," said Mascarin, "and please do not interrupt me. Are you known to the domestics at the house of the Viscountess?"

"Not at all."

"Well, then, at three o'clock sharp, the day after to-morrow, call on her. Her footman will say that Madame has a visitor with her."

"I will say I will wait."

"Not at all. You must almost force your way in, and you will find the Viscountess talking to the Marquis de Croisenois. You know him, I suppose?"

"By sight—nothing more."

"That is sufficient. Take no notice of him; but at once present your bill, and violently insist upon immediate payment."

"What can you be thinking of? She will have me kicked out of doors."

"Quite likely; but you must threaten to take the bill to her husband. She will command you to leave the house, but you will sit down doggedly and declare that you will not move until you get the money."

"But that is most unbusinesslike behavior."

"I quite agree with you; but the Marquis de Croisenois will interfere; he will throw a pocketbook in your face, exclaiming, ' There is your money, you impudent scoundrel! ' "

" Then I am to slink away? "

" Yes; but before doing so, you will give a receipt in this form—' Received from the Marquis de Croisenois, the sum of so many francs, in settlement of the account of the Viscountess Bois Arden.' "

" If I could only understand the game," muttered the puzzled Van Klopen.

" There is no necessity for that now; only act up to your instructions."

" I will obey, but remember that we shall not only lose her custom, but that of all her acquaintance."

Again the same angry sounds were heard in the corridor.

" It is scandalous," cried a voice. " I have been waiting an hour; my sword and armor. What, ho, lackeys; hither, I say. Van Klopen is engaged, is he? Hie to him and say I must see him at once."

The two accomplices exchanged looks, as though they recognized the shrill, squeaky voice.

" That is our man," whispered Mascarin, as the door was violently flung open, and Gaston de Gandelu burst in. He was dressed even more extravagantly than usual, and his face was inflamed with rage.

" Here am I," cried he; " and an awful rage I am in. Why, I have been waiting twenty minutes. I don't care a curse for your rules and regulations."

The tailor was furious at this intrusion; but as Mascarin was present, and he felt that he must respect his orders, he by a great effort controlled himself.

" Had I known, sir," said he sulkily, " that you were here——"

These few words mollified the gorgeous youth, who at once broke in.

" I accept your apologies," cried he; " the lackeys remove our arms, the joust is over. My horses have been standing all this time, and may have taken cold. Of course you have seen my horses. Splendid animals, are they not? Zora is in the other room. Quick, fetch her here."

With these words he rushed into the passage and shouted out, " Zora, Mademoiselle de Chantemille, my dear one, come hither."

The renowned tailor was exquisitely uncomfortable at so terrible a scene in his establishment. He cast an appealing glance at Mascarin, but the face of the agent seemed carved in marble. As to Paul, he was quite prepared to accept this young gentleman as a perfect type of the glass of fashion and the mould of form, and could not forbear pitying him in his heart. He went across the room to Mascarin.

" Is there no way," whispered he, " of saving this poor young fellow?"

Mascarin smiled one of those livid smiles which chilled the hearts of those who knew him thoroughly.

" In fifteen minutes," said he, " I will put the same question to you, leaving you to reply to it. Hush, this is the first real test that you have been subjected to; if you are not strong enough to go through it, then we had better say farewell. Be firm, for a thunderbolt is about to fall!"

The manner in which these apparently trivial words were spoken startled Paul, who, by a strong effort, recovered his self-possession; but, prepared as he was, it was with the utmost difficulty that he stifled the expression of rage and surprise that rose to his lips at the sight of the woman who entered the room. The Madame de Chantemille, the Zora of the youthful Gandelu, was there, attired in what to his eyes seemed a most dazzling costume. Rose seemed a little timid as Gandelu almost dragged her into the room.

" How silly you are ! " said he. " What is there to be frightened at? He is only in a rage with his flunkies for having kept us waiting."

Zora sank negligently into an easy chair, and the gorgeously attired youth addressed the all-powerful Van Klopen.

" Well, have you invented a costume that will be worthy of Madame's charms? "

For a few moments Van Klopen appeared to be buried in profound meditation.

" Ah," said he, raising his hand with a grandiloquent gesture, " I have it; I can see it all in my mind's eye."

" What a man ! " murmured Gaston in deep admiration.

" Listen," resumed the tailor, his eye flashing with the fire of genius. " First, a walking costume with a polonaise and a cape *à la pensionnaire;* bodice, sleeves, and underskirt of a brilliant chestnut——"

He might have continued in this strain for a long time, and Zora would not have heard a word, for she had caught sight of Paul, and in spite of all her audacity, she nearly fainted. She was so ill at ease, that young Gandelu at last perceived it; but not knowing the effect that the appearance of Paul would necessarily cause, and being also rather dull of comprehension he could not understand the reason for it.

"Hold hard, Van Klopen, hold hard! the joy has been too much for her, and I will lay you ten to one that she is going into hysterics."

Mascarin saw that Paul's temper might blaze forth at any moment, and so hastened to put an end to a scene which was as absurd as it was dangerous.

"Well, Van Klopen, I will say farewell," said he. "Good morning, madame; good morning, sir;" and taking Paul by the arm, he led him away by a private exit which did not necessitate their passing through the great reception-room.

It was time for him to do so, and not until they were in the street did the wily Mascarin breathe freely.

"Well, what do you say, now?" asked he.

Paul's vanity had been so deeply wounded, and the effort that he had made to restrain himself so powerful, that he could only reply by a gasp.

"He felt it more than I thought he would," said Mascarin to himself. "The fresh air will revive him."

Paul's legs bent under him, and he staggered so that Mascarin led him into a little *café* hard by, and ordered a glass of cognac, and in a short time Paul was himself once again.

"You are better now," observed Mascarin; and then, believing it would be best to finish his work, he added, "A quarter of an hour ago I promised that I would ask you to settle what our intentions were to be regarding M. de Gandelu."

"That is enough," broke in Paul, violently.

Mascarin put on his most benevolent smile.

"You see," remarked he, "how circumstances change ideas. Now you are getting quite reasonable."

"Yes, I am reasonable enough now; that is, that I

mean to be wealthy. You have no need to urge me on any more. I am willing to do whatever you desire, for I will never again endure degradation like that I have gone through to-day."

"You have let temper get the better of you," returned Mascarin, with a shrug of his shoulders.

"My anger may pass over, but my determination will remain as strong as ever."

"Do not decide without thinking the matter well over," answered the agent. "To-day you are your own master; but if you give yourself up to me, you must resign your dearly loved liberty."

"I am prepared for all."

Victory had inclined to the side of Mascarin, and he was proportionally jubilant.

"Good," said he. "Then Dr. Hortebise shall introduce you to Martin Rigal, the father of Mademoiselle Flavia, and one week after your marriage I will give you a duke's coronet to put on the panels of your carriage."

CHAPTER XII.

A STARTLING REVELATION.

WHEN Sabine de Mussidan told her lover that she would appeal to the generosity of M. de Breulh-Faverlay, she had not calculated on the necessity she would have for endurance, but had rather listened to the dictates of her heart; and this fact came the more strongly before her, when, in the solitude of her own chamber, she inquired of herself how she was to carry out her

promise. It seemed to her very terrible to have to
lay bare the secrets of her soul to any one, but the
more so to M. de Breulh-Faverlay, who had asked for
her hand in marriage. She uttered no word on her
way home, where she arrived just in time to take her
place at the dinner table, and never was a more dismal
company assembled for the evening meal. Her own
miseries occupied Sabine, and her father and mother
were suffering from their interviews with Mascarin
and Dr. Hortebise. What did the liveried servants,
who waited at table with such an affectation of interest, care for the sorrows of their master or mistress?
They were well lodged and well fed, and nothing save
their wages did they care for. By nine o'clock Sabine
was in her own room trying to grow accustomed to
the thoughts of an interview with M. de Breulh-Faverlay. She hardly closed her eyes all night, and felt
worn out and dispirited by musing; but she never
thought of evading the promise she had made to André,
or of putting it off for a time. She had vowed to
lose no time, and her lover was eagerly awaiting a letter from her, telling him of the result. In the perplex-
ity in which she found herself, she could not confide in
either father or mother, for she felt that a cloud hung
over both their lives, though she knew not what it
was. When she left the convent where she had been
educated, and returned home, she felt that she was in
the way, and that the day of her marriage would be
one of liberation to her parents from their cares and re-
sponsibilities. All this preyed terribly upon her mind,
and might have driven a less pure-minded girl to desperate measures. It seemed to her that it would be
less painful to fly from her father's house than to have
this interview with M. de Breulh-Faverlay. Luckily

for her, frail as she looked, she possessed an indomitable will, and this carried her through most of her difficulties.

For André's sake, as well as her own, she did not wish to violate any of the unwritten canons of society, but she longed for the hour to come when she could acknowledge her love openly to the world. At one moment she thought of writing a letter, but dismissed the thought as the height of folly. As the time passed Sabine began to reproach herself for her cowardice. All at once she heard the clang of the opening of the main gates. Peeping from her window, she saw a carriage drive up, and, to her inexpressible delight, M. de Breulh-Faverlay alighted from it.

" Heaven has heard my prayer, and sent him to me," murmured she.

" What do you intend to do, Mademoiselle? " asked the devoted Modeste; " will you speak to him now? "

" Yes, I will. My mother is still in her dressing-room, and no one will venture to disturb my father in the library. If I meet M. de Breulh-Faverlay in the hall and take him into the drawing-room, I shall have time for a quarter of an hour's talk, and that will be sufficient."

Calling up all her courage, she left her room on her errand. Had André seen the man selected by the Count de Mussidan for his daughter's husband, he might well have been proud of her preference for him. M. de Breulh-Faverlay was one of the best known men in Paris, and fortune had showered all her blessings on his head. He was not forty, of an extremely aristocratic appearance, highly educated, and witty; and, in addition, one of the largest landholders in the country.

He had always refused to enter public life. "For," he would say to those who spoke to him on the matter, "I have enough to spend my money on without making myself ridiculous." He was a perfect type of what a French gentleman should be—courteous, of unblemished reputation, and full of chivalrous devotion and generosity. He was, it is said, a great favorite with the fair sex; but, if report spoke truly, his discretion was as great as his success. He had not always been wealthy, and there was a mysterious romance in his life. When he was only twenty, he had sailed for South America, where he remained twelve years, and returned no richer than he was before; but shortly afterward his aged uncle, the Marquis de Faverlay, died, bequeathing his immense fortune to his nephew on the condition that he should add the name of Faverlay to that of De Breulh. De Breulh was passionately fond of horses; but he was really a lover of them, and not a mere turfite, and this was all that the world knew of the man who held in his hands the fates of Sabine de Mussidan and André. As soon as he caught sight of Sabine he made a profound inclination.

The girl came straight up to him.

"Sir," said she, in a voice broken by conflicting emotions, "may I request the pleasure of a short private conversation with you?"

"Mademoiselle," answered De Breulh, concealing his surprise beneath another bow, "I am at your disposal."

One of the footmen, at a word from Sabine, threw open the door of the drawing-room in which the Countess had thrown down her arms in her duel with Dr. Hortebise. Sabine did not ask her visitor to be seated, but, leaning her elbow on the marble mantelpiece, she said, after a silence equally trying to both,—

"This strange conduct on my part, sir, will show you, more than any explanation, my sincerity, and the perfect confidence with which you have inspired me."

She paused, but De Breulh made no reply, for he was perfectly mystified.

"You are," she continued, "my parents' intimate friend, and must have seen the discomforts of our domestic hearth, and that though both my father and mother are living, I am as desolate as the veriest orphan."

Fearing that M. de Breulh might not understand her reason for speaking thus, she threw a shade of haughtiness into her manner as she resumed,—

"My reason, sir, for seeing you to-day is to ask,— nay, to entreat you, to release me from my engagement to you, and to take the whole responsibility of the rupture on yourself."

Man of the world as he was, M. de Breulh could not conceal his surprise, in which a certain amount of wounded self-love was mingled.

"Mademoiselle!" commenced he—

Sabine interrupted him.

"I am asking a great favor, and your granting it will spare me many hours of grief and sadness, and," she added, as a faint smile flickered across her pallid features, "I am aware that I am asking but a trifling sacrifice on your part. You know scarcely anything of me, and therefore you can only feel indifference toward me."

"You are mistaken," replied the young man gravely; "and you do not judge me rightly. I am not a mere boy, and always consider a step before I take it; and if I asked for your hand, it was because I had learned to appreciate the greatness both of your heart and intellect; and I believe that if you would condescend to accept me, we could be very happy together."

The girl seemed about to speak, but De Breulh continued,—

" It seems, however, that I have in some way displeased you,—I do not know how; but, believe me, it will be a source of sorrow to me for the rest of my life."

De Breulh's sincerity was so evident, that Mademoiselle de Mussidan was deeply affected.

" You have not displeased me in any way," answered she softly, " and are far too good for me. To have become your wife would have made me a proud and happy woman."

Here she stopped, almost choked by her tears, but M. de Breulh wished to fathom this mystery.

" Why then this resolve? " asked he.

" Because," replied Sabine faintly, as she hid her face,—" because I have given all my love to another."

The young man uttered an exclamation so full of angry surprise, that Sabine turned upon him at once.

" Yes, sir," answered she, " to another; one utterly unknown to my parents, yet one who is inexpressibly dear to me. This ought not to irritate you, for I gave him my love long before I met you. Besides, you have every advantage over him. He is at the foot, while you are at the summit, of the social ladder. You are of aristocratic lineage,—he is one of the people. You have a noble name,—he does not even know his own. Your wealth is enormous,—while he works hard for his daily bread. He has all the fire of genius, but the cruel cares of life drag and fetter him to the earth.

He carries on a workman's trade to supply funds to study his beloved art."

Incautiously, Sabine had chosen the very means to wound this noble gentleman most cruelly, for her whole beauty blazed out as, inflamed by her passion, she spoke so eloquently of André and drew such a parallel between the two young men.

"Now, sir," said she, "do you comprehend me? I know the terrible social abyss which divides me from the man I love, and the future may hold in store some terrible punishment for my fidelity to him, but no one shall ever hear a word of complaint from my lips, for——" she hesitated, and then uttered these simple words—"for I love him."

M. de Breulh listened with an outwardly impassible face, but the venomed tooth of jealousy was gnawing at his heart. He had not told Sabine the entire truth, for he had studied her for a long time, and his love had grown firm and strong. Without an unkind thought the girl had shattered the edifice which he had built up with such care and pain. He would have given his name, rank, and title to have been in this unknown lover's place, who, though he worked for his bread, and had no grand ancestral name, was yet so fondly loved. Many a man in his position would have shrugged his shoulders and coldly sneered at the words, "I love him," but he did not, for his nature was sufficiently noble to sympathize with hers. He admired her courage and frankness, which, disdaining all subterfuges, went straight and unhesitatingly to the point she desired to reach. She might be imprudent and reckless, but in his eyes these seemed hardly to be faults, for it is seldom that convent-bred young ladies err in this way.

"But this man," said he, after a long pause,—"how do you manage ever to see him?"

"I meet him out walking," replied she, "and I sometimes go to his studio."

"To his studio?"

"Yes, I have sat to him several times for my portrait; but I have never done anything that I need blush to own. You know all now, sir," continued Sabine; "and it has been very hard for a young girl like me to say all this to you. It is a thing that ought to be confided to my mother."

Only those who have heard a woman that they are ardently attached to say, "I do not love you," can picture M. de Breulh's frame of mind. Had any one else than Sabine made this communication he would not have withdrawn, but would have contested the prize with his more fortunate rival. But now that Mademoiselle de Mussidan had, as it were, thrown herself upon his mercy, he could not bring himself to take advantage of her confidence.

"It shall be as you desire," said he, with a faint tinge of bitterness in his tone. "To-night I will write to your father, and withdraw my demand for your hand. It is the first time that I have ever gone back from my word; and I am sure that your father will be highly indignant."

Sabine's strength and firmness had now entirely deserted her. "From the depth of my soul, sir," said she, "I thank you; for by this act of generosity I shall avoid a contest that I dreaded."

"Unfortunately," broke in De Breulh, "you do not see how useless to you will be the sacrifice that you exact from me. Listen! you have not appeared much in society; and when you did, it was in the character of my betrothed; as soon as I withdraw hosts of aspirants for your hand will spring up."

Sabine heaved a deep sigh, for André had foreseen the same result.

"Then," continued De Breulh, "your situation will become even a more trying one; for if your noble qualities are not enough to excite admiration in the bosoms of the other sex, your immense wealth will arouse the cupidity of the fortune-hunters."

When De Breulh referred to fortune-hunters, was this a side blow at André? With this thought rushing through her brain, she gazed upon him eagerly, but read no meaning in his eyes.

"Yes," answered she dreamily, "it is true that I am very wealthy."

"And what will be your reply to the next suitor, and to the one after that?" asked De Breulh.

"I know not; but I shall find some loophole of escape when the time comes; for if I act in obedience to the dictates of my heart and conscience, I cannot do wrong, for Heaven will come to my aid."

This phrase sounded like a dismissal; but De Breulh, man of the world as he was, did not accept it.

"May I permit myself to offer you a word of advice?"

"Do so, sir."

"Very well, then; why not permit matters to remain as they now are? So long as our rupture is not public property, so long will you be left in peace. It would be the simplest thing in the world to postpone all decisive steps for a twelvemonth, and I would withdraw as soon as you notified me that it was time."

Sabine put every confidence in this proposal, believing that everything was in good faith. "But," said she, "such a subterfuge would be unworthy of us all."

M. de Breulh did not urge this point; a feeling of deep sympathy had succeeded to his wounded pride; and, with all the chivalrous instinct of his race, he determined to do his best to assist these lovers.

"Might I be permitted," asked he, "now that you have placed so much confidence in me, to make the acquaintance of the man whom you have honored with your love?"

Sabine colored deeply. "I have no reason to conceal anything from you: his name is André, he is a painter, and lives in the Rue de la Tour d'Auvergne."

De Breulh made a mental note of the name, and continued,—

"Do not think that I ask this question from mere idle curiosity; my only desire is to aid you. I should be glad to be a something in your life. I have influential friends and connections——"

Sabine was deeply wounded. Did this man propose patronizing André, and thus place his position and wealth in contrast with that of the obscure painter? In his eagerness De Breulh had made a false move.

"I thank you," answered she coldly; "but André is very proud, and any offer of assistance would wound him deeply. Forgive my scruples, which are perhaps exaggerated and absurd. All he has of his own are his self-respect and his natural pride."

As she spoke, Sabine rang the bell, to show her visitor that the conversation was at an end.

"Have you informed my mother of M. de Breulh-Faverlay's arrival?" asked she, as the footman appeared at the door.

"I have not, mademoiselle; for both the Count and

Countess gave the strictest order that they were not
to be disturbed on any pretext whatsoever."

"Why did you not tell me that before?" demanded
M. de Breulh; and, without waiting for any explanation, he bowed gravely to Sabine, and quitted the room,
after apologizing for his involuntary intrusion, and by
his manner permitted all the domestics to see that he
was much put out.

"Ah!" sighed Sabine, "that man is worthy of some
good and true woman's affection."

As she was about to leave the room, she heard some
one insisting upon seeing the Count de Mussidan. Not
being desirous of meeting strangers, she remained
where she was. The servant persisted in saying that
his master could receive no one.

"What do I care for your orders?" cried the visitor;
"your master would never refuse to see his friend the
Baron de Clinchain;" and, thrusting the lackey on one
side, he entered the drawing-room; and his agitation
was so great that he hardly noticed the presence of
the young girl.

M. de Clinchain was a thoroughly commonplace looking personage in face, figure, and dress, neither tall
nor short, handsome nor ill-looking. The only notice-
able point in his attire was that he wore a coral hand
on his watch chain; for the Baron was a firm believer
in the evil eye. When a young man, he was most
methodical in his habits; and, as he grew older, this
became an absolute mania with him. When he was
twenty, he recorded in his diary the pulsations of his
heart, and at forty he added remarks regarding his
digestion and general health.

"What a fearful blow!" murmured he; "and to
fall at such a moment when I had indulged in a more

hearty dinner than usual. I shall feel it for the next six months, even if it does not kill me outright."

Just then M. de Mussidan entered the room, and the excited man ran up to him, exclaim. r,—

"For Heaven's sake, Octave, save both, by cancelling your daughter's engagement with M. de——"

The Count laid his hand upon his friend's lips.

"Are you mad?" said he; "my daughter is here."

In obedience to a warning gesture, Sabine left the room; but she had heard enough to fill her heart with agitation and terror. What engagement was to be cancelled, and how could such a rupture affect her father or his friend? That there was some mystery, was proved by the question with which the Count had prevented his friend from saying any more. She was sure that it was the name of M. de Breulh-Faverlay with which the Baron was about to close his sentence, and felt that the destiny of her life was to be decided in the conversation about to take place between her father and his visitor. It was deep anxiety that she felt, not mere curiosity; and while these thoughts passed through her brain, she remembered that she could hear all from the card-room, the doorway of which was only separated from the drawing-room by a curtain. With a soft, gliding step she gained her hiding-place and listened intently. The Baron was still pouring out his lamentations.

"What a fearful day this has been!" groaned the unhappy man. "I ate much too heavy a breakfast, I have been terribly excited, and came here a great deal too fast. A fit of passion caused by a servant's insolence, joy at seeing you, then a sudden interruption to what I was going to say, are a great deal more than sufficient to cause a serious illness at my age."

But the Count, who was usually most considerate of his friend's foibles, was not in a humor to listen to him.

"Come, let us talk sense," said he sharply; "tell me what has occurred."

"Occurred!" groaned De Clinchain; "oh, nothing, except that the whole truth is known regarding what took place in the little wood so many years back. I had an anonymous letter this morning, threatening me with all sorts of terrible consequences if I do not hinder you from marrying your daughter to De Breulh. The rogues say that they can prove everything."

"Have you the letter with you?"

De Clinchain drew the missive from his pocket. It was to the full as threatening as he had said; but M. de Mussidan knew all its contents beforehand.

"Have you examined your diary, and are the three leaves really missing?"

"They are."

"How were they stolen? Are you sure of your servants?"

"Certainly; my valet has been sixteen years in my service. You know Lorin? The volumes of my diary are always locked up in the escritoire, the key of which never leaves me. And none of the other servants ever enter my room."

"Some one must have done so, however."

Clinchain struck his forehead, as though an idea had suddenly flashed across his brain.

"I can partly guess," said he. "Some time ago Lorin went for a holiday, and got drunk with some fellows he picked up in the train. Drink brought on fighting, and he was so knocked about that he was laid up for some weeks. He had a severe knife wound in the shoulder, and was much bruised."

" Who took his place? "

" A young fellow that my groom got at a servants' registry office."

M. de Mussidan felt that he was on the right track, for he remembered that the man who had called on him had had the audacity to leave a card, on which was marked:

" B. MASCARIN,
Servants' Registry Office,
Rue Montorgueil."

" Do you know where this place is? " asked he.

" Certainly; in the Rue du Dauphin nearly opposite to my house."

The Count swore a deep oath. " The rogues are very wily; but, my dear fellow if you are ready, we will defy the storm together."

De Clinchain felt a cold tremor pass through his whole frame at this proposal.

" Not I," said he; " do not try and persuade me. If you have come to this decision, let me know at once, and I will go home and finish it all with a pistol bullet."

He was just the sort of nervous, timorous man to do exactly as he said, and would sooner have killed himself than endure all kinds of annoyance, which might impair his digestion.

" Very well," answered his friend, with sullen resignation, " then I will give in."

De Clinchain heaved a deep sigh of relief, for he, not knowing what had passed before, had expected to have had a much more difficult task in persuading his friend.

"You are acting like a reasonable man for once in your life," said he.

"You think so, because I give ear to your timorous advice. A thousand curses on that idiotic habit of yours of putting on paper not only your own secrets, but those of others."

But at this remark Clinchain mounted his hobby.

"Do not talk like that," said he. "Had you not committed the act, it would not have appeared in my diary."

Chilled to the very bone, and quivering like an aspen leaf, Sabine had listened to every word. The reality was even more dreadful than she had dreamed of. There was a hidden sorrow, a crime in her father's past life.

Again the Count spoke. "There is no use in re-crimination. We cannot wipe out the past, and must, therefore, submit. I promise you, on my honor, that this day I will write to De Breulh, and tell him that this marriage must be given up."

These words threw the balm of peace and safety into De Clinchain's soul, but the excess of joy was too much for him, and murmuring, "Too much breakfast, and the shock of too violent an emotion," he sank back, fainting, on a couch.

The Count de Mussidan was terrified; he pulled the bell furiously, and the domestics rushed in, followed by the Countess. Restoratives were applied, and in ten minutes the Baron opened one eye, and raised him-self on his elbow.

"I am better now," said he, with a faint smile. "It is weakness and dizziness. I know what I ought to take—two spoonfuls of *eau des carmes* in a glass of sugar and water, with perfect repose of both mind and body. Fortunately, my carriage is here. Pray, be prudent, Mussidan." And, leaning upon the arm of one of the lackeys, he staggered feebly out, leaving the Count and Countess alone, and Sabine still listening from her post of espial in the card-room.

CHAPTER XIII.

HUSBAND AND WIFE.

EVER since Mascarin's visit, the Count de Mussidan had been in a deplorable state of mind. Forgetting the injury to his foot, he passed the night pacing up and down the library, cudgelling his brains for some means of breaking the meshes of the net in which he was entangled. He knew the necessity for immediate action, for he felt sure that this demand would only be the forerunner of numerous others of a similar character. He thought over and dismissed many schemes. Sometimes he had almost decided to go to the police authorities and make a clean breast; then the idea of placing the affair in the hands of a private detective occurred to him; but the more he deliberated, the more he realized the strength of the cord that bound him, and the scandal which exposure would cause. This long course of thought had in some measure softened the bitterness of his wrath, and he was able to receive his old friend M. de Clinchain with some degree of calmness. He was not at all surprised at the receipt of the anonymous letter,—indeed, he had expected that a blow would be struck in that direction. Still immersed in thought, M. de Mussidan hardly took heed of his wife's presence, and he still paced the room, uttering a string of broken phrases. This excited the attention of the Countess, for her own threatened position caused her to be on the alert.

"What is annoying you, Octave?" asked she. "Surely, not M. de Clinchain's attack of indigestion?"

For many years the Count had been accustomed to that taunting and sarcastic voice, but this feeble joke at such a moment was more than he could endure.

"Don't address me in that manner," said he angrily.

"What is the matter—are you not well?"

"Madame!"

"Will you have the kindness to tell me what has taken place?"

The color suffused the Count's face, and his rage burst forth the more furiously from his having had to suppress it so long; and coming to a halt before the chair in which the Countess was lounging, his eyes blazing with hate and anger, he exclaimed,—

"All I wish to tell you is, that De Breulh-Faverlay shall not marry our daughter."

Madame de Mussidan was secretly delighted at this reply, for it showed her that half the task required of her by Dr. Hortebise had been accomplished without her interference; but in order to act cautiously, she began at once to object, for a woman's way is always at first to oppose what she most desires.

"You are laughing at me, Count!" said she. "Where can we hope to find so good a match again?"

"You need not be afraid," returned the Count, with a sneer; "you shall have another son-in-law."

These words sent a pang through the heart of the Countess. Was it an allusion to the past? or had the phrase dropped from her husband's lips accidentally? or had he any suspicion of the influence that had been brought to bear upon her? She, however, had plenty of courage, and would rather meet misfortune face to face than await its coming in dread.

"Of what other son-in-law are you speaking?" asked she negligently. "Has any other suitor presented himself? May I ask his name? Do you intend to settle my child's future without consulting me?"

"I do, madame."

A contemptuous smile crossed the face of the Countess, which goaded the Count to fury.

"Am I not the master here?" exclaimed he in accents of intense rage. "Am I not driven to the exercise of my power by the menaces of a pack of villains who have wormed out the hidden secrets which have overshadowed my life from my youth upward? They can, if they desire, drag my name through the mire of infamy."

Madame de Mussidan bounded to her feet, asking herself whether her husband's intellect had not given way.

"You commit a crime!" gasped she.

"I, madame, I, myself! Does that surprise you? Have you never had any suspicion? Perhaps you have not forgotten a fatal accident which took place out shooting, and darkened the earlier years of our married life? Well, the thing was not an accident, but a deliberate murder committed by me. Yes, I murdered him, and this fact is known, and can be proved."

The Countess grew deadly pale, and extended her

hand, as though to guard herself from some coming danger.

"You are horrified, are you?" continued the Count, with a sneer. "Perhaps I inspire you with horror; but do not fear; the blood is no longer on my hands, but it is here, and is choking me." And as he spoke he pressed his fingers upon his heart. "For twenty-three years I have endured this hideous recollection, and even now when I wake in the night I am bathed in cold sweat, for I fancy I can hear the last gasps of the unhappy man."

"This is horrible, too horrible!" murmured Madame de Mussidan faintly.

"Ah, but you do not know why I killed him,—it was because the dead man had dared to tell me that the wife that I adored with all the passion of my soul was unfaithful to me."

Words of eager denial rose to the lips of the Countess; but her husband went on coldly, "And it was all true, for I heard all later on.

"Poor Montlouis! *he* was really loved. There was a little shop-girl, who toiled hard for daily bread, but she was a thousand times more honorable than the haughty woman of noble race that I had just married."

"Have mercy, Octave."

"Yes, and she fell a victim to her love for Montlouis. Had he lived, he would have made her his wife. After his death, she could no longer conceal her fault. In small towns the people are without mercy; and when she left the hospital with her baby at her breast, the women pelted her with mud. But for me," continued the Count, "she would have died of hunger. Poor girl! I did not allow her much, but with it she managed to give her son a decent education. He has now grown up, and whatever happens, his future is safe."

Had M. de Mussidan and his wife been less deeply engaged in this hideous recital, they would have heard the stifled sobs that came from the adjoining room.

The Count felt a certain kind of savage pleasure in venting the rage, that had for years been suppressed, upon the shrinking woman before him. "Would it not be a cruel injustice, madame, to draw a comparison between you and this unhappy girl? Have you always been deaf to the whisperings of conscience? and have you never thought of the future punishment which most certainly awaits you? for you have failed in the duties of daughter, wife, and mother."

Generally the Countess cared little for her husband's reproaches, well deserved as they might be, but to-day she quailed before him.

"With your entrance into my life," continued the Count, "came shame and misfortune. When people saw you so gay and careless under the oak-trees of your ancestral home, who could have suspected that your heart contained a dark secret? When my only wish was to win you for my wife, how did I know that you were weaving a hideous conspiracy against me? Even when so young, you were a monster of dissimulation and hypocrisy. Guilt never overshadowed your brow, nor did falsehood dim the frankness of your eyes. On the day of our marriage I mentally reproached myself for my unworthiness. Wretched fool that I was, I was happy beyond all power of expression, when you, madame, completed the measure of your guilt by adding infidelity to it."

"It is false," murmured the Countess. "You have been deceived."

M. de Mussidan laughed a grim and terrible laugh.

"Not so," answered he; "I have every proof. This seems strange to you, does it? You have always looked upon me as one of those foolish husbands that may be duped without suspicion on their parts. You thought that you had placed a veil over my eyes, but I could see through it when you little suspected that I could do so. Why did I not tell you this before? Because I had not ceased to love you, and this fatal love was stronger than all honor, pride, and even self-respect." He poured out this tirade with inconceivable rapidity, and the Countess listened to it in awestruck silence. "I kept silence," continued the Count, "because I knew that on the day I uttered the truth you would be entirely lost to me. I might have killed you; I had every right to do so, but I could not live apart from you. You will never know how near the shadow of death has been to you. When I have kissed you, I have fancied that your lips were soiled with the kisses of others, and I could hardly keep my hands from clutching your ivory neck until life was extinct, and failed utterly to decide whether I loved you or hated you the most."

"Have mercy, Octave! have mercy!" pleaded the unhappy woman.

"You are surprised, I can see," answered he, with a dark smile; "yet I could give you further food for wonder if I pleased, but I have said enough now."

A tremor passed over the frame of the Countess. Was her husband acquainted with the existence of the letters? All hinged upon this. He could not have read them, or he would have spoken in very different terms, had he known the mystery contained in them.

"Let me speak," began she.

" Not a word," replied her husband.

" On my honor——"

" All is ended; but I must not forget to tell you of one of my youthful follies. You may laugh at it, but that signifies nothing. I actually believed that I could gain your affection. I said to myself that one day you would be moved by my deep passion for you. I was a fool. As if love or affection could ever penetrate the icy barriers that guarded your heart."

" You have no pity," wailed she.

He gazed upon her with eyes in which the pent-up anger of twenty years blazed and consumed slowly. " And you, what are you? I drained to the bottom the poisoned cup held out to a deceived husband by an unfaithful wife. Each day widened the breach between us, until at last we sank into this miserable existence which is wearing out my life. I kept no watch on you; I was not made for a jailer. What I wanted was your soul and heart. To imprison the body was easy, but your soul would still have been free to wander in imagination to the meeting-place where your lover expected you. I know not how I had the courage to remain by your side. It was not to save an honor that had already gone, but merely to keep up appearances; for as long as we were nominally together the tongue of scandal was forced to remain silent."

Again the unhappy woman attempted to protest her innocence, and again the Count paid no heed to her. " I wished too," resumed he, " to save some portion of our property, for your insatiable extravagance swallowed up all like a bottomless abyss. At last your trades-people, believing me to be ruined, refused you credit, and this saved me. I had my daughter to think of, and have gathered together a rich dowry for her, and yet——" he hesitated, and ceased speaking for a moment.

" And yet," repeated Madame de Mussidan.

" I have never kissed her," he burst forth with a fresh and terrible explosion of wrath, " without feeling a hideous doubt as to whether she was really my child."

This was more than the Countess could endure.

" Enough," she cried, " enough! I have been guilty, Octave; but not so guilty as you imagine."

" Why do you venture to defend yourself? "

" Because it is my duty to guard Sabine."

" You should have thought of this earlier," answered the Count with a sneer. " You should have moulded her mind—have taught her what was noble and good, and have perused the unsullied pages of the book of her young heart."

In the deepest agitation the Countess answered,—

"Ah, Octave, why did you not speak of this sooner, if you knew all; but I will now tell you everything."

By an inconceivable error of judgment the Count corrected her speech. " Spare us both," said he. " If I have broken through the silence that I have maintained for many a year, it is because I know that no word you could utter would touch my heart."

Feeling that all hope had fled, Madame de Mussidan fell backward upon the couch, while Sabine, unable to listen to any more terrible revelations, had crept into her own chamber. The Count was about to leave the drawing-room, when a servant entered, bearing a letter on a silver salver. De Mussidan tore it open; it was from M. de Breulh-Faverlay, asking to be released from his engagement to Sabine de Mussidan. This last stroke was almost too much for the Count's nerves, for in this act he saw the hand of the man who had come to him with such deadly threats, and terror filled his soul as he thought of the far-stretching arm of him whose bondslave he found himself to be; but before he could collect his thoughts, his daughter's maid went into the room crying with all her might, "Help, help; my poor mistress is dying!"

CHAPTER XIV.

FATHER AND DAUGHTER.

VAN KLOPEN, the man-milliner, knew Paris and its people thoroughly like all tradesmen who are in the habit of giving large credit. He knew all about the business of his customers, and never forgot an item of information when he received one. Thus, when Mascarin spoke to him about the father of the lovely Flavia, whose charms had set the susceptible heart of Paul Violaine in a blaze, the arbiter of fashion had replied,—

"Martin Rigal; yes, I know him; he is a banker." And a banker, indeed, Martin Rigal was, dwelling in a magnificent house in the Rue Montmartre. The bank was on the ground floor, while his private rooms were in the story above. Though he did not do business in a very large way, yet he was a most respectable man, and his connection was chiefly with the smaller tradespeople, who seem to live a strange kind of hand-to-mouth existence, and who might be happy were it not for the constant reappearance of that grim phantom— bills to be met. Nearly all these persons were in the banker's hands entirely. Martin Rigal used his power despotically and permitted no arguments, and speedily quelled rebellion on the part of any new customer who ventured to object to his arbitrary rules. In the morning the banker was never to be seen, being engaged in his private office, and not a clerk would venture to knock at his door. Even had one done so, no reply would have been returned; for the experiment had been tried, and it was believed that nothing short of an alarm of fire would have brought him out.

The banker was a big man, quite bald, his face was clean shaved, and his little gray eyes twinkled incessantly. His manner was charmingly courteous, and he said the most cruel things in the most honied accents, and invariably escorted to the door the man whom he would sell up the next day. In his dress he affected a fashionable style, much used by the modern school of Shylocks. When not in business, he was a pleasant, and, as some say, a witty companion. He was not looked on as an ascetic, and did not despise those little pleasures which enable us to sustain life's tortuous journey. He liked a good dinner, and had always a smile ready for a young and attractive face. He was a widower, and all his love was concentrated on his daughter. He did not keep a very extravagant establishment, but the report in the neighborhood was that Mademoiselle Flavia, the daughter of the eminent banker, would one day come into millions. The banker always did his business on foot, for the sake of his health, as he said; but Flavia had a sweet little Victoria, drawn by two thoroughbred horses, to drive in the Bois de Boulogne, under the protection of an old woman, half companion and half servant, who was driven half mad by her charge's caprices. As yet her father has never denied her anything. He worked harder than all his clerks put together, for, after having spent the morning in his counting house over his papers, he received all business clients.

On the day after Flavia and Paul Violaine had met at Van Klopen's, M. Martin Rigal was, at about half-past five, closeted with one of his female clients. She was young, very pretty, and dressed with simple elegance, but the expression of her face was profoundly melancholy. Her eyes were overflowing with tears, which she made vain efforts to restrain.

"If you refuse to renew our bill, sir, we are ruined," said she. "I could meet it in January. I have sold all my trinkets, and we are existing on credit."

"Poor little thing!" interrupted the banker.

Her hopes grew under these words of pity.

"And yet," continued she, "business has never been so brisk. New customers are constantly coming in, and though our profits are small, the returns are rapid."

As Martin Rigal heard her exposition of the state of affairs, he nodded gravely.

"That is all very well," said he at last, "but this does not make the security you offer me of any more value. I have more confidence in you."

"But remember, sir, that we have thirty thousand francs' worth of stock."

"That is not what I was alluding to," and the banker accompanied these words with so meaning a look, that the poor woman blushed scarlet and almost lost her nerve. "Your stock," said he, "is of no more value in my eyes than the bill you offer me. Suppose, for instance, you were to become bankrupt, the landlord might come down upon everything, for he has great power."

He broke off abruptly, for Flavia's maid, as a privileged person, entered the room without knocking.

"Sir," said she, "my mistress wishes to see you at once."

The banker got up directly. "I am coming," said he; then, taking the hand of his client, he led her to the door, repeating: "Do not worry yourself; all the difficulties shall be got through. Come again, and we will talk them over;" and before she could thank him he was half way to his daughter's apartment. Flavia had summoned her father to show him a new costume which had just been sent home by Van Klopen, and which pleased her greatly. Flavia's costume was a masterpiece of fashionable bad taste, which makes women look all alike and destroys all appearance of individuality. It was a mass of frills, furbelows, fringes, and flutings of rare hue and form, making a series of wonderful contrasts. Standing in the middle of the room, with every available candle alight, for the day was fading away, she was so dainty and pretty that even the *bizarre* dress of Van Klopen's was unable to spoil her appearance. As she turned round, she caught sight of her father in a mirror, panting with the haste he had made in running up-stairs.

"What a time you have been!" said she pettishly.

"I was with a client," returned he apologetically.

"You ought to have got rid of him at once. But never mind that; look at me and tell me plainly what you think of me."

She had no need to put the question, for the most intense admiration beamed in his face.

"Exquisite, delicious, heavenly!" answered he.

Flavia, accustomed as she was to her father's compliments, was highly delighted. "Then you think that he will like me?" asked she.

She alluded to Paul Violaine, and the banker heaved a deep sigh as he replied,—

" Is it possible that any human being exists that you cannot please ? "

" Ah ! " mused she, " if it were any one but he, I should have no doubts or misgivings."

Martin Rigal took a seat near the fire, and, drawing his daughter to him, pressed a fond kiss upon her brow, while she with the grace and activity of a cat, nestled upon his knee. " Suppose, after all, that he should not like me," murmured she ; " I should die of grief."

The banker turned away his face to hide the gloom that overspread it. " Do you love him, then, even now ? " asked he.

She paused for a moment, and he added, " More than you do me ? "

Flavia pressed her father's hand between both her palms and answered with a musical laugh, " How silly you are, papa ! Why, of course I love you. Are you not my father ? I love you too because you are kind and do all I wish, and because you are always telling me that you love me. Because you are like the cupids in the fairy stories—dear old people who give their children all their heart's desire ; I love you for my carriage, my horses, and my lovely dresses ; for my purse filled with gold, for my beautiful jewelry, and for all the lovely presents you make me."

Every word she spoke betrayed the utter selfishness of her soul, and yet her father listened with a fixed smile of delight on his face.

" And why do you love him ? " asked he.

" Because—because," stammered the girl, " first, because he is himself ; and then,—well, I can't say, but I *do* love him."

Her accents betrayed such depth of passion that the father uttered a groan of anguish.

Flavia caught the expression of his features, and burst into a fit of laughter.

"I really believe that you are jealous," said she, as if she were speaking to a spoiled child. "That is very naughty of you; you ought to be ashamed of yourself. I tell you that the first time I set eyes upon him at Van Klopen's, I felt a thrill of love pierce through my heart, such love as I never felt for a human being before. Since then, I have known no rest. I cannot sleep, and instead of blood, liquid fire seems to come through my veins."

Martin Rigal raised his eyes to the ceiling in mute surprise at this outburst of feeling.

"You do not understand me," went on Flavia. "You are the best of fathers, but, after all, you are but a man. Had I a mother, she would comprehend me better."

"What could your mother have done for you more than I? Have I neglected anything for your happiness?" asked the banker, with a sigh.

"Perhaps nothing; for there are times when I hardly understand my own feelings."

In gloomy silence the banker listened to the narrative of his daughter's state of mind; then he said,—

"All shall be as you desire, and the man you love shall be your husband."

The girl was almost beside herself with joy, and, throwing her arms around his neck, pressed kiss upon kiss on his cheeks and forehead.

"Darling," said she, "I love you for this more than for anything that you have given me in my life."

The banker sighed again; and Flavia, shaking her

DRAWING HIS DAUGHTER TO HIM, SHE, WITH THE GRACE AND ACTIVITY
OF A CAT, NESTLED UPON HIS KNEE

pretty little fist at him, exclaimed, " What is the meaning of that sigh, sir? Do you by any chance regret
your promise? But never mind that. How do you
mean to bring him here without causing any suspicion?"

A benevolent smile passed over her father's face, as
he answered,—

" That, my pet, is my secret."

" Very well, keep it; I do not care what means you
use, as long as I see him soon, very soon,—to-night
perhaps, in an hour, or even in a few minutes. You
say Dr. Hortebise will bring him here; he will sit at
our table. I can look at him without trouble, I shall
hear his voice——"

" Silly little puss!" broke in the banker; " or, rather,
I should say, unhappy child."

" Silly, perhaps; but why should you say unhappy?"

" You love him too fondly, and he will take advantage of your feeling for him."

" Never; I do not believe it," answered the girl.

" I hope to heaven, darling, that my fears may never
be realized. But he is not the sort of husband that I
intended for you; he is a composer."

" And is that anything against him!" exclaimed
Flavia in angry tones; " one would think from your
sneers that this was a crime. Not only is he a composer, but he is a genius. I can read that in his face.
He may be poor, but I am rich enough for both, and
he will owe all to me; so much the better, for then
he will not be compelled to give lessons for his livelihood, and he will have leisure to compose an opera
more beautiful than any that Gounod has ever written,
and I shall share all his glory. Why, perhaps, he may
even sing his own songs to me alone."

Her father noticed her state of feverish excitement and gazed upon her sadly. Flavia's mother had been removed from this world at the early age of twenty-four by that insidious malady, consumption, which defies modern medical science, and in a brief space changes a beautiful girl into a livid corpse, and the father viewed her excited manner, flushed cheeks, and sparkling eyes with tears and dismay.

"By heavens!" cried he, bursting into a sudden fit of passion; "'f ever he ill treats you, he is a dead man."

The girl was startled at the sudden ferocity of his manner.

"What have I done to make you angry?" asked she; "and why do you have such evil thoughts of him?"

"I tremble for you, in whom my whole soul is wrapped up," answered the banker. "This man has robbed me of my child's heart, and you will be happier with him than you are with your poor old father. I tremble because of your inexperience and his weakness, which may prove a source of trouble to you."

"If he is weak, all the better; my will can guide him."

"You are wrong," replied her father, "as many other women have been before you. You believe that weak and vacillating dispositions are easily controlled, but I tell you that this is an error. Only determined characters can be influenced, and it is on substantial foundations that we find support."

Flavia made no reply, and her father drew her closer to him.

"Listen to me, my child," said he. "You will never have a better friend than I am. You know that I would shed every drop of blood in my veins for you.

He is coming, so search your heart to discover if this is not some mere passing fancy."

" Father ! " cried she.

" Remember that your happiness is in your own hands now, so be careful and conceal your feelings, and do not let him discover how deep your love is for him. Men's minds are so formed that while they blame a woman for duplicity, they complain far more if she acts openly and allows her feelings to be seen——"

He paused, for the door-bell rang. Flavia's heart gave a bound of intense joy.

" He has come ! " gasped she, and, with a strong effort to retain her composure, she added, " I will obey you, my dear father; I will not come here again until I have entirely regained my composure. Do not fear, and I will show you that your daughter can act a part as well as any other woman."

She fled from the room as the door opened, but it was not Paul who made his appearance, but some other guests—a stout manufacturer and his wife, the latter gorgeously dressed, but with scarcely a word to say for herself. For this evening the banker had issued invitations to twenty of his friends, and among this number Paul would scarcely be noticed. He in due time made his appearance with Dr. Hortebise, who had volunteered to introduce him into good society. Paul felt ill at ease; he had just come from the hands of a fashionable tailor, who, thanks to Mascarin's influence, had in forty-eight hours prepared an evening suit of such superior cut that the young man hardly knew himself in it. Paul had suffered a good deal from conflicting emotions after the visit to Van Klopen's, and more than once regretted the adhesion that he had given to

Mascarin's scheme; but a visit the next day from
Hortebise, and the knowledge that the fashionable
physician was one of the confederates, had reconciled
him to the position he had promised to assume.

He was moreover struck with Flavia's charms, and
dazzled with the accounts of her vast prospective fortune. To him, Hortebise, gay, rich, and careless,
seemed the incarnation of happiness, and contributed
greatly to stifle the voice of Paul's conscience. He
would, however, perhaps have hesitated had he known
what the locket contained that dangled so ostentatiously
from the doctor's chain.

Before they reached the banker's door, driven in the
doctor's elegant brougham, a similar one to which Paul
mentally declared he would have, as soon as circumstances would permit, the young man's mentor spoke.

" Let me say a few words to you. You have before
you a chance which is seldom afforded to any young
man, whatever his rank and social standing. Mind
that you profit by it."

" You may be sure I will," said Paul, with a smile
of self-complacency.

" Good, dear boy; but let me fortify your courage
with a little of my experience. Do you know what
an heiress really is ? "

" Well, really——"

" Permit me to continue. An heiress and more so
if she is an only child, is generally a very disagreeable
person, headstrong, capricious, and puffed up with her
own importance. She is utterly spoiled by the flattery
to which she has been accustomed from her earliest
years, and thinks that all the world is made to bend
before her."

" Ah ! " answered Paul, a little discomfited. " I hope

it is not Mademoiselle Flavia's portrait that you have been sketching?"

"Not exactly," answered the doctor, with a laugh. "But I must warn you that even she has certain whims and fancies. For instance, I am quite sure that she would give a suitor every encouragement, and then repulse him without rhyme or reason."

Paul, who up to this time had only seen the bright side of affairs, was a good deal disconcerted.

"But why should you introduce me to her then?"

"In order that you may win her. Have you not everything to insure success? She will most likely receive you with the utmost cordiality; but beware of being too sanguine. Even if she makes desperate love to you, I say, take care; it may be only a trap; for, between ourselves, a girl who has a million stitched to her petticoats is to be excused if she endeavors to find out whether the suitor is after her or her money."

Just then the brougham stopped, and Dr. Hortebise and his young friend entered the house in the Rue Montmartre, where they were cordially greeted by the banker.

Paul glanced round, but there were no signs of Flavia, nor did she make her appearance until five minutes before the dinner hour, when the guests flocked round her. She had subdued all her emotions, and not a quiver of the eyelids disclosed the excitement under which she was laboring. Her eye rested on Paul, and he bowed ceremoniously. The banker was delighted, for he had not believed much in her self-command. But Flavia had taken his advice to heart, and when seated at table abstained from casting a glance in Paul's direction. When dinner was over and many of the guests had sat down to whist, Flavia ventured to approach

Paul, and in a low voice, which shook a little in spite of her efforts, said,—

"Will you not play me one of your own compositions, M. Violaine?"

Paul was but a medium performer, but Flavia seemed in the seventh heaven, while her father and Dr. Hortebise, who had taken their seats not far away, watched the young couple with much anxiety.

"How she adores him!" whispered the banker. "And yet I cannot judge of the effect that she has produced upon him.

"Surely Mascarin will worm it all out of him to-morrow," returned the doctor. "To-morrow the poor fellow will have his hands full, for there is to be a general meeting, when we shall hear all about Catenac's ideas, and I shall be glad to know what Croisenois's conduct will be when he knows what he is wanted for."

It was growing late, and the guests began to drop off. Dr. Hortebise signalled to Paul, and they left the house together. According to the promise to her father, Flavia had acted her part so well, that Paul did not know whether he had made an impression or not.

CHAPTER XV.

MASTER CHUPIN.

BEAUMARCHEF, when Mascarin called a general meeting of his associates, was in the habit of assuming his very best attire; for as he was often called into the inner office to answer questions, he was much impressed with the importance of the occasion. This time, however, the subordinate, although he had received due

notice of the meeting, was still in his every-day dress.
This discomposed him a good deal, though he kept
muttering to himself that he meant no disrespect by it.
Early in the morning he had been compelled to make
up the accounts of two cooks, who, having obtained
situations, were leaving the servants' lodging-house.
When this matter was completed, he had hoped for half
an hour's leisure. As he was crossing the courtyard,
however, he fell in with Toto Chupin bringing in his
daily report, which Beaumarchef thought would be
what it usually was—a mere matter of form. He was,
however, much mistaken; for though outwardly Toto
was the same, yet his ideas had taken an entirely new
direction; and when Beaumarchef urged him to look
sharp, the request was received with a great deal of
sullenness.

" I ain't lost no time," said he, " and have fished up
a thing or two fresh; but before saying a word——"

He stopped, and seemed a little confused

" Well, go on."

" I want a fresh arrangement."

Beaumarchef was staggered.

" Arrangement ! " he echoed.

" Of course you can lump it if yer don't like it," said
the boy. " Do you think as how I'm going to work like
a horse, and not get a wink of sleep, just for a ' thank
ye, Chupin? ' No fear. I'm worth a sight more nor
that."

Beaumarchef flew into a rage.

" Then you are not worth a pinch of salt," said he.

" All right, my cove."

" And you are an ungrateful young villain to talk
like this after all the kindness your master has shown
you."

Chupin gave a sarcastic laugh.

"Goodness!" cried he. "To hear you go on, one would think that the boss had ruined himself for my sake."

"He took you out of the streets, and has given you a room ever since."

"A room, do you say? I call it a dog kennel."

"You have your breakfast and dinner every day regularly."

"I know that, and half a bottle of wine at each meal, which has so much water in it that it cannot even stain the tablecloth."

"You are an ungrateful young hound," exclaimed Beaumarchef, "and forget that, in addition to this, he has set you up in business as a hot chestnut seller."

"Good old business! I am allowed to stand all day under the gateway, roasted on one side, and frozen on the other, and gain, perhaps twenty sous."

"You know that in summer he has promised to set you up in the fried potato line."

"Thank ye for nothing; I don't like the smell of grease."

"What is it you want, then?"

"Nothing. I feels that I ought to be a gentleman at large."

Beaumarchef cast a furious glance at the shameless youth, and told him that he would report everything to his master. The boy, however, did not seem to care a pin.

"I intends to see Master Mascarin myself presently," remarked Chupin.

"You are an idiot."

"Why so? Do you think I didn't live better before

I had anything to do with this blooming old cove? I never worked then. I used to sing in front of the pubs, and easily made my three francs a day. My pal and I soon check 'em though, and then off we went to the theatre. Sometimes we'd make tracks for Ivry, and take our doss in a deserted factory, into which the crushers never put their noses. In the winter we used to go to the glass houses and sleep in the warm ashes. All these were good times, while now——"

"Well, what have you to grumble at now? Don't I hand you a five-franc piece every day that you are at work?"

"But that ain't good enough. Come, don't get shirty; all I asks for is a rise of salary. Only say either Yes or No; and if you say No, why, I sends in my resignation."

Beaumarchef would have given a five-franc piece out of his own pocket for Mascarin to have heard the boy's impertinence.

"You are a young rascal!" said he, "and keep the worst of company. There is no use in denying it, for a hang-dog fellow, calling himself Polyte, has been here asking after you."

"My company ain't any business of yours."

"Well, I give you warning, you will come to grief."

"How?" returned Toto Chupin sulkily. "How can I come to grief? If old Mascarin interferes, I'll shut up his mouth pretty sharp. I wish you and your master wouldn't poke their noses into my affairs. I'm sick of you both. Don't you think I'm up to you? When you make me follow some one for a week at a time, it isn't to do 'em a kindness, I reckon. If things turn out badly, I've only to go before a beak and speak up; I should get off easily enough then; and if I do so, you will be sorry for not having given me more than my five francs a day."

Beaumarchef was an old soldier and a bold man, but he was easily upset, for the lad's insolence made him believe that he was uttering words that had been put in his mouth by some wily adviser; and not knowing how to act, the ex-soldier thought it best to adopt a more conciliating demeanor.

" How much do you want? " asked he.

" Well, seven francs to start with."

" The deuce you do! Seven francs a day is a sum. Well, I'll give it you myself to-day and will speak about you to the master."

" You won't get me to loosen my tongue for that amount to-day; you may bet your boots on that," answered the lad insolently. " I wants one hundred francs down on the nail."

" One hundred francs," echoed Beaumarchef, scandalized at such a demand.

" Yes, my cove, that and no less."

" And what will you give in return? No, no, my lad; your demand is a preposterous one; besides, you wouldn't know how to spend such a sum."

" Don't you flurry yourself about that; but of one thing you may be sure, I sha'n't spend my wages as you do—in wax for your mustache."

Beaumarchef could not endure an insult to his mustache, and Chupin was about to receive the kick he had so richly earned, when Daddy Tantaine suddenly made his appearance, looking exactly as he did when he visited Paul in his garret.

" Tut, tut; never quarrel with the door open."

Beaumarchef thanked Providence for sending this

sudden reinforcement to his aid, and began in a tone
of indignation,—

"Toto Chupin——"

"Stop! I have heard every word," broke in Tantaine.

On hearing this, Toto felt that he had better make
himself scarce; for though he hardly knew Mascarin,
and utterly despised Beaumarchef, he trembled before
the oily Tantaine, for in him he recognized a being who
would stand no nonsense. He therefore began in an
apologetic tone,—

"Just let me speak, sir; I only wanted——"

"Money, of course, and very natural too. Come,
Beaumarchef, hand this worthy lad the hundred francs
that he has so politely asked for."

Beaumarchef was utterly stupefied, and was about
to make some objection when he was struck by a signal
which Toto did not perceive, and, drawing out his
pocketbook, extracted a note which he offered to the
lad. Toto glanced at the note, then at the faces of
the two men, but was evidently afraid to take the
money.

"Take the money," said Tantaine. "If your information is not worth the money, I will have it back
from you; come into the office, where we shall not be
disturbed."

Tantaine took a chair, and glancing at Toto, who
stood before him twirling his cap leisurely, said,—

"I heard you."

The lad had by this time recovered his customary
audacity.

"Five days ago," he began, "I was put on to Caroline Schimmel; I have found out all about her by this
time. She is as regular as clockwork in her duties at

least. She wakes at ten and takes her absinthe. Then she goes to a little restaurant she knows, and has her breakfast and a game at cards with any one that will play with her. At six in the evening she goes to the Grand Turk, a restaurant and dancing-shop in the Rue des Poisonnières. Ain't it a swell ken just! You can eat, drink, dance, or sing, just as you like; but you must have decent togs on, or they won't let you in."

" Wouldn't they let you through then ? "

Toto pointed significantly to his rags as he replied,—

" This rig out wouldn't pass muster, but I have a scheme in hand."

Tantaine took down the address of the dancing-saloon, and then, addressing Toto with the utmost severity,—

" Do you think," said he, " that this report is worth a hundred francs ? "

Toto made a quaint grimace.

" Do you think," asked he, " that Caroline can lead the life she does without money? No fear. Well, I have found out where the coin comes from."

The dim light in the office enabled Tantaine to hide the pleasure he felt on hearing these words.

" Ah," answered he carelessly, as if it was a matter of but little moment, " and so you have found out all that, have you ? "

" Yes, and a heap besides. Just you listen. After her breakfast, my sweet Carry began to play cards with some chaps who had been grubbing at the next table. ' Regular right down card sharpers and macemen,' said I to myself, as I watched the way in which they faked the pasteboards. ' They'll get everything out of you, old gal.' I was in the right, for in less than an hour she had to go up to the counter and leave one of her rings as security for the breakfast. He said he knew her, and would give her credit. 'You are a trump,' said she. 'I'll just trot off to my own crib and get the money.'"

"Did she go home?"

"Not she; she went to a real swell house in a bang up part of Paris, the Rue de Varennes. She knocked at the door, and in she went, while I lounged about outside."

"Do you know who lives there?"

"Of course I do. The grocer round the corner told me that it was inhabited by the Duke —— what was his blessed name? Oh, the Duke ——"

"Was it the Duke de Champdoce?"

"That is the right one, a chap they say as has his cellars chock full of gold and silver."

"You are rather slow, my lad," said Tantaine, with his assumed air of indifference. "Get on a bit, do."

Toto was much put out; for he had expected that his intelligence would have created an immense sensation.

"Give a cove time to breathe in. Well, in half an hour out comes my Carry as lively as a flea. She got into a passing cab and away she went. Fortunately I can run a bit, and reached the Palais Royal in time to see Caroline change two notes of two hundred francs each at the money-changers."

"How did you find out that?"

"By looking at 'em. The paper was yellow."

Tantaine smiled kindly. "You know a banknote then?"

"Yes, but I have precious few chances of handling them. Once I went into a money-changer's shop and

asked them just to let me feel one, and they said, ' Get
out sharp.' "

" Is that all? " demanded Tantaine.

" No; I have kept the best bit for a finish. I want
to tell you that there are others on the lookout after
Caroline."

Toto had no reason this time to grumble at the effect
he had produced, for the old man gave such a jump
that his hat fell off.

" What are you saying? " said he.

" Simply that for the last three days a big chap with
a harp on his back has been keeping her in view. I
twigged him at once, and he too saw her go into the
swell crib that you say belongs to that Duke."

Tantaine pondered a little.

" A street musician," muttered he. " I must find out
all about this. Now, Toto, listen to me; chuck Caroline over, and stick to the fellow with the harp; be
off with you, for you have earned your money well."

As Chupin went off, the old man shook his head.

" Too sharp by a good bit," said he; " he won't have
a long lease of life."

Beaumarchef was about to ask Tantaine to remain
in the office while he went off to put on his best clothes,
but the old man stopped this request by saying,—

" As M. Mascarin does not like to be disturbed, I
will just go in without knocking. When the other gentlemen arrive, show them in; for look you here, my
good friend, the pear is so ripe that if it is not plucked,
it will fall to the ground."

CHAPTER XVI.

A TURN OF THE SCREW.

DR. HORTEBISE was the first to arrive. It was a terrible thing for him to get up so early; but for Mascarin's sake he consented even to this inconvenience. When he passed through the office, the room was full of clients; but this did not prevent the doctor from noticing the negligence of Beaumarchef's costume.

"Aha!" remarked the doctor, "on the drunk again, I am afraid."

"M. Mascarin is within," answered the badgered clerk, endeavoring to put on an air of dignity; "and M. Tantaine is with him."

A brilliant idea flashed across the doctor's mind, but it was with great gravity that he said,—

"I shall be charmed to meet that most worthy old gentleman."

When, however, he entered the inner sanctum, he found Mascarin alone, occupied in sorting the eternal pieces of pasteboard.

"Well, what news?" asked he.

"There are none that I know of."

"What, have you not seen Paul?"

"No."

"Will he be here?"

"Certainly."

Mascarin was often laconic, but he seldom gave such short answers as this.

"What is the matter?" asked the doctor. "Your greeting is quite funereal. Are you not well?"

"I am merely preoccupied, and that is excusable on the eve of the battle we are about to fight," returned Mascarin.

He only, however, told a portion of the truth; for there was more in the background, which he did not wish to confide to his friend. Toto Chupin's revolt had disquieted him. Let there be but a single flaw in the axletree, and one day it will snap in twain; and Mascarin wanted to eliminate this flaw.

"Pooh!" remarked the doctor, playing with his locket, "we shall succeed. What have we to fear, after all,—opposition on Paul's part?"

"Paul may resent a little," answered Mascarin disdainfully; "but I have decided that he shall be present at our meeting of to-day. It will be a stormy one, so be prepared. We might give him his medicine in minims, but I prefer the whole dose at once."

"The deuce you do! Suppose he should be frightened, and make off with our secret."

"He won't make off," replied Mascarin in a tone which froze his listener's blood. "He can't escape from us any more than the cockchafer can from the string that a child has fastened to it. Do you not understand weak natures like his? He is the glove, I the strong hand beneath it."

The doctor did not argue this point, but merely murmured,—

"Let us hope that it is so."

"Should we have any opposition, resumed Mascarin, "it will come from Catenac. I may be able to force him into co-operation with us, but his heart will not be in the enterprise."

"Do you propose to bring Catenac into this affair?" asked Hortebise in great surprise.

" Assuredly."

" Why have you changed your plan? "

" Simply because I have recognized the fact that, if we dispensed with his services, we should be entirely at the mercy of a shrewd man of business, because——"

He broke off, listened for a moment, and then said,—
Hush! I can hear his footstep."

A dry cough was heard outside, and in another moment Catenac entered the room.

Nature, or profound dissimulation, had gifted Catenac with an exterior which made every one, when first introduced to him, exclaim, " This is an honest and trustworthy man." Catenac always looked his clients boldly in the face. His voice was pleasant, and had a certain ring of joviality in it, and his manner was one of those easy ones which always insure popularity. He was looked upon as a shrewd lawyer; but yet he did not shine in court. He must therefore, to make those thirty thousand francs a year which he was credited with doing, have some special line of business. He assayed rather risky matters, which might bring both parties into the clutches of the criminal law, or, at any rate, leave them with a taint upon both their names. A sensational lawsuit is begun, and the public eagerly await the result; suddenly the whole thing collapses, for Catenac has acted as mediator. He has even settled the disputes of murderers quarrelling over their booty. But he has even gone farther than this. More than once he has said of himself, " I have passed through the vilest masses of corruption." In his office in the Rue Jacob he has heard whispered conferences which were enough to bring down the roof above his head. Of course this was the most lucrative

business that passed into Catenac's hands. The client
conceals nothing from his attorney, and he belongs to
him as absolutely as the sick man belongs to his physician or the penitent to his confessor.

"Well, my dear Baptiste," said he, "here I am; you
summoned me, and I am obedient to the call."

"Sit down," replied Mascarin gravely.

"Thanks, my friend, many thanks, a thousand
thanks; but I am much hurried; indeed I have not a
moment to spare. I have matters on my hands of life
and death."

"But for all that," remarked Hortebise, "you can
sit down for a moment. Baptiste has something to say
to you which is as important as any of your matters
can be."

With a frank and genial smile Catenac obeyed; but
in his heart were anger and an abject feeling of alarm.

"What is it that is so important?" asked he.

Mascarin had risen and locked the door. When he
had resumed his seat he said,—

"The facts are very simple. Hortebise and I have
decided to put our great plan into execution, which
we have as yet only discussed generally with you. We
have the Marquis de Croisenois with us."

"My dear sir," broke in the lawyer.

"Wait a little; we must have your assistance,
and——"

Catenac rose from his seat. "That is enough," said
he. "You have made a very great mistake if it is on
this matter that you have sent for me; I told you this
before."

He was turning away, and, looking for his hat, proposed to beat a retreat; but Dr. Hortebise stood between him and the door, gazing upon him with no

friendly expression of countenance. Catenac was not
a man to be easily alarmed, but the doctor's appearance
was so threatening, and the smile upon Mascarin's lips
was of so deadly a character, that he stood still, posi-
tively frightened into immobility.

" What do you mean? " stammered he; " what is it
you say now? "

" First," replied the doctor, speaking slowly and distinctly,—" first, we wish that you should listen to us
when we speak to you."

" I am listening."

" Then sit down again, and hear what Baptiste has
to say."

The command Catenac had over his countenance was
so great that it was impossible to see to what conclusion he had arrived from the words and manner of his
confederates.

" Then let Baptiste explain himself," said he.

" Before entering into matters completely," said he
coolly, " I first want to ask our dear friend and associate if he is prepared to act with us? "

" Why should there be any doubt on that point? "
asked the lawyer. " Do all my repeated assurances
count as nothing? "

" We do not want promises now; what we do want
is good faith and real co-operation."

" Can it be that you——"

" I ought to inform you," continued Mascarin, un-
heeding the interruption, " that we have every prospect of success; and, if we carry the matter through,
we shall certainly have a million apiece."

Hortebise had not the calm patience of his confederate, and exclaimed,—

" You understand it well enough. Say Yes or No."

Catenac was in the agonies of indecision, and for fully a minute made no reply.

" *No,* then! " he broke out in a manner which betrayed his intense agitation. " After due consideration, and having carefully weighed the chances for and against, I answer you decidedly, No."

Mascarin and Hortebise evidently expected this reply, and exchanged glances.

" Permit me to explain," said Catenac, " what you consider as a cowardly withdrawal upon my part——"

" Call it treachery."

" I will not quibble about words. I wish to be perfectly straightforward with you."

" I am glad to hear it," sneered the doctor, " though that is not your usual form."

" And yet I do not think that I have ever concealed my real opinion from you. It is fully ten years ago since I spoke to you of the necessity of breaking up this association. Can you recall what I said? I said only our extreme need and griping poverty justified our acts. They are now inexcusable."

" You talked very freely of your scruples," observed Mascarin.

" You remember my words then? "

" Yes, and I remember too that those inner scruples never hindered you from drawing your share of the profits."

" That is to say," burst in the doctor, " you repudiated the work, but shared the booty. You wished to play the game without staking anything."

Catenac was in no way disconcerted at this trenchant argument.

" Quite true," said he, " I always received my share; but I have done quite as much as you in putting the agency in its present prosperous condition. Does it not work smoothly like a perfect piece of mechanism? Have we not succeeded in nearly all our schemes? The income comes in monthly with extreme regularity, and I, according to my rights, have received one-third. If you desire to throw up this perilous means of livelihood, say so, and I will not oppose it."

"You are really too good," sneered the doctor, with a look of menace in his glance.

"Nor," continued Catenac, "will I oppose you if you prefer to let matters stand as they are; but if you start on fresh enterprises, and embark on the tempestuous sea of danger, then I put down my foot and very boldly 'halt.' I will not take another step with you. I can see by the looks of both of you that you think me a fool and a coward. Heaven grant that the future may not show you only too plainly that I have been in the right. Think over this. For twenty years fortune has favored us, but, believe me, it is never wise to tempt her too far, for it is well known that at some time or other she always turns."

"Your imagery is really charming," remarked Hortebise sarcastically.

"Good, I have nothing else to say but to repeat my warning: *reflect*. Grand as your hopes and expectations may be, they are as nothing to the perils that you will encounter."

This cold flood of eloquence was more than the doctor could bear.

"It is all very well for you," exclaimed he, "to reason like this, for you are a rich man."

"I have enough to live on, I allow; for in addition to the income derived from my profession, I have saved two hundred thousand francs; and if you can be induced to renounce your projects, I will divide this sum with you. You have only to think."

Mascarin, who had taken no part in the dispute, now judged it time to interfere.

" And so," said he, turning to Catenac, " you have only two hundred thousand francs? "

" That or thereabouts."

" And you offer to divide this sum with us. Really we ought to be deeply grateful to you, but——."

Mascarin paused for a moment; then settling his spectacles more firmly, he went on,—

" But even if you were to give us what you propose, you would still have eleven hundred francs remaining! "

Catenac burst into a pleasant laugh. " You are jesting," said he.

" I can prove the correctness of my assertion;" and as he spoke, Mascarin unlocked a drawer, and taking a small notebook from it, turned over the pages, and leaving it open at a certain place, handed it to the lawyer.

" There," said he, " that is made up to December last, and shows precisely how you stand financially. Twice, then, you have increased your funds. These deposits you will find in an addenda at the end of the book."

Catenac started to his feet; all his calmness had now disappeared.

" Yes," he said, " I have just the sum you name; and I, for that very reason, refuse to have anything further to do with your schemes. I have an income of sixty thousand francs; that is to say, sixty thousand good reasons for receiving no further risks. You envy me my good fortune, but did we not all start penniless?

I have taken care of my money, while you have squandered yours. Hortebise has lost his patients, while I have increased the number of my clients; and now you want me to tread the dangerous road again. Not I; go your way, and leave me to go home."

Again he took up his hat, but a wave of the hand from Mascarin detained him.

"Suppose," said he coldly, "that I told you that your assistance was necessary to me."

"I should say so much the worse for you."

"But suppose I insist?"

"And how can you insist? We are both in the same boat, and sink or swim together."

"Are you certain of that?"

"So certain that I repeat from this day I wash my hands of you."

"I am afraid you are in error."

"How so?"

"Because for twelve months past, I have given food and shelter to a girl of the name of Clarisse. Do you by any chance know her?"

At the mention of this name, the lawyer started, as a man starts who, walking peacefully along, suddenly sees a deadly serpent coiled across his path.

"Clarisse," stammered he, "how did you know of her? who told you?"

But the sarcastic sneer upon the lips of his two confederates wounded his pride so deeply, that in an instant he recovered his self-possession.

"I am getting foolish," said he, "to ask these men how they learned my secret. Do they not always work by infamous and underhand means?"

"You see I know all," remarked Mascarin, "for I foresaw the day would come when you would wish to sever our connection, and even give us up to justice, if you could do so with safety to yourself. I therefore took my precautions. One thing, however, I was not prepared for, and that was, that a man of your intelligence should have played so paltry a game, and even twelve months back thought of betraying us. It is almost incredible. Do you ever read the *Gazette des Tribunaux?* I saw in its pages yesterday a story nearly similar to your own. Shall I tell it to you? A lawyer who concealed his vices beneath the mantle of joviality and candor, brought up from the country a pretty, innocent girl to act as servant in his house. This lawyer occupied his leisure time in leading the poor child astray, and the moment at last came when the consequences of her weakness were too apparent. The lawyer was half beside himself at the approaching scandal. What would the neighbors say? Well, to cut the story short, the infant was suppressed,—you understand, suppressed, and the mother turned into the street."

" Baptiste, have mercy ! "

" It was a most imprudent act, for such things always leak out somehow. You have a gardener at your house at Champigny, and suppose the idea seized upon this worthy man to dig up the ground round the wall at the end of the garden."

" That is enough," said Catenac, piteously. " I give in."

Mascarin adjusted his spectacles, as he always did in important moments.

" You give in, do you? Not a bit. Even now you are endeavoring to find a means of parrying my home thrusts."

" But I declare to you——"

"Do not be alarmed; dig as deeply as he might, your gardener would discover nothing."

The lawyer uttered a stifled exclamation of rage as he perceived the pit into which he had fallen.

"He would find nothing," resumed Mascarin, "and yet the story is all true. Last January, on a bitterly cold night, you dug a hole, and in it deposited the body of a new-born infant wrapped in a shawl. And what shawl? Why the very one that you purchased at the *Bon Marché,* when you were making yourself agreeable to Clarisse. The shopman who sold it to you has identified it, and is ready to give evidence when called upon. You may look for that shawl, Catenac, but you will not find it."

"Have you got that shawl?" asked Catenac hoarsely.

"Am I a fool?" asked Mascarin contemptuously. "Tantaine has it; but *I* know where the body is, and will keep the information to myself. Do not be alarmed; act fairly, and you are safe; but make one treacherous move, and you will read in the next day's papers a paragraph something to this effect: 'Yesterday some workmen, engaged in excavations near so-and-so, discovered the body of a new-born infant. Every effort is being made to discover the author of the crime.' You know me, and that I work promptly. To the shawl I have added a handkerchief and a few other articles belonging to Clarisse, which will render it an easy matter to fix the guilt on you."

Catenac was absolutely stunned, and had lost all power of defending himself. The few incoherent words that he uttered showed his state of utter despair.

"You have killed me," gasped he, "just as the prize, that I have been looking for for twenty years, was in my grasp."

"Work does a man no harm," remarked the doctor sententiously.

There was, however, little time to lose; the Marquis de Croisenois and Paul might be expected to arrive at any moment, and Mascarin hastened to restore a certain amount of calmness to his prostrate antagonist.

"You make as much noise as if we were going to hand you over to the executioner on the spot. Do you think that we are such a pair of fools as to risk all these hazards without some almost certain chance of success? Hortebise was as much startled as yourself when I first spoke to him of this affair, but I explained everything fully to him, and now he is quite enthusiastic in the matter. Of course you can lay aside all fear, and, as a man of the world, will bear no malice against those who have simply played a better game than yourself."

"Go on," said Catenac, forcing a smile. "I am listening."

Mascarin made a short pause.

"What we want of you," answered he, "will not compromise you in the slightest degree. I wish you to draw up a document, the particulars of which I will give you presently, and you will outwardly have no connection with the matter."

"Very good."

"But there is more yet. The Duke of Champdoce has placed a difficult task in your hands. You are engaged in a secret on his behalf."

"You know that also?"

"I know everything that may be made subservient to our ends. I also know that instead of coming direct to me you went to the very man that we have every reason to dread, that fellow Perpignan, who is nearly as sharp as we are."

" Go on," returned Catenac impatiently. " What do you expect from me on this point? "

" Not much; you must only come to me first, and report any discovery you may have made, and never give any information to the Duke without first consulting us."

" I agree."

The contending parties seemed to have arrived at an amicable termination, and Dr. Hortebise smiled complacently.

" Now," said he, " shall we not confess, after all, that there was no use in making such a fuss? "

" I allow that I was in the wrong," answered Catenac meekly; and, extending his hands to his two associates with an oily smile, he said: "Let us forget and forgive."

Was he to be trusted? Mascarin and the doctor exchanged glances of suspicion. A moment afterward a knock came to the door, and Paul entered, making a timid bow to his two patrons.

" My dear boy," said Mascarin, " let me present you to one of my oldest and best friends." Then, turning to Catenac, he added: " I wish to ask you to help and assist my young friend here. Paul Violaine is a good fellow, who has neither father nor mother, and whom we are trying to help on in his journey through life."

The lawyer started as he caught the strange, meaning smile which accompanied these words.

" Great heavens! " said he, " why did you not speak sooner? "

Catenac at once divined Mascarin's project, and understood the allusion to the Duke de Champdoce.

CHAPTER XVII.

SOME SCRAPS OF PAPER.

THE Marquis de Croisenois was never punctual. He had received a note asking him to call on Mascarin at eleven o'clock, and twelve had struck some time before he made his appearance. Faultlessly gloved, his glass firmly fixed in his eye, and a light walking cane in his hand, and with that air of half-veiled insolence that is sometimes affected by certain persons who wish the world to believe that they are of great importance, the Marquis de Croisenois entered the room.

At the age of twenty-five Henry de Croisenois affected the airs and manners of a lad of twenty, and so found many who looked upon his escapades with lenient eyes, ascribing them to the follies of youth. Under this youthful mask, however he concealed a most astute and cunning intellect, and had more than once got the better of the women with whom he had had dealings. His fortune was terribly involved, because he had insisted on living at the same rate as men who had ten times his income. Forming one of the recklessly extravagant band of which the Duke de Saumeine was the head, Croisenois, too, kept his racehorses, which was certainly the quickest way to wreck the most princely fortune. The Marquis had found out this, and was utterly involved, when Mascarin extended a helping hand to him, to which he clung with all the energy of a drowning man.

Whatever Henry de Croisenois' anxieties may have been on the day in question, he did not allow a symptom of them to appear, and on his entrance negligently drawled, " I have kept you waiting, I fear ; but really my time is not my own. I am quite at your service now, and will wait until these gentlemen have finished their business with you." And as he concluded, he again placed the cigar which he had removed while saying these words, to his lips.

His manner was very insolent, and yet the amiable Mascarin did not seem offended, although he loathed the scent of tobacco.

" We had begun to despair of seeing you, Marquis," answered he politely. " I say so, because these gentlemen are here to meet you. Permit me to introduce to you, Dr. Hortebise, M. Catenac of the Parisian bar, and our secretary," pointing as he spoke, to Paul.

As soon as Croisenois had taken his seat, Mascarin went straight to the point, as a bullet to the target. " I do not intend," began he, " to leave you in doubt for a moment. Beatings about the bush would be absurd among persons like ourselves."

At finding himself thus classed with the other persons present, the Marquis gave a little start, and then drawled out, " You flatter me, really."

" I may tell you, Marquis," resumed Mascarin, "that your marriage has been definitely arranged by myself and my associates. All you have to do is to get the young lady's consent, for that of the Count and Countess has already been secured."

" There will be no difficulty in that," lisped the Marquis. " I will promise her the best horsed carriage in the Bois, a box at the opera, unlimited credit at Van Klopen's, and perfect freedom. There will be no difficulty, I assure you. Of course, however, I must be presented by some one who holds a good position in society."

"Would the Viscountess de Bois Arden suit you?"

"No one better; she is a relation of the Count de Mussidan."

"Good; then when you wish, Madame de Bois Arden will introduce you as a suitor for the young lady's hand, and praise you up to the skies."

The Marquis looked very jubilant at hearing this. "All right," cried he; "then that decides the matter."

Paul wondered whether he was awake or dreaming. He too had been promised a rich wife, and here was another man who was being provided for in the same manner. "These people," muttered he, "seem to keep a matrimonial agency as well as a servants' registry office!"

"All that is left, then," said the Marquis, "is to arrange the—shall I call it the commission?"

"I was about to come to that," returned Mascarin.

"Well, I will give you a fourth of the dowry, and on the day of my marriage will hand you a cheque for that amount."

Paul now imagined that he saw how matters worked. "If I marry Flavia," thought he, "I shall have to share her dowry with these highly respectable gentlemen."

The offer made by the Marquis did not, however, seem to please Mascarin. "That is not what we want," said he.

"No,—well, must I give you more? Say how much."

Mascarin shook his head.

"Well then, I will give you a third; it is not worth while to give you more."

"No, no; I would not take half, nor even the whole of the dowry. You may keep that as well as what you owe us."

"Well, but tell me what you *do* want."

"I will do so," answered Mascarin, adjusting his spectacles carefully; "but before doing so, I feel that I must give you a short account of the rise and progress of this association."

At this statement Hortebise and Catenac sprang to their feet in surprise and terror. "Are you mad?" said they at length, with one voice.

Mascarin shrugged his shoulders.

"Not yet," answered he gently, "and I beg that you will permit me to go on."

"But surely we have some voice in the matter," faltered Catenac.

"That is enough," exclaimed Mascarin angrily. "Am not I the head of this association? Do you think," he continued in tones of deep sarcasm, "that we cannot speak openly before the Marquis?"

Hortebise and the lawyer resignedly resumed their seats. Croisenois thought that a word from him might reassure them.

"Among honest men——" began he.

"We are not honest men," interrupted Mascarin. "Sir," added he in a severe tone, "nor are you either."

This plain speaking brought a bright flush to the face of the Marquis, who had half a mind to be angry, but policy restrained him, and he affected to look on the matter as a joke. "Your joke is a little personal," said he.

But Mascarin took no heed of his remark. "Listen to me," said he, "for we have no time to waste, and do you," he added, turning to Paul, " pay the greatest attention."

A moment of perfect silence ensued, broken only by the hum of voices in the outer office.

" Marquis," said Mascarin, whose whole face blazed with a gleam of conscious power, " twenty-five years ago I and my associates were young and in a very different position. We were honest then, and all the illusions of youth were in full force; we had faith and hope. We all then tenanted a wretched garret in the Rue de la Harpe, and loved each other like brothers."

" That was long, long ago," murmured Hortebise.

" Yes," rejoined Mascarin; " and yet the effluxion of times does not hinder me from seeing things as they then were, and my heart aches as I compare the hopes of those days with the realities of the present. Then, Marquis, we were poor, miserably poor, and yet we all had vague hopes of future greatness."

Croisenois endeavored to conceal a sneer; the story was not a very interesting one.

" As I said before, each one of us anticipated a brilliant career. Catenac had gained a prize by his ' Treatise on the Transfer of Real Estate,' and Hortebise had written a pamphlet regarding which the great Orfila had testified approval. Nor was I without my successes. Hortebise had unluckily quarrelled with his family. Catenac's relatives were poor, and I, well, I had no family. I stood alone. We were literally starving, and I was the only one earning money. I prepared pupils for the military colleges, but as I only earned thirty-five sous a day by cramming a dull boy's brain with algebra and geometry, that was not enough to feed us all. Well, to cut a long story short, the day came when we had not a coin among us. I forgot to tell you that I was devotedly attached to a young girl who was dying of consumption, and who had neither food nor fuel. What could I do? I knew not. Half mad, I rushed from the house, asking myself if I had better plead for charity or take the money I required by force from the first passer-by. I wandered along the quays, half inclined to confide my sorrow to the Seine, when suddenly I remembered it was a holiday at the Polytechnic School, and that if I went to the *Café Semblon* or the Palais Royal, I should most likely meet with some of my old pupils, who could perhaps lend me a few sous. Five francs perhaps, Marquis,—that is a very small sum, but in that day it meant the life of my dear Marie and of my two friends. Have you ever been hungry, M. de Croisenois?"

De Croisenois started; he had never suffered from hunger, but how could he tell what the future might bring? for his resources were so nearly exhausted, that even to-morrow he might be compelled to discard his fictitious splendor and sink into the abyss of poverty.

"When I reached the *Café Semblon,*" continued Mascarin, "I could not see a single pupil, and the waiter to whom I addressed my inquiries looked at me with the utmost contempt, for my clothes were in tatters; but at length he condescended to inform me that the young gentlemen had been and gone, but that they would return. I said that I would wait for them. The man asked me if I would take anything, and when I replied in the negative, contemptuously pointed to a chair in a distant corner, where I patiently took my seat. I had sat for some time, when suddenly a young man entered the *café*, whose face, were I to live for a century, I shall never forget. He was perfectly livid, his features rigid, and his eyes wild and full of anguish.

He was evidently in intense agony of mind or body. Evidently, however, it was not poverty that was oppressing him, for as he cast himself upon a sofa, all the waiters rushed forward to receive his orders. In a voice that was almost unintelligible, he asked for a bottle of brandy, and pen, ink, and paper. In some mysterious manner, the sight of this suffering brought balm to my aching heart. The order of the young man was soon executed, and pouring out a tumbler of brandy, he took a deep draught. The effect was instantaneous, he turned crimson, and for a moment almost fell back insensible. I still kept my eyes on him, for a voice within me kept crying out that there was some mysterious link connecting this man and myself, and that his life was in some manner interwoven with mine, and that the influence he would exercise over me would be for evil. So strongly did this idea become rooted, that I should have left the *café*, had not my curiosity been so great. In the meantime the stranger had recovered himself, and seizing a pen, scrawled a few lines on a sheet of paper. Evidently he was not satisfied with his composition, for after reading it over, he lit a match and burnt the paper. He drank more brandy, and wrote a second letter, which, too, proved a failure, for he tore it to fragments, which he thrust into his waistcoat pocket. Again he commenced, using greater care. It was plain that he had forgotten where he was, for he gesticulated, uttered a broken sentence or two and evidently believed that he was in his own house. His last letter seemed to satisfy him, and he recopied it with care. He closed and directed it; then, tearing the original into pieces, he flung it under the table; then calling the waiter, he said, 'Here are twenty francs; take this letter to the address on the envelope. Bring the answer to my house; here is my card.' The man ran out of the room, and the nobleman, only waiting to pay his bill, followed almost immediately. The morsels of white paper beneath the table had a strange fascination for me; I longed to gather them up, to put them together, and to learn the secret of the strange drama that had been acted before me. But, as I have told you, then I was honest and virtuous, and the meanness of such an act revolted all my instincts; and I should have overcome this temptation, had it not been for one of those trifling incidents which too often form the turning-point of a life. A draught from a suddenly opened door caught one of these morsels of paper, and wafted it to my feet. I stooped and picked it up, and read on it the ominous words, 'blow out my brains!' I had not been mistaken, then, and was face to face with some coming tragedy. Having once yielded, I made no further efforts at self-control. The waiters were running about; no one paid any attention to me; and creeping to the place that the unknown had occupied, I obtained possession of two more scraps of paper. Upon one I read, 'shame and horror!' upon the other, 'one hundred thousand francs by to-night.' The meaning of these few words were as clear as daylight to me; but for all that, I managed to collect every atom of the torn paper, and piecing them together, read this:—

" ' CHARLES,—
' I must have one hundred thousand francs to-night, and you are the only one to whom I can apply. The shame and horror of my position are too much for me. Can you send it me in two hours? As you act, so I regulate my conduct. I am either saved, or I blow out my brains.'

    *   *   *   *   *   *

"You are probably surprised, Marquis, at the accuracy of my memory, and even now I can see this scrawl as distinctly as if it were before me. At the end of this scrawl was a signature, one of the best known commercial names, which, in common with other financial houses, was struggling against a panic on the Bourse. My discovery disturbed me very much. I forgot all my miseries, and thought only of his. Were not our positions entirely similar? But by degrees a hideous temptation began to creep into my heart, and, as the minutes passed by, assume more vivid color and more tangible reality. Why should I not profit by this stolen secret? I went to the desk and asked for some wafers and a Directory. Then, returning, I fastened the torn fragments upon a clean sheet of paper, discovered the address of the writer, and then left the *café*. The house was situated in the Rue Chaussée d'Autin. For fully half an hour I paced up and down before his magnificent dwelling-place. Was he alive? Had the reply of Charles been in the affirmative? I decided at last to venture, and rang the bell. A liveried domestic appeared at my summons, and said that his master did not receive visitors at that hour; besides, he was at dinner. I was exasperated at the man's insolence, and replied hotly, ' If you want to save your master from a terrible misfortune, go and tell him that a man has brought him the rough draft of the letter he wrote a little time back at the *Café Semblon.*' The man obeyed me without a word, no doubt impressed by the earnestness of my manner. My message must have caused intense consternation, for in a moment the footman reappeared, and, in an obsequious manner, said, ' Follow at once, sir; my master is waiting for you.' He led me into a large room, magnificently furnished as a library, and in the centre of this room stood the man of the *Café Semblon*. His face was deadly pale, and his eyes blazed with fury. I was so agitated that I could hardly speak.

"'You have picked up the scraps of paper I threw away?' exclaimed he.

"I nodded, and showed him the fragments fastened on to the sheet of note-paper.

"'How much do you want for that?' asked he. 'I will give you a thousand francs.'

"I declare to you, gentlemen, that up to this time I had no intention of making money by the secret. My intention in going had been simply to say, 'I bring you this paper, of which some one else might have taken an undue advantage. I have done you a service; lend me a hundred francs.' This is what I meant to say, but his behavior irritated me, and I answered,—

"'No, I want two thousand francs.'

"He opened a drawer, drew out a bundle of banknotes, and threw them in my face.

"'Pay yourself, you villain!' said he.

"I can, I fear, never make you understand what I felt at this undeserved insult. I was not myself, and Heaven knows that I was not responsible for any crime that I might have committed in the frenzy of the moment, and I was nearly doing so. That man will, perhaps, never see death so near him, save at his last hour. On his writing table lay one of those Catalan daggers, which he evidently used as a paper-cutter. I snatched it up, and was about to strike, when the recollection of Marie dying of cold and starvation occurred to me. I dashed the knife to the ground, and rushed from the house in a state bordering on insanity. I went into

that house an honest man, and left it a degraded scoundrel. But I must finish. When I reached the street,
the two banknotes which I had taken from the packet
seemed to burn me like coals of fire. I hastened to a
money-changer, and got coin for them. I think, from
my demeanor, he must have thought that I was insane.
With my plunder weighing me down, I regained our
wretched garret in the Rue de la Harpe. Catenac and
Hortebise were waiting for me with the utmost anxiety.
You remember that day, my friends. Marquis, my
story is especially intended for you. As soon as I
entered the room, my friends ran up to me, delighted
at seeing me return in safety, but I thrust them
aside.

" 'Let me alone!' cried I; 'I am no longer fit to
take an honest man's hand; but we have money,
money!' And I threw the bags upon the table. One
of them burst, and a flood of silver coins rolled to
every part of the room.

" Marie started from her chair with upraised hands.
'Money!' she repeated, 'money! we shall have food,
and I won't die.'

" My friends, Marquis, were not as they are now,
and they started back in horror, fearing that I had
committed some crime.

" ' No,' said I, 'I have committed no crime, not one,
at least, that will bring me within the reach of the
strong arm of the law. This money is the price of
our honor, but no one will know that fact but ourselves.'

" Marquis, there was no sleeping in the garret all that
night; but when daylight peered through the broken
windows, it beamed on a table covered with empty
bottles, and round it were seated three men, who, hav-

ing cast aside all honorable scruples, had sworn that
they would arrive at wealth and prosperity by any
means, no matter how foul and treacherous they might
be. That is all."

———

CHAPTER XVIII.

AN INFAMOUS TRADE.

MASCARIN, who was anxious to make as deep an impression as possible upon Croisenois and Paul, broke
off his story abruptly, and paced up and down the
room. Had his intention been to startle his audience,
he had most certainly succeeded. Paul was breathless
with interest, and Croisenois broke down in attempting to make one of his usual trivial remarks. He was
not particularly intelligent, except as regarded his self-
interests, and though, of course, he knew that there
must be some connection between his interests and the
recital that Mascarin had just made, he could not for
the life of him make out what it was. Mascarin seemed
utterly careless of the effect that he had produced.
But the next time that his walk brought him to his
desk he stopped, and, adjusting his glasses, said, " I
trust, Marquis, that you will forgive this long preliminary address, which would really make a good sensational novel; but we have now arrived at the really
practical part of the business." As he said these
words, he took up an imposing attitude, with his elbow
resting on the mantelpiece.

" On the night of which I have spoken, I and my
friends released ourselves from all the bonds of virtue

and honor, and freed ourselves from all the fetters of
duty to our fellow-men. The plan emanated from my
brain complete in all its details in the will I made
twenty years ago to my friends. Marquis, as the summer goes on, you know that the ripest and reddest
cherries are the fullest flavored, just so, in the noblest
and wealthiest of families in Paris there is not one
that has not some terrible and ghostly secret which is
sedulously concealed. Now, suppose that one man
should gain possession of all of them, would he not
be sole and absolute master? Would he not be more
powerful than a despot on his throne? Would he not
be able to sway society in any manner he might think
fit? Well, I said to myself, I will be that man!"

Ever since the Marquis had been in relation with
Mascarin, he had shrewdly suspected that his business
was not conducted on really fair principles.

"What you mention," said he, "is nothing but an
elaborate and extended system of blackmail."

Mascarin bowed low, with an ironical smile on his
face. "Just so, Marquis, just so; you have hit on the
very name. The word is modern, but the operation
doubtless dates from the earliest ages. The day upon
which one man began to trade upon the guilty secret
of another was the date of the institution of this line
of business. If antiquity makes a thing respectable,
then blackmailing is worthy of great respect."

"But, sir," said the Marquis, with a flush upon his
face, "but, sir——"

"Pshaw!" broke in Mascarin, "does a mere word
frighten you? Who has not done some of it in his
time? Why, look at yourself. Do you not recollect
this winter that you detected a young man cheating at
cards? You said nothing to him at the time, but you

found out that he was rich, and, calling upon him the next day, borrowed ten thousand francs. When do you intend to repay that loan?"

Croisenois sank back in his chair, overcome with surprise at this display of knowledge on Mascarin's part. "This is too terrible," muttered he, but Mascarin went on,—

"I know, at least, two thousand persons in Paris who only exist by the exercise of this profession; for I have studied them all, from the convict who screws money out of his former companions, in penal servitude, to the titled villain, who, having discovered the frailty of some unhappy woman, forces her to give him her daughter as his wife. I know a mere messenger in the Rue Douai, who in five years amassed a comfortable fortune. Can you guess how? When he was intrusted with a letter, he invariably opened it, and made himself master of the contents, and if there was a compromising word in it, he pounced down upon either the writer or the person to whom it was addressed. I also know of one large limited company which pays an annual income to a scoundrel with half a dozen foreign orders, who has found out that they have broken their statutes of association, and holds proofs of their having done so. But the police are on the alert, and our courts deal very severely with blackmailers."

Mascarin went on: "The English, however, are our masters, for in London a compromising servant is as easily negotiable as a sound bill of exchange. There is in the city a respectable jeweller, who will advance money on any compromising letter with a good name at the foot. His shop is a regular pawnshop of infamy. In the States it has been elevated to the dignity of a profession, and the citizen at New York dreads the blackmailers more than the police, if he is meditating some dishonorable action. Our first operations did not bring in any quick returns, and the harvest promised to be a late one; but you have come upon us just as we are about to reap our harvest. The professions of Hortebise and Catenac—the one a doctor and the other a lawyer—facilitated our operations greatly. One administered to the diseases of the body, and the other to that of the purse, and, of course, thus they became the possessors of many secrets. As for me, the head and chief, it would not do to remain an idle looker-on. Our funds had dwindled down a good deal, and, after mature consideration, I decided to hire this house, and open a Servants' Registry Office. Such an occupation would not attract any attention, and in the end it turned out a perfect success, as my friends can testify."

Catenac and Hortebise both nodded assent.

" By the system which I have adopted," resumed Mascarin, " the wealthy and respectable man is as strictly watched in his own house as is the condemned wretch in his cell; for no act of his escapes the eyes of the servants whom we have placed around him. He can hardly even conceal his thoughts from us. Even the very secret that he has murmured to his wife with closed doors reaches our ears."

The Marquis gave a supercilious smile.

" You must have had some inkling of this," observed Mascarin, " for you have never taken a servant from our establishment; but for all that, I am as well posted up in your affairs as yourself. You have even now about you a valet of whom you know nothing."

" Morel was recommended to me by one of my most intimate friends—Sir Richard Wakefield."

" But for all that I have my suspicions of him; but we will talk of this later, and we will now return to the subject upon which we have met. As I told you, I conceal the immense power I had attained through our agency, and use it as occasion presents itself, and after twenty years' patient labor, I am about to reap a stupendous harvest. The police pay enormous sums to their secret agents, while I, without opening my purse, have an army of devoted adherents. I see perhaps fifty servants of both sexes daily; calculate what this will amount to in a year."

There was an air of complacency about the man as he explained the working of his system, and a ring of triumph in his voice.

" You must not think that all my agents are in my secrets, for the greater part of them are quite unaware of what they are doing, and in this lies my strength. Each of them brings me a slender thread, which I twine into the mighty cord by which I hold my slaves. These unsuspecting agents remind me of those strange Brazilian birds, whose presence is a sure sign that water is to be found near at hand. When one of them utters a note, I dig, and I find. And now, Marquis, do you understand the aim and end of our association? "

" It has," remarked Hortebise quietly, " brought us in some years two hundred and fifty thousand francs apiece."

If M. de Croisenois disliked prosy tales, he by no means underrated the eloquence of figures. He knew quite enough of Paris to understand that if Mascarin threw his net regularly, he would infallibly catch many fish. With this conviction firmly implanted in his mind, he did not require much urging to look with favor on the scheme, and, putting on a gracious smile, he now asked, "And what must I do to deserve admission into this association?"

Paul had listened in wonder and terror, but by degrees all feelings of disgust at the criminality of these men faded away before the power that they unquestionably possessed.

"If," resumed Mascarin, "we have up to this met with no serious obstacles, it is because, though apparently acting rashly, we are in reality most prudent and cautious. We have managed our slaves well, and have not driven any one to desperation. But we are beginning to weary of our profession; we are getting old, and we have need of repose. We intend, therefore, to retire, but before that we wish to have all matters securely settled. I have an immense mass of documentary evidence, but it is not always easy to realize the value they represent, and I wait upon your assistance to enable me to do so."

Croisenois' face fell. Was he to take compromising letters round to his acquaintances and boldly say, "Your purse or your honor?" He had no objection to share the profits of this ignoble trade, but he objected strongly to showing his connection with it openly. "No, no," cried he hastily, "you must not depend upon me."

He seemed so much in earnest that Hortebise and Catenac exchanged glances of dismay.

"Let us have no nonsense," returned Mascarin sternly, "and wait a little before you display so much fierceness. I told you that my documentary evidence was of a peculiar kind. We very often find among our fish married people who cannot deal with their personal property. A husband, for instance, will say, 'I can't take ten thousand francs without my wife knowing of it.' Women say, 'Why, I get all my money through my husband,' and both are telling the truth. They kneel at my feet and entreat me to have mercy, saying, 'Find me some excuse for using a portion of my funds and you shall have more than you ask.' For a long time I have sought for this means, and at last I have found it in the Limited Company, which you, Marquis, will float next month."

"Really!" returned the Marquis. "I do not see——"

"I beg your pardon; you see it all clearly. A husband who cannot, without fear of disturbing his domestic peace, put in five thousand francs, can put in ten thousand if he tells his wife, 'It is an investment;' and many a wife who has not any money of her own will persuade her husband to bring in the money we require by the proposal to take shares. Now, what do you say to the idea?"

"I think that it is an excellent one, but what part am I to play in it?"

"In taking the part of Chairman of the Company. I could not do so, being merely the proprietor of a Servants' Registry Office. Hortebise, as a doctor, and more than all a homœopath, would inspire no confidence, and Catenac's legal profession prevents him appearing in the matter openly. He will act as our legal adviser."

"But really I do not see anything about me that would induce people to invest," remarked De Croisenois.

"You are too modest; you have your name and rank, which, however we may look upon them, have a great effect upon the general public. There are many

Companies who pay directors of rank and creditable connection very largely. Before starting this enterprise you can settle all your debts, and the world will then conclude that you are possessed of great wealth, while, at the same time, the news of your approaching marriage with Mademoiselle de Mussidan will be the general talk of society. What better position could you be in?"

"But I have the reputation of being a reckless spend-thrift."

"All the better. The day the prospectus comes out with your name at the head of it, there will be a universal burst of laughter. Men will say, ' Do you see what Croisenois is at now? What on earth possessed him to go into Company work? ' But as this proceeding on your part will have paid your debts and given you Mademoiselle Sabine's dowry, I think that the laugh will be on your side."

The prospect dazzled De Croisenois.

"And suppose I accept," asked he, "what will be the end of the farce?"

"Very simple. When all the shares are taken up, you will close the office and let the Company look after itself."

Croisenois started to his feet angrily. "Why," cried he, "you intend to make a catspaw of me! Such a proceeding would send me to penal servitude."

"What an ungrateful man he is!" said Mascarin, appealing to his audience, "when I am doing all I can to prevent his going there."

"Sir!"

But Catenac now felt it time to interfere. "You do not understand," remarked he, addressing Croisenois. "You will start a Company for the development of some native product, let us say Pyrenean marble, for instance, issue a prospectus, and the shares will be at once taken up by Mascarin's clients."

" Well, what happens then?"

" Why, out of the funds thus obtained we will take care when the crash comes to reimburse any outsiders who may have taken shares in the concern, telling them that the thing has been a failure, and that we are ruined; while Mascarin will take care to obtain from all his clients a discharge in full, so the Company will quietly collapse."

" But," objected the Marquis, " all the shareholders will know that I am a rogue."

" Naturally."

" They would hold me in utter contempt."

" Perhaps so, but they would never venture to let you see it. I never thought that you would make objections; and whose character, however deep, will bear investigation?"

" Are you sure that you hold your people securely?" asked he; " and that none of them will turn surly?"

Mascarin was waiting for this question, and taking from his desk the pieces of cardboard which he took so much pains to arrange, he replied, " I have here the names of three hundred and fifty people who will each invest ten thousand francs in the Company. Listen to me, and judge for yourself."

He put all three pieces of cardboard together, and then drawing out one he read,—

" ' N——, civil engineer. Five letters written by him to the gentleman who procured his appointment for him: worth fifteen thousand francs.'

" ' P——, merchant. Absolute proof that his last bankruptcy was a fraudulent one, and that he kept back from his creditors two hundred thousand francs. Good for twenty thousand francs.'

"'Madame V——. A photograph taken in very light and airy costume. Poor, but can pay three thousand francs.'

"'M. H——. Three letters from her mother, proving that the daughter had compromised herself before marriage. Letter from a monthly nurse appended. Can be made to pay ten thousand francs.'

"'L——. A song both impious and obscene. Good for two thousand francs.'

"'S——, head clerk in a Limited Company; proof of a false account. Can be made to pay fifteen thousand francs.'

"'X——, a portion of his correspondence with L—— in 1848. Three thousand francs.'

"'Madame M. de M——. A true history of her adventure with M. J——.'"

This sample was quite sufficient to satisfy M. de Croisenois. "Enough," cried he, "I yield. I bow before your gigantic power, which utterly surpasses that of the police. Give me your orders."

Before this Mascarin had conquered Hortebise and Paul Violaine, and now he had the Marquis at his feet. Many times during this conversation the Marquis had more than once endeavored to make up his mind to withdraw entirely from the business, but he had been unable to resist the strange fascination of that mysterious person who had been laying bare his scheme with such extraordinary audacity. The few vestiges of honesty that were still left in his corrupted soul revolted at the thought of the shameful compact into which he was about to enter, but the dazzling prospect held out before his eyes silenced his scruples, and he felt a certain pride in being the associate of men who possessed such seemingly illimitable power. Mascarin saw that there was no longer any necessity for the extreme firmness with which he had before spoken, and it was with the most studied courtesy that he replied: " I have no orders to give you, Marquis, our interests are identical, and we must all have a voice in the deliberations as to the best means of carrying them out."

This change from *hauteur* to suavity gratified Croisenois' pride immensely.

" Now," continued Mascarin, " let us speak of your own circumstances. You wrote to me recently that you had nothing, and I am aware that you have no expectations for the future."

" Excuse me, but there is the fortune of my poor brother George, who disappeared so mysteriously."

" Let me assure you," answered Mascarin, " that we had better be perfectly frank with each other."

" And am I not so? " answered the Marquis.

" Why, in talking of this imaginary fortune? "

" It is not imaginary; it is real, and a very large one, too, about twelve or fourteen hundred thousand francs, and I can obtain it, for, by Articles 127 and 129 of the Code Napoleon——"

He interrupted himself, as he saw an expression of hardly-restrained laughter upon the features of Dr. Hortebise.

" Do not talk nonsense," answered Mascarin. " You could at first have filed an affidavit regarding your brother's disappearance, and applied to the Court to appoint you trustee, but this is now exactly what you wish to avoid."

" Why not, pray? Do you think——"

" Pooh, pooh, but you have raised so much money

on this inheritance that there is nothing of it left hardly, certainly not sufficient to pay your debts. It is the bait you used to allure your tradespeople into giving you credit."

At finding himself so easily fathomed, Croisenois burst into a peal of laughter. Mascarin had by this time thrown himself into an armchair, as though utterly worn out by fatigue.

"There is no necessity, Marquis," said he, "to detain you here longer. We shall meet again shortly, and settle matters. Meanwhile Catenac will draw up the prospectus and Articles of Association of the proposed Company, and post you up in the financial slang of which you must occasionally make use."

The Marquis and the lawyer at once rose and took their leave. As soon as the door had closed behind them, Mascarin seemed to recover his energy.

"Well, Paul," said he, "what do you think of all this?"

Like all men with weak and ductile natures, Paul, after being almost prostrated by the first discovery of his master's villainy, had now succeeded in smothering the dictates of his conscience, and adopted a cynical tone quite worthy of his companions.

"I see," said he, "that you have need of me. Well, I am not a Marquis, but you will find me quite as trustworthy and obedient."

Paul's reply did not seem to surprise Mascarin, but it is doubtful whether he was pleased by it, for his countenance showed traces of a struggle between extreme satisfaction and intense annoyance, while the doctor was surprised at the cool audacity of the young man whose mind he had undertaken to form.

Paul was a little disturbed by the long and continued

silence of his patron, and at last he ventured to say timidly,—

" Well, sir, I am anxious to know under what conditions I am to be shown the way to make my fortune and marry Mademoiselle Flavia Rigal, whom I love."

Mascarin gave a diabolical smile.

" Whose dowry you love," he observed. " Let us speak plainly."

" Pardon me, sir, I said just what I meant."

The doctor, who had not Mascarin's reasons for gravity, now burst into a jovial laugh.

" And that pretty Rose," said he, " what of her? "

" Rose is a creature of the past," answered Paul. " I can now see what an idiot I was, and I have entirely effaced her from my memory, and I am half inclined to deplore that Mademoiselle Rigal is an heiress, the more so if it is to form a barrier between us."

This declaration seemed to make Mascarin more easy.

" Reassure yourself, my boy," said he, " we will remove that barrier; but I will not conceal from you that the part you have to play is much more difficult than that assigned to the Marquis de Croisenois; but if it is harder and more perilous, the reward will be proportionately greater."

" With your aid and advice I feel capable of doing everything necessary," returned Paul.

" You will need great self-confidence, the utmost self-possession, and as a commencement you must utterly destroy your present identity."

" That I will do with the utmost willingness."

" You must become another person entirely; you must adopt his name, his gait, his behavior, his virtues, and even his failings. You must forget all that you

have either said or done. You must always think that
you are in reality the person you represent yourself to
be, for this is the only way in which you can lead
others into a similar belief. Your task will be a heavy
one."

"Ah, sir," cried the young man, enthusiastically,
"can you doubt me?"

"The glorious beam of success that shines ahead
of you will take your attention from the difficulties and
dangers of the road that you are treading."

The genial Dr. Hortebise rubbed his hands.

"You are right," cried he, "quite right."

"When you have done this," resumed Mascarin,
"we shall not hesitate to acquaint you with the secret
of the lofty destiny that awaits you. Do you understand me fully?"

Here the speaker was interrupted by the entrance of
Beaumarchef, who had signified his desire to come in
by three distinct raps upon the door. He was now
gorgeous to look upon, for having taken advantage of
a spare half hour, he had donned his best clothes.

"What is it?" demanded Mascarin.

"Here are two letters, sir."

"Thank you; hand them to me, and leave us."

As soon as they were once more alone, Mascarin examined the letters.

"Ah," cried he, "one from Van Klopen, and the
other from the Hôtel de Mussidan. Let us first see
what our friend the man-milliner has to say.

"Dear Sir,—
"You may be at ease. Our mutual friend Verminet
has executed your orders most adroitly. At his instiga-
tion Gaston de Gandelu has forged the banker Martin
Rigal's signature on five different bills. I hold them,

and awaiting your further orders regarding them, and also with respect to Madame de Bois Arden,

"I remain your obedient servant,

"VAN KLOPEN."

Tossing it on the table, Mascarin opened the other letter, which he also read aloud.

"SIR,—

"I have to report to you the breaking off of the marriage between Mademoiselle Sabine and M. de Breulh-Faverlay. Mademoiselle is very ill, and I heard the medical man say that she might not survive the next twenty-four hours.

"FLORESTAN."

Mascarin was so filled with rage on learning this piece of news, which seemed likely to interfere with his plans, that he struck his hand down heavily on the table.

"Damnation!" cried he. "If this little fool should die now, all our work will have to be recommenced."

He thrust aside his chair, and paced hurriedly up and down the room.

"Florestan is right," said he; "this illness of the girl comes on at the date of the rupture of the engagement. There is some secret that we must learn, for we dare not work in the dark."

"Shall I go to the Hôtel de Mussidan?" asked Hortebise.

"Not a bad idea. Your carriage is waiting, is it not? You can go in your capacity as a medical man."

The doctor was preparing to go, when Mascarin arrested his progress.

"No," said he, "I have changed my mind. We must neither of us be seen near the place. I expect that one of our mines has exploded; that the Count and

Countess have exchanged confidences, and that between the two the daughter has been struck down."

" How shall we find this out? "

" I will see Florestan and try and find out."

In an instant he vanished into his inner room, and as he changed his dress, continued to converse with the doctor.

" This blow would be comparatively trifling, if I had not so much on hand, but I have Paul to look after. The Champdoce affair must be pressed on, for Catenac, the traitor, has put the Duke and Perpignan into communication. I must see Perpignan and discover how much has been told him, and how much he has guessed. I will also see Caroline Schimmel, and extract something from her. I wish to heaven that there were thirty-six hours in the day instead of only twenty-four."

By this time he had completed his change of costume and called the doctor into his room.

" I am off, now," whispered he; " do not lose sight of Paul for a single instant, for we are not sufficiently sure of him to let him go about alone with our secret in his possession. Take him to dine at Martin Rigal's, and then make some excuse for keeping him all night at your rooms. See me to-morrow."

And he went out so hurriedly that he did not hear the cheery voice of the doctor calling after him,—

" Good luck; I wish you all good luck."

CHAPTER XIX.

A FRIENDLY RIVAL.

ON leaving the Hôtel de Mussidan, M. de Breulh-Faverlay dismissed his carriage, for he felt as a man often does after experiencing some violent emotion, the absolute necessity for exercise, and to be alone with his thoughts, and by so doing recover his self-possession. His friends would have been surprised if they had seen him pacing hurriedly along the Champs Elysées. The usual calm of his manner had vanished, and the generally calm expression of his features was entirely absent. As he walked, he talked to himself, and gesticulated.

" And this is what we call being a man of the world. We think ourselves true philosophers, and a look from a pair of beautiful, pleading eyes scatters all our theories to the winds."

He had loved Sabine upon the day on which he had asked for her hand, but not so fondly as upon this day when he had learned that she could no longer be his wife, for, from the moment he had made this discovery, she seemed to him more gifted and fascinating than ever. No one could have believed that he, the idol of society, the petted darling of the women, and the successful rival of the men, could have been refused by the young girl to whom he had offered his hand.

" Yes," murmured he with a sigh, " she is just the companion for life that I longed for. Where could I find so intelligent an intellect and so pure a mind, united with such radiant beauty, so different from the women of society, who live but for dress and gossip. Has Sabine anything in common with those giddy girls who look upon life as a perpetual valse, and who take a husband as they do a partner, because they cannot dance without one? How her face lighted up as she spoke of him, and how thoroughly she puts faith in him! The end of it all is that I shall die a bachelor. In my old age I will take to the pleasures of the table, for an excellent authority declares that a man can enjoy his four meals a day with comfort. Well, that is something to look forward to certainly, and it will not impair my digestion if my heirs and expectants come and squabble round my armchair. Ah," he added, with a deep sigh, "my life has been a failure."

M. de Breulh-Faverlay was a very different type of man to that which both his friends and his enemies popularly supposed him to be. Upon the death of his uncle, he had plunged into the frivolous vortex of Parisian dissipation, but of this he had soon wearied.

All that he had cared for was to see the doings of his racehorse chronicled in the sporting journals, and occasionally to expend a few thousand francs in presents of jewelry to some fashionable actress. But he had secretly longed for some more honorable manner of fulfilling his duties in life, and he had determined that before his marriage he would sell his stud and break with his old associates entirely; and now this wished-for marriage would never take place.

When he entered his club, the traces of his agitation were so visible upon his face, that some of the card-players stopped their game to inquire if Chambertin, the favorite for the Chantilly cup, had broken down.

"No, no," replied he, as he hurriedly made his way

to the writing-room, "Chambertin is as sound as a bell."

"What the deuce has happened to De Breulh?" asked one of the members.

"Goodness gracious!" remarked the man to whom the question was addressed, "he seems in a hurry to write a letter."

The gentleman was right. M. de Breulh was writing a withdrawal from his demand for Sabine's hand to M. de Mussidan, and he found the task by no means an easy one, for on reading it over he found that there was a valid strain of bitterness throughout it, which would surely attract attention and perhaps cause embarrassing questions to be put to him.

"No," murmured he, "this letter is quite unworthy of me." And tearing it up, he began another, in which he strung together several conventional excuses, alleging the difficulty of breaking off his former habits and of an awkward entanglement which he had been unable to break with, as he had anticipated. When this little masterpiece of diplomacy was completed, he rang the bell, and, handing it to one of the club servants, told him to take it to the Count de Mussidans' house. When this unpleasant duty was over, M. de Breulh had hoped to experience some feeling of relief, but in this he was mistaken. He tried cards, but rose from the table in a quarter of an hour; he ordered dinner, but appetite was wanting; he went to the opera, but there he did nothing but yawn, and the music grated on his nerves. At length he returned home. The day had seemed interminable, and he could not sleep, for Sabine's face was ever before him. Who could this man be whom she so fondly loved and preferred before all others? He respected her too much not to feel assured that her choice was a worthy one, but his experience had taught him that when so many men of the world fell into strange entanglements, a poor girl without knowledge of the dangers around her might easily be entrapped. "If he is worthy of her," thought he, "I will do my best to aid her; but if not, I will open her eyes."

At four o'clock in the morning he was still seated musing before the expiring embers of his fire; he had made up his mind to see André—there was no difficulty in this, for a man of taste and wealth can find a ready excuse for visiting the studio of a struggling artist. He had no fixed plan as to what he would say or do, he left that all to chance, and with this decision he went to bed, and by two in the afternoon he drove straight to the Rue de la Tour d'Auvergne.

André's discreet portress was as usual leaning on her broom in the gallery as M. de Breulh's magnificent equipage drew up.

"Gracious me!" exclaimed the worthy woman, dazzled by the gorgeousness of the whole turnout; "he can't be coming here, he must have mistaken the house."

But her amazement reached its height when M. de Breulh, on alighting, asked for André.

"Fourth story, first door to the right," answered the woman; "but I will show you the way."

"Don't trouble yourself;" and with these words M. de Breulh ascended the staircase that led to the painter's studio and knocked at the door. As he did so, he heard a quick, light step upon the stairs, and a young and very dark man, dressed in a weaver's blouse and carrying a tin pail which he had evidently just filled with water from the cistern, came up.

" Are you M. André? " asked De Breulh.

" That is my name, sir."

" I wish to say a few words to you."

" Pray come in," replied the young artist, opening the door of his studio and ushering his visitor in. André's voice and expression had made a favorable impression upon his visitor; but he was, in spite of his having thrown aside nearly all foolish prejudices, a little startled at his costume. He did not, however, allow his surprise to be visible.

" I ought to apologize for receiving you like this," remarked André quickly, " but a poor man must wait upon himself." As he spoke, he threw off his blouse and set down the pail in a corner of the room.

" I rather should offer my excuse for my intrusion," returned M. de Breulh. " I came here by the advice of one of my friends; " he stopped for an instant, endeavoring to think of a name.

" By Prince Crescensi, perhaps," suggested André.

" Yes, yes," continued M. de Breulh, eagerly snatching at the rope the artist held out to him. " The Prince sings your praises everywhere, and speaks of your talents with the utmost enthusiasm. I am, on his recommendation, desirous of commissioning you to paint a picture for me, and I can assure you that in my gallery it will have no need to be ashamed of its companions."

André bowed, coloring deeply at the compliment.

" I am obliged to you," said he, " and I trust that you will not be disappointed in taking the Prince's opinion of my talent."

" Why should I be so? "

" Because, for the last four months I have been so busy that I have really nothing to show you."

"That is of no importance. I have every confidence in you."

"Then," returned André, "all that we have to do is to choose a subject."

André's manner had by this time so captivated De Breulh that he muttered to himself, "I really ought to hate this fellow, but on my word I like him better than any one I have met for a long time."

André had by this time placed a large portfolio on the table. "Here," said he, "are some twenty or thirty sketches; if any of them took your fancy, you could make your choice."

"Let me see them," returned De Breulh politely, for having made an estimate of the young man's character, he now wished to see what his artistic talents were like. With this object in view he examined all the sketches in the portfolio minutely, and then turned to those on the walls. André said nothing, but he somehow felt that this visit would prove the turning-point of his misfortunes. But for all that the young man's heart was very sad, for it was two days since Sabine had left him, promising to write to him the next morning regarding M. de Breulh-Faverlay, but as yet he had received no communication, and he was on the tenterhooks of expectation, not because he had any doubt of Sabine, but for the reason that he had no means of obtaining any information of what went on in the interior of the Hôtel de Mussidan. M. de Breulh had now finished his survey, and had come to the conclusion that though many of André's productions were crude and lacking in finish, yet that he had the true artistic metal in him. He extended his hand to the young man and said forcibly, "I am no longer influenced by the opinion of a friend. I have seen and judged for myself, and am more desirous than ever of possessing one of your pictures. I have made my choice of a subject, and now let us discuss the details."

As he spoke he handed a little sketch to André. It was a view of everyday life, which the painter had entitled, " Outside the Barrier." Two men with torn garments and wine-flushed faces were struggling in tipsy combat, while on the right hand side of the picture lay a woman, bleeding profusely from a cut on the forehead, and two of her terrified companions were bending over her, endeavoring to restore her to consciousness. In the background were some flying figures, who were hastening up to separate the combatants. The sketch was one of real life, denuded of any sham element of romance, and this was the one that M. de Breulh had chosen. The two men discussed the size of the picture, and not a single detail was omitted.

" I am sure that you will do all that is right," remarked De Breulh. " Let your own inspiration guide you, and all will be well." In reality he was dying to get away, for he felt in what a false position he was, and with a violent effort he approached the money part of the matter.

" Monsieur," said André, " it is impossible to fix a price; when completed, a picture may only be worth the canvas that it is painted on, or else beyond all price. Let us wait."

" Well," broke in M. de Breulh, " what do you say to ten thousand francs?"

" Too much," returned André with a deprecatory wave of his hand; " far too much. If I succeed in it, as I hope to do, I will ask six thousand francs for it."

"Agreed!" answered De Breulh, taking from his pocket an elegant note-case with his crest and monogram upon it and extracting from it three thousand francs. "I will, as is usual, deposit half the price in advance."

André blushed scarlet. "You are joking," said he.

"Not at all," answered De Breulh quietly; "I have my own way of doing business, from which I never deviate."

In spite of this answer André's pride was hurt.

"But," remarked he, "this picture will not be ready for perhaps six or seven months. I have entered into a contract with a wealthy builder, named Candéle, to execute the outside decorations of his house."

"Never mind that," answered M. de Breulh; "take as long as you like."

Of course, after this, André could offer no further opposition; he therefore took the money without another word.

"And now," said De Breulh, as he paused for a moment at the open doorway, "let me wish you my good luck, and if you will come and breakfast with me one day, I think that I can show you some pictures which you will really appreciate." And handing his card to the artist, he went downstairs.

At first André did not glance at the card, but when he did so, the letters seemed to sear his eyeballs like a red-hot iron. For a moment he could hardly breathe, and then a feeling of intense anger took possession of him, for he felt that he had been trifled with and deceived.

Hardly knowing what he was doing, he rushed out on the landing, and, leaning over the banister, called out loudly, "Sir, stop a moment!"

De Breulh, who had by this time reached the bottom of the staircase, turned round.

" Come back, if you please," said André.

After a moment's hesitation, De Breulh obeyed; and when he was again in the studio, André addressed him in a voice that quivered with indignation.

" Take back these notes, sir; I will not accept them."

" What do you mean?"

" Only that I have thought the matter over, and that I will not accept your commission."

" And why this sudden change?"

" You know perfectly well, M. de Breulh-Faverlay."

The gentleman at once saw that Sabine had mentioned his name to the young artist, and with a slight lacking of generous feeling said,—

" Let me hear your reasons, sir."

" Because, because——" stammered the young man.

" Because is no answer."

André's confusion became greater. He would not tell the whole truth, for he would have died sooner than bring Sabine's name into the discussion; and he could only see one way out of his difficulty.

" Suppose I say that I do not like your manner or appearance," returned he disdainfully.

" Is it your wish to insult me, M. André?"

" As you choose to take it."

M. de Breulh was not gifted with an immense stock of patience. He turned livid, and made a step forward; but his generous impulses restrained him, and it was in a voice broken by agitation that he said,—

" Accept my apologies, M. André; I fear that I have played a part unworthy both of you and of myself. I ought to have given you my name at once. I know everything."

"I do not comprehend you," answered André in a glacial voice.

"Why doubt, then, if you do not understand? However, I have given you cause to do so. But, let me reassure you, Mademoiselle Sabine has spoken to me with the utmost frankness; and, if you still distrust me, let me tell you that this veiled picture is her portrait. I will say more," continued De Breulh gravely, as the artist still kept silent; "yesterday, at Mademoiselle de Mussidan's request, I withdrew from my position as a suitor for her hand."

André had been already touched by De Breulh's frank and open manner, and these last words entirely conquered him.

"I can never thank you enough," began he.

But De Breulh interrupted him.

"A man should not be thanked for performing his duty. I should lie to you if I said that I am not painfully surprised at her communication; but tell me, had you been in my place, would you not have acted in the same manner?"

"I think that I should."

"And now we are friends, are we not?" and again De Breulh held out his hand, which André clasped with enthusiasm.

"Yes, yes," faltered he.

"And now," continued De Breulh, with a forced smile, "let us say no more about the picture, which was, after all, merely a pretext. As I came here I said to myself, 'If the man to whom Mademoiselle de Mussidan has given her heart is worthy of her, I will do all I can to advance his suit with her family!' I came here to see what you were like; and now I say to you, do me a great honor, and permit me to place myself, my fortune, and the influence of my friends, at your disposal."

The offer was made in perfect good faith, but André shook his head.

"I shall never forget your kindness in making this offer, but——"; he paused for a moment, and then went on: "I will be as open as you have been, and will tell you the whole truth. You may think me foolish; but remember, though I am poor, I have still my self-respect to maintain. I love Sabine, and would give my life for her. Do not be offended at what I am about to say. I would, however, sooner give up her hand than be indebted for it to you."

"But this is mere madness."

"No, sir, it is the purest wisdom; for were I to accede to your wishes, I should feel deeply humiliated by the thought of your self-denial; for I should be madly jealous of the part you were playing. You are of high birth and princely fortune, while I am utterly friendless and unknown; all that I am deficient in you possess."

"But I have been poor myself," interposed De Breulh, "and perhaps endured even greater miseries than ever you have done. Do you know what I was doing at your age? I was slowly starving to death at Sonora, and had to take the humblest position in a cattle ranch. Do you think that those days taught me nothing?"

"You will be able to judge me all the more clearly then," returned André. "If I raise myself up to Sabine's level, as she begged me to, then I shall feel that I am your equal; but if I accept your aid, I am your dependent; and I will obey her wishes or perish in the effort."

Up to this moment the passion which stirred André's inmost soul had breathed in every word he uttered; but, checking himself by a mighty effort, he resumed in a tone of greater calmness,—

"But I ought to remember how much we already owe you, and I hope that you will allow me to call myself your friend?"

M. de Breulh's noble nature enabled him to understand André's scruples; his feelings, however, would not for the instant enable him to speak. He slowly put the notes back in their receptacle, and then said in a low voice,—

"Your conduct is that of an honorable man; and remember this, at all times and seasons you may rely upon De Breulh-Faverlay. Farewell!"

As soon as he was alone, André threw himself into an armchair, and mused over this unexpected interview, which had proved a source of such solace to his feelings. All that he now longed for was a letter from Sabine. At this moment the portress entered with a letter. André was so occupied with his thoughts that he hardly noticed this act of condescension on the part of the worthy woman.

"A letter!" exclaimed he; and, tearing it open, he glanced at the signature. But Sabine's name was not there; it was signed Modeste. What could Sabine's maid have to say to him? He felt that some great misfortune was impending, and, trembling with excitement, he read the letter.

"Sir,—

"I write to tell you that my mistress has succeeded in the matter she spoke of to you; but I am sorry to say that I have bad news to give you, for she is seriously ill."

"Ill!" exclaimed André, crushing up the letter in his hands, and dashing it upon the floor. "Ill! ill!" he repeated, not heeding the presence of the portress; "why, she may be dead;" and, snatching up his hat, he dashed downstairs into the street.

As soon as the portress was left alone, she picked up the letter, smoothed it out, and read it.

"And so," murmured she, "the little lady's name was Sabine—a pretty name; and she is ill, is she? I expect that the old gent who called this morning, and asked so many questions about M. André, would give a good deal for this note; but no, that would not be fair."

CHAPTER XX.

A COUNCIL OF WAR.

MAD with his terrible forebodings, André hurried through the streets in the direction of the Hôtel de Mussidan, caring little for the attention that his excited looks and gestures caused. He had no fixed plan as to what to do when he arrived there, and it was only on reaching the Rue de Matignon that he recovered sufficient coolness to deliberate and reflect.

He had arrived at the desired spot; how should he set to work to obtain the information that he required? The evening was a dark one, and the gas-lamps showed a feeble light through the dull February fog. There were no signs of life in the Rue de Matignon, and the silence was only broken by the continuous surge of carriage wheels in the Faubourg Saint Honoré. This gloom, and the inclemency of the weather, added to the young painter's depression. He saw his utter helplessness, and felt that he could not move a step without compromising the woman he so madly adored. He walked to the gate of the house, hoping to gain some information even from the exterior aspect of the house; for it seemed to him that if Sabine were dying, the very stones in the street would utter sounds of woe and lamentation; but the fog had closely enwrapped the house, and he could hardly see which of the windows were lighted. His reasoning faculties told him that there was no use in waiting, but an inner voice warned him to stay. Would Modeste, who had written to him, divine, by some means that he was there, in an agony of suspense, and come out to give him information and solace? All at once a thought darted across his mind, vivid as a flash of lightning.

" M. de Breulh will help me," cried he; " for though I cannot go to the house, he will have no difficulty in doing so."

By good luck, he had M. de Breulh's card in his pocket, and hurried off to his address. M. de Breulh had a fine house in the Avenue de l'Impératrice, which he had taken more for the commodiousness of the stables than for his own convenience.

" I wish to see M. de Breulh," said André, as he stopped breathless at the door, where a couple of footmen were chatting.

The men looked at him with supreme contempt. "He is out," one of them at last condescended to reply.

André had by this time recovered his coolness, and taking out De Breulh's card, wrote these words on it in pencil: " One moment's interview. ANDRÉ."

" Give this to your master as soon as he comes in,"
said he.

Then he descended the steps slowly. He was certain that M. de Breulh was in the house, and that he
would send out after the person who had left the card
almost at once. His conclusion proved right; in five
minutes he was overtaken by the panting lackey, who,
conducting him back to the house, showed him into a
magnificently furnished library. De Breulh feared
that some terrible event had taken place.

" What has happened? " said he.

" Sabine is dying; " and André at once proceeded to
inform De Breulh of what had happened since his departure.

" But how can I help you? "

" You can go and make inquiries at the house."

" Reflect; yesterday I wrote to the Count, and broke
off a marriage, the preliminaries of which had been
completely settled; and within twenty-four hours to
send and inquire after his daughter's health would be
to be guilty of an act of inexcusable insolence; for it
would look as if I fancied that Mademoiselle de Mussidan had been struck down by my rupture of the engagement."

" You are right," murmured André dejectedly.

" But," continued De Breulh, after a moment's reflection, " I have a distant relative, a lady who is also
a connection of the Mussidan family, the Viscountess
de Bois Arden, and she will be glad to be of service
to me. She is young and giddy, but as true as steel.
Come with me to her; my carriage is ready."

The footmen were surprised at seeing their master
on such terms of intimacy with the shabbily dressed
young man, but ventured, of course, on no remarks.

Not a word was exchanged during the brief drive to Madame de Bois Arden's house.

"Wait for me," exclaimed De Breulh, springing from the vehicle as soon as it drew up; "I will be back directly."

Madame de Bois Arden is justly called one of the handsomest women in Paris. Very fair, with masses of black hair, and a complexion to which art has united itself to the gifts of nature, she is a woman who has been everywhere, knows everything, talks incessantly, and generally very well. She spends forty thousand francs per annum on dress. She is always committing all sorts of imprudent acts, and scandal is ever busy with her name. Half a dozen of the opposite sex have been talked of in connection with her, while in reality she is a true and faithful wife, for, in spite of all her frivolity, she adores her husband, and is in great awe of him. Such was the character of the lady into whose apartment M. de Breulh was introduced. Madame de Bois Arden was engaged in admiring a very pretty fancy costume of the reign of Louis XV., one of Van Klopen's masterpieces, when M. de Breulh was announced, which she was going to wear, on her return from the opera, at a masquerade ball at the Austrian Ambassador's. Madame de Bois Arden greeted her visitor with effusion, for they had been acquaintances from childhood, and always addressed each other by their Christian names.

"What, you here at this hour, Gontran!" said the lady. "Is it a vision, or only a miracle?" But the smile died away upon her lips, as she caught a glimpse of her visitor's pale and harassed face. "Is there anything the matter?" asked she.

"Not yet," answered he, "but there may be, for

I hear that Mademoiselle de Mussidan is dangerously ill."

"Is she really? Poor Sabine! what is the matter with her?"

"I do not know; and I want you, Clotilde, to send one of your people to inquire into the truth of what we have heard."

Madame de Bois Arden opened her eyes very wide.

"Are you joking?" said she. "Why do you not send yourself?"

"It is impossible for me to do so; and if you have any kindness of heart, you do as I ask you; and I want you also to promise me not to say a word of this to any one."

Excited as she was by this mystery, Madame de Bois Arden did not ask another question.

"I will do exactly what you want," replied she, "and respect your secret. I would go at once, were it not that Bois Arden will never sit down to dinner without me; but the moment we have finished I will go."

"Thanks, a thousand times; and now I will go home and wait for news from you."

"Not at all,—you will remain here to dinner."

"I must,—I have a friend waiting for me."

"Do as you please, then," returned the Viscountess, laughing. "I will send round a note this evening."

De Breulh pressed her hand, and hurried down, and was met by André at the door, for he had been unable to sit still in the carriage.

"Keep up your courage. Madame de Bois Arden had not heard of Mademoiselle Sabine's illness, and this looks as if it was not a very serious matter. We shall have the real facts in three hours."

"Three hours!" groaned André, "what a lapse of time!"

"It is rather long, I admit; but we will talk of her while we wait, for you must stay and dine with me."

André yielded, for he had no longer the energy to contest anything. The dinner was exquisite, but the two men were not in a condition of mind to enjoy it, and scarcely consumed anything. Vainly did they endeavor to speak on indifferent subjects, and when the coffee had been served in the library, they relapsed into utter silence. As the clock struck ten, however, a knock was heard at the door, then whisperings, and the rustle of female attire, and lastly Madame de Bois Arden burst upon them like a tornado.

"Here am I," cried she.

It was certainly rather a hazardous step to pay such a late visit to a bachelor's house, but then the Viscountess de Bois Arden did exactly as she pleased.

"I have come here, Gontran," exclaimed she, with extreme vehemence, "to tell you that I think your conduct is abominable and ungentlemanly."

"Clotilde!"

"Hold your tongue! you are a wretch! Ah! now I can see why you did not wish to write and inquire about poor Sabine. You well knew the effect that your message would have on her."

M. de Breulh smiled as he turned to André and said,—

"You see that I was right in what I told you."

This remark for the first time attracted Madame de Bois Arden's attention to the fact that a stranger was present, and she trembled lest she had committed some grave indiscretion.

"Gracious heavens!" exclaimed she, with a start, "why, I thought that we were alone!"

"This gentleman has all my confidence," replied M. de Breulh seriously; and as he spoke he laid his hand upon André's shoulder. "Permit me to introduce M. André to you, my dear Clotilde; he may not be known to-day, but in a short time his reputation will be European."

André bowed, but for once in her life the Viscountess felt embarrassed, for she was surprised at the extremely shabby attire of this confidential friend, and then there seemed something wanting to the name.

"Then," resumed De Breulh, "Mademoiselle de Mussidan is really ill, and our information is correct."

"She is."

"Did you see her?"

"I did, Gontran; and had you seen her, your heart would have been filled with pity, and you would have repented your conduct toward her. The poor girl did not even know me. She lay in her bed, whiter than the very sheets, cold and inanimate as a figure of marble. Her large black eyes were staring wildly, and the only sign of life she exhibited was when the great tears coursed down her cheeks."

André had determined to restrain every token of emotion in the presence of the Viscountess, but her recital was too much for him.

"Ah!" said he, "she will die; I know it."

There was such intense anguish in his tone that even the practised woman of the world was softened.

"I assure you, sir," said she, "that you go too far; there is no present danger; the doctors say it is catalepsy, which often attacks persons of a nervous temperament upon the receipt of a sudden mental shock."

"But what shock has she received?" asked André.

"No one told me," answered she after a short pause, "that Sabine's illness was caused by the breaking off of her engagement; but, of course, I supposed that it was."

"That was not the reason, Clotilde; but you have told us nothing; pray, go on," interposed De Breulh.

The extreme calmness of her cousin, and a glance which she observed passing between him and André, enlightened the Viscountess somewhat.

"I asked as much as I dared," she replied, "but I could only get the vaguest answers. Sabine looked as if she were dead, and her father and mother hovered around her couch like two spectres. Had they slain her with their own hands, they could not have looked more guilty; their faces frightened me."

"Tell me precisely what answers were given to your questions," broke in he impatiently.

"Sabine had seemed so agitated all day, that her mother asked her if she was suffering any pain."

"We know that already."

"Indeed!" replied the Viscountess, with a look of surprise. "It seems, cousin, that you saw Sabine that afternoon, but what became of her afterward no one appears to know; but there is positive proof that she did not leave the house, and received no letters. At all events, it was more than an hour after her maid saw her enter her own room. Sabine said a few unintelligible words to the girl, who, seeing the pallor upon her mistress's face, ran up to her. Just as she did so, Sabine uttered a wild shriek, and fell to the ground. She was raised up and laid upon the bed, but since then she has neither moved nor spoken."

"That is not all," said De Breulh, who had watched his cousin keenly.

The Viscountess started, and avoided meeting her cousin's eye.

"I do not understand," she faltered. "Why do you look at me like that?"

De Breulh, who had been pacing up and down the room, suddenly halted in front of the Viscountess.

"My dear Clotilde," said he, "I am sure when I tell you that the tongue of scandal has often been busy with your name, I am telling you nothing new."

"Pooh!" answered the Viscountess. "What do I care for that?"

"But I always defended you. You are indiscreet— your presence here to-night shows this; but you are, after all, a true woman,—brave and true as steel."

"What do you mean by this exordium, Gontran?"

"This, Clotilde,—I want to know if I dare venture to intrust to you a secret which involves the honor of two persons, and, perhaps, the lives of more."

"Thank you, Gontran," answered she calmly. "You have formed a correct judgment of me."

But here André felt that he must interpose, and, taking a step forward, said, "Have you the right to speak?"

"My dear André," said De Breulh, "this is a matter in which my honor is as much concerned as yours. Will you not trust me?" Then turning to the Viscountess, he added, "Tell us all you heard."

"It is only something I heard from Modeste. You had hardly left the house, when the Baron de Clinchain made his appearance."

"An eccentric old fellow, a friend of the Count de Mussidan's. I know him."

" Just so; well, they had a stormy interview, and at the end of it, the Baron was taken ill, and it was with difficulty that he regained his carriage."

" That seems curious."

" Wait a bit.   After that Octave and his wife had a terrible scene together, and Modeste thinks that her mistress must have heard something, for the Count's voice rang through the house like thunder."

Every word that the Viscountess uttered strengthened De Breulh's suspicions.   " There is something mysterious in all this, Clotilde," said he, " as you will say when you know the whole truth," and, without omitting a single detail, he related the whole of Sabine and André's love story.

Madame de Bois Arden listened attentively, sometimes thrilled with horror, and at others pleased with this tale of innocent love.

" Forgive me," said she, when her cousin had concluded; " my reproaches and accusations were equally unfounded."

" Yes, yes; never mind that; but I am afraid that there is some hidden mystery which will place a fresh stumbling-block in our friend André's path."

" Do not say that," cried André, in terror.   " What is it?"

" That I cannot tell; for Mademoiselle de Mussidan's sake, I have withdrawn all my pretensions to her hand,—not to leave the field open to any other intruder, but in order that she may be your wife."

" How are we to learn what has really happened?" asked the Viscountess.

" In some way or other we shall find out, if you will be our ally."

Most women are pleased to busy themselves about a

marriage, and the Viscountess was cheered to find herself mixed up in so romantic a drama.

"I am entirely at your beck and call," answered she. "Have you any plan?"

"Not yet, but I will soon. As far as Mademoiselle de Mussidan is concerned, we must act quite openly. André will write to her, asking for an explanation, and you shall see her to-morrow, and if she is well enough, give her his note."

The proposal was a startling one, and the Viscountess did not entertain it favorably.

"No," said she, "I think that would not do at all."

"Why not? However, let us leave it to André."

André, thus addressed, stepped forward, and said,—

"I do not think that it would be delicate to let Mademoiselle de Mussidan know that her secret is known to any one else than ourselves."

The Viscountess nodded assent.

"If," continued André, "the Viscountess will be good enough to ask Modeste to meet me at the corner of the Avenue de Matignon; I shall be there."

"A capital idea, sir," said the lady, "and I will give your message to Modeste." She broke off her speech suddenly, and uttered a pretty little shriek, as she noticed that the hands of the clock on the mantelpiece pointed to twenty to twelve. "Great heavens!" cried she, "and I am going to a ball at the Austrian Embassy, and now not even dressed." And, with a coquettish gesture, she drew her shawl around her, and ran out of the room, exclaiming as she descended the stairs, "I will call here to-morrow, Gontran, on my way to the Bois," and disappeared like lightning.

André and his host sat over the fire, and conversed for a long time. It seemed strange that two men who had met that morning for the first time should now be on such intimate terms of friendship; but such was the case, for a mutual feeling of admiration and respect had sprung up in their hearts.

M. de Breulh wished to send André home in his carriage, but this the young man declined, and merely borrowed an overcoat to protect him from the inclemency of the weather.

"To-morrow," said he, as he made his way home, "Modeste shall tell all she knows, provided always that that charming society dame does not forget all about our existence before then."

Madame de Bois Arden, however, could sometimes be really in earnest. Upon her return from the ball she would not even go to bed, lest she should oversleep herself, and the next day André found Modeste waiting at the appointed spot, and learnt, to his great grief, that Sabine had not yet regained consciousness.

The family doctor betrayed no uneasiness, but expressed a wish for a consultation with another medical man. Meanwhile, the girl promised to meet André morning and evening in the same place, and give him such scraps of information as she had been able to pick up. For two whole days Mademoiselle de Mussidan's condition remained unchanged, and André spent his whole time between his own studio, the Avenue de Matignon, and M. de Breulh's, where he frequently met Madame de Bois Arden.

But on the third day Modeste informed him, with tears in her eyes, that though the cataleptic fit had passed away, Sabine was struggling with a severe attack of fever. Modeste and André were so interested in their conversation, that they did not perceive Florestan, who had gone out to post a letter to Mascarin.

"Listen, Modeste," whispered André, "you tell me that she is in danger,—very great danger."

"The doctor said that the crisis would take place to-day; be here at five this evening."

André staggered like a madman to De Breulh's house; and so excited was he that his friend insisted upon his taking some repose, and would not, when five o'clock arrived, permit André to go to the appointment alone. As they turned the corner, they saw Modeste hurrying toward them.

"She is saved, she is saved!" said she, "for she has fallen into a tranquil sleep, and the doctor says that she will recover."

André and De Breulh were transported by this news; but they did not know that they were watched by two men, Mascarin and Florestan, who did not let one of their movements escape them. Warned by a brief note from Florestan, Mascarin had driven swiftly to Father Canon's public-house, where he thought he was certain to find the domestic, but the man was not there, and Mascarin, unable to endure further suspense, sent for him to the Hôtel de Mussidan. When the servant informed Mascarin that the crisis was safely passed, he drew a deep breath of relief; for he no longer feared that the frail structure that he had built up with such patient care for twenty long years would be shattered at a blow by the chill hand of death. He bent his brow, however, when he heard of Modeste's daily interviews with the young man whom Florestan termed "Mademoiselle's lover."

"Ah," muttered he, "if I could only be present at one of those interviews!"

"And, as you say," returned Florestan, drawing out, as he spoke, a neat-looking watch, "it is just the hour of their meeting; and as the place is always the same, you——"

" Come, then," broke in his patron. They went out accordingly, and reached the Champs Elysées by a circuitous route. The place was admirably suited to their purpose, for close by were several of those little wooden huts, occupied in summer by the vendors of cakes and playthings.

" Let us get behind one of these," said Florestan. Night was drawing in, but objects could still be distinguished, and in about five minutes Florestan whispered, " Look, there comes Modeste, and there is the lover, but he has a pal with him to-night. Why, what can she be telling him? He seems quite overcome."

Mascarin divined the truth at once, and found that it would be a difficult task to interfere with the love of a man who displayed such intensity of feeling.

" Then," remarked Mascarin, savagely, " that great booby, staggering about on his friend's arm, is your young lady's lover?"

" Just so, sir."

" Then we must find out who he is."

Florestan put on a crafty air, and replied in gentle accents.

" The day before yesterday, as I was smoking my pipe outside, I saw this young bantam swaggering down the street—not but what he seemed rather crestfallen; but I knew the reason for that, and should look just as much in the dumps if my young woman was laid up. I thought, as I had nothing to do, I might as well see who he was and where he lived; so, sticking my hands in my pockets, after him I sloped. He walked such a long way, that I got precious sick of my job, but at last I ran him to earth in a house. I went straight up to the lodge, and showed the portress my tobacco pouch, and said, 'I picked up this; I think that the gentleman who has just gone in dropped it. Do you know him?' 'Of course I do,' said she. 'He is a painter; lives on the fourth floor; and his name is M. André.'"

"Was the house in the Rue de la Tour d'Auvergne?" broke in Mascarin.

"You are right, sir," returned the man, taken a little aback. "It seems, sir, that you are better informed than I am."

Mascarin did not notice the man's surprise, but he was struck with the strange persistency with which this young man seemed to cross his plans, for he found that the acquaintance of Rose and the lover of Mademoiselle de Mussidan were one and the same person, and he had a presentiment that he would in some way prove a hindrance to his plans.

The astute Mascarin concentrated all his attention upon André.

The latter said something to Modeste, which caused that young woman to raise her hands to heaven, as though in alarm.

"But who is the other?" asked he,—"the fellow that looks like an Englishman?"

"Do you not know?" returned the lackey. "Why, that is M. de Breulh-Faverlay."

"What, the man who was to marry Sabine?"

"Certainly."

Mascarin was not easily disconcerted, but this time a blasphemous oath burst from his lips.

"Do you mean," said he, "that De Breulh and this painter are friends?"

"That is more than I can tell. You seem to want to know a lot," answered Florestan, sulkily.

Modeste had now left the young men, who walked arm in arm in the direction of the Avenue de l'Impératrice.

"M. de Breulh takes his dismissal easily enough," observed Mascarin.

"He was not dismissed; it was he that wrote and broke off the engagement."

This time Mascarin contrived to conceal the terrible blow that this information caused to him, and even made some jesting remark as he took leave of Florestan; but he was in truth completely staggered, for after thoroughly believing that the game was won, he saw that, though perhaps not lost, his victory was postponed for an indefinite period.

"What!" said he, as he clenched his hand firmly, "shall the headstrong passion of this foolish boy mar my plans? Let him take care of himself; for if he walks in my path, he will find it a road that leads to his own destruction."

CHAPTER XXI.

AN ACADEMY OF MUSIC.

DR. HORTEBISE had for some time back given up arguing with Mascarin as to the advice the latter gave him. He had been ordered not to let Paul out of his sight, and he obeyed this command literally. He had taken him to dine at M. Martin Rigal's, though the host himself was absent; from there he took Paul to his

club, and finally wound up by forcing the young man
to accept a bed at his house. They both slept late, and
were sitting down to a luxurious breakfast, when the
servant announced M. Tantaine, and that worthy man
made his appearance with the same smile upon his face
which Paul remembered so well in the Hôtel de Perou.
The sight of him threw the young man into a state of
fury. "At last we meet," cried he. "I have an account to settle with you."

"You have an account to settle with me?" asked
Daddy Tantaine with a puzzled smile.

"Yes; was it not through you that I was accused of
theft by that old hag, Madame Loupins?"

Tantaine shrugged his shoulders.

"Dear me," said he; "I thought that M. Mascarin had explained everything, and that you were
anxious to marry Mademoiselle Flavia, and that, above
all, you were a young man of intelligence and
tact."

Hortebise roared with laughter, and Paul, seeing his
folly, blushed deeply and remained silent.

"I regret having disturbed you, doctor," resumed
Tantaine, "but I had strict orders to see you."

"Is there anything new then?"

"Yes; Mademoiselle de Mussidan is out of danger,
and M. de Croisenois can commence proceedings at
once."

The doctor drank off a glass of wine. "To the
speedy marriage of our dear friend the Marquis and
Mademoiselle Sabine," said he gayly.

"So be it," said Tantaine; "I am also directed to
beg M. Paul not to leave this house, but to send for
his luggage and remain here."

Hortebise looked so much annoyed that Tantaine

hastened to add: " Only as a temporary measure, for I am on the lookout for rooms for him now."

Paul looked delighted at the idea of having a home of his own.

" Good! " exclaimed the doctor merrily. " And now, my dear Tantaine, as you have executed all your commissions, you can stay and breakfast with us."

" Thanks for the honor; but I am very busy with affairs of the Duke de Champdoce and must see Perpignan at once." As he spoke he rose, making a little sign which Paul did not catch, and Hortebise accompanied him to the door of the vestibule. " Don't leave that lad alone," said Tantaine; " I will see about him to-morrow; meanwhile prepare him a little."

" I comprehend," answered Hortebise; " my kind regards to that dear fellow, Perpignan."

This Perpignan was well known—some people said too well known—in Paris. His real name was Isidore Crocheteau, and he had started life as a cook in a Palais Royal restaurant. Unfortunately a breach of the Eighth Commandment had caused him to suffer incarceration for a period of three years, and on his release he bloomed out into a private inquiry agent. His chief customers were jealous husbands, but as surely as one of these placed an affair in his hands, he would go to the erring wife and obtain a handsome price from her for his silence.

Mascarin and Perpignan had met in an affair of this kind; and as they mutually feared each other, they had tacitly agreed not to cross each other's path in that great wilderness of crime—Paris. But while Perpignan knew nothing of Mascarin's schemes and operations, the former was very well acquainted with the ex-cook's doings. He knew, for instance, that the income from the Inquiry Office would not cover Perpignan's expenses, who dressed extravagantly, kept a carriage, affected artistic tastes, played cards, betted on races, and liked good dinners at the most expensive restaurants. "Where can he get his money from?" asked Mascarin of himself; and, after a long search, he succeeded in solving the riddle.

Daddy Tantaine, after leaving the doctor's, soon arrived at the residence of M. Perpignan, and rang the bell.

A fat woman answered the door. "M. Perpignan is out," said she.

"When will he be back?"

"Some time this evening."

"Can you tell me where I can find him, as it is of the utmost importance to both of us that I should see him at once?"

"He did not say where he was going to?"

"Perhaps he is at the factory," said Tantaine blandly.

The fat woman was utterly taken aback by this suggestion. "What do you know about that?" faltered she.

"You see I *do* know, and that is sufficient for you. Come, is he there?"

"I think so."

"Thank you, I will call on him then. An awfully long journey," muttered Tantaine, as he turned away; "but, perhaps, if I catch the worthy man in the midst of all his little business affairs, he will be more free in his language, and not so guarded in his actual admissions."

The old man went to his task with a will. He passed down the Rue Toumenon, skirted the Luxemburg, and

made his way into the Rue Guy Lussac; from thence
he walked down the Rue Mouffetard, and thence direct
into one of those crooked lanes which run between the
Gobelins Factory and the Hôpital de l'Oursine. This
is a portion of the city utterly unknown to the greater
number of the Parisians. The streets are narrow and
hardly afford room for vehicles. A valley forms the
centre of the place, down which runs a muddy, sluggish
stream, the banks of which are densely crowded with
tanyards and iron works. On the one side of this
valley is the busy Rue Mouffetard, and on the other
one of the outer boulevard, while a long line of sickly-
looking poplars mark the course of the semi-stagnant
stream. Tantaine seemed to know the quarter well,
and went on until he reached the Champs des Alouettes.
Then, with a sigh of satisfaction, he halted before a
large, three-storied house, standing on a piece of
ground surrounded by a mouldering wooden fence. The
aspect of the house had something sinister and gloomy
about it, and for a moment Tantaine paused as if he
could not make up his mind to enter it; but at last he
did so. The interior was as dingy and dilapidated as
the outside. There were two rooms on the ground
floor, one of which was strewn with straw, with a few
filthy-looking quilts and blankets spread over it. The
next room was fitted up as a kitchen; in the centre was
a long table composed of boards placed on trestles, and
a dirty-looking woman with her head enveloped in a
coarse red handkerchief, and grasping a big wooden
spoon, was stirring the contents of a large pot in which
some terrible-looking ingredients were cooking. On a
small bed in a corner lay a little boy. Every now and
then a shiver convulsed his frame, his face was deadly
pale, and his hands almost transparent, while his great

black eyes glittered with the wild delirium of fever.
Sometimes he would give a deep groan, and then the
old beldame would turn angrily and threaten to strike
him with her wooden spoon.

"But I am so ill," pleaded the boy.

"If you had brought home what you were told, you
would not have been beaten, and then you would have
had no fever," returned the woman harshly.

"Ah, me! I am sick and cold, and want to go away,"
wailed the child; "I want to see mammy."

Even Tantaine felt uneasy at this scene, and gave a
gentle cough to announce his presence. The old woman
turned round on him with an angry snarl. "Who do
you want here?" growled she.

"Your master."

"He has not yet arrived, and may not come at all,
for it is not his day; but you can see Poluche."

"And who may he be?"

"He is the professor," answered the hag contemptuously.

"And where is he?"

"In the music-room."

Tantaine went to the stairs, which were so dingy and
dilapidated as to make an ascent a work of danger and
difficulty. As he ascended higher, he became aware
of a strange sound, something between the grinding of
scissors and the snarling of cats. Then a moment's
silence, a loud execration, and a cry of pain. Tantaine passed on, and coming to a rickety door, he
opened it, and in another moment found himself in
what the old hag downstairs had called the music-room.
The partitions of all the rooms on the floor had been
roughly torn down to form this apartment; hardly a
pane of glass remained intact in the windows; the

dingy, whitewashed walls were covered with scrawls and drawings in charcoal. A suffocating, nauseous odor rose up, absolutely overpowering the smell from the neighboring tanyards. There was no furniture except a broken chair, upon which lay a dog whip with plaited leather lash. Round the room, against the wall, stood some twenty children, dirty, and in tattered clothes. Some had violins in their hands, and others stood behind harps as tall as themselves. Upon the violins Tantaine noticed there were chalk marks at various distances. In the middle of the room was a man, tall and erect as a dart, with flat, ugly features and lank, greasy hair hanging down on his shoulders. He, too, had a violin, and was evidently giving the children a lesson. Tantaine at once guessed that this was Professor Poluche.

"Listen," said he; "here, you Ascanie, play the chorus from the *Château de Marguerite.*" As he spoke he drew his bow across his instrument, while the little Savoyard did his best to imitate him, and in a squeaking voice, in nasal tone, he sang:

"Ah! great heavens, how fine and grand
    Is the palace!"

"You young rascal!" cried Poluche. "Have I not bid you fifty times that at the word 'palace' you are to place your bow on the fourth chalkmark and draw it across? Begin again."

Once again the boy commenced, but Poluche stopped him.

"I believe, you young villain, that you are doing it on purpose. Now, go through the whole chorus again; and if you do not do it right, look out for squalls."

Poor Ascanie was so muddled that he forgot all his instructions. Without any appearance of anger, the professor took up the whip and administered half a dozen severe cuts across the bare legs of the child, whose shouts soon filled the room.

"When you have done howling," remarked Poluche, "you can try again; and if you do not succeed, no supper for you to-night, my lad. Now, Giuseppe, it is your turn."

Giuseppe, though younger than Ascanie, was a greater proficient on the instrument, and went through his task without a single mistake.

"Good!" said Poluche; "if you get on like that, you will soon be fit to go out. You would like that, I suppose?"

"Yes," replied the delighted boy, "and I should like to bring in a few coppers too."

But the Professor did not waste too much time in idle converse.

"It is your turn, now Fabio," said he.

Fabio, a little mite of seven, with eyes black and sparkling as those of a dormouse, had just seen Tantaine in the doorway and pointed him out to the professor.

Poluche turned quickly round and found himself face to face with Tantaine, who had come quickly forward, his hat in his hand.

Had the professor seen an apparition, he could not have started more violently, for he did not like strangers.

"What do you want?" asked he.

"Reassure yourself, sir," said Tantaine, after having for a few seconds enjoyed his evident terror; "I am the intimate friend of the gentleman who employs you, and have come here to discuss an important matter of business with him."

Poluche breathed more freely.

"Take a chair, sir," said he, offering the only one in the room. "My master will soon be here."

But Daddy Tantaine refused the offer, saying that he did not wish to intrude, but would wait until the lesson was over.

"I have nearly finished," remarked Poluche; "it is almost time to let these scamps have their soup."

Then turning to his pupils, who had not dared to stir a limb, he said,—

"There, that is enough for to-day; you can go."

The children did not hesitate for a moment, but tumbled over each other in their eagerness to get away, hoping, perhaps, that he might omit to execute certain threats that he had held out during the lesson. The hope was a vain one, for the equitable Poluche went to the head of the stairs and called out in a loud voice,—

"Mother Butor, you will give no soup to Monte and put Ravillet on half allowance."

Tantaine was much interested, for the scene was an entirely new one.

The professor raised his eyes to heaven.

"Would," said he, "that I might teach them the divine science as I would wish; but the master would not allow me; indeed, he would dismiss me if I attempted to do so."

"I do not understand you."

"Let me explain to you. You know that there are certain old women who, for a consideration, will train a linnet or a bullfinch to whistle any air?"

Tantaine, with all humility, confessed his ignorance of these matters.

"Well," said the professor, the only difference between those old women and myself is, that they teach birds and I boys; and I know which I had rather do."

Tantaine pointed to the whip.

"And how about this?" asked he.

Poluche shrugged his shoulders.

"Put yourself in my place for a little while," remarked he. "You see my master brings me all sorts of boys, and I have to cram music into them in the briefest period possible. Of course the child revolts, and I thrash him; but do not think he cares for this; the young imps thrive on blows. The only way that I can touch them is through their stomachs. I stop a quarter, a half, and sometimes the whole of their dinner. That fetches them, and you have no idea how a little starvation brings them on in music."

Daddy Tantaine felt a cold shiver creep over him as he listened to this frank exposition of the professor's mode of action.

"You can now understand," remarked the professor, "how some airs become popular in Paris. I have forty pupils all trying the same thing. I am drilling them now in the *Marguerite,* and in a little time you will have nothing else in the streets."

Poluche was proceeding to give Tantaine some further information, when a step was heard upon the stairs, and the professor remarked,—

"Here is the master; he never comes up here, because he is afraid of the stairs. You had better go down to him."

CHAPTER XXII.

DIAMOND CUT DIAMOND.

THE ex-cook appeared before Tantaine in all his appalling vulgarity as the latter descended the stairs. The proprietor of the musical academy was a stout, red-faced man, with an insolent mouth and a cynical eye. He was gorgeously dressed, and wore a profusion of jewelry. He was much startled at seeing Tantaine, whom he knew to be the redoubtable Mascarin's right-hand man. "A thousand thunders!" muttered he. "If these people have sent him here for me, I must take care what I am about," and with a friendly smile he extended his hand to Tantaine.

"Glad to see you," said he. "Now, what can I do for you, for I hope you have come to ask me to do something?"

"The veriest trifle," returned Tantaine.

"I am sorry that it is not something of importance, for I have the greatest respect for M. Mascarin."

This conversation had taken place in the window, and was interrupted every moment by the shouts and laughter of the children; but beneath these sounds of merriment came an occasional bitter wail of lamentation.

"What is that?" inquired Perpignan, in a voice of thunder. "Who presumes to be unhappy in this establishment?"

"It is two of the lads that I have put on half ration," returned Poluche. "I'll make them learn somehow or——"

A dark frown on the master's face arrested his further speech. "What do I hear?" roared Perpignan. "Do you dare, under my roof, to deprive those poor children of an ounce of food? It is scandalous, I may say, infamous, on your part, M. Poluche."

"But, sir," faltered the professor, "have you not told me hundreds of times——"

"That you were an idiot, and would never be anything better. Go and tell Mother Butor to give these poor children their dinner."

Repressing further manifestations of rage, Perpignan took Tantaine by the arm and led him into a little side-room, which he dignified by the name of his office. There was nothing in it but three chairs, a common deal table, and a few shelves containing legers. "You have come on business, I presume," remarked Perpignan.

Tantaine nodded, and the two men seated themselves at the table, gazing keenly into each other's eyes, as though to read the thoughts that moved in the busy brain.

"How did you find out my little establishment down here?" asked Perpignan.

"By a mere chance," remarked Tantaine carelessly. "I go about a good deal, and hear many things. For instance, you have taken every precaution here, and though you are really the proprietor, yet the husband of your cook and housekeeper, Butor, is supposed to be the owner of the house—at least it stands in his name. Now, if anything untoward happened, you would vanish, and only Butor would remain a prey for the police."

Tantaine paused for a moment, and then slowly added, "Such tactics usually succeed unless a man has some secret enemy, who would take advantage of his knowledge, to do him an injury by obtaining irrefragable proofs of his complicity."

The ex-cook easily perceived the threat that was hidden under these words. "They know something," muttered he, "and I must find out what it is."

"If a man has a clear conscience," said he aloud, "he is all right. I have nothing to conceal, and therefore nothing to fear. You have now seen my establishment; what do you think of it?"

"It seems to me a very well-conducted one."

"It may have occurred to you that a factory at Roubaix might have been a better investment, but I had not the capital to begin with."

Tantaine nodded. "It is not half a bad trade," said he.

"I agree with you. In the Rue St. Marguerite you will find more than one similar establishment; but I never cared for the situation of the Faubourg St. Antoine. My little angels find this spot more salubrious."

"Yes, yes," answered Tantaine amicably, "and if they howl too much when they are corrected, there are not too many neighbors to hear them."

Perpignan thought it best to take no notice of this observation. "The papers are always pitching into us," continued he. "They had much better stick to politics. The fact is, that the profits of our business are tremendously exaggerated."

"Well, you manage to make a living out of it?"

"I don't lose, I confess, but I have six little cherubs in hospital, besides the one in the kitchen, and these, of course, are a dead loss to me."

"That is a sad thing for you," answered Tantaine gravely.

Perpignan began to be amazed at his visitor's coolness.

"Damn it all," said he, "if you and Mascarin think the business such a profitable one, why don't you go in for it. You may perhaps think it easy to procure the kids; just try it. You have to go to Italy for most of them, then you have to smuggle them across the frontier like bales of contraband goods."

Perpignan paused to take breath, and Tantaine asked,—

"What sum do you make each of the lads bring in daily?"

"That depends," answered Perpignan hesitatingly.

"Well, you can give an average?"

"Say three francs then."

"Three francs!" repeated Tantaine with a genial smile, "and you have forty little cherubs, so that makes one hundred and twenty francs per day."

"Absurd!" retorted Perpignan; "do you think each of the lads bring in such a sum as that?"

"Ah! you know the way to make them do so."

"I don't understand you," answered Perpignan, in whose voice a shade of anxiety now began to appear.

"No offence, no offence," answered Tantaine; "but the fact is, the newspapers are doing you a great deal of harm, by retailing some of the means adopted by your colleague to make the boys do a good day's work. Do you recollect the sentence on that master who tied one of his lads down on a bed, and left him without food for two days at a stretch?"

"I don't care about such matters; no one can bring a charge of cruelty against me," retorted Perpignan angrily.

" A man with the kindest heart in the world may be the victim of circumstances."

Perpignan felt that the decisive moment was at hand.

" What do you mean? " asked he.

" Well, suppose, to punish one of your refractory lads, you were to shut him in the cellar. A storm comes on during the night, the gutter gets choked up, the cellar fills with water, and next morning you find the little cherub drowned like a rat in his hole? "

Perpignan's face was livid.

" Well, and what then? " asked he.

" Ah! now the awkward part of the matter comes. You would not care to send for the police, that might excite suspicion; the easiest thing is to dig a hole and shove the body into it."

Perpignan got up and placed his back against the door.

" You know too much, M. Tantaine,—a great deal too much," said he.

Perpignan's manner was most threatening; but Tantaine still smiled pleasantly, like a child who has just committed some simply mischievous act, the results of which it cannot foresee.

" The sentence isn't heavy," he continued; " five years' penal servitude, if evidence of previous good conduct could be put in; but if former antecedents were disclosed, such as a journey to Nancy——"

This was the last straw, and Perpignan broke out,—

" What do you mean? " said he; " and what do you want me to do? "

" Only a trifling service, as I told you before. My dear sir, do not put yourself in a rage," he added, as Perpignan seemed disposed to speak again. " Was it not you who first began to talk of your, 'em—well, let us say business? "

"Then you wanted to make yourself agreeable by talking all this rot to me. Well, shall I tell you in my turn what I think?"

"By all means, if it will not be giving you too much trouble."

"Then I tell you that you have come here on an errand which no man should venture to do alone. You are not of the age and build for business like this. It is a misfortune—a fatal one perhaps—to put yourself in my power, in such a house as this."

"But, my dear sir, what is likely to happen to me?"

The features of the ex-cook were convulsed with fury; he was in that mad state of rage in which a man has no control over himself. Mechanically his hand slipped into his pocket; but before he could draw it out again, Tantaine who had not lost one of his movements, sprang upon him and grasped him so tightly by the throat that he was powerless to adopt any offensive measures, in spite of his great strength and robust build. The struggle was not a long one; the old man hurled his adversary to the ground, and placed his foot on his chest, and held him down, his whole face and figure seemingly transfigured with the glories of strength and success.

"And so you wished to stab me,—to murder a poor and inoffensive old man. Do you think that I was fool enough to enter your cut-throat door without taking proper precautions?" And as he spoke he drew a revolver from his bosom. "Throw away your knife," added he sternly.

In obedience to this mandate, Perpignan, who was now entirely demoralized, threw the sharp-pointed weapon which he had contrived to open in his pocket into a corner of the room.

"Good," said Tantaine. "You are growing more reasonable now. Of course I came alone, but do you think that plenty of people did not know where I was going to? Had I not returned to-night, do you think that my master, M. Mascarin, would have been satisfied? and how long do you think that it would have been before he and the police would have been here? If you do not do all that I wish for the rest of your life, you will be the most ungrateful fellow in the world."

Perpignan was deeply mortified; he had been worsted in single combat, and now he was being found out, and these things had never happened to him before.

"Well, I suppose that I must give in," answered he sulkily.

"Quite so; it is a pity that you did not think of that before."

"You vexed me and made me angry."

"Just so; well, now, get up, take that chair, and let us talk reasonably."

Perpignan obeyed without a word.

"Now," said Tantaine, "I came here with a really magnificent proposal. But I adopted the course I pursued because I wished to prove to you that *you* belonged more absolutely to Mascarin than did your wretched foreign slaves to you. You are absolutely at his mercy, and he can crush you to powder whenever he likes."

"Your Mascarin is Satan himself," muttered the discomfited man. "Who can resist him?"

"Come, as you think thus, we can talk sensibly at last."

"Well," answered Perpignan ruefully, as he adjusted his disordered necktie, "say what you like, I have no answer to make."

" Let us begin at the commencement," said Tantaine.
" For some days past your people have been following
a certain Caroline Schimmel.   A fellow of sixteen,
called Ambrose, a lad with a harp, was told off for this
duty.   He is not to be trusted.   Only a night or two
ago one of my men made him drunk; and fearing lest
his absence might create surprise, drove him here in a
cab, and left him at the corner."

The ex-cook uttered an oath.

" Then you too are watching Caroline," said he.   " I
knew well that there was some one else in the field, but
that was no matter of mine."

" Well, tell me why you are watching her? "

" How can you ask me?   You know that my motto
is silence and discretion, and that this is a secret intrusted to my honor."

Tantaine shrugged his shoulders.

" Why do you talk like that, when you know very
well that you are following Ambrose on your own account, hoping by that means to penetrate a secret, only
a small portion of which has been intrusted to you? "
remarked he.

" Are you certain of this statement? " asked the
man, with a cunning look.

" So sure that I can tell you that the matter was
placed in your hands by a certain M. Catenac."

The expression in Perpignan's face changed from
astonishment to fear.

"Why, this Mascarin knows everything," muttered he.

" No," replied Tantaine, " my master does not know
everything, and the proof of this is, that I have come
to ask you what occurred between Catenac's client and
yourself, and this is the service that we expect from
you."

"Well, if I must, I must. About three weeks ago, one morning, I had just finished with half a dozen clients at my office in the Rue de Fame, when my servant brought me Catenac's card. After some talk, he asked me if I could find out a person that he had utterly lost sight of. Of course I said, yes, I could. Upon this he asked me to make an appointment for ten the next morning, when some one would call on me regarding the affair. At the appointed time a shabbily dressed man was shown in. I looked at him up and down, and saw that, in spite of his greasy hat and threadbare coat, his linen was of the finest kind, and that his shoes were the work of one of our best bootmakers. 'Aha,' said I to myself, 'you thought to take me in, did you!' I handed him a chair, and he at once proceeded to let me into his reasons for coming. 'Sir,' said he, 'my life has not been a very happy one, and once I was compelled to take to the Foundling Asylum a child that I loved very dearly, the son of a woman whom I adored. She is dead now, and I am old and solitary. I have a small property, and would give half of it to recover the child. Tell me, is there any chance of my doing so?' You must imagine, my dear sir," continued he, after a slight pause, "that I was much interested in this story, for I said to myself, that the man's fortune must be a very small one if half of it would not amply repay me for making a journey to the Foundling Hospital. So I agreed to undertake the business, but the old fellow was too sharp for me. 'Stop a bit, and let me finish,' said he, 'and you will see that your task will not be so easy as you seem to think it.' I, of course, bragged of my enormous sources of information, and the probability of ultimate success."

" Keep to your story," said Tantaine impatiently, " I
know all about that."

" I will leave you, then, to imagine all I said to the
old man, who listened to me with great satisfaction.
' I only hope that you are as skilful as M. Catenac says
you are, and have as much influence and power as you
assert, for no man has a finer chance than you now
have. I have tried all means up to this, but I have
failed.' I went first to the hospital where the child
had been placed, and they showed me the register containing the date of his admission, but no one knew what
had become of him, for at twelve years of age he had
left the place, and no one had heard of him since;
and in spite of every effort, I have been unable to discover whether he was alive or dead."

" A pretty riddle to guess," remarked Tantaine.

" An enigma that it is impossible to solve," returned
Perpignan. " How is one to get hold of a boy who
vanished ten years ago, and who must now be a grown-
up man? "

" We could do it."

Tantaine's tone was so decided, that the other man
looked sharply at him with a vague suspicion rising in
his breast that the affair had also been placed in Mascarin's hands; and if so, whether he had worked it
with more success than himself.

" You might, for all I know; but I felt that the clue
was absolutely wanting," answered Perpignan sulkily.
" I put on a bold face, however, and asked for the boy's
description. The man told me that he could provide
me with an accurate one, for that many people, notably
the lady superior, remembered the lad. He could also
give other details which might be useful."

" And these you obtained, of course? "

" Not yet."

" Are you joking? "

" Not a bit. I do not know whether the old man
was sharp enough to read in the expression of my
features that I had not the smallest hope of success;
be that as it may, he could give me no further information that day, declaring that he came in only to consult
me, and that everything must be done in a most confidential way. I hastened to assure him that my office
was a perfect tomb of secrets. He told me that he took
that for granted. Then telling me that he wished me
to draw up a *précis* of my intended course, he took out
a note for five hundred francs, which he handed to me
for my time. I refused to take it, though it cost me
a struggle to do so, for I thought that I should make
more out of him later on. But he insisted on my taking it, saying that he would see me again soon, and
that Catenac would communicate with me. He left
me less interested in the search than in who this old
man could possibly be."

Tantaine felt that Perpignan was telling the truth.

" Did you not try and find out that? " asked he.

Perpignan hesitated; but feeling convinced that there
was no loophole for escape, he answered, " Hardly had
my visitor left than, slipping on a cap and a workman's
blouse, I followed in his track, and saw him enter one
of the finest houses in the Rue de Varennes."

" He lived there then? "

" He did, and he was a very well-known man—the
Duke de Champdoce."

" Yes, I know all that," answered Tantaine, placidly,
" but I can't, for the life of me, imagine the connection
between the Duke and Caroline Schimmel."

Perpignan raised his eyebrows.

"Why did you put a man to watch her?" asked Tantaine.

"My reasons for doing so were most simple. I made every inquiry regarding the Duke; learned that he was very wealthy, and lived a very steady life. He is married, and loves his wife dearly. They had one son, whom they lost a year ago, and have never recovered from the shock. I imagine that this Duke, having lost his legitimate heir, wishes me to find his other son. Do you not think that I am right?"

"There is something in it; but, after all, you have not explained your reasons for watching Caroline."

Perpignan was no match for Mascarin's right-hand man, but he was keen enough to discern that Tantaine was putting a string of questions to him which had been prepared in advance. This he, however, was powerless to resent.

"As you may believe," said he, "I made every inquiry into the past as well as the present of the Duke, and also tried to discover who was the mother of the child, but in this I entirely failed."

"What! not with all your means?" cried Tantaine, with a sneer.

"Laugh at me as much as you like; but out of the thirty servants in the Champdoce establishment, not one has been there more than ten years. Nor could I anywhere lay my hands upon one who had been in the Duke's service in his youth. Once, however, as I was in the wineshop in the Rue de Varennes, I quite by chance heard allusion made to a woman who had been in the service of the Duke twenty-five years ago, and who was now in receipt of a small allowance from him. This woman was Caroline Schimmel. I easily found out her address, and set a watch on her."

" And of what use will she be to you? "

" Very little, I fear. And yet the allowance looks as
if she had at one time done something out of the way
for her employers. Can it be that she has any knowledge of the birth of this natural child? "

" I don't think much of your idea," returned Tantaine carelessly.

" Since then," continued Perpignan, " the Duke has
never put in an appearance at my office."

" But how about Catenac? "

" I have seen him three times."

" Has he told you nothing more? Do you not even
know in which hospital the child was placed? "

" No; and on my last visit I plainly told him that I
was getting sick of all this mystery; and he said that
he himself was tired, and was sorry that he had ever
meddled in the affair."

Tantaine was not surprised at hearing this, and ac-
counted for Catenac's change of front by the threats
of Mascarin.

" Well, what do you draw from this? " asked he.

" That Catenac has no more information than I have.
The Duke most likely proposes to drop the affair; but,
were I in his place, I should be afraid to find the boy,
however much I might at one time have desired to do
so. He may be in prison—the most likely thing for a
lad who, at twelve years of age, ran away from a place
where he was well treated. I have, however, planned
a mode of operation, for, with patience, money, and
skill, much might be done."

" I agree with you."

" Then let me tell you. I have drawn an imaginary
circle round Paris. I said to myself, ' I will visit every
house and inn in the villages round within this radius;

I will enter every isolated dwelling, and will say to the inhabitants, "Do any of you remember at any time sheltering and feeding a child, dressed in such and such a manner?"' giving at the same time a description of him. I am sure that I should find some one who would answer in the affirmative. Then I should gain a clue which I would follow up to the end."

This plan appeared so ingenious to Tantaine, that he involuntarily exclaimed,—

"Good! excellent!"

Perpignan hardly knew whether Tantaine was praising or blaming him. His manner might have meant either.

"You are very fast," returned he dismally. "Perhaps presently you will be good enough to allow that I am not an absolute fool. Do you really think that I am an idiot? At any rate, I sometimes hit upon a judicious combination. For example, with regard to this boy, I have a notion which, if properly worked might lead to something."

"Might I ask what it is?"

"I speak confidentially. If it is impossible to lay our hands upon the real boy, why should we not substitute another?"

At this suggestion, Tantaine started violently.

"It would be most dangerous, most hazardous," gasped he.

"You are afraid, then?" said Perpignan, delighted at the effect his proposal had made.

"It seems it is you who were afraid," retorted Tantaine.

"You do not know me when you say that," said Perpignan.

"If you were not afraid," asked Tantaine, in his

most oily voice, "why did you not carry out your plan?"

"Because there was one obstacle that could not be got over."

"Well, I can't see it myself," returned Tantaine, desirous of hearing every detail.

"Ah, there is one thing that I omitted in my narrative. The Duke informed me that he could prove the identity of the boy by certain scars."

"Scars? And of what kind, pray?"

"Now you are asking me too much. I do not know."

On receiving this reply, Tantaine rose hastily from his chair, and thus concealed his agitation from his companion.

"I have a hundred apologies to make for taking up so much of your valuable time. My master has got it into his head that you were after the same game as ourselves. He was mistaken, and now we leave the field clear to you."

Before Perpignan could make any reply, the old man had passed through the doorway. On the threshold he paused, and said,—

"Were I in your place, I would stick to my first plan. You will never find the boy, but you will get several thousand francs out of the Duke, which I am sure will come in handy."

"There are scars now, then," muttered Tantaine, as he moved away from the house, "and that Master Catenac never said a word about them!"

CHAPTER XXIII.

FATHER AND SON.

Two hours after André had left the Avenue de Matignon, one of Mascarin's most trusty emissaries was at his heels, who could watch his actions with the tenacity of a bloodhound. André, however, now that he had heard of Sabine's convalescence, had entirely recovered the elasticity of his spirits, and would never have noticed that he was being followed. His heart, too, was much rejoiced at the friendship of M. de Breulh and the promise of assistance from the Viscountess de Bois Arden; and with the assistance of these two, he felt that he could end his difficulties.

"I must get to work again," muttered he, as he left M. de Breulh's hospitable house. "I have already lost too much time. To-morrow, if you look up at the scaffolding of a splendid house in the Champs Elysées, you will see me at work."

André was busy all night with his plans for the rich contractor, M. Gandelu, who wanted as much ornamental work on the outside of his house as he had florid decorations within. He rose with the lark, and having gazed for a moment on Sabine's portrait, started for the abode of M. Gandelu, the proud father of young Gaston. This celebrated contractor lived in a splendid house in the Rue Chasse d'Antin, until his more palatial residence should be completed.

When André presented himself at the door, an old servant, who knew him well, strongly urged him not to go up.

" Never," said he, " in all the time that I have been with master, have I seen him in such a towering rage. Only just listen!"

It was easy to hear the noise alluded to, mingled with the breaking of glass and the smashing of furniture.

" The master has been at this game for over an hour," remarked the servant, " ever since his lawyer, M. Catenac, has left him."

André, however, decided not to postpone his visit. " I must see him in spite of everything; show me up," said he.

With evident reluctance the domestic obeyed, and threw open the door of a room superbly furnished and decorated, in the centre of which stood M. Gandelu waving the leg of a chair frantically in his hand. He was a man of sixty years of age, but did not look fifty, built like a Hercules, with huge hands and muscular limbs which seemed to fret under the restraint of his fashionable garments. He had made his enormous fortune, of which he was considerably proud, by honest labor, and no one could say that he had not acted fairly throughout his whole career. He was coarse and violent in his manner, but he had a generous heart and never refused aid to the deserving and needy. He swore like a trooper, and his grammar was faulty; but for all that, his heart was in the right place, and he was a better man than many who boast of high birth and expensive education.

" What idiot is coming here to annoy me?" roared he, as soon as the door was opened.

" I have come by appointment," answered André, and the contractor's brow cleared as he saw who his visitor was.

"Ah, it is you, is it? Take a seat; that is, if there is a sound chair left in the room. I like you, for you have an honest face and don't shirk hard work. You needn't color up, though; modesty is no fault. Yes, there is something in you, and when you want a hundred thousand francs to go into business with, here it is ready for you; and had I a daughter, you should marry her, and I would build your house for you."

"I thank you much," said André; "but I have learned to depend entirely on myself."

"True," returned Gandelu, "you never knew your parents; you never knew what a kind father would do for his child. Do you know my son?" asked he, suddenly turning upon André.

This question at once gave André the solution of the scene before him. M. Gandelu was irritated at some folly that his son had committed. For a moment André hesitated; he did not care to say anything that might revive the old man's feeling of anger, and therefore merely replied that he had only met his son Gaston two or three times.

"Gaston," cried the old man, with a bitter oath; "do not call him that. Do you think it likely that old Nicholas Gandelu would ever have been ass enough to call his son Gaston? He was called Peter, after his grandfather, but it wasn't a good enough one for the young fool; he wanted a swell name, and Peter had too much the savor of hard work in it for my fine gentleman. But that isn't all; I could let that pass," continued the old man. "Pray, have you seen his cards? Over the name of Gaston de Gandelu is a count's coronet. He a count indeed! the son of a man who has carried a hod for years!"

"Young people will be young people," André ventured to observe; but the old man's wrath would not be assuaged by a platitude like this.

"You can find no excuse for him, only the fellow is absolutely ashamed of his father. He consorts with titled fools and is in the seventh heaven if a waiter addresses him as 'Count,' not seeing that it is not he that is treated with respect, but the gold pieces of his old father, the working man."

André's position was now a most painful one, and he would have given a good deal not to be the recipient of a confidence which was the result of anger.

"He is only twenty, and yet see what a wreck he is," resumed Gandelu. "His eyes are dim, and he is getting bald; he stoops, and spends his nights in drink and bad company. I have, however, only myself to blame, for I have been far too lenient; and if he had asked me for my head, I believe that I should have given it to him. He had only to ask and have. After my wife's death, I had only the boy. Do you know what he has in this house? Why, rooms fit for a prince, two servants and four horses. I allow him, monthly, fifteen hundred francs, and he goes about calling me a niggard, and has already squandered every bit of his poor mother's fortune." He stopped, and turned pale, for at that moment the door opened, and young Gaston, or rather Peter, slouched into the room.

"It is the common fate of fathers to be disappointed in their offspring, and to see the sons who ought to have been their honor and glory the scourge to punish their worldly aspirations," exclaimed the old man.

"Good! that is really a very telling speech," murmured Gaston approvingly, "considering that you have not made a special study of elocution."

Fortunately his father did not catch these words, and

continued in a voice broken by emotion, "That, M. André, is my son, who for twenty years has been my sole care. Well, believe it or not, as you like, he has been speculating on my death, as you might speculate on a race-horse at Vincennes."

"No, no," put in Gaston, but his father stopped him with a disdainful gesture.

"Have at least the courage to acknowledge your fault. You thought me blind because I said nothing, but your past conduct has opened my eyes."

"But, father!"

"Do not attempt to deny it. This very morning my man of business, M. Catenac, wrote to me, and with that real courage which only true friends possess, told me all. I must tell you, M. André," resumed the contractor, "I was ill. I had a severe attack of the gout, such as a man seldom recovers from, and my son was constant in his attendance at my sick couch. This consoled me. 'He loves me after all,' said I. But it was only my testamentary arrangements that he wanted to discover, and he went straight to a money-lender called Clergot and raised a hundred thousand francs, assuring the blood-sucker that I had not many hours to live."

"It is a lie!" cried Gaston, his face crimsoning with shame.

The old man raised the leg of the chair in his hand, and made so threatening a movement that André flung himself between father and son. "Great heavens!" cried he, "think what you are doing, sir, and forbear."

The old man paused, passed his hand round his brow, and flung the weapon into a remote corner of the room. "I thank you," said he, grasping André's hand; "you have saved me from a great crime. In another moment I should have murdered him."

Gaston was no coward, and he still retained the position he had been in before.

"This is quite romantic," muttered he. "The governor seems to be going in for infanticide."

André did not allow him to finish the sentence, for, grasping the young man's wrist, he whispered fiercely, "Not another word; silence!"

"But I want to know what it all means?" answered the irrepressible youth.

"I had in my hands," said the old man, addressing André, and ignoring the presence of his son, the important paper he had copied. Yes; not more than an hour ago I read it. These were the terms: if I died within eight days from the date of signature, my son agreed to pay a bonus of thirty thousand francs; but if I lived for one month, he would take up the bill by paying one hundred and fifty thousand. If, however, by any unforeseen chance, I should recover entirely, he bound himself to pay Clergot the hundred thousand francs."

The old man tore the cravat from his swelling throat, and wiped the beads of cold sweat that bedewed his brow.

"When this man recovers his self-command," thought André, "he will never forgive me for having been the involuntary listener to this terrible tale." But in this André was mistaken, for unsophisticated nature requires sympathy, and Nicholas Gandelu would have said the same to the first comer.

"Before, however, delivering the hundred thousand francs, the usurer wished to make himself more secure, and asked for a certificate from some one who had seen me. This person was his friend. He spoke to me of a medical man, a specialist, who would understand my

case at once. Would I not see him? Never had I seen
my son so tender and affectionate. I yielded to his
entreaties at last, and one evening I said to him, 'Bring
in this wonderful physician, if you really think he can
do anything for me,' and he did bring him.

"Yes, M. André, he found a medical man base and
vile enough to become the tool of my son, and a money-
lender; and if I choose, I can expose him to the loathing of the world, and the contempt of his brethren.

"The fellow came, and his visit lasted nearly an
hour. I can see him now, asking questions and feeling
my pulse. He went away at last, and my son followed
him. They both met Clergot, who was waiting in the
street. 'You can pay him the cash; the old man won't
last twenty-four hours longer,' said the doctor; and
then my son came back happy and radiant, and assured
me that I should soon be well again. And strange as
it may seem, a change for the better took place that very
night. Clergot had asked for forty-eight hours in
which to raise the sum required. He heard of my convalescence, and my son lost the money.

"Was it courage you lacked?" asked the old man,
turning for the first time to his son. "Did you not
know that ten drops instead of one of the medicine I
was taking would have freed you from me for ever?"

Gaston did not seem at all overwhelmed. Indeed, he
was wondering how the matter had reached his father's
ears, and how Catenac had discovered the rough draft
of the agreement.

The contractor had imagined that his son would im-
plore forgiveness; but seeing that he remained ob-
durate, his violence burst forth again. "And do you
know what use my son would make of my fortune?
He would squander it on a creature he picked up out

of the streets,—a woman he called Madame de Chantemille,—a fit companion for a noble count!"

The shaft had penetrated the impassibility which Gaston had up to this displayed. "You shall not insult Zora," said he.

"I shall not," returned his father with a grim laugh, "take the trouble to do that; you are not of age, and I shall clap your friend Madame de Chantemille into prison."

"You would not do that!"

"Would I not? You are a minor; but your Zora, whose real name is Rose, is much older; the law is wholly on my side."

"But father——"

"There is no use in crying; my lawyer has the matter in hand, and by nightfall your Zora will be securely caged."

This blow was so cruel and unexpected, that the young man could only repeat,—

"Zora in prison!"

"Yes, in the House of Correction, and from thence to Saint Lazare. Catenac told me the very things to be done."

"Shameful!" exclaimed Gaston, "Zora in prison! Why, I and my friends will lay siege to the place. I will go to the Court, stand by her side, and depose that this all comes from your devilish malignity. I will say that I love and esteem her, and that as soon as I am of age I will marry her; the papers will write about us. Go on, go on; I rather like the idea."

However great a man's self-control may be, it has its limits. M. Gandelu had restrained himself even while he told his son of his villainous conduct; but these revolting threats were more than he could endure, and André seeing this, stepped forward, opened the door, and thrust the foolish youth into the corridor.

" What have you done? " cried the contractor; " do you not see that he will go and warn that vile creature, and that she will escape from justice? "

And as André, fearing he knew not what, tried to restrain him, the old man, exerting all his muscular strength, thrust him on one side with perfect ease, and rushed from the room, calling loudly to his servants.

André was horrified at the scene at which, in spite of himself, he had been compelled to assist as a witness. He was not a fool, and had lived too much in the world of art not to have witnessed many strange scenes and met with many dissolute characters; but, as a rule, the follies of the world had amused rather than disgusted him. But this display of want of feeling on the part of a son toward a father absolutely chilled his blood. In a few minutes M. Gandelu appeared with a calmer expression upon his face.

" I will tell you how matters now stand," said he, in a voice that quivered in spite of his efforts. " My son is locked up in his room, and a trustworthy servant whom he cannot corrupt has mounted guard over him."

" Do you not fear, sir, that in his excitement and anger he may——? "

The contractor shrugged his shoulders.

" You do not know him," answered he, " if you imagine that he resembles me in any way. What do you think that he is doing now? Lying on his bed, face downward, yelling for his Zora. Zora, indeed! As if that was a name fit for a Christian. How is it that these creatures are enabled to drug our boys and lead them anywhere? Had his mother not been a saint on earth, I should scarcely believe that he was my son."

The contractor sank into a chair and buried his face in his hands.

"You are in pain, sir?" said André.

"Yes; my heart is deeply wounded. Up to this time I have only felt as a father; now I feel as a man. To-morrow I send for my family and consult with them; and I shall advertise that for the future I will not be responsible for any debts that my son may contract. He shall not have a penny, and will soon learn how society treats a man with empty pockets. As to the girl, she will disappear in double quick time. I have thoroughly weighed the consequences of sending this girl to gaol, and they are very terrible. My son will do as he has threatened, I am sure of that; and I can picture him tied to that infamous creature for life, looking into her face, and telling her that he adores her, and glorying in his dishonor, which will be repeated by every Parisian newspaper."

"But is there no other way of proceeding?" asked André.

"No, none whatever. If all modern fathers had my courage, we should not have so many profligate sons. It is impossible that this conferring with the doctor and the money-lender could have originated in my son's weak brain. He is a mere child, and some one must have put him up to it."

The poor father was already seeking for some excuse for the son's conduct.

"I must not dwell on this longer," continued Gandelu, "or I shall get as mad as I was before. I will look at your plans another day. Now, let us get out of the house. Come and look at the new building in the Champs Elysées."

The mansion in question was situated at the corner of the Rue de Chantilly, near the Avenue des Champs Elysées, and the frontage of it was still marked by scaffolding, so that but little of it could be seen. A dozen workmen, engaged by André, were lounging about. They had expected to see him early, and were surprised at his non-appearance, as he was usually punctuality itself. André greeted them in a friendly manner, but M. Gandelu, though he was always on friendly terms with his workmen, passed by them as if he did not even notice their existence. He walked through the different rooms and examined them carelessly, without seeming to take any interest in them, for his thoughts were with his son,—his only son.

After a short time he turned to André.

" I cannot stay longer," said he; " I am not feeling well; I will be here to-morrow; " and he went away with his head bent down on his chest.

The workmen noticed his strange and unusual manner.

" He does not look very bright," remarked one to his comrade. " Since his illness he has not been the same man. I think he must have had some terrible shock."

CHAPTER XXIV.

AN ARTFUL TRICK.

ANDRÉ had removed his coat and donned his blouse, the sleeves of which were rolled up to his shoulders. "I must get to business," murmured he, "to make up for lost time." He set to work with great vigor, but had hardly got into the swing, when a lad came actively up the ladder and told him that a gentleman wished to see him, "and a real swell, too," added the boy. André was a good deal put out at being disturbed, but when he reached the street and saw that it was M. de Breulh-Faverlay who was waiting for him, his ill-humor disappeared like chaff before the wind.

"Ah, this is really kind of you," cried he; for he could never forget the debt of gratitude he owed to the gentleman. "A thousand thanks for remembering me. Excuse my not shaking hands, but see;" and he exhibited his palms all white with plaster. As he did so the smile died away on his lips, for he caught sight of his friend's face.

"What is the matter?" exclaimed he, anxiously. "Is Sabine worse? Has she had a relapse?"

De Breulh shook his head, but the expression of his face clearly said,—

"Would to heavens it were only that!"

But the news that Sabine was not worse had relieved André at once, and he patiently waited for his friend to explain.

"I have seen her twice for you," answered De Breulh; "but it is absolutely necessary that you should come to a prompt decision on an important affair."

" I am quite at your service," returned André a good deal surprised and troubled.

" Then come with me at once. I did not drive here, but we shall not be more than a quarter of an hour in reaching my house."

" I will follow you almost immediately. I only ask five minutes' grace to go up to the scaffold again."

" Have you any orders to give? "

" No, I have none."

" Why should you go, then? "

" To make myself a little more presentable."

" Is it an annoyance or inconvenience for you to go out in that dress? "

" Not a bit, I am thoroughly used to it; but it was for your sake."

" If that is all, come along."

" But people will stare at seeing you in company with a common workman."

" Let them stare." And drawing André's arm through his, M. de Breulh set off.

André was right; many persons did turn round to look at the fashionably dressed gentleman walking arm in arm with a mason in his working attire, but De Breulh took but little heed, and to all André's questions simply said, " Wait till we reach my house."

At length they arrived, without having exchanged twenty words, and entering the library closed the door. M. de Breulh did not inflict the torture of suspense upon his young friend a moment longer than was necessary.

" This morning, about twelve o'clock, as I was crossing the Avenue de Matignon, I saw Modeste, who had been waiting for you more than an hour."

" I could not help it."

"I know that. As soon as she saw me, she ran up
to me at once. She was terribly disappointed at not
having seen you; but knowing our intimacy, she intrusted me with a letter for you from Mademoiselle de
Mussidan."

André shuddered; he felt that the note contained
evil tidings, with which De Breulh was already acquainted. "Give it to me," said he, and with trembling hands he tore open the letter and perused its
contents.

"DEAREST ANDRÉ,—

"I love you, and shall ever continue to do so, but
I have duties—most holy ones—which I must fulfil;
duties which my name and position demand of me,
even should the act cost me my life. We shall never
meet again in this world, and this letter is the last one
you will ever receive from me. Before long you will
see the announcement of my marriage. Pity me, for
great as your wretchedness will be, it will be as nothing
compared to mine. Heaven have mercy upon us both!
André, try and tear me out of your heart. I have not
even the right to die, and oh, my darling, this—this is
the last word you will ever receive from your poor
unhappy   SABINE."

If M. de Breulh had insisted upon taking André
home with him before he handed him the letter, it was
because Modeste had given him some inkling of its
contents. He feared that the effect would be tremendous upon nerves so highly strung and sensitive
as those of André. But he need not have been alarmed
on this point. As the young painter mastered the contents of the letter his features became ghastly pale,
and a shudder convulsed every nerve and muscle of
his frame. With a mechanical gesture he extended the
paper to M. de Breulh, uttering the one word, "Read."

His friend obeyed him, more alarmed by André's laconism than he would have been by some sudden explosion of passion.

"Do not lose heart," exclaimed he.

But André interrupted him. "Lose heart!" said he; "you do not know me. When Sabine was ill, perhaps dying, far away from me, I did feel cast down; but now that she tells me that she loves me, my feelings are of an entirely different nature."

M. de Breulh was about to speak, but André went on.

"What is this marriage contract which my poor Sabine announces to me, as if it was her death-warrant? Her parents must all along have intended to break with you, but you were beforehand with them. Can they have received a more advantageous offer of marriage already? It is scarcely likely. When she confided the secret of her life to you, she certainly knew nothing of this. What terrible event has happened since then? My brave Sabine would never have submitted unless some coercion had been used that she could not struggle against; she would rather have quitted her father's house for ever."

As André uttered these words De Breulh's mind was busy with similar reflections, for Modeste had given him some hint of the approaching marriage, and had begged him to be most careful how he communicated the facts to André.

"You must have noticed," continued the young painter, "the strange coincidence between Sabine's illness and this note. You left her happy and full of hope, and an hour afterward she falls senseless, as though struck by lightning; as soon as she recovers a little she sends me this terrible letter. Do you remember that Madame de Bois Arden told us that during Sabine's illness her father and mother never left her bedside? Was not this for fear lest some guilty secret of theirs might escape her lips in a crisis of delirium?"

"Yes, I remember that, and I have long had reason to imagine that there is some terrible family secret in the Mussidans' family, such as we too often find among the descendants of noble houses."

"What can it be?"

"That I have no means of ascertaining, but that there is one I am sure."

André turned away and paced rapidly up and down the room. "Yes," said he, suddenly, "there is a mystery; but you and I will leave no stone unturned until we penetrate it." He drew a chair close to the side of his friend, who was reclining on a couch. "Listen," said he, "and correct me if you fancy that I am not right in what I am saying. Do you believe that the most terrible necessity alone has compelled Sabine to write this letter?"

"Most certainly."

"Both the Count and Countess were willing to accept you as their son-in-law?"

"Exactly so."

"Could M. de Mussidan have found a more brilliant match for his daughter, one who could unite so many advantages of experience and education to so enormous a fortune?"

De Breulh could hardly repress a smile.

"I am not wishing to pay you a compliment," said André impatiently. "Reply to my question."

"Very well then, I admit that according to the opinion of the world, I was a most eligible suitor, and that M. de Mussidan would find it hard to replace me."

" Then tell me how it comes about that neither the Count nor Countess has made any effort to prevent this rupture? "

Their pride, perhaps, has been wounded."

Not so, for Modeste tells us that on the very day you sent the letter the Count was going to call on you to break off the engagement."

" Yes, that is so, if we are to believe Modeste."

As if to give more emphasis to his words, André started to his feet. " This," cried he, " this man, who has so suddenly appeared upon the scene, will marry Sabine, not only against her own will, but against that of her parents, and for what reason? Who is this man, and what is the mysterious power that he possesses? His power is too great to spring from an honorable source. Sabine is sacrificing herself to this man for some reason or other, and he, like a dastardly cur, is ready to take advantage of the nobleness of her heart."

" I admit the correctness of your supposition," said he; " and now, how do you propose to act? "

" I shall do nothing as yet," answered the young man, with a fierce gleam in his eyes. " Sabine asks me to tear her from my heart. I will affect to do so for the time. Modeste believes in me, and will help me. I have patience. The villain who has wrecked my life does not know me, and I will only reveal myself upon the day that I hold him helpless in my hand."

" Take care, André," urged De Breulh; " a false step would ruin your hopes for ever."

" I will make none; as soon as I have this man's name, I will insult him; there will be a duel, and I shall kill him—or he me."

"A duel will be the height of madness, and would ruin all your hopes of marriage with Sabine."

"The only thing that holds me back is that I do not wish that there should be a corpse between Sabine and myself. Blood on a bridal dress, they say, brings misery; and if this man is what I suspect him to be, I should be doing him too much honor if I crossed swords with him. No, I must have a deeper vengeance than this, for I can never forget that he nearly caused Sabine's death."

He paused for a few seconds, and once again broke the silence which reigned in the room.

"To abuse the power that he must possess shows what a miserable wretch he must be; and men do not attain such a height of infamy by a single bound. The course of his life must be full of similar crimes, growing deeper and deadlier as he moves on. I will make it my business to unmask him and to hold him up to the scorn and contempt of his fellow-men."

"Yes; that is the plan to pursue."

"And we will do so, sir. Ah! heaven help me! I say 'we,' for I have relied on you. The generous offer that you made to me I refused, and I was in the right in doing so; but I should now be a mere madman if I did not entreat you to grant me your aid and advice. We have both known hardship and are capable of going without food or sleep, if necessity requires it of us. We have both graduated in the school of poverty and sorrow. We can keep our plans to ourselves and act."

André paused, as if waiting for a reply, but his friend remained silent.

"My plan is most simple," resumed the young painter. "As soon as we know the fellow's name we shall be able to act. He will never suspect us, and we can follow him like his very shadow. There are pro-

fessional detectives who, for a comparatively small sum,
will lay bare a man's entire life. Are we not as clever
as this fine fellow? We can work well together in our
different circles; you, in the world of fashion, can pick
up intelligence that I could not hope to gain; while I,
from my lowly position, will study the hidden side of
his life, for I can talk to the servants lounging at the
front doors or the grooms at the public-houses without
suspicion."

M. de Breulh was delighted at finding that he could
have some occupation which would fill up the dreary
monotony of his life.

"I am yours!" cried he; "and will work with you
heart and soul."

Before the artist could reply a loud blow was struck
upon the library door, and a woman's voice exclaimed,—

"Let me in, Gontran, at once."

"It is Madame de Bois Arden," remarked De
Breulh, drawing the bolt back; and the Viscountess
rushed hastily into the room and threw herself into a
low chair.

Her beautiful face was bedewed with tears, and she
was in a terrible state of excitement.

"What is the matter, Clotilde?" asked De Breulh
kindly, as he took her hand.

"Something terrible," answered she with a sob; "but
you may be able to help me. Can you lend me twenty
thousand francs?"

De Breulh smiled; a heavy weight had been lifted
from his heart.

"If that is all you require, do not shed any more
tears."

"But I want them at once."

"Can you give me half an hour?"

"Yes; but lose no time."

De Breulh drew a check and despatched his valet for the money.

"A thousand thanks!" said the Viscountess; "but money is not all that I require, I want your advice."

André was about to leave the cousins together, but the lady stopped him.

"Pray remain, M. André," said she; "you are not at all in the way; besides, I shall have to speak of some one in whom you take a very deep interest—of Mademoiselle de Mussidan, in short.

"I never knew such a strange occurrence," continued the Viscountess, recovering her spirits rapidly, "as that to which, my dear Gontran, you owe my visit. Well, I was just going up to dress, for I had been detained by visitor after visitor, when at two o'clock another came before I could give my order, 'Not at home.' This was the Marquis de Croisenois, the brother of the man who twenty years ago disappeared in so mysterious a manner. I hardly knew him at all, though of course we have met in society, and he bows to me in the Bois, but that is all."

"And yet he called on you to-day?" remarked De Breulh.

"Don't interrupt me," said the Viscountess. "Yes, he called, and that is enough. He is good-looking, faultlessly dressed, and talks well. He brought a letter from an old friend of my grandmother's, the Marchioness d'Arlanges. She is a dear old thing, she uses awful language, and some of her stories are quite too——you know what I mean. In the letter the old lady said that the Marquis was one of her friends, and begged me for her sake to do him the service he required. Of course I asked him to be seated, and assured him that I would do anything that lay in my power. Then he began talking about M. de Clinchain, and told me a funny story about that eccentric man and a little actress, when I heard a great noise in the anteroom. I was about to ring and inquire the cause, when the door flew open and in came Van Klopen, the ladies' tailor, with a very inflamed countenance. I thought that he had come in a hurry because he had hit on something extremely fetching and wished me to be the first to see it. But do you know what the impudent fellow wanted?"

A smile shone in De Breulh's eyes, as he answered,—
" Money, perhaps!"

" You are right," returned the Viscountess, gravely; " he brought my bill into my very drawing-room, and handed it in before a stranger. I never thought that a man who supplies the most aristocratic portion of society could have been guilty of such a piece of impertinence. I ordered him to leave the room, taking it for granted that he would do so with an apology, but I was wrong. He flew into a rage and threatened me, and swore that if I did not settle the bill on the spot, he would go to my husband. The bill was nearly twenty thousand francs; imagine my horror! I was so thunderstruck at the amount that I absolutely entreated him to give me time. But my humility added to his annoyance, and taking a seat in an armchair, he declared that he would not move from it until he received his money, or had seen my husband."

" What was Croisenois doing all this time?" asked M. de Breulh.

" He did nothing at first, but at this last piece of audacity he took out his pocketbook, and throwing it in Van Klopen's face, said: 'Pay yourself, you insolent scoundrel, and get out of this.'"

"And the tailor went off?"

"No. 'I must give you a receipt,' said he, and taking writing materials from his pocket, he wrote at the foot of the bill, 'Received from the Marquis de Croisenois, on account of money owing by the Viscountess de Bois Arden, the sum of twenty thousand francs.'"

"Well," said De Breulh, looking very grave, "and after Van Klopen's departure, I suppose Croisenois remained to ask the favor regarding which he had called?"

"You are mistaken," answered his cousin. "I had great difficulty in making him speak; but at last he confessed that he was deeply in love with Mademoiselle de Mussidan, and entreated me to present him to her parents and exert all my influence in his behalf."

Both the young men started.

"That is the man!" cried they.

"What do you mean?" asked the Viscountess, looking from one to the other.

"That yon Marquis de Croisenois is a despicable scoundrel, who has imposed upon the Marchioness d'Arlanges. Just you listen to our reasons for coming to this conclusion." And with the most perfect clearness De Breulh laid the whole state of the case before the Viscountess.

The lady listened attentively, and then said,—

"Your premises are wrong; just let me say a word on the matter. You say that there is some man who, by means of the influence which he exercises over the Count and Countess, can coerce them into granting him Sabine's hand. But, my dear Gontran, an utter stranger to the family could not exercise this power.

Now M. de Croisenois has never entered the doors of the house, and came to me to ask for an introduction."

The justness of this remark silenced De Breulh, but André took another view of the matter.

" This seems all right at a first glance, but still, after the extraordinary scene that the Viscountess has described, I should like to ask a few questions. Was not Van Klopen's behavior very unexpected? "

"It was brutal and infamous."

" Are you not one of his best customers? "

" I am, and I have spent an enormous sum with him."

" But Van Klopen is nasty sometimes; did he not sue Mademoiselle de Riversac? " asked De Breulh.

" But he did not, I expect, force his way into her drawing-room and behave outrageously before a perfect stranger. Do you know M. de Croisenois? " returned André.

" Very slightly; he is of good family, and his brother George was much esteemed by all who knew him."

" Has he plenty of money? "

" I do not think so, but in time he will inherit a large fortune; very likely he is over head and ears in debt."

" And yet he had twenty thousand francs in his pocketbook; is not that rather a large sum to carry when you are simply making a morning call? and it is curious, too, that it should have been the exact sum wanted. Then there is another point; the pocketbook was hurled into Van Klopen's face. Did he submit without a word to such treatment? "

" He certainly said nothing," replied Madame de Bois Arden.

" One question more, if you please. Did Van Klopen

open the book and count the notes before he gave the receipt?"

The Viscountess thought for a moment.

"I was a good deal excited," said she at length, but I am almost sure that I saw no notes in Van Klopen's hands."

André's face grew radiant.

"Good, very good; he was told to pay himself, and yet he never looked to see if the money was there, but gave a receipt at once. Of course, as Van Klopen kept the pocketbook, the Marquis could have had nothing in it besides the exact sum that was required."

"It does seem odd," muttered De Breulh.

"But," said André, "your bill was not exactly twenty thousand francs, was it?"

"No," answered the Viscountess. "I ought to have had change to the amount of a hundred or a hundred and twenty francs, but I suppose he was too much excited to give it me."

"But for all that he could remember that he had writing materials with him, and give you a receipt?"

The Viscountess was utterly bewildered.

"And," continued André, "how was it that Van Klopen knew De Croisenois' name? And now, lastly, where is the receipt?"

Madame de Bois Arden turned very pale and trembled violently.

"Ah," said she, "I felt sure that something was going to happen, and it was on this very point that I wanted your advice. Well, I have not got this receipt. M. de Croisenois crumpled it up in his hand and threw it on the table. After a while, however, he took it up and put it in his pocket."

"It is all perfectly clear," said André in jubilant

tones; "M. de Croisenois had need of your aid, he saw that he could not easily obtain it, and so sought to bind you by the means of a loan made to you at a time of great need."

"You are right," said De Breulh.

The Viscountess' giddy mode of action had brought her into many scrapes, but never into so terrible a one as this.

"Great heavens!" cried she, "what do you think that M. de Croisenois will do with this receipt?"

"He will do nothing," answered M. de Breulh, "if you do everything to advance his suit; but pause for an instant, and he will show the hand of steel which has up to now been covered by the velvet glove."

"I am not alarmed at a new slander?" returned the Viscountess.

"And why not?" answered De Breulh. "You know very well that in these days of lavish expenditure and unbridled luxury there are many women in society who are so basely vile that they ruin their lovers with as little compunction as their frailer sisters. To-morrow even De Croisenois may say at the club, 'On my word that little Bois Arden costs me a tremendous lot,' and hands about this receipt for twenty thousand francs. What do you imagine that people will think then?"

"The world knows me too well to think so ill of me."

"No, no, Clotilde, there is no charity in society; they will simply say that you are his mistress, and finding that the allowance from your husband is not enough for your needs, you are ruining your lover. There will be a significant laugh among the members, and in time, a very short time, the scandal in a highly sensational form will come to the ears of your husband."

The Viscountess wrung her hands.

"It is too horrible," wailed she. "And do you know that Bois Arden would put the worst construction on the whole affair, for he declares that a woman will sacrifice anything in order to outshine her sex in dress. Ah, I will never run up another bill anywhere; tell me, Gontran, what I had better do. Can you not get the receipt from De Croisenois?"

M. de Breulh paused for a moment and then replied, "Of course I could do so, but such a step would be very damaging to your reputation. I have no proof; and if I went to him, he would deny everything of course, and it would make him your enemy for life."

"Besides," added André, "you would put him on his guard, and he would escape us."

The unhappy woman glanced from one to the other in utter despair.

"Then I am lost," she exclaimed. "Am I to remain for the rest of my days in this villain's power?"

"Not so," returned André, "for I hope soon to put it out of M. de Croisenois' power to injure any one. What did he say when he asked you to introduce him to the Mussidans?"

"Nothing pointed."

"Then, madame, do not disturb yourself to-night. So long as he hopes you will be useful, so long he will stay his hand. Do as he wishes; never allude to the receipt; introduce him and speak well of him, while I, aided by M. de Breulh, will do my utmost to unmask this scoundrel; and as long as he believes himself to be in perfect security, our task will be an easy one."

Just then the servant returned from the bank, and

as soon as the man had left the room De Breulh took the notes and placed them in his cousin's hand.

"Here is the money for De Croisenois," said he. "Take my advice, and give it to him this evening with a polite letter of thanks."

"A thousand thanks, Gontran; I will act as you advise."

"Remember you must not allude in your letter to his introduction to the Mussidans. What do you think, André?"

"I think a receipt for the money would be a great thing," answered he.

"But such a demand would arouse his suspicions."

"I think not, madame, and I see a way of doing it; have you a maid upon whom you could rely?"

"Yes, I have one."

"Good, then give the girl a letter and the notes done up in a separate parcel, and tell her exactly what she is to do. When she sees the Marquis, let her pretend to be alarmed at the great responsibility that she is incurring in carrying this large sum, and insist upon a receipt for her own protection."

"There is sound sense in that," said De Breulh.

"Yes, yes," said the Viscountess, "Josephine will do—as sharp a girl as you could find in a day's journey—and will manage the thing admirably. Trust to me," she continued, as a smile of hope spread over her face; "I will keep De Croisenois in a good humor; he will confide in me, and I will tell you everything. But, oh dear! what shall I do without Van Klopen? Why, there is not another man in Paris fit to stand in his shoes."

With these words the Viscountess rose to leave.

"I am completely worn out," remarked she; "and

I have a dinner-party to-night. Good-bye then, until we meet again;" and with her spirits evidently as joyous as ever, she tripped into her carriage.

"Now," said André, as soon as they were once more alone, "we are on the track of De Croisenois. He evidently holds Madame de Mussidan as he holds Madame de Bois Arden. His is a really honorable mode of action; he surprises a secret, and then turns extortioner."

CHAPTER XXV.

A NEW SKIN.

DR. HORTEBISE'S private arrangements were sadly upset by his being compelled to accede to the desire of Tantaine and Mascarin, and in granting hospitality to Paul Violaine; and in spite of the brilliant visions of the future, he often devoutly wished that Mascarin and his young friend were at the other side of the world; but for all that he never thought of attempting to evade the order he had received. He therefore set himself steadily to his task, endeavoring to form Paul's mind, blunt his conscience, and prepare him for the inevitable part that he would soon have to play.

Paul found in him a most affable companion, pleasant, witty, and gifted with great conversational powers. Five days were thus spent breakfasting at well-known restaurants, driving in the Bois, and dining at clubs of which the doctor was a member, while the evenings were passed at the banker's. The doctor played cards with his host, while Paul and Flavia conversed together in low whispers, or else hung over the piano together. But every kind of agreeable existence comes to an end, and one day Daddy Tantaine entered the room, his face radiant with delight.

" I have secured you the sweetest little nest in the world," cried he merrily. " It is not so fine as this, but more in accordance with your position."

" Where is it? " asked Paul.

Tantaine waited. " You won't wear out much shoe leather," said he, " in walking to a certain banker's, for your lodgings are close to his house."

That Tantaine had a splendid talent for arrangement Paul realized as soon as he entered his new place of abode, which was in the Rue Montmartre, and consisted of some neat, quiet rooms, just such as an artist who had conquered his first difficulties would inhabit. The apartments were on the third floor, and comprised a tiny entrance hall, sitting-room, bed and dressing room. A piano stood near the window in the sitting-room. The furniture and curtains were tasteful and in good order, but nothing was new. One thing surprised Paul very much; he had been told that the apartments had been taken and furnished three days ago, and yet it seemed as if they had been inhabited for years, and that the owner had merely stepped out a few minutes before. The unmade bed, and the half-burnt candles in the sleeping-room added to this impression, while on the rug lay a pair of worn slippers. The fire had not gone out entirely, and a half-smoked cigar lay on the mantelpiece.

On the table in the sitting-room was a sheet of music paper, with a few bars jotted down upon it. Paul felt so convinced that he was in another person's rooms, that he could not help exclaiming, " But surely some one has been living in these chambers."

"We are in your own home, my dear boy," said Tantaine.

"But you took over everything, I suppose, and the original proprietor simply walked out?"

Tantaine smiled, as though an unequivocal compliment had been paid him.

"Why, do you not know your own home?" asked he; "you have been living here for the last twelve months."

"I can't understand you," answered Paul, opening his eyes in astonishment; "you must be jesting."

"I am entirely in earnest; for more than a year you have been established here. If you want a proof of the correctness of my assertion, call up the porter." He ran to the head of the staircase and called out, "Come up, Mother Brigaut."

In a few moments a stout old woman came panting into the room.

"And how are you, Mother Brigaut?" said Tantaine gayly. "I have a word or two to say to you. You know that gentleman, do you not?"

"What a question? as if I did not know one of the gentlemen lodging here?"

"What is his name?"

"M. Paul."

"What, plain M. Paul, and nothing else?"

"Well, sir, it is not his fault if he did not know his father or mother."

"What does he do?"

"He is a musician; he gives lessons on the piano, and composes music."

"Does he do a good business?"

"I can't say, sir, but I should guess about two or three hundred francs a month; and he makes that do, for he is economical and quiet, and as modest as a young girl."

Tantaine's face shone all over with satisfaction.

"You must have known M. Paul for some time, as you seem so thoroughly acquainted with his habits?" said he.

"Well, I ought to, for he has been here nearly fifteen months, and all that time I have looked after his room."

"Do you know where he lived before he came here?"

"Of course I do, for I went to inquire about him in the Rue Jacob. The people there were quite cut up at his leaving, but you see this was more handy for the music publisher in the Rue Richelieu, for whom he works."

"Good, Mother Brigaut; that will do; you can leave us now."

As Paul listened to this brief conversation, he wondered if he was awake or asleep. Tantaine stood at the door and watched the woman down stairs; then he closed it carefully, and coming up to Paul, said,—

"Well, what do you think of all this?"

At first Paul was so astounded that he could hardly find words in which to express himself; but he remembered the words that Dr. Hortebise had so often dinned into his ears during the last five days,—

"Let nothing astonish you."

"I suppose," said he at last, "that you had taught the old woman her lesson beforehand."

"Merciful powers!" exclaimed Tantaine in tones of extreme disgust. "If these are all the ideas you have gained from what you have heard, our task will not be by any means an easy one."

Paul was wounded by Tantaine's contemptuous manner.

" I understand well enough, sir," answered he sulkily, "that this is merely a prologue to a romantic drama."

" You are right, my lad," cried he in a more satisfied voice; " and it is one that is quite indispensable.
The plot of the drama will be revealed to you later on,
and also the reward you will receive if you play your
part well."

" But why cannot you tell me everything now? "

Tantaine shook his head.

" Have patience, you rash boy! " said he.   " Rome
was not built in a day. Be guided by me, and follow
blindly the orders of those interested in you. This is
your first lesson; think it over seriously."

" My first lesson! What do you mean? "

" Call it a rehearsal if you like. All that the good
woman told you," continued Tantaine, " you must look
upon as true; nay, it is true, and when you believe this
thoroughly, you are quite prepared for the fray, but
until then you must remain quiescent. Remember this,
you cannot impress others unless you firmly believe
yourself. The greatest impostors of all ages have
ever been their own dupes."

At the word impostor, Paul seemed about to speak,
but a wave of Tantaine's hand silenced him.

" You must cast aside your old skin, and enter that
of another. Paul Violaine, the natural son of a woman
who kept a small drapery shop at Poitiers, Paul Violaine, the youthful lover of Rose, no longer exists. He
died of cold and hunger in a garret in the Hôtel de
Perou, as M. de Loupins will testify when necessary."

The tone in which Tantaine spoke showed his intense earnestness, and with emphatic gestures he drove
each successive idea into Paul's brain.

" You will rid yourself of your former recollections

as you do of an old coat, which you throw aside, and forget the very existence of. And not only that, but you must lose your memory, and that so entirely, that if any one in the street calls out Violaine, you will never even dream of turning round."

Paul's brain seemed to tremble beneath the crime that his companion was teaching him.

" Who am I then?" asked he.

A sardonic smile crossed Tantaine's face.

" You are just what the portress told you, Paul, and nothing more. Your first recollections are of a Foundling Hospital, and you never knew your parents. You have lived here fifteen months, and before that you resided in the Rue Jacob. The portress knows no more; but if you will come with me to the Rue Jacob, the people there can tell you more about your life when you were a lodger in the house. Perhaps, if you are careful, we may take you back to your more childish days, and even find you a father."

" But," said Paul, " I might be questioned regarding my past life: what then? M. Rigal or Mademoiselle Flavia might interrogate me at any moment?"

" I see; but do not disquiet yourself. You will be furnished with all necessary papers, so that you can account for all your life during the twenty-five years you spent in this world."

" Then I presume that the person into whose shoes I have crept was a composer and a musician like myself?"

Again Tantaine's patience gave way, and it was with an oath that he exclaimed,—

" Are you acting the part of a fool, or are you one in reality? No one has ever been here except you. Did you not hear what the old woman said? She told you that you were a musician, a self-made one, and while waiting until your talents are appreciated, you give lessons in music."

" And to whom do I *give* them? "

Tantaine took three visiting cards from a china ornament on the mantelshelf.

" Here are three pupils of yours," said he, " who can pay you one hundred francs per month for two lessons a week, and two of them will assure you that you have taught them for some time. The third, Madame Grandorge, a widow, will vow that she owes all her success, which is very great, to your lessons. You will go and give these pupils their lessons at the hours noted on their cards, and you will be received as if you had often been to the house before; and remember to be perfectly at your ease."

" I will do my best to follow your instructions."

" One last piece of information. In addition to your lessons, you are in the habit of copying for certain wealthy amateurs the fragments of old and almost obsolete operas, and on the piano lies the work that you are engaged on for the Marquis de Croisenois, a charming composition by Valserra. You see," continued Tantaine, taking Paul by the arm, and showing him round the room, " that nothing has been forgotten, and that you might have lived here for years past. You have always been a steady young man, and have saved up a little money. In this drawer you will find eight certificates of scrip of the Bank of France."

Paul would have put many more questions, but the visitor was already on the threshold, and only paused to add these words,—

" I will call here to-morrow with Dr. Hortebise." Then, with a strange smile playing on his lips, he added, as Mascarin had before, "You will be a duke yet."

The old portress was waiting for Tantaine, and as soon as she saw him coming down the stairs immersed in deep thought, out she ran toward him with as much alacrity as her corpulency would admit.

"Did I do it all right?" asked she.

"Hush!" answered he, pushing her quickly into her lodge, the door of which stood open. "Hush! are you mad or drunk, to talk like this, when you do not know who is listening?"

"I hope you were pleased with my success," continued the woman, aghast at his sudden anger.

"You did well—very well; you piled up the evidence perfectly. I shall have an excellent report to make of you to M. Mascarin."

"I am so glad; and now my husband and I are quite safe?"

The old man shook his head with an air of doubt.

"Well, I can hardly say that yet; the master's arm is long and strong; but you have numerous enemies. All the servants in the house hate you, and would be glad to see you come to grief."

"Is that really so, sir? How can that be, for both I and my husband have been very kind to all of them?"

"Yes, perhaps you have been lately, but how about the times before? You and your husband both acted very foolishly. Article 386 cannot be got now, and two women can swear that they saw you and your husband, with a bunch of keys in your hand, on the second floor."

The fat woman's face turned a sickly yellow, she clasped her hands, and whined in tones of piteous entreaty,—

"Don't speak so loud, sir, I beg of you."

"You made a terrible mistake in not coming to my master earlier, for there had been then so much talk that the matter had reached the ears of the police."

"But for all that, if M. Mascarin pleased——"

"He does please, my good woman, and is quite willing to serve you. I am sure that he will manage to break the inquiry; or if it must go on, he has several witnesses who will depose in your favor; but, you know, he gives nothing for nothing, and must have implicit obedience."

"Good, kind man that he is, my husband and I would go through fire and water for him, while my daughter, Euphenice, would do anything in the world for him."

Tantaine recoiled uneasily, for the old woman's gratitude was so demonstrative that he feared she was about to embrace him.

"All you have to do is to stick firmly to what you have said about Paul," continued he, when he found himself at a safe distance; "and if ever you breathe a word of what you have been doing, he will hand you over to the law, and then take care of Article 386."

It was evident that this portion of the Code, that had reference to the robbery of masters by servants, struck terror into the woman's soul.

"If I stood on the scaffold," said she, "I would tell the story about M. Paul exactly as I have been taught."

Her tone was so sincere, that Tantaine addressed her in a kindlier voice.

"Stick to that," said he, "and I can say to you, 'Hope.' Upon the day on which the young man's business is settled you will get a paper from me, which will prove your complete innocence, and enable you to say, ' I have been grossly maligned.' "

" May the dear young man's business be settled sharp," said she.

" It will not be long before it is so; but, remember, in the meantime you must keep an eye upon him."

" I will do so."

" And, remember, report to me whoever comes to see him, no matter who it may be."

" Not a soul can go upstairs without my seeing or hearing him."

" Well, if any one, save the master, Dr. Hortebise, or myself comes, do not lose a moment, but come and report."

" You shall know in five minutes."

" I wonder if that is all I have to say?" mused Tantaine. " Ah! I remember: note exactly the hour at which this young man comes and goes. Do not have any conversation with him; answer all questions he addresses you with a simple ' Yes,' or ' No,' and, as I said before, watch his every movement."

And Tantaine turned to go away, paying no attention to the woman's eager protestations.

" Keep a strict watch," were his last words, " and, above all, see that the lad gets into no scrape."

In Tantaine's presence Paul had endeavored to assume an air of bravado, but as soon as he was left alone he was seized with such mortal terror, that he sank in a half fainting condition into an easy-chair. He felt that he was not going to put on a disguise for a brief period, but for life, and that now, though he rose in life, wealth, title, even a wife would all have been obtained by a shameful and skilfully planned deception, and this deception he must keep up until the day of his death. He shuddered as he recalled Tantaine's words, " Paul Violaine is dead." He recalled the incidents in the life of the escaped galley-slave Coignard, who, under the name of Pontis de St. Hélène, absolutely assumed the rank of a general officer, and took command of a domain. Coignard was recognized and betrayed by an old fellow-prisoner, and this was exactly the risk that Paul knew he must run, for any of his old companions might recognize and denounce him. Had he on such an occasion sufficient presence of mind to turn laughingly to his accuser, and say, " Really, my good fellow, you are in error, for I never set eyes on you before?"

He felt that he could not do it, and had he any means of existence, he would have solved the difficulty by taking to flight. But he knew that men like Mascarin, Hortebise, and Tantaine were not easily eluded, and his heart sank within him as he remembered the various crumbs of information that each of these men had dropped before him. To agree to their sordid proposals, and to remain in the position in which he was, was certainly to incur a risk, but it was one that was a long way off, and might never eventually come to pass; while to change his mind would be as sure to bring down swift and condign punishment upon his head; and the weak young man naturally chose the more remote contingency, and with this determination the last qualms of his conscience expired.

The first night he slept badly in his new abode, for it seemed to him as if the spectre of the man whose place he was to usurp was hovering over his couch. But with the dawn of day, and especially when the hour arrived for him to go out and give his lessons, he felt his courage return to him, though rashness perhaps would be the more correct word. And with a mien of perfect confidence he repaired to the house of Mademoiselle Grandorge, the oldest of his pupils. Impelled by the same feeling of curiosity as to how Paul would comport himself, both Dr. Hortebise and Father Tantaine had been hanging about the Rue Montmartre, and taking advantage of a heavy dray that was passing, caught a good glimpse of the young man.

"Aha," chuckled Tantaine, delighted at seeing Paul look so brisk and joyous, "our young cock is in full feather; last night he was decidedly rather nervous."

"Yes," answered the doctor, "he is on the right road, and I think that we shall have no further trouble with him."

They then thought it would be as well to see Mother Brigaut, and were received by the old woman with slavish deference.

"No one has been near the dear young gentleman," said she, in reply to their questions. "Last night he came down about seven o'clock, and asked where the nearest eating-house was. I directed him to Du Val's, and he was back by eight, and by eleven I saw that he had put out his light."

"How about to-day?"

"I went up stairs at nine, and he had just finished dressing. He told me to get his breakfast ready, which I did. He ate well, and I said to myself, 'Good; the bird is getting used to its cage.'"

"And then?"

"Then he commenced singing like a very bird, the dear fellow. His voice is as sweet as his face; any woman would fall in love with him. I'm precious glad that my girl, Euphenice, is nowhere near."

" And after that he went out?" continued Tantaine. " Did he say how long he would be away?"

" Only to give his lessons. I suppose he expected that you would call."

" Very good," remarked the old man; then, addressing Dr. Hortebise, he said, " Perhaps, sir, you are going to the Registry Office?"

" Yes; I want to see Mascarin."

" He is not there; but if you want to see him on any special matter, you had better come to our young friend's apartment, and await his arrival."

" Very well, I will do so," answered the doctor.

Hortebise was much more impressed than Paul with the skill of the hand which had imparted such a look of long occupation to the rooms.

" On my word, the quiet simplicity of these rooms would induce any father to give his daughter to this young fellow."

The old man's silence surprised him, and, turning sharply round, he was struck by the gloomy look upon his features.

" What is the matter?" asked Hortebise, with some anxiety. "What is troubling you?"

Tantaine had thrown himself into a chair, and for a moment made no reply; then, springing to his feet, he gave the expiring embers a furious kick, and faced the doctor with folded arms.

" I see much trouble before us," said he at last.

The doctor's face grew as gloomy as that of his companion.

" Is it Perpignan who interferes?" asked he.

" No, Perpignan is only a fool; but he will do what I tell him."

" Then I really do not see——"

"Do not see," exclaimed Tantaine; "but luckily for us all, I am not so blind. Have you forgotten this marriage of De Croisenois? There lies the danger. All had gone so smoothly, every combination had been arranged, and every difficulty foreseen, and now——"

"Well, you had made too sure, that was all; and you were unprepared for the slightest check."

"Not so, but I had made no attempt to guard against the impossible."

"Of course, there are limits to all human intelligence, but pray explain yourself."

"This is it, then, doctor. The most adroit energy could never have put in our way such an obstacle as now threatens us. Have you in your experience of society ever come across a wealthy heiress who is indifferent to all the allurements of luxury, and is capable of disinterested love?"

The doctor smiled an expressive denial.

"But such an heiress does exist," said Tantaine, "and her name is Sabine de Mussidan. She loves— and whom do you think?—why a mere painter, who has crossed my path three times already. He is full, too, of energy and perseverance, and for these qualities I have never met his equal."

"What, a man without friends, money, or position, what can——"

A rapid gesture of Tantaine's checked his companion's speech.

"Unfortunately he is not without friends," remarked the genial Tantaine. "He has one friend at least; can you guess who it is? No less a personage than the man who was to have married Sabine, M. de Breulh-Faverlay."

At this unexpected news Hortebise remained silent and aghast.

" How on earth those two met I cannot imagine. It must have been Sabine who brought them together, but the facts remain the same. They are close friends anyhow. And these two men have in their interests the very woman that I had selected to push De Croise-nois' suit."

" Is it possible? "

" That is my present belief. At any rate, these three had a long interview last night, and doubtless came to a decision hostile to the interests of the Marquis."

" What do you mean? " asked Hortebise, his lips tightly compressed with anxiety. " Do you mean that they are aware of the manner by which De Croisenois hopes to succeed? "

" Look here? " answered Tantaine. " A general, on the eve of a battle, takes every precaution, but among his subordinates there are always fools, if not traitors. I had arranged a pretty little scene between Croisenois and Van Klopen, by which the Viscountess would be securely trapped. Unfortunately, though the rehearsal was excellent, the representation was simply idiotic. Neither of the actors took the least trouble to enter into the spirit of his part. I had arranged a scene full of delicacy and *finesse,* and they simply made a low, coarse exhibition of it and themselves. Fools! they thought it was the easiest thing in the world to de-ceive a woman; and finally the Marquis, to whom I had recommended the most perfect discretion, opened fire, and actually spoke of Sabine and his desire to press his suit. The Viscountess found, with a woman's keen perceptions, that there was something arranged between Van Klopen and her visitor, and hurried off to her cousin, M. de Breulh-Faverlay for advice and assistance."

The doctor listened to this recital, pallid and trembling.

" Who told you all this?" gasped he.

" No one; I discovered it; and it was easy to do so. When we have a result, it is easy to trace it back to the cause. Yes, this is what took place."

" Why don't you say at once that the whole scheme is knocked on the head?" asked the doctor.

" Because I do not think that it is; I know that we have sustained a very severe check; but when you are playing *écarté* and your adversary has made five points to your one, you do not necessarily throw down the cards and give up the game? Not a bit; you hold on and strive to better your luck."

The worthy Dr. Hortebise did not know whether the most to admire the perseverance or deplore the obstinacy of the old man, and exclaimed,—

" Why, this is utter madness; it is like plunging headlong into a deep pit, which you can easily see in your path."

Tantaine gave a long, low whistle.

" My friend," said he, " what in your opinion would be the best course to pursue?"

" I should say, without a moment's hesitation, turn up the whole scheme, and look out for another one, which, if less lucrative, would not be so full of danger. You had hoped to win the game, and with good reason too. Now throw aside all feelings of wounded vanity, and accept your defeat. After all, it does not matter to us who Mademoiselle de Mussidan marries. The great enterprise fortunately does not lie in this alliance. We have still the idea of the Company to which all old people must subscribe remaining to us, and we can work it up at once."

He stopped short, abashed by the look on Tantaine's face.

"It strikes me," resumed the doctor, a little mortified, "that my proposal is not utterly ridiculous, and certainly deserves some consideration."

"Perhaps so; but is it a practical one?"

"I see no reason why it should not be."

"Indeed, then, you look at the thing in a very different manner to myself. We are too far advanced, my dear doctor, to be our own masters. We must go on, and have no option to do otherwise. To beat a retreat would simply be to invite our enemies to fall upon our disorganized battalions. We must give battle; and as the first to strike has always the best chance of victory, we must strive to take the initiative."

"The idea is good, but these are mere words."

"Was the secret that we confided to De Croisenois only words?"

This thrust went home.

"Do you mean that you think he would betray us?" said he.

"Why should he not if it were to his interests to do so? Reflect, Croisenois is almost at the end of his tether. We have dangled the line of a princely fortune before his eyes. Do you think he would do nothing if we were to say, 'Excuse us, but we made a mistake; poor as you are, so you must remain, for we do not intend to help you?'"

"But is it necessary to say that at all?"

"Well, at any rate, whatever we choose to say, what limit do you think he will place upon his extortions

now that he holds our secret? We have taught him
his music, and he will make us do our part in the
chorus, and can blackmail us as well as we can others."

"We played a foolish game," answered Dr. Hortebise moodily.

"No; we had to confide in some one. Besides, the
two affairs, that of Madame de Mussidan and the
Duke de Champdoce, ran so well together. They were
the simultaneous emanations of my brain. I worked
them up together, and together they must stand or fall."

"Then you are determined to go on?"

"Yes; more determined than ever."

The doctor had been playing with his locket for some
time, and the contact of the cold metal seemed to have
affected his nerves; for it was in a trembling voice that
he replied,—

"I vowed long ago that we should sink or swim
together." He paused, and then, with a melancholy
smile upon his face, continued,—"I have no intention
of breaking my oath, you see; but I repeat, that your
road seems to be a most perilous one, and I will add
that I consider you headstrong and self-opinionated;
but for all that, I will follow you, even though the
path you have chosen leads to the grave. I have at
this moment a something between my fingers that will
save me from shame and disgrace—a little pill to be
swallowed, a gasp, a little dizziness, and all is over."

Tantaine did not seem to care for the doctor's explanation.

"There, that will do," said he. "If things come to
the worst, you can use the contents of your locket as
much as you like, but in the meantime leave it alone,
and do not keep jingling it in that distracting manner.
For people of our stamp a danger well known is a

comparatively slight peril, for threats furnish us with means of defence. Woe, I say, woe to the man who crosses my path, for I will hold my hand from nothing!" He stopped for a little, opened every door, and assured himself that there were no eavesdroppers, and then, in a low whisper, he said to Hortebise, " Do you not see that there is but one obstacle to our success, and that is André? Remove him, and the whole of our machinery will work as smoothly as ever."

Hortebise winced, as if suffering from a sudden pain.

" Do you mean——? " asked he.

But Tantaine interrupted him with a low laugh, terrible to listen to.

" And why not?" said he. " Is it not better to kill than to be killed? "

Hortebise trembled from head to foot. He had no objection to extorting money by the basest threats, but he drew the line at murder.

" And suppose we were found out?" muttered he.

" Nonsense! How could we be discovered? Justice always looks for a motive; how, then, could they bring it home to us? They could only find out that a young lady adored by De Breulh had thrown him over in order to marry André."

" Horrible! " murmured the doctor, much shocked.

" I daresay that it is horrible, and I have no wish to proceed to extremities. I only wish to speak of it as a remote possibility, and one that we may be compelled to adopt. I hate violence just as much as you do, and trust that it may not be necessary."

Just then the door opened, and Paul entered, a letter in his hand. He seemed in excellent spirits, and shook hands with both his visitors.

Tantaine smiled sarcastically as he contrasted Paul's

high spirits with the state of depression in which he had left him not many hours ago.

"Things are evidently going well with you," remarked the doctor, forcing a smile.

"Yes; I cannot find any reason for complaint."

"Have you given your lesson?"

"Yes; what a delightful woman Madame Grandorge is! she has treated me so kindly."

"That is a good reason for your being so happy," remarked the doctor, with a tinge of irony in his voice.

"Ah, that is not the only reason," returned Paul.

"Shall I be indiscreet if I ask the real cause, then?"

"I am not quite sure whether I ought to speak on this matter," said he fatuously.

"What! a love adventure already?" laughed the doctor.

The vanity of Paul's nature beamed out in a smile.

"Keep your secret, my boy," said Tantaine, in louder accents.

This, of course, was enough to loosen Paul's tongue.

"Do you think, sir," said he, "that I would keep anything from you?" He opened the letter he held in his hand, continuing: "The portress handed this to me as I came in; she said it was left by a bank messenger. Can you guess where it came from? Let me tell you—it is from Mademoiselle Flavia Rigal, and leaves no room to doubt of her sentiments toward me."

"Is that a fact?"

"It is so; and whenever I choose, Mademoiselle Flavia will be only too ready to become Madame Paul."

For an instant a bright flush crimsoned old Tantaine's wrinkled face, but it faded away almost as soon as it appeared.

" Then you feel happy?" asked he, with a slight quiver in his voice.

Paul threw back his coat, and, placing his fingers in the armholes of his waistcoat, remarked carelessly,—

" Yes, of course, I am happy, as you may suppose; but the news is not particularly startling to me. On my third visit to M. Rigal's, the girl let me know that I need not sigh in vain."

Tantaine covered his face with his hands as Paul passed his fingers through his hair, and, striking what he considered an imposing attitude, read as follows :—

" MY DEAR PAUL,—

" I was very naughty, and I repent of it. I could not sleep all night, for I was haunted by the look of sorrow I saw in your face when you took leave of me. Paul, I did it to try you. Can you forgive me? You might, for I suffered much more than you could have done. Some one who loves me—perhaps more than you do—has told me that when a girl shows all the depths of her heart to a man she runs the risk of his despising her. Can this be true? I hope not, Paul, for never—no, never—can I conceal my feelings; and the proof of my faith in you is that I am going now to tell you all. I am sure that if your good friend and mine, Dr. Hortebise, came to my father with a certain request from you, it would not be rejected.

"Your own
"FLAVIA."

" Did not this letter go straight to your heart?" asked Tantaine.

" Of course it did. Why, she will have a million for her wedding portion ! "

On hearing these words, Tantaine started up with so threatening an aspect that Paul recoiled a step, but a warning look from the doctor restrained the old man's indignation.

" He is a perfect sham! " muttered he; " even his vices are mere pretence."

" He is our pupil, and is what we have made him," whispered Tantaine.

Meanwhile Tantaine had gone up to Paul, and, placing his hand caressingly on his shoulder, said,—

" My boy, you will never know how much you owe to Mademoiselle Flavia."

Paul could not understand the meaning of this scene. These men had done their best to pervert his morals, and to deaden the voice of his conscience, and now that he had hoped to earn their praise by an affectation of cynicism they were displeased with him. Before, however, he could ask a question, Tantaine had completely recovered his self-command.

" My dear boy," said he, " I am quite satisfied with you. I came here to-day expecting to find you still undecided, and I am pleased with the change."

" But, sir——" said Paul.

" On the contrary, you are firm and strong."

" Yes, he has got on so well," said the doctor, " that we should now treat him as one of ourselves, and confide more in him. To-night, my young friend, M. Mascarin will get from Caroline Schimmel the solution of the riddle that has for so long perplexed us. Be at the office to-morrow at ten o'clock, and you shall be told everything."

Paul would have asked more questions, but Tantaine cut him short with a brief good-morning, and went off hurriedly, taking the doctor with him, and seemingly wishing to avoid a hazardous and unpleasant explanation.

" Let us get out of this," whispered he. " In another moment I should have knocked the conceited ass down. Oh, my Flavia! my poor Flavia! your weakness of to-day will yet cost you very dear!"

Paul remained rooted to the ground, with an expression of surprise and confusion upon every line of his face. All his pride and vanity had gone. "I wonder," muttered he, "what these disagreeable persons are saying about me? Perhaps laughing at my inexperience and ridiculing my aspirations." The idea made him grind his teeth with rage; but he was mistaken, for neither Tantaine nor the doctor mentioned his name after they had left his apartment. As they walked up the Rue Montmartre, all their ideas were turning upon how it would be easiest to checkmate André.

"I have not yet got sufficient information to act on," remarked Tantaine meditatively. "My present plan is to remain perfectly quiescent, and I have told Croisenois not to make a move of any kind. I have, however, set a watch upon all three—André, the Countess, and De Breulh, and not one can take a step without my hearing of it. I have an eye and ear watching and listening when they think themselves in perfect privacy. Very soon I shall fathom their plans, and then——, but in the meantime have faith in me, and do not let the matter worry you."

On the boulevard Tantaine took leave of his friend.

"I shall very likely not see you to-night, for I have an appointment at the Grand Turk with that precious young rascal, Toto Chupin. I *must* find Caroline, for I am sure that with her lies the Champdoce secret. She is very cunning, but has a weakness for drink, and, with Satan's help, I hope to find out the special liquor which will make her open her lips freely."

CHAPTER XXVI.

AT THE GRAND TURK.

TANTAINE took a cab, and, promising the cabman a handsome gratuity if he would drive fast, stopped at the spot where the Rue Blanche intersects the Rue de Douai, and told the coachman to wait for him, and entered the house where the younger Gandelu had installed the fair Madame de Chantemille. It was some time before his ring at the door was answered, but at last the door was opened by a stout, red-faced girl, with an untidy cap. Upon seeing Tantaine, she uttered an exclamation of delight, for it was the cook that had been placed in Zora's employment by M. Mascarin's agency.

"Ah, Daddy Tantaine," said she, "you are as welcome as the sun in winter."

"Hush, hush," returned the old man, gazing cautiously round him.

"Don't be frightened," returned the girl. "Madame has gone to a place from whence there is no return ticket, at least, for some time. You know the greater the value of an article the closer we keep it under lock and key."

Tantaine gathered from this that Rose had been arrested, and his astonishment appeared to be unmeasured.

"Surely you don't mean that she has gone to quod?" said he.

"It is as I tell you," answered she; "but come in, and have a glass of wine, while you hear all about it."

She led the old man into the dining-room, round the table in which half a dozen guests were seated, just concluding a late breakfast. Tantaine at once recognized four of the several guests as servants whom he knew from their having applied for situations at the office, and there were two men of a very unprepossessing exterior.

"We are having a regular spree to-day," observed the cook, handing a bottle to Tantaine; "but yesterday there was not much of a jollification here, for just as I was setting about getting the dinner two fellows came in and asked for my mistress, and as soon as they saw her they clapped their hands on her and said that she must come to the stone jug. When madame heard this she shrieked so loud as to have been heard in the next street. She would not go a foot with them, clung to the furniture and banisters, so they just took her up by the head and feet, and carried her down to a cab that was standing at the door. I seem to bring ill luck wherever I go, for this is the fourth mistress I have seen taken off in this way; but come, you are taking nothing at all."

But Tantaine had had enough, and making an excuse, retired from a debauch which he saw would continue as long as the wine held out.

"All is going well," muttered he, as he climbed into the cab; "and now for the next one."

He drove straight to the house that the elder Gandelu was building in the Champs Elysées, and putting his head out of the window, he accosted a light, active young fellow who was warning the foot passengers not to pass under the scaffolding.

"Anything new, La Cordille?" enquired the old man.

" No, nothing; but tell the master I am keeping a good watch."

From there Tantaine visited a footman in De Breulh's employment, and a woman in the service of Madame de Bois Arden. Then, paying his fare, he started on foot for Father Canon's wine shop, in the Rue St. Honoré, where he met Florestan, who was as saucy and supercilious to Tantaine as he was obsequious to Mascarin. But although he paid for Florestan's dinner, all that he could extort from him was, that Sabine was terribly depressed. It was fully eight o'clock before Tantaine had got rid of Florestan, and hailing another cab, he ordered the driver to take him to the Grand Turk, in the Rue des Poissonniers.

The magnificent sign of the Grand Turk dances in the breeze, and invites such youths as Toto Chupin and his companions. The whole aspect of the exterior seemed to invite the passers-by to step in and try the good cheer provided within,—a good *table d'hôte* at six p.m., coffee, tea, liquors, and a grand ball to complete the work of digestion. A long corridor leads to this earthly Eden, and the two doors at the end of it open, the one into the dining, and the other into the ball-room. A motley crew collected there for the evening meal, and on Sundays it is next to impossible to procure a seat. But the dining-room is the Grand Turk's brightest attraction, for as soon as the dessert is over the head waiter makes a sign, and dishes and tablecloths are cleared away in a moment. The dining-room becomes a *café,* and the click of dominoes gives way to rattle of forks, while beer flows freely. This, however, is nothing, for, at a second signal, huge folding doors are thrown open, and the strains of an orchestra ring out as an invitation to the ball, to which all diners are allowed free entrance. Nothing is danced but round dances, polkas, mazurkas, and waltzes.

The German element was very strong at the Grand Turk, and if a gentleman wished to make himself agreeable to his fair partners, it was necessary for him, at any rate, to be well up in the Alsatian dialect. The master of the ceremonies had already called upon the votaries of Terpsichore to take their places for the waltz as Daddy Tantaine entered the hall. The scene was a most animated one, and the air heavy with the scent of beer and tobacco, and would have asphyxiated any one not used to venture into such places.

It was the first time that he had ever visited the Grand Turk, and yet any one observing would have sworn that he was one of the regular frequenters as he marched idly through the rooms, making constant pauses at the bar. But glance around him as he might, he could see neither Toto Chupin nor Caroline Schimmel.

" Have I come here for nothing," muttered he, " or is the hour too early ? "

It was hard to waste time thus, but at last he sat down and ordered some beer. His eyes wandered to a large picture on the wall, representing a fat, eastern-looking man, with a white turban and loose, blue garments, seated in a crimson chair, with his feet resting upon a yellow carpet. One hand was caressing his protuberant paunch, while the other was extended toward a glass of beer. Evidently this is the Grand Turk. And finally by an odalisque, who fills his goblet with the foaming infusion of malt and hops. This odalisque is very fair and stout, and some fair Alsatian damsel has evidently sat as the model. As Tantaine was gazing upon this wondrous work of art he heard a squeaking voice just behind him.

"That is certainly that young rogue Chupin," muttered he.

He turned sharply round, and two tables off, in a dark corner, he discovered the young gentleman that he had been looking for. As he gazed on the lad, he was not surprised that he had not recognized him at first, for Toto had been strangely transmogrified, and in no degree resembled the boy who had shivered in a tattered blouse in the archway near the Servants' Registry Office. He was now gorgeous to behold. From the moment that he had got his hundred francs he had chalked out a new line of life for himself, and was busy pursuing it. He had found that he could make all his friends merry, and he had succeeded. He had made a selection from the most astounding wares that the Parisian tailor keeps on hand. He had sneered at young Gaston de Gandelu, and called him an ape; but he had aped the ape. He wore a very short, light coat, a waistcoat that was hideous from its cut and brilliancy, and trousers strapped tightly under his feet. His collar was so tall and stiff, that he had the greatest difficulty in turning his head. He had gone to a barber, and his lank hair had been artistically curled. The table in front of him was covered with glasses and bottles. Two shocking looking-scamps of the true barrier bully type, with loose cravats and shiny-peaked caps, were seated by him, and were evidently his guests. Tantaine's first impulse was to catch the debauched youth by the ear, but he hesitated for an instant and reflection conquered the impulse. With the utmost caution so that he might not attract Toto's attention, he crept down to him, concealing himself as best he could behind one of the pillars that supported the gallery, and by this manœuvre found himself so close to the lad that he could catch every word he said.

Chupin was talking volubly.

" Don't you call me a swell, nor yet say that I brag," said he. " I shall always make this kind of appearance, for to work in the manner I propose, a man must pay some attention to dress."

At this his companions roared with laughter.

" All right," returned Toto. " I'm precious sharp, though you may not think so, and shall go in for all kinds of elegant accomplishments, and come out a regular masher."

" Wonders will never cease," answered one of the men. " When you go on your trip for action in the Bois among the toffs, will you take me with you? "

" Any one can go to the Bois who has money: and just tell me who are those who make money. Why, those who have plenty of cheek and a good sound business. Well, I have learned my business from some real downy cards, who made it pay well. Why should I not do the same? "

With a sickening feeling of terror, Tantaine saw that the lad was half drunk. What could he be going to say? and how much did he know? Toto's guests evidently saw that he had taken too much; but as he seemed ready to let them into a secret, they paid great attention, and exchanged a look of intelligence. The young rogue's new clothes and his liberality all proved that he had found a means of gaining money; the only question was what the plan could be. To induce him to talk they passed the bottle rapidly and flattered him up. The younger man of the two shook his head with a smile.

"I don't believe you have any business at all," said he.

CHUPIN WAS TALKING VOLUBLY. "DON'T YOU CALL ME A SWELL. . . .
I SHALL ALWAYS MAKE THIS KIND OF APPEARANCE"

"Nor have I, if by business you mean some low handicraft. It is brain work I mean, my boy; and that's what I do."

"I don't doubt that a bit," answered the elder guest coaxingly.

"Come on! Tell us what it is," broke in the other. "You can't expect us to take your word."

"It is as easy as lying," replied Toto. "Listen a bit, and you shall have the whole bag of tricks. Suppose I saw Polyte steal a couple of pairs of boots from a trotter-case seller's stall——"

Polyte interrupted the narrator, protesting so strongly that he would not commit such an act, that Tantaine perceived at once that some such trifling act of larceny weighed heavily on his conscience.

"You needn't kick up such a row," returned Toto. "I am only just putting it as a thing that might happen. We will say you had done the trick, and that I had twigged you. Do you know what I should do? Well, I would hunt up Polyte, and say quietly, 'Halves, old man, or I will split.'"

"And I should give you a crack in the jaw," returned Polyte angrily.

Forgetting his fine dress, Toto playfully put his thumb to his nose and extended his fingers.

"You would not be such an ass," said he. "You would say to yourself, 'If I punch this chap, he will kick up no end of a row, and I shall be taken up, and perhaps sent to the mill.' No; you would be beastly civil, and would end by doing just as I wished."

"And this is what you call your business, is it?"

"Isn't it a good one—the mugs stand the racket, and the downy cards profit by it?"

"But there is no novelty in this; it is only blackmail after all."

"I never said it wasn't; but it is blackmailing perfected into a system."

As Toto made this reply he hammered on the table, calling for more drink.

"But," remarked Polyte, with an air of disappointment, "you don't get chances every day, and the business is often a precious poor one. You can't always be seeing chaps prigging boots."

"Pooh! pooh!" answered Toto, "if you want to make money in this business, you must keep your eyes about you. Our customers don't come to you, but there is nothing to prevent you going to them. You can hunt until you find them."

"And where are you to hunt, if you please?"

"Ah, that's tellings."

A long silence ensued, during which Tantaine was half tempted to come forward. By doing so he would assuredly nip all explanations in the bud; but, on the other hand, he wanted to hear all the young rascal had to say. He therefore only moved a little nearer, and listened more intently.

Forgetting his curls, Toto was abstractedly passing his fingers through his hair, and reflecting with all the wisdom of a muddled brain. Finally, he came to the conclusion that he might speak, and, leaning forward, he whispered,—

"You won't peach if I tell you the dodge?"

His companions assured him that he might have every confidence in them.

"Very well; I make my money in the Champs Elysées, and sometimes get a harvest twice a day."

"But there are no shoemakers' shops there."

"You are a fool," answered Toto contemptuously. "Do you think I blackmail thieves? That wouldn't be half good enough. Honest people, or at least people who call themselves honest, are my game. These are the ones who can be made to pay up."

Tantaine shuddered; he remembered that Mascarin had made use of the same expression, and at once surmised that Toto must have had an occasional ear to the keyhole.

"But," objected Polyte, "honest people have no occasion to pay up."

Toto struck his glass so heavily on the table that it flew to shivers.

"Will you let me speak?" said he.

"Go on, go on, my boy," returned his friend.

"Well, when I'm hard up for cash, I go into the Champs Elysées, and take a seat on one of the benches. From there I keep an eye on the cabs, and see who get out of them. If a respectable woman does so, I am sure of my bird."

"Do you think you know a respectable woman when you see her?"

"I should just think that I did. Well, when a respectable woman gets out of a cab where she ought not to have been, she looks about her on all sides, first to the right and then to the left, settles her veil, and, as soon as she is sure that no one is watching her, sets off as if old Nick was behind her."

"Well, what do you do then?"

"Why, I take the number of the cab, and follow the lady home. Then I wait until she has had time to get to her own rooms, and go to the porter and say, 'Will you give me the name of the lady who has just come in?'"

" And do you think the porter is fool enough to do so ? "

" Not a bit; I always take the precaution of having a delicate little purse in my pocket; and when the man says, as he always does, ' I don't know,' I pull out the purse and say, ' I am sorry for that, for she dropped this as she came in, and I wanted to return it to her.' The porter at once becomes awfully civil; she gives the name and number, and up I go. The first time I content myself with finding out if she is married or single. If she is single, it is no go; but if the reverse, I go on with the job."

" Why, what do you do next? "

" Next morning I go there, and hang about until I see the husband go out. Then I go upstairs, and ask for the wife. It is ticklish work then, my lads; but I say, ' Yesterday, madame, I was unlucky enough to leave my pocketbook in cab number so-and-so. Now, as I saw you hail the vehicle immediately after I had left it, I have come to ask you if you saw my pocketbook.' The lady flies into a rage, denies all knowledge of the book, and threatens to have me turned out. Then, with the utmost politeness, I say, ' I see, madame, that there is nothing to be done but to communicate the matter to your husband.' Then she gets alarmed, and —she pays."

" And you don't see any more of her? "

" Not that day; but when the funds are low, I call and say, ' It is I again, madame; I am the poor young man who lost his money in such and such a cab on a certain day of the month.' And so the game goes on. A dozen such clients give a fellow a very fair income. Now, perhaps, you understand why I am always so well dressed, and always have money in my pocket.

When I was shabbily attired, they offered me a five-franc piece, but now they come down with a flimsy."

The young wretch spoke the truth; for to many women, who in a mad moment of passion may have forgotten themselves, and been tracked to their homes by some prowling blackmailer, life has been an endless journey of agony. Every knock at the door makes them start, and every footfall on the staircase causes a tremor as they think that the villain has come to betray their guilty secret.

" That is all talk," said Polyte; " such things are never done."

" They *are* done," returned Toto sulkily.

" Have you ever tried the dodge yourself, then? " sneered Polyte.

At another time Chupin would have lied, but the fumes of the drink he had taken, added to his natural self-conceit, had deprived him of all judgment.

" Well," muttered he, " if I have not done it myself exactly, I have seen others practise it often enough—on a much larger scale, it is true; but one can always do things in a more miniature fashion with perhaps a better chance of success."

" What! *you* have seen this done? "

" Of course I have."

" And had you a share in the swag? "

" To a certain extent. I have followed the cabs times without number, and have watched the goings on of these fine ladies and gentlemen; only I was working for others, like the dog that catches the hare, and never has a bit of it to eat. No, all I got was dry bread, with a kick or a cuff for dessert. I sha'n't put up with it any longer, and have made up my mind to open on my own account."

"And who has been employing you?"

A flash of sense passed through Chupin's muddled brain. He had never wished to injure Mascarin, but merely to increase his own importance by extolling the greatness of his employer.

"I worked for people who have no equal in Paris," said he proudly. "They don't mince matters either, I can tell you; and they have more money than you could count in six months. There is not a thing they cannot do if they desire; and if I were to tell you——"

He stopped short, his mouth wide open, and his eyes dilated with terror, for before him stood old Daddy Tantaine.

Tantaine's face had a most benign expression upon it, and in a most paternal voice he exclaimed,—

"And so here you are at last, my lad; and, bless me, how fine! why, you look like a real swell."

But Toto was terribly disconcerted. The mere appearance of Tantaine dissipated the fumes of liquor which had hitherto clouded the boy's brain, and by degrees he recollected all that he had said, and, becoming conscious of his folly, had a vague idea of some swift-coming retribution. Toto was a sharp lad, and he was by no means deceived by Tantaine's outward semblance of friendliness, and he almost felt as if his life depended on the promptness of his decision. The question was, had the old man heard anything of the preceding conversation?

"If the old rogue has been listening," said he to himself, "I am in a hole, and no mistake."

It was, therefore, with a simulated air of ease that he answered,—

"I was waiting for you, sir, and it was out of respect to you that I put on my very best togs."

"That was very nice of you; I ought to thank you very much. And now, will you——"

Toto's courage was coming back to him rapidly.

"Will you take a glass of beer, or a liquor of brandy, sir?" said he.

But Daddy Tantaine excused himself on the plea that he had just been drinking.

"That is all the more reason for being thirsty," remarked Toto. "My friends and I have drunk the contents of all these bottles since dinner."

Tantaine raised his shabby hat at this semi-introduction, and the two roughs bowed uncouthly. They were not entirely satisfied with the appearance of the new-comer, and thought that this would be a good moment for taking leave of their host. The waltz had just concluded, and the master of the ceremonies was repeating his eternal refrain of—

"Take your places, ladies and gentlemen;" and taking advantage of the noise, Toto's friends shook hands with their host and adroitly mixed with the crowd.

"Good fellows! jolly fellows;" muttered Toto, striving to catch a last glimpse of them.

Tantaine gave a low, derisive whistle. "My lad," said he, "you keep execrable company, and one day you will repent it."

"I can look after myself, sir."

"Do as you like, my lad; it is no business of mine. But, take my word for it, you will come to grief some day. I have told you that often enough."

"If the old rascal suspected anything," thought Toto, "he would not talk in this way."

Wretched Toto! he did not know that when his spirits were rising the danger was terribly near, for Tantaine was just then saying to himself,—

" Ah! this lad is much too clever—too clever by half.
If I were going on with the business, and could make
it worth his while, how useful he would be to me! but
just now it would be most imprudent to allow him to
wander about and jabber when he gets drunk."

Meanwhile Toto had called a waiter, and, flinging a
ten-franc piece on the table, said haughtily: "Take
your bill out of that." But Tantaine pushed the money
back toward the lad, and, drawing another ten-franc
piece from his pocket, gave it to the waiter.

This unexpected act of generosity put the lad in the
best possible humor. " All the better for me," exclaimed he; "and now let us hunt up Caroline Schimmel."

" Is she here? I could not find her."

" Because you did not know where to look for her.
She is at cards in the coffee-room. Come along, sir."

But Tantaine laid his hand upon the boy's arm.

" One moment," said he. " Did you tell the woman
just what I ordered you to say?"

" I did not omit a single word."

" Tell me what you said, then."

" For five days," began the lad solemnly, " your Toto
has been your Caroline's shadow. We have played
cards until all sorts of hours, and I took care that she
should always win. I confided to her that I had a
jolly old uncle,—a man not without means, a widower,
and crazy to be married again,—who had seen her and
had fallen in love with her."

" Good! my lad, good! and what did she say?"

" Why, she grinned like half a dozen cats; only she
is a bit artful, and I saw at once that she thought I
was after her cash, but the mention of my uncle's property soon chucked her off that idea."

" Did you give my name? "

" Yes, at the end, I did. I knew that she had seen you, and so I kept it back as long as I could; but as soon as I mentioned it she looked rather confused, and cried out: 'I know him quite well.' So you see, sir, all you have now is to settle a day for the marriage. Come on; she expects you."

Toto was right. The late domestic of the Duke de Champdoce was playing cards; but as soon as she caught sight of Toto and his pretended uncle, in spite of her holding an excellent hand, she threw up her cards, and received him with the utmost civility. Toto looked on with delight. Never had he seen the old rascal (as he inwardly called him in his heart) so polite, agreeable, and talkative. It was easy to see that Caroline Schimmel was yielding to his fascinations, for she had never had such extravagant compliments whispered in her ear in so persuasive a tone. But Tantaine did not confine his attentions to wine only: he first ordered a bowl of punch, and then followed that up by a bottle of the best brandy. All the old man's lost youth seemed to have come back to him: he sang, he drank, and he danced. Toto watched them in utter surprise, as the old man whirled the clumsy figure of the woman round the room.

And he was rewarded for this tremendous exertion, for by ten o'clock she had consented, and Caroline left the Grand Turk on the arm of her future husband, having promised to take supper with him.

Next morning, when the scavengers came down from Montmartre to ply their matutinal avocations, they found the body of a woman lying on her face on the pavement. They raised her up and carried her to an hospital. She was not dead, as had been at first

supposed; and when the unhappy creature came to her
senses, she said that her name was Caroline Schimmel,
that she had been to supper at a restaurant with her betrothed, and that from that instant she remembered
nothing. At her request, the surgeon had her conveyed
to her home in the Rue Mercadet.

CHAPTER XXVII.

THE LAST LINK.

FOR some days M. Mascarin had not shown himself at
the office, and Beaumarchef was terribly harassed with
inquiries regarding his absent master. Mascarin, on
the day after the evening on which Tantaine had met
Caroline Schimmel at the Grand Turk, was carefully
shut up in his private room; his face and eyes were
red and inflamed, and he occasionally sipped a glass of
some cooling beverage which stood before him, and his
compressed lips and corrugated brow showed how
deeply he was meditating. Suddenly the door opened,
and Dr. Hortebise entered the room.

"Well!" exclaimed Mascarin, "have you seen the
Mussidans, as I told you to do."

"Certainly," answered Hortebise briskly; "I saw
the Countess, and told her how pressing the holders of
her letters were growing, and urged on her the necessity for immediate action. She told me that both she
and her husband had determined to yield, and that
Sabine, though evidently broken-hearted, would not oppose the marriage."

"Good," said Mascarin; "and now, if Croisenois

only follows out the orders that I have given him, the marriage will take place without the knowledge of either De Breulh or André. Then we need fear them no longer. The prospectus of the new Company is ready, and can be issued almost immediately; but we meet to-day to discuss not that matter, but the more important one of the heir to the Champdoce title."

A timid knock at the door announced the arrival of Paul who came in hesitatingly, as if doubtful what sort of a reception he might receive; but Mascarin gave him the warmest possible welcome.

" Permit me," said he, " to offer you my congratulations on having won the affections of so estimable and wealthy a young lady as Mademoiselle Flavia. I may tell you that a friend of mine has informed me of the very flattering terms in which her father, M. Rigal, spoke of you, and I can assure you that if our mutual friend Dr. Hortebise were to go to the banker with an offer of marriage on your part, you have no cause to dread a refusal."

Paul blushed with pleasure, and as he was stammering out a few words, the door opened for the third time, and Catenac made his appearance. To cover the lateness of his arrival, he had clothed his face in smiles, and advanced with outstretched hands toward his confederates; but Mascarin's look and manner were so menacing, that he recoiled a few steps and gazed on him with an expression of the utmost wonder and surprise.

" What is the meaning of this reception? " asked he.

" Can you not guess? " returned Mascarin, his manner growing more and more threatening. " I have sounded the lowest depths of your infamy. I was sure the other day that you meant to turn traitor, but you swore to the contrary, and you——"

" On my honor——"

" It is useless.   One word from Perpignan set us on the right track.   Were you or were you not ignorant that the Duke de Champdoce had a certain way of recognizing his son, and that was by a certain ineffaceable scar? "

" It had escaped my memory——"

The words faded from his lips, for even his great self-command failed him under Mascarin's disdainful glance.

" Let me tell you what I think of you," said the latter.   " I knew that you were a coward and a traitor. Even convicts keep faith with each other, and I had not thought you so utterly infamous."

" Then why have you forced me to act contrary to my wishes? "

This reply exasperated Mascarin so much that he grasped Catenac by the throat, and shook him violently.

" I made use of you, you viper," said he, " because I had placed you in such a position that you could not harm us.   And now you will serve me because I will show you that I can take everything from you—name, money, liberty, and *life*.   All depends upon our success.   If we fail, you fall into an abyss of the depth and horrors of which you can have no conception.   I knew with whom I had to deal, and took my measures accordingly.   The most crushing proofs of your crime are in the hands of a person who has precise orders how to act.   When I give the signal, he moves; and when he moves, you are utterly lost."

There was something so threatening in the silence

that followed this speech that Paul grew faint with apprehension.

"And," went on Mascarin, "it would be an evil
day for you if anything were to happen to Hortebise,
Paul, or myself; for if one of us were to die suddenly,
your fate would be sealed. You cannot say that you
have not been warned."

Catenac stood with his head bent upon his breast,
rooted to the ground with terror. He felt that he was
bound, and gagged, and fettered hand and foot. Mascarin swallowed some of the cooling draught that stood
before him, and tranquilly commenced,—

"Suppose, Catenac, that I were to tell you that I
know far more of the Champdoce matter than you do;
for, after all, your knowledge is only derived from
what the Duke has told you. You think that you have
hit upon the truth; you were never more mistaken in
your life. I, perhaps you are unaware, have been many
years engaged in this matter. Perhaps you would like
to know how I first thought of the affair. Do you remember that solicitor who had an office near the Law
Courts, and did a great deal of blackmail business?
If you do, you must remember that he got two years'
hard labor."

"Yes, I remember the man," returned Catenac in a
humble voice.

"He used," continued Mascarin, "to buy up waste
paper, and search through the piles he had collected for
any matters that might be concealed in the hetero-
geneous mass. And many things he must have found.
In what sensational case have not letters played a
prominent part? What man is there who has not at
one time or other regretted that he has had pen and
ink ready to his hand? If men were wise, they would

use those patent inks, which fade from the paper in a
few days. I followed his example, and, among other
strange discoveries, I made this one."

He took from his desk a piece of paper—ragged,
dirty, and creased—and, handing it to Hortebise and
Paul, said,—

" Read! "

They did so, and read the following strange word:
"TNAFNEERTONIOMZEDNEREITIPZEYAETN
ECONNISIUSEJECARG;" while underneath was
written in another hand the word, " Never."

" It was evident that I had in my hands a letter
written in cipher, and I concluded that the paper contained some important secret."

Catenac listened to this narrative with an air of contempt, for he was one of those foolish men who never
know when it is best for them to yield.

" I daresay you are right," answered he with a
slight sneer.

" Thank you," returned Mascarin coolly. " At any
rate, I was deeply interested in solving this riddle, the
more as I belonged to an association which owes its
being and position to its skill in penetrating the secrets
of others. I shut myself up in my room, and vowed
that I would not leave it until I had worked out the
cipher."

Paul, Hortebise, and Catenac examined the letter
curiously, but could make nothing of it.

" I can't make head or tail of it," said the doctor impatiently.

Mascarin smiled as he took back the paper, and
remarked,—

" At first I was as much puzzled as you were, and
more than once was tempted to throw the document

into the waste-paper basket, but a secret feeling that it
opened a way to all our fortunes restrained me. Of
course there was the chance that I might only decipher
some foolish jest, and no secret at all, but still I went
on. If the commencement of the word was written in
a woman's hand, the last word had evidently been
added by a man. But why should a cryptogram have
been used? Was it because the demand was of so dangerous and compromising a character that it was impossible to put it in plain language? If so, why was
the last word not in cipher? Simply because the mere
rejection of what was certainly a demand would in no
manner compromise the writer. You will ask how it
happens that demand and rejection are both on the
same sheet of paper. I thought this over, and came to
the conclusion that the letter had once been meant for
the post, but had been sent by hand. Perhaps the
writers may have occupied rooms in the same house.
The woman, in the anguish of her soul, may have sent
the letter by a servant to her husband, and he, transported by rage, may have hurriedly scrawled this word
across it, and returned it again: 'Take this to your
mistress.' Having settled this point, I attacked the
cipher, and, after fourteen hours' hard work, hit upon
its meaning.

"Accidentally I held the piece of paper between myself and the light, with the side on which the writing
was turned from me, and read it at once. It was a
cryptogram of the simplest kind, as the letters forming
the words were simply reversed. I divided the letters
into words, and made out this sentence: '*Grace, je suis
innocente. Ayez pitiè; rendez-moi notre enfant*
(Mercy, I am innocent. Give me back our son).'"

Hortebise snatched up the paper and glanced at it.

" You are right," said he; " it is the art of cipher writing in its infancy."

" I had succeeded in reading it,—but how to make use of it! The mass of waste paper in which I found it had been purchased from a servant in a country house near Vendôme. A friend of mine, who was accustomed to drawing plans and maps, came to my aid, and discovered some faint signs of a crest in one corner of the paper. With the aid of a powerful magnifying glass, I discovered it to be the cognizance of the ducal house of Champdoce. The light that guided me was faint and uncertain, and many another man would have given up the quest. But the thought was with me in my waking hours, and was the companion of my pillow during the dark hours of the night. Six months later I knew that it was the Duchess who had addressed this missive to her husband, and why she had done so. By degrees I learned all the secret to which this scrap of paper gave me the clue; and if I have been a long while over it, it is because one link was wanting which I only discovered yesterday."

" Ah," said the doctor, " then Caroline Schimmel has spoken."

" Yes; drink was the magician that disclosed the secret that for twenty years she had guarded with unswerving fidelity."

As Mascarin uttered these words he opened a drawer, and drew from it a large pile of manuscript, which he waved over his head with an air of triumph.

" This is the greatest work that I have ever done," exclaimed he. " Listen to it, Hortebise, and you shall see how it is that I hold firmly, at the same time, both the Duke and Duchess of Champdoce, and Diana the Countess of Mussidan. Listen to me, Catenac,—you who distrusted me, and were ready to play the traitor, and tell me if I do not grasp success in my strong right hand." Then, holding out the roll of papers to Paul, he cried, "And do you, my dear boy, take this and read it carefully. Let nothing escape you, for there is not one item, however trivial it may seem to you, that has not its importance. It is the history of a great and noble house, and one in which you are more interested than you may think."

Paul opened the manuscript, and, in a voice which quivered with emotion, he read the facts announced by Mascarin, which he had entitled "The Mystery of Champdoce."

The conclusion of this exciting narrative will be found in the volume called "The Mystery of Champdoce."